WHETSTONES

WHETSTONES
MOSTLY FRONTIER GRIT
AND
SPUN-FUNNERY

Robert E. Enlow

WHETSTONES
MOSTLY FRONTIER GRIT
AND
SPUN-FUNNERY

Robert E. Enlow

Rutledge Books, Inc.   Bethel, CT

All Rights Reserved.
Rutledge Books, Inc.
8 F. J. Clarke Circle, Bethel, CT 06801

Printed in the United States of America

Library of Congress Cataloging-in-Publication Data
Enlow, Robert E.
　　Whetstones : mostly frontier grit and
spunfunnery / Robert E. Enlow
　　　　p.　cm.
　　ISBN 1-887750-11-8
　　　　1. Frontier and pioneer life--Kentucky--Fiction.
2. Frontier and pioneer life--Indian--Fiction.　I.
Title.
813.54--dc20

95–71651

Acknowledgements

The author is grateful to his wife, Helen T. Enlow, for her support as first reviewer-editor and to senior citizens who reviewed and reacted to chapters of *Whetstones*: Thor Kommedahl, professor emeritus, University of Minnesota; Robert B. Rathbone, a retired journalist, Gaithersburg, Maryland; Mrs. Midge Lewis, homemaker and active church and community leader, West Des Moines, Iowa; Harley Danforth, retired businessman, River Falls, Wisconsin; The Rev. Edward J. Campbell, White Bear Lake, Minnesota; and Mrs. Christie Shannon, California school executive secretary, now retired at White Bear Lake, Minnesota.

Cover Art: Harold L. Enlow, a distant cousin of the author of this novel, sketched the cover for WHETSTONES. Harold is an artist, as you can see; he is also a woodcarver-instructor who puts on workshops throughout the USA and parts of Canada. To learn more about Harold, read his profile in Chapter VIII. He authored it himself.

CONTENTS

Facts in Fiction — Dream or Reality?
(Check one each, below.)

(1) An earliest Kentucky family adopted two Indian brothers who were left stranded. Dream ___ Reality ___

(2) John Fitch, a "Tucky" pioneer, invented steam power for boats and sold land to a family herein. Dream ___ Reality ___

(3) A woman character was the midwife at the birth of A. Lincoln in Kentucky. Dream ___ Reality ___

(4) A pioneer woman chose the name Jasper for a town in southwest Indiana. Dream ___ Reality ___

(5) A. Lincoln, ll, and father, Tom, visited an Indiana mill owned by the lead family in this book. Dream ___ Reality ___

(6) The maneuver to dislodge a kernel of corn from a child's windpipe was discovered in a chapter of this book by a pioneer Kentucky woman. Dream ___ Reality ___

(7) At age 71, a man cited herein was the eldest sent to Vietnam by the U. S. Government just prior to the TET attack by the North Vietnamese.
Dream ___ Reality ___

(See how you fared at bottom of column.)

I reckon I had a dream that was so real I was sure I was there. It was in May 1987, somewhat short, and about ancestral times.

The place: Enlow Hill in an area to be named Indiana, later subdivided into counties, like Dubois. The characters in the dream: My Great[3] Grandparents Joseph "Josh" and Ellandor "Nelly" Enlow (Plowman, in chapters) and a reddish cow named "Tucky" for Kentucky, from whence she came as a calf. And, oh yes, the author was there, either being ignored or invisible.

Recall of the dream came in pieces taking me back close to two centuries to a family that lived on a hill. It was reflective of a visit there by the author and his wife, Helen, of nearly 50 years, and the initial reactor and reviewer of my writings. We visited the Dubois County Library, a first of its kind in Indiana; the graveyard on Enlow Hill (Plowman Hill, herein); the mill site with its historical marker; and Jasper and the countryside in general. The visit added many facts about this family to a large and ever growing pool of knowledge.

Nothing strange about living on a hill, except that Enlow today means "dwellers on a hill." I learned this recently from the New Dictionary of Family

Names, (Harper Row) which also states the name belongs to a rare clan in the hilly Lake District of northwestern England.

That's where earliest known roots of characters in this book began to grow and spread from England to what is now Holland, perhaps a few decades before 1658 when the four or five families, then Enloes, migrated across the Atlantic to a "new" land. A kin of one of these families began tracking these four brothers, their wives, children, grandchildren and great grandchildren.

For more than 30 years, U.S. Air Force Col. Thomas A. Enlow of Annandale, Virginia, hunted down Enloes-Enloe-Enlow-Inlow family lines now going back 12 to 14 generations here. Before his death in the early 1960s, he made repeated surveys and studies, coast to coast, in all of the United States. He kept three huge typewritten ledgers filled with family trees, limbs and twigs of which branched in the author's line from the original Enloe families, I believe. One link, however, between the author's third and fourth generations in this nation, has not been documented.

The first Enloe arrivals initially settled along the coasts of Delaware Bay and decades later some generations moved on to the Colony of Maryland. From there, the author's roots spread to locations where WHETSTONES evolved — Penn Province, mid-1700s; the "dark country" of western-most Virginia (now Kentucky), late 1790s; and onto Indiana Territory, early 1800s.

They had dreams and some, like the Plowman families, preserved diaries and letters, to pass down to new generations. Their primary dreams were of owning land, raising large families and surviving. Some of these dreams and writings became reality — and the basis of WHETSTONES. The author's dream is that type: Grampa Joseph was consoling Tucky, the family milk cow. . . (Read Chapter I to find out why Tucky needed consoling.)

My dream started me thinking of a fact-fiction book, the first I had written. It is factual and true to the times (See Reference Quiz, page 180). Each main character lives a life following threads of historical accuracy, enjoying or disliking human interplay and situations in frontier times.

In the beginning, the real life characters were ill-prepared to farm: Two of the five men arrived on this continent as goldsmiths, so stated the director of the Amsterdam Archives in a letter to Col. Enloe. No job openings were available to them. Early records indicate that the others may have been mariners and a carpenter, both then important vocations that they probably pursued, at least until they could rent or own land. Like others, many farmed out as apprentices.

Ultimately, most such pioneers became farmers, hunters, tradesmen and soldiers whose lifestyles were tied firmly to community and family mores and the urgency of survival — against hunger, sickness, wars. Most had courage and honor and senses of humor and direction, as you'll see on meeting them.

Chapters herein open with letter-type diary writings involving happenings that then meld into tales of real lives and times, reflecting sadness, success, failure, suspense, joy, danger, achievement and heroism. Each chapter then unfolds as a series of progressive events and conditions that end with a suspenseful climax — not all with happy endings.

Men and women, boys and girls, pioneers and Native Americans play active roles. All characters are patterns of those of the times, conditions and places. The exceptions are those rascal-like characters who play surrogate roles as barber Billy, Brutus, DeCur, Hanger, "Fatlandowner", Levey, Nunbender and attorney Upton. All Indian characters also are surrogates, except for Pisquetomen.

Women play pivotal roles among pioneers and often provide the backbone, and definitely the spirit, in families.

Many more women than men read, wrote and communicated orally. They often taught their children and grandchildren the basics in areas where frontier schools had not been built and school "masters" were not available.

Two of the Plowman main characters, Louicie (Enlow) Plowman and her husband, Henry, probably could both read and write; however, they did not sign their August 13, 1802 bill of sale of their 300-acre farm on Cox's Creek, near Salem, Virginia (now Bardstown, Kentucky). Instead, their signatures appear to be those of County Clerk Benjamin Grayson. He also penned a deed of sale on Jan. 21, 1805 for Joseph, Henry's brother, and Sarah who sold their 300-acre farm, also on Cox's Creek. Joseph signed with an X and Sarah with the symbol of a dove, perhaps designating a sign of peace.

Frontier women had to learn or were taught midwifery where doctors were not present. Indian ways helped, not only in doctoring, but also in harvesting and storing food from forests and meadows.

The women taught religion and family values by word and actions. All of these were duties of love and responsibility, not to mention cooking, mending, gardening, canning and weaving.

The men cleared land, built cabins and farmed, mostly; they also protected and negotiated against uprisings, some started by pioneers themselves. Yes, pioneers did take over Indian hunting grounds, but infrequent efforts were made to teach Indians to farm and learn the pioneer "tongue," efforts that were resented at times by both Native Americans and pioneers.

Both men and women of those days had to be intuitive and imaginative to the extent of making and repairing brooms, hoes, looms, harnesses and musical instruments, as examples. Thanks to the ingenious blacksmith and his forge and sledge, most needs of farm and home could be met or replaced. But:

How could a pioneer woman save the life of a child who had inhaled a kernel of corn? . . . How does one float a flatbottom boat that was completed on land? . . . How could families make peace with Indians while taking over their land? . . . Why did pioneers with large families move so frequently?

What are the best ways to measure the height of a tree or find wild honey? . . What entertainment did pioneers enjoy most? . . . Were there conflicts between fundamentalists and so-called high church members? . . . Did pioneers take politics seriously?

All of these questions — and others — are discussed through fictional and actual situations and anecdotes that replicate real life during frontier times. The characters in WHETSTONES not only recognize and accept challenges, they look for or initiate humorous and unusual situations and anecdotes to balance out their lives. And so it is, or should be, today.

Consider the incident about the author's family and its Dalmatian's search and find of our daughter's cameo ring in the snow where the day before she had been building a snowman.

Shelley, then 8, her brother, Tom, 16, and her parents, Helen and Bob, searched the area of play thoroughly, no doubt concentrating on and visualizing the ring continuously. After we walked away from the search, Calyph, our Dalmatian, began barking enthusiastically — like the yelps of a child finding her first Easter egg — and excitedly nudging something across the patio with his nose. . . . . . It was the ring.

Even 28 years later, that ring sports Calyph's teeth marks from tugging it from the snow following an overnight freeze. . Calyph's mental telepathic reaction is part of a true and factual anecdote (not told in WHETSTONES), just as true as the fact that readers have the right to file it away as fiction.

• Dream-Reality Answer: Read ensuing chapters and find out. You gotta remember, this book, in part, is spun-fun, including the "Bibliography," ibid Reference Quiz.

• One answer (#4): Nelly did name the town, Jasper.

Did she upright a canoe, counsel the council?

Louicie read through her December 1810 diary-letters and laughed quietly as she recalled, Benjamin Plowman, 4, her great nephew, awakened early on Christmas morning, at a time when his parents were up and around haying their beef cattle. Benjie couldn't wait to see how his older sister and brother had decorated the tree and how many presents Santa had brought.

First, though, he saw that the cookies were gone from the plate; only crumbs remained, so he knew Santa had been there. Viewed by his hidden sister, Betsy, he walked around the tree, strung with dried wild berries, popcorn and pine cones, like the family had always chosen to do. Then he stopped, looked up, down and around, grinned broadly and said, 'Just look at dat. Look at dat twee!', as Betsy burst into uncontrollable laughter.

Louicie (Enlow) Plowman, the family historian for several decades, liked to read her letters that went back in time and were organized by months and stored in a worn sea trunk. Benjie's grandmother and grandfather, Nelly and Josh, Jr., helped Louicie from their farm at Plowman Hill[1], Indiana Territory, in her attempt at a round-robin exchange. So did infrequent participants, Bell Plowman, her niece, at Turkey Foot, Pennsylvania, and her Uncle Zack Enloes, 90, at Baltimore "Town", Maryland, before returning the letters to Louicie and Henry's farm at Cox's Creek, Kentucky.

This time her letter made the rounds in three months, she was pleased to see, from December 29, 1809 to March 30, 1810. It began with a story about Bull Josher and his giggling court, involving a dairy cow named "Tucky", from Kentucky. . . .

* * *

Tucky's moo sounded quietly mournful.

She nestled her head forlornly against Joseph's chest while Josh, as he was called, stroked Tucky's neck. Kent lay nearby with his head resting on his paws, tail not wagging.

Josh, 33, had tears in his eyes. So did Ellandor, his wife, known to everyone as Nelly, 31, who knelt and scratched their black lab's back.

"It's just not fair," Nelly said as her voice broke. . . "That's her third dead calf born in jest . . . in just that number of years. She's only a mite over bein' five years old.. . . It isn't fair at all . . . Not fair, at all."

"No, it's not a damned bit fair, mostly only for Tucky, but for us, too," Josh said, then quickly remembering that two days ago Jed Martin's cow, Salem, had dropped twin heifer calves.

"Say, one of Salem's dairy twins would be fine for Tucky," Josh said aloud, without giving Nelly the benefit of his thoughts.

"What twins? Who in the world is Salem?" Nelly asked.

"Jed Martin's twins. . . I mean his cow, Salem, bore twin heifer calves two or three days ago, an' I hear tell he's lookin' for a home for one of 'em."

"Josh, I don't believe Tucky would have a particle to do with a strange calf. You know how stand-offish she can be."

"That's so. But I've in mind a way to fool Tucky into acceptin' a calf that's not her own."

At that instant, a series of rifle shots pierced the air, immediately severing talk between Josh and Nelly who raced toward their log house for Josh's rifle and pistol. He hoped he never had to use his guns again, "exceptin' for huntin' meat for the table," he said frequently.

"Those ain't huntin' shots!" Josh said. "Unless someone's tryin' to make a sieve out of a deer. . ."

"Nelly, you wait in the cabin while I check it out."

"Most assuredly not! I'm takin' your pistol. I'll protect your hinder from a ways back," Nelly commanded. "You move out first and I'll be close behind . . . and close behind the biggest oak I can find. . . You be special careful, Joseph."

Josh knew Ellander Plowman's stubbornness and how useless it was to try to argue her out of a position she had taken.

He arrived at the scene of the shooting just in time to see his cousin, Captain John Plowman, take bead and topple an Indian brave from his horse. The brave fell into the Patoka River and swam to the opposite bank where he was immediately taken prisoner, along with his horse, by Capt. Plowman's men[2].

Josh dodged in and out amongst trees, running low in a circuitous route to where his nephew crouched in the brush. Nelly held her breath and gripped her pistol in readiness, at the same time peering intensely into the underbrush for a sign of braves.

The woods took on an eerie silence: No birds were fluttering by, nor were they calling or responding to their mates; crickets were quiet; even the leaves were stilled, void of their usual waving and dancing.

Then, a wild turkey called.

Was it a turkey? Or was it an Indian signal? . . .

A second turkey gobbled in answer to the first, followed by another intense, but prolonged silence. A breeze then stirred leaves and put Kent on his

Did she upright a canoe, counsel the council?

master's scent and that of others in the woods. As a labrador retriever, he had a very keen sense of smell.

Josh whispered to his nephew, John, "You sure picked the right time for a turkey hunt. . . How are you friend and nephew, aside from your skirmish with these braves? . . . I take it there's more than one."

"I'm fine, Josh. Good to see you, even in the middle of this," John said, as they shook hands firmly.

"One Indian's dead, one's wounded and captured and three more surrendered to my men without injury, a bit south of here. If our count's right, two are still on the loose."

Nelly, in the meantime, had moved to where Josh and John were secluded, just as Josh asked, "Why in tarnation are these braves marauding up here?"

"They're Shawnee from eastern Kentucky, more than 50 miles away from your community of Plowman Hill," Captain John explained. "They were misjudged for an action they never committed, so they reacted by taking three pioneer women captive. Thank God we were able to free them unharmed yesterday morning. They're lodged, for now, with the Bill Robertson family."

Nelly squeezed in between the two men, breathed a sigh of relief, hugged her nephew strongly about the head and neck and kissed him warmly. Then she gave Josh's hand a squeeze.

"I declare, Captain John Plowman, this is the first time I've seen you wearing your captain's bars. Congratulations on your promotion! Here's another hug and a kiss on the cheek, which you duly deserve," and which Nelly provided.

At that point, Kent trotted forth after swimming across the Patoka River. He was soaking wet but proud, erect and tense, his nose held high sniffing the breeze.

"I wonder if Kent has taken scent of the braves," Josh said, just as the labrador shook his thick, furry hide vigorously, spraying water over the three.

Captain John laughed with the others and said, "Kent, you must know I need a bath. After this is over, I'm gonna shuck all my clothes and dive right into the Patoka River for a swim."

Kent wagged his tail, then began sniffing again. This time, however, it was combined with a low, quiet growl and an intense visual search of the thick underbrush. He then whined softly and raked Josh's leg with his forepaw.

John came alert instantly as did Nelly and Josh.

"He's got wind of something, and I think it could be one or both of the Indian braves still at large," John said.

Josh reached out and tugged Kent to him, then stroked the retriever's head, saying, "Kent, boy, what do you smell? Can you round 'em up; bring 'em in. Roundup! Good boy!"

Kent understood and began his routine as if he were about to sort the Plowman beef cattle out of the woods and herd them home before a heavy snowstorm hit the area.

Did she upright a canoe, counsel the council?

Nose alternating between ground and air, Kent worked the area in a large spiraling pattern, moving ever closer to the center target. Soon, he sniffed out a fresh trail and began his usual signals, growling and barking loudly — as he would when he let the herd know who's boss.

His tracking ended at a bluff, where growling and barking ceased, and quiet, rigid pointing began.

When the Plowman arrived at the bluff, Kent stood rigidly except for a slight wag of the tip of his tail. His nose-point was aimed directly at the bluff and a cave opening about a ten-foot climb from where the three stood.

John called out in the few Shawnee words he knew, translating in English to:

"Come out! Soldiers not hurt you."

Kent remained silent, except for a quiet, continuing growl. His tail tip no longer wagged.

John called out again in Shawnee, "You hear what I say. Come out! Come out!"

By this time, the captain's men had heard Kent's earlier growling and barking and had gathered below the cave opening with the others.

"If these two have no rifles," Josh offered, "I'll dispatch Kent into the cave. He'll not harm them unless they attack first. Can you assure the warriors of this?"

"I'm not sure, but it's worth a try," Captain John said, then called out again in Shawnee:

"You know bear dog. This one is named Kent. You hear? You use bear dogs to hunt . . . like pioneers. This one named Kent! . . . He not like angry bear with cub."

On hearing his name repeated several times, Kent stirred uneasily but stood patiently nevertheless, awaiting further action.

Nelly was uneasy for the sake of the braves and Kent. To assist, she offered to go with Kent to the mouth of the cave.

"No, Nelly! No!" Josh exclaimed. "If anybody's goin' up, I'll take Kent myself."

"Nelly, Josh is right," John said. "You have no notion about how these two warriors will react."

John's troops murmured in agreement.

"Listen to me," Nelly snapped sharply. "The fact that I'm a woman — and not a militiaman — will work to our advantage. Don't you see that?"

"All the Indians I've ever known, and that's a lot, treat their women with love and respect. At this point, you men are their enemies and not to be trusted. They'll believe me, not you."

Without another word, Nelly commanded, "Come, Kent!"

Kent at her side, she strode to the bluff and climbed up to the cave opening where she used her own knowledge of Shawnee words to convince the warriors to surrender. She told the two that she was "strong for peace" and one of the "she chiefs" in her community. Then she told them she would counsel the soldiers and pioneer leaders to insure them just treatment.

Nelly then climbed down and strode back with Kent to where the men stood and where Josh took her hand, put his arm around her waist and squeezed her tightly without speaking a word.

Once the two warriors left the cave, they were taken captive and later secured temporarily in the Plowman loft above the cattle shelter. There the unit's medical aide treated the injured brave as others buried the dead beside the Patoka... The four captured earlier were being held at the Robertson farm. The three women hostages, now freed, lodged with the Robertson family.

John turned then to his aunt, took her hand, and said, "Nelly, we owe you a debt of gratitude, but I've got to say that luck was on your side. I'll do my utmost as a captain in the Kentucky militia to see these men are treated justly.

"However, I'm under Kentucky orders to bring them back for trial and I'll do my best to see they get a fair one. As I told Josh, I don't believe they are guilty of any crime. For that reason, I'm as sorry as sin that we had to kill one and wound another of the seven."

"Thanks Captain John, I know you'll treat them fairly," Nelly responded, giving him another hug.

Josh then invited John to bunk at their cabin and his men in the loft of their log cattle shelter. He accepted happily.

Nelly and Josh were anxious to get back to Tucky and her problem of losing her third calf. Nelly was very curious about how Josh would get Tucky to "cuddle up to a strange calf."

They also wanted John to see his cousins, Benjamin and Jacob, and their wives and kids and to tell him about their plans to rebuild the squatters' grist mill they hoped to buy some day from Andrew and Mary Evans.[3]

On arriving at Plowman Hill, Captain John skinned down to a naked body and dove into the Patoka to swim with his men.

Time to rejoice, except for the Indians, Josh and Nelly knew.

That evening, as the family ate supper and later sat around the hearth, John renewed acquaintances with his cousins, Benjamin and Jacob, and their wives, Fanny and Elizabeth, and met for the first time their young offspring. The glow of the hearth made it difficult to distinguish between that caused by the hearth and that of happy faces.

While eating, Josh asked Nelly, "Can you put your finger on pa's old wool militia blanket?"

"What in tarnation do you want with that? It's in near shreds. Smells like Tucky after her last dead birthing," Nelly answered. "Anyway, you stuffed it in one of the feed mangers last summer. Why do you want it now?"

"I'm gonna strap it on Tucky's back, so's, so it'll pick up more odor, Tucky's fresh odor."

Did she upright a canoe, counsel the council?

That brought laughter to everyone.

"To quote Nelly," John responded, grinningly and a bit gloatingly, "What in tarnation do you want with that?"

Then Fanny laughed and said, "Josh, you'll exasperate Tucky, herself, if you keep on dragging this thing out. I hope one of these days you'll come clean, cleaner than that old blanket of yours."

Nelly laughed with the others and remarked, "Josh is a bit like his Uncle Henry, as a teaser. Henry once told his nephew, Mordecai, that their horse, Whinny, stole his hat and hid it under a stack of hay."

"Truth is, Henry went to sleep by the stack, then went back to work without his hat."

Then Elizabeth entered, saying, "Aunt Nelly, you left out part of Henry's best punchline. "Henry claims, 'That horse plain and simple stole it, then walked off awearin' it.'"

Family members, except for youngins having gone to bed, then changed subjects to livelihoods . . . . Benjamin, who detested being called "Ben," talked of timber and the need for a water powered, upright sawmill. . . . Jacob told of a way to plow and plant that would lessen loss of top soil. . . . Elizabeth who would stomp out of the room if someone called her "Lizzy," said she felt strongly that "pioneer women should toss their hats and hearts into politics" and "run some of them men blowhards out of office," to which Nelly said, "Ahhmen!"

Then with a twinkle, Bessie, who liked her nickname, said "I think it's time we all thought of growing veggies — like lettuce, turnip and pea, followed by guffaws by all present, except Nelly, a more serious type, who said, "Bessie, it's no laughing matter about men in politics. I heard one last month at the bureau meeting answer a serious question about Indians, something like this:

"'Well, ifen I'da known you was gonna ax a question like that, I'da brung my notes."

"The pitiful part about that man is that he is highly intelligent. . . can speak kings' English fluently. . . except when he hasn't done his schoolwork. Then, he dodges into a backcountry language that few can understand."

"Nelly, why don't you challenge him at the polls?" John asked.

"Matter of fact, I'm planning on. . . I'm thinking about it." Josh then said, "I'm thinking" — with strong emphasis on the word, thinking — "about hittin' the hay. What about the rest of you?" All agreed, even if each of the women wanted to talk about what will happen to the Indian prisoners, particularly Nelly who felt it best to speak to John alone.

On the way to bed, John asked Josh if there were chores his men, including the prisoners, could work at to keep busy and out of mischief for the next few days. Josh jumped at the offer by suggesting the men work at clearing a mix of hardwood trees from the lowland for growing more hay and corn, adding that they could fell, unlimb and saw them into lengths of twelve and sixteen feet, "if you've a mind they should do that."

Did she upright a canoe, counsel the council?

John agreed, except for one man to remain, of course, to care for and guard the injured prisoner.

Just after daybreak the next morning, Nelly was up with dawn as usual to milk Tucky while Josh hayed down their cattle. She found Tucky standing head first into a thick bramble bush, as though she couldn't put up with looking around at the world.

"I've never seen a sadder critter in all my born days," Nelly said aloud.

"Tucky, dear young thing, I know why you feel the way you do," she said teary eyed as she stroked Tucky's rump. She then sat down on her three-legged stool and began milking Tucky as she continued her soothing words.

"I know how you feel 'cause I lost one child at birth and another from choking on a kernel of corn. It's the toughest thing for a mamma to have to face.

"But maybe Josh will fix you up with a calf of your own, one that you can nurse, if you are willing. . . . one you can nuzzle and tongue clean and slick so that . . . ."

John broke in at that moment, a bit choked up on hearing Nelly talk about losing her children and previously about the treatment of the Indian prisoners, saying, "Nelly, I have a strong feeling that you still object to my taking the prisoners back down to Kentucky.[4] Am I right?"

"Yes, you're right. Even though I know you are following orders from your militia commander, as you should. I'm fearful. . . . not because you won't treat them fairly. I'm fearful because of emotional reactions of those close to the women who were taken hostage. I'm fearful the Indians will be hornswoggled by those in command. They're apt to rig nooses and hang them.

"I just believe strongly that we have to upright their canoes, not flip them over a tall waterfall."

At that point Tucky let go with a mournful mooing sound as she exhaled. It reminded Nelly instantly of her own tearful moan of many years ago when she was told she had lost her first child to a kernel of corn lodged in the six-year-old's windpipe.

"I just wish I had been with Trixie at the time. Maybe I could have laid her down and trounsed her chest and forced the kernel out of her breath pipe."

"Nelly, stop taking the blame for something you couldn't have avoided even if you had been there," John said.

"I know. . . I know." Nelly said as she sighed deeply. Let's change the subject. I have something else to suggest about your captive Indians. You do have a responsibility to your State of Kentucky, I agree. But did you ever think that we have no government locally. We're just known as the Northwest Territory. Why? I'll never know. We aren't even northwest, more like northeast, insofar as this country is known geographically.

"My point is this, as you prob'ly already figured: Who do we answer to, if we keep the captive Indians here for trial, rather than in western Kentucky?"

By now, Nelly had finished milking Tucky, as much milk going on the

Did she upright a canoe, counsel the council?

ground as in the pail, John noticed, and told Nelly so with a chuckle. Nelly forced a pleasant smile.

Josh was back by noon from Jed Martin's dairy farm with a sturdy, healthy-looking calf. For the trip over, he had strapped one of his young beef calves across the roan back of his horse, Pioneer, for bartering. He now had returned with the dairy calf strapped the same way.

After the noon meal, he invited all adults and children to join him at the "Northwest Cattle Corral, grandest in the whole northeast," for the adorning of Tucky, the dairy queen.

The youngsters giggled and clapped enthusiastically, as did the adults, who marveled at Josh's joshings.

Josh came forward with one of Nelly's best wooden trays held high on fingertips. He bowed regally, and with a dramatic flourish unfurled and swept the air with the tattered and straw-covered militia blanket.

Tucky snorted and jumped to her left.

Children laughed and cheered and clapped; adults hooted and hollered and applauded, including both the militiamen, who interpreted for the Indian captives, out for an exercise stroll.

"Now, ladies and gentlemen, be aware that, here and now, I do anoint Tucky with this blanket of scent . . . in the name of Bull Josher and his giggling court."

Josh kissed Tucky on each cheek and hugged and stroked her head and neck. Josh then fanned the blanket over Tucky's back, tied it in place, kissed Tucky again on each cheek and gave her a final hug around the neck.

Tucky mooed softly and shook her head up and down.

The youngsters then ganged around Tucky to hug her legs and chest. Tucky lowered her head so that she could be hugged and kissed around her neck and cheeks by the youngsters.

Captain John, who also had been interpreting the game for the Indians, summed it all up when he said, "Josh, that's an all-time best bunch of hilarious blarney I've ever witnessed in my whole lifetime. That beats even Uncle Henry's fawning."

While the youngsters and adults were still gathered, Josh explained what would come next. Looking directly into their eyes he told them, "This blanket will be worn by Tucky for two sunsets. On the following sunrise, I'll remove it and put it on the back of the calf. Then Tucky will smell her own self and let the calf nurse. Meantime, you can nipple feed her.

"And by the by, she'll also be needin' a name. All of you youngsters get together and come up with the best names you can think of. Betsy, you write 'em down and then you all can vote for the name you think is best. That be all right?"

They agreed enthusiastically and followed Betsy, 10, oldest child of Betsy and Benjamin Sr. into the cabin for chalk and her chalkboard. Once they had voted, they planned and later put on an early evening "Name the Calf" event for the adults and Captain John's militiamen and Indian captives.

They even wrote out invitations to each and every person, including the captives, whose names were given them by their Uncle John, who would serve as interpreter of the invitations and the event of "Name the Calf." They named the calf "Pucky" because of how she'd pucker up when ready to nurse.

Captain John was ecstatic, until he realized how such comaradarie would make it more difficult for him to return the captives south for judgment, partly because of Nelly's fear of a trumped-up court and her view on which of the "counselors" would hold the high cards.

Emotionally, he took Nelly's side but he really had doubts. The next morning Betsy was up at dawn with the adults, all brightly washed and sparkly in attitude and attention. She peppered the adults with "why" questions about Tucky and then about the word, breakfast.

After they had eaten, looking very serious and studious, Betsy asked, "Why do we call this meal breakfast?"

"Split the word in two parts, Betsy," Mamma Fanny suggested.

"Then you can come up with your own answer."

"Break . . . fast? But what is the hurry?" she asked, then bursting into laughter, joined by the adults. . . "Wait! I know. We fasted. We didn't eat all night, so this morning we breaked the fast. Oops, we broke the fast."

The adults' laughter, then the clapping, awoke the other children, bunking mostly in corners or wheresoever they were not to be trampled. They wanted to know what was funny; their parents then took the time to tell them all in good spirits.

* * *

"Here's Louicie again from Salem,[5] quill in hand writing about Plowman women and men. You may be happy to hear how smart they were in handling their problems. Here's what happened:

"The Plowman family invited a councilman, name of Pilot Nunbender, to leave the farm; they found a way to stop water and mud from running strong off hillsides; Nelly and Jacob each ran for the same council office; the women ganged up on the men and the men stuck close together; and Straight Feather, nicknamed Beaver, helped Nelly and the Indians."

Louicie then wrote that early of a morning . . . .

* * *

The Plowman men were out clearing mixed-oak from land for cropping. They were working shoulder-to-shoulder with the Indian captives when along

Did she upright a canoe, counsel the council?

came a far-neighbor, surnamed Nunbender of German extraction. He was known to the Plowman people only by reputation and by his delayed-told election.

At that very moment, Nelly, Elizabeth and Fanny brought cookies and hot sassafras tea to the workers.

Nunbender surveyed the gathering, peering above his cloudy, half-moon spectacles, and wearing a mixed look of disgust and feigned shock.

"I'm Councilman Nunbender, representing my pioneer council up at White River. My councilmen voted me to check on what you are doing with these captive injun redskins," at which Nelly bristled angrily, then cooled down and asked, forcefully:

"Sir! . . . Councilman! . . . If you are referring to these Indian friends, who happen to be temporary captives, you should remember that these are native Americans who came here hundreds, yes, even thousands, of years before you and I did."

"I'm not int'rested in the slightest in your recall of prehistoric times," Nunbender snapped.

"Didn't these redskins, you call your friends, kidnap three lady pioneers from western Virginia, and didn't they . . ."

Interrupting angrily, Nelly responded, "If you knew any history, you'd know that western Virginia no longer exists. The women are from western Kentucky, so named 18 years ago. There is no need for you to talk about not knowing history."

"Who's in charge of these injun prisoners?" Nunbender demanded. . . . . .
Dressed in work clothes, John responded in a forced friendly tone: "I'm Captain John Plowman, under order to take these prisoners back to Kentucky. I'm in full charge, which brings to mind two questions I'd like you to answer."

"I ain't a bit interested in . . . ."

John interrupted, "Where and when did the council meet?"

"And two, why are you talking like you own the council, when it's a fact you were just elected as one of the councilmen?"

"Another fact, Mister Counselorman," Nelly injected, "We Plowman people know most all of the other councilmen — by first name and by their good reputations.

"For those reasons, I don't believe a single word you've said."

"Now, mister so-called councilman, you have a strong invitation from the owners to take leave now, immediately," said Josh, standing at a full six-foot, one inch.

"You haven't heard the last of this," Nunbender said sharply, parting quickly with an angry escort, the family dog, Kent.

John had been interpreting for the captive Indians, as best he could, but not all that was said. He skipped over any reference to 'injuns' and 'redskins' but he knew they heard.

Did she upright a canoe, counsel the council?

Later the Plowman adults learned Nunbender's nickname: "Pilot."

Nelly brought up the name, Pilot Nunbender after supper that evening, saying, "I heard a while back that Bill Kingsley had announced he would withdraw from the Pioneer Council. Then he'd stay on for a while to help initiate the land protection program. I didn't think much of it then, but now I'm concerned."

"Why, Nelly?" Elizabeth asked.

"We never know what's going on because the seat of the council isn't centrally located from a population standpoint. White River citizens, nice people, I'm sure, but they have an edge over us. They know what's going on. We don't most of the time. . . . . "For example: Did we get word that Bill Kingsley was resigning from the Council? Did we know that Pilot had filed to fill the vacancy? Did we hear that Pilot had been elected to fill Bill's spot?

"The answers, of course are no, no and no.

"And have we heard that Pilot Nunbender has only four months before he has to file to run again? The answer again is no."

"Nelly, you plannin' to run for that seat?" Josh asked.

"Maybe, and maybe not. I'm really not equipped to work on land protection . . . if I was elected and assigned that role."

Benjamin then said, "You could get a lot of help from Jacob, here. He's hell bent on stoppin' land from wastin' down creeks and rivers. We all know he's come up with at least one good idea that works."

"Why shouldn't Jacob run?" Josh asked.

"Hold on! I ain't . . . I'm not gonna be stampeded into this. My first love is farmin'. And that's where I'm gonna stay put."

"You gonna run for that office?" Josh again asked Nelly.

"I've not made up my mind."

Cap John then asked Jacob about his idea on stopping erosion.

"It's maybe my idea, but it's not all my doin'. 'Sledge' Hammler is due most of the credit," Jacob said.

"Sledge Hammler? You've got to be joshing," John said amidst a gale of laughter. . . . "His mamma surely didn't pin that one on him. Next you're going to say he's a blacksmith. Right?"

"What else?" others responded in unison, still laughing.

John's thoughts then drifted down Kentucky way, saying, "That name's about as funny as the doc that Henry and Louicie have at near Salem . . . . I mean Bardstown, now.

"His name's Stitchler. . . Doc Stitchler."

They all laughed heartily until John interrupted, saying, "Let's get serious for a bit. I haven't heard about Jacob's way of land protection. What is it and how does it work?"

Jacob set out to describe it. . . . "You've seen how muddy streams run, like the Patoka, during and after a good rain. That muddy run costs us dearly over

Did she upright a canoe, counsel the council?

a time, 'specially on corn land. . . . I know, I've been out watching during heavy falls."

Jacob continued, his devotion whelming ever stronger as he spoke, "I watched during one very heavy fall. A big wash of water gathered and tore out a sapling. Then it gored a gulley down a hill in less than an hour's time.

"That water runs from my land through Branch Creek and onto Benjamin's, then into Patoka River, which should and could run clear of mud. It even skirts the land we're on here."

"How would you and Sledge help prevent water gullying like that?" Cap. John asked.

"Only the good Lord knows the answer to that. But we can help out by plowin' around a hill, instead of up and down it."

"You bet. That'd help a lot," Benjamin interrupted. "But there'd be a lot of plow horses around with shorter legs on one flank than the other."

The men laughed; the women looked perplexed.

"The fact is," Benjamin continued, "if horses pulled plows around and around hills, in the same direction, they'd all wind up short legged on the uphill side."

That brought groans from the women, laughter from the men.

"I'm almost afraid to ask this," Cap. John said, "But what part does our folkman, Sledge Hammler, play in this tale?"

"Cap. John, I know you'll recall that seaman's spyglass that's been handed down from generation to generation in our family line," Jacob said. "It first was owned by Jan Plowman, a seaman, I believe when the earliest of his family arrived in this country.

"Well, I've got the spyglass now, and I asked Sledge if he thought it could be mounted on a three-legged, stool-like stand . . . to use like a transit in layin' out level planes along hillsides. Sledge said he thought it could be done.

"About three weeks later," Jacob said, "here came Sledge ridin' up our farm path with his invention he called a 'hillspy transit' strapped securely to his back.

"He was twice as proud as a cow birthing twin calves."

"How'd he put it all together?" Cap. John wanted to know, as the women excused themselves to chat while doing the dishes. Nelly kept an ear cocked in the direction of the men.

"I should have the piece here for you to see the beauty of it. . . and how well it works. It's almost like a real transit." Jacob then explained that Sledge had mounted the spyglass on a swivel in the center of a round, wooden disk on which he had engraved calibrations for north, east, south and west, plus some degrees between. Sledge then attached a small carpenter's level parallel to the spyglass and put tripod legs on the base of the disk.

"So I can tilt the spyglass vertically, Sledge strapped eight-inch metal spikes on each of the three legs. The sharp spikes can be pressed into the ground, or raised up, to view different planes up and down the hill."

Did she upright a canoe, counsel the council?

On conclusion, Jacob appologized for "providin' too much detail" and invited them to stop by his farm the following day. There, John and Josh saw Jacob and Benjamin in action with the "hillspy transit," including staking out level planes around Jacob's hill being readied for plowing and planting corn the following spring.

Jacob promised to observe and keep records on his project, as best he could, and report results now and again. He didn't say anything about keeping the Pioneer Council informed, Josh noted, but hoped he would later on.

On the way home with John, Josh quietly puzzled over Nelly's future. He had the greatest respect for her straight forward approach and fortitude. Besides that, he knew Nelly was bright and made the right decisions, mostly. She reminded Josh of his Aunt Louicie's determination, down south at Salem.

Nelly's only problem, he felt, was that she frequently let emotions enter her activities, particularly when pitted against men. If she was a member of the Pioneer Council, for example, she'd badger male members like a mama bear protecting her cub on such issues as seeing that Indians get fair treatment.

Josh strongly agreed with Nelly on being fair, but he knew many men in the area, particularly members of the Council, had battled Indians frequently. Even though they hated fighting — the loss of blood and lives of family and friends, including Indians — pioneer men were compelled to protect loved ones and their land and stock.

True, now was the time for peace and reconciliation, Josh knew, but didn't hold out much hope. He did have hope that Jacob would agree to run for council, even though he didn't believe Jacob had the persistence of Nelly.

Josh was aware, however, that if Nelly ran she'd have an uphill battle — in a political scene dominated by men. And most men in this part of Northwest Territory feared or felt uneasy about strong women like Nelly.

He knew that pioneer women mostly ran the homes, but that included their families, without excluding husbands and sons. Josh knew, too, that women like Nelly could rally and organize support from most women, particularly if an issue was tied emotionally to humans, like that of fairness to Indians.

Josh was torn of mind. He wanted, on the one hand, for Nelly to run for office and to win; but at the same time, he knew the torment that would ensue both in a campaign and later as a council member, should she win.

John enjoyed the silent walk but interrupted and interjected into Josh's thoughts, almost as though he had been reading his mind, when he asked:

"Josh, is Jacob in the same voting district as Nelly?"

"Strange you should ask. Jacob's farm is divided by South Branch Creek. Most of Jacob's farm is in the same district as ours, but his cabin and out buildings are in a different district."

"Are you thinkin' what I think you're thinkin', that both Nelly and Jacob could file and run for the council seat?"

John laughed and said that he'd not been known for mind reading, but,

Did she upright a canoe, counsel the council?

"Yes, that's exactly what I had in mind. You know from militia experience that a diversionary tactic is one of the best military moves a unit can initiate."

"True , but just who would be diverted, Jacob or Nelly?"

"I can't answer to that," John responded. "You know them better than I, particularly Nelly; but any diversion has to be planned and timed carefully by both units and their leaders. They must be of one mind and of one goal."

"Jacob and Nelly are of one mind, particularly on Indian rights. No doubt about that," Josh said. "But I wouldn't bet either way on whether or not Jacob would be willing to play a part in political decisions. You heard how devoted he is to farming and protecting the land.

"Jacob holds you in highest regard, John. Would you be willin' to talk with him about this?"

John remained silent, thinking.

"John, I'd be the one to speak to Nelly, once you learn how close or far away Jacob is from agreein' or disagreein', but you might agree on condition . . . that you and I then meet with Nelly and Jacob after we've talked tactics with both.

"If they agree, the whole family must understand and support what we're doing — much like platoons and their leaders."

Then, much alike philosophically, the two shook hands and followed through with their tactics.

On arriving home, they found the militia and their captives had tied a rope high in a tree beside the Patoka and were taking turns swinging and plunging into the river. Cap. John was pleased to see such comaraderie, but it nagged at his mind, just the same. How would his men react in battle against Indians, should skirmishes ever again take place? If they think of all Indians as friends, would they revolt? He then dismissed the thought, telling himself he knew better. First he believed the fighting was over; second, he knew that neither his men nor Indians in general wanted any more conflicts.

For that reason, John became even more resolute in support of Nelly's strong desire for fairness. Without it, John knew, there would be no peace.

Later, John told his ensign that he would be in charge during the two months John had been ordered to report to his Kentucky commander. He looked forward to the visit, but he was certain it would be a challenging encounter over the Indian captives. He would tell his superior the truth and how he felt about the Indian captives.

John's questioning mind then pondered: What if he was ordered to return with the captives immediately? What effect would this have on Nelly and family and their relationships with him? Then he knew the answer.

"Hell! I'll use Nelly's reasoning," he said quietly but   firmly. "If it means confrontation, so be it. I want to return to farming, anyway. I'll buy a farm close by here."

John's ensign, who had begun walking away, turned and asked, "Were you speakin' to me, sir?" John grinned and shook his head.

Did she upright a canoe, counsel the council?

Meanwhile, Nelly, Bessie and Elizabeth contacted pioneer women to drum up support among them and some of their husbands. The Plowman men joined their wives to gather support for more effective communications in keeping citizens informed quickly of all Council activities. The approach was based totally on family discussions and agreements.

This activity extended into the Pioneer Fair, held annually. A booth was tended by women who were most dedicated to the correct causes, and where six women, and two men, paraded the grounds with signs that read:

Pioneer Councilmen!
Keep Citizens Informed

BE FAIR TO INDIANS:
Help Upright Canoes

Bessie and Elizabeth had taken charge of the Fair booth and the placard "parades," including doing all of the artwork. They were as enthusiastic as Nelly could ever have dreamed, enjoying the work as great fun. They even thought up and circulated petitions to be signed in support of their two issues.

All of this activity and results of petitions were relayed by Captain John to Kentucky, some of which angered his commander to the point of threatening to decommission him. John backed off sufficiently to hold his captaincy, at least until after the Indian affair was settled. After that, he didn't care.

He'd move close to Plowman Hill, where he would purchase a farm and commit to buying Evans' squatters mill[6] when Evans was ready to sell. John asked Joanne Millert, 30, five years his junior, to marry him. She accepted, but no date was set.

Three weeks before the Pioneer Council election, both Nelly and Jacob agreed to run for Nunbender's office. Neither Josh nor John had spoken with them about running. To their surprise, Nelly and Jacob had already met and agreed to file as candidates. After filing, they developed platforms and strategies together, then combed their districts for support leaders and campaigners.

Nelly, of course, stressed the human element in support of Indians and, particularly, the captives. She was a direct, honest and ferocious campaigner. She got her message across to women without doubt and to more men than she had hoped for. Because of Nelly's nature, she alienated a large body of men, which caused some women to stay away from the polls.

Jacob was straightforward and convincing about protecting land and waterways, and he had fiendish support from Sledge Hammler, who promised to build six more hillspy transits. These six would be shared by farmers in the area.

Jacob was lucky for more than one reason. Besides help from Sledge, a torrential rain gullied lands and muddied all local waterways three days before voting time. Following the rains, all of his gatherings were scheduled on banks of rivers or streams as a negative farming backdrop, but positive for Jacob.

Jacob won by a decisive edge; Nelly lost by a large margin.

But Nelly didn't pout or lose spirit for a minute. Instead, she called a meeting of constituents and family members three days later at which she thanked her supporters and layed out a plan of action for the captives and Indians affairs in general.

Surprisingly, three of the councilmen, without counting Jacob, turned out, providing a majority on Nelly's side.

"Thank you. Thank you. Thank you," Nelly said. "I'm so proud and grateful for your successful support. Don't you fret or worry for a minute about not winning. We won in principle, and we'll be victors in the long run. You can bet on that . . . if any of you are bettors.

"I have a dream . . . and a strategy.

"You don't know a man in Kentucky that we call Beaver, a close friend of ours. He's now a lawyer assistant to a judge and a strong supporter of Indians and pioneers, alike. His Indian name is Straight Feathers. And believe me, he stands tall at five feet, ten inches and thirty or so years.

"I sent a message to Lawyer Straight Feathers a time ago, asking him to come here and make a case for our Indian friends. He agreed and should be here in a week or so. In fact, before that, he advised not to send the captives back to Kentucky."

The crowd, including the councilmen, applauded and cheered.

Nelly then said, "Beaver pulled himself up by his own stirrup strap. He is a successful farmer, and formerly managed a farm and home apprenticeship program for young Indians and pioneers. It still exists, for both men and women," she emphasized.

"For more background, you should know that Straight Feathers was first trained to farm by my Uncle Henry and Aunt Louicie Plowman, farmers on Cox's Creek in Kentucky. They took him in and adopted him as a teen at the time his tribe moved west. Our Beaver, now legally a Plowman, didn't go west because of his love for farming."

Nelly then told the crowd that, "Captain John Plowman sent word that he resigned his Kentucky Captaincy and he's enthused to be arriving here in a month to take up farming — with his wife to be, Joanne Millert."

At the close of Nelly's talk, and following prolonged applause, a teary-eyed Josh took Nelly in his arms and without a word, hugged her close and hard. That brought cheers from the crowd.

Lawyer Plowman came north and argued and won freedom for all of the captives. Later, he told the Indians: "I have asked, as you may know, to have you and your families accepted as members of my father's tribe — Chief Tall Feather's tribe. I've received word from my Pa Chief that, and I quote the Chief, 'You and your wives and children are most welcome to our rocky mountainous area in the west — where trout bite, deer are plentiful and gardening and farming are good, between rocks.'"

Did she upright a canoe, counsel the council?

WHETSTONES

The freed Indians, whose families had rejoined them, accepted the Chief's offer to go west, where they established their own community a few miles south of the Chief's encampment.

Before Beaver and the freed Indians left, the Plowman families pooled their food with neighbors and put on a community picnic to celebrate their victories. The families of freed Indians all were guests of honor.

As usual before eating, Benjamin gave thanks to "the Almighty, to the Holy Ghost, for being on the side of justice, particularly that of our good Indian friends and to Nelly, Josh and Beaver. And may thy blessings be upon us all." Everyone then said, "AAAmen," especially Benjamin.

That evening, as the parents began putting the children to bed, Patricia, 4, daughter of Jacob and Elizabeth, began to cry and squirm nervously.

"What's the matter, Patty, honey?" her mother asked.

"I'm afraid of ghosts, like Uncle said, 'the Holy Ghost'." "Don't be afraid, Patty. This is a very friendly ghost, an imaginary friend you can't see, a friend that is part of people, like your Uncle Benjamin, and all the rest of us. . . But now it's bedtime. If you'd like to talk more about the Holy Ghost, we can do so in the morning. Tell everyone good night."

Patty and the other children said good night and trundled off to bed, all keenly absorbed in Elizabeth's message. Once the children were in bed, the adults could hear Patty and other youngsters talking of a friendly ghost who was inside of them.

The adults then began discussing a rumor they had heard about possible uprisings within a few months by warriors of Tecumpseh and his brother, The Prophet[7] who was considered the most dangerous. John said of The Prophet, "He thinks he has supernatural powers; so do most of his warriors."

Then they dropped back in time to 1776, and before, to rehash battles Josh's father fought in Penn Province in Captain Cresap's Maryland company. But the most popular subject was land and how often it was stolen away by men who Joseph, Sr., called, "Dogs that don't know their mothers."

"Even Governor Tom Penn tried to run Henry, Jacob, and Pa Joseph off their land at Turkey Foot in the late 1760s." Josh said. "Tom Penn issued a decree years ago to pioneers to vacate land that they didn't own, so that it could be given back to the Indians."[8] He never cancelled it.

"Hard to believe a governor would do that to his own citizens," Jacob said, "but it's written down in history volumes."

Did she upright a canoe, counsel the council?

Did they squat it, own it or lose it?

To remind relatives about their roots, Louicie Plowman often wrote letter based on facts passed down from generation to generation and from her diarie and letters beginning in the 1760s. This time she began her letter with earliest known ancestors, writing that they moved to Amsterdam from the lake distric of NW England,[9] sometime in the early 1600s.

"They wanted to get away from the church power of bishops," she wrote "For a few decades, they were happy living among friends at Amsterdam mostly working as silversmiths, fishers and carpenters; but they wanted to ow land, and land there wasn't to be had for settling. So our ancestral families se sail in 1657 across the huge Atlantic to another land. As they neared the coast the story goes, a group of about 20 Plowman and Enloes (my kinfolk) men an women, ganged up on the bow and yelled out, 'Farmland ahoy!'

"On arriving they found it was hard earning a living and too often skir mishing with Indians. So, looking for better days, they moved from Delawar Bay to the Province of Maryland and later to Penn Province,[10] where this stor continues in the middle 1760s."

Louicie's husband, Henry, was fretting about losing land they were squat ting at Turkey Foot while doing some soldiering there. He and his brothe Joseph Senior, and his cousin, Isaac, had reason enough to worry; so did thei families still in Maryland Province. The men were confused and down in spir it, until good friends knocked at their door. It was Feather and her husband Scout, a Monongahela Indian point man for the Virginia militia; before that, fo the English. Henry was saying . . .

* * *

"I gotta wonder whether it's all worth it. Here we are away from our wive and youngsters, soldierin' on call, and squattin' land we most likely will lose, Henry said and asked:

"What caused Governor Tom Penn to issue such a decree?"

"Damned if I know," Joseph said.

18

"Like a big, lightnin' bolt shot down amidst us," Isaac added.

Their miserable thoughts and words were interrupted by the rap at the cabin door. Scout and Bright Feather, his wife, and in many ways his quiet mentor, entered carrying a gift of fresh trout from Turtle Branch.

"Good fishin' this mornin', I'd say," Scout said in an oblique greeting. He then added quickly and laughingly, "Bright Feather caught all but the small one. But you should have seen the big one of mine that flipped free of the hook."

Their presence immediately rolled dark clouds away and allowed bright smiles to beam through, as the three standing men greeted and thanked their Indian friends.

Bright Feather, usually called Feather, for short, said abruptly and haltingly, "We want you know we are friends. . . . We don't want you leave. We want you stay close . . .as our ponies and bear-dog do."

Pride spread over Scout's face, as he said:

"Feather thinks a two-trail way. While fishing, she planned to catch fish and how to help you, our good friends, who once saved my skin," then adding with a smile, "Redskin, at that."

Joseph responded, "Your skin color doesn't matter. We are your friends.[11] We hope to stay here. What is your plan?"

Isaac, momentarily, had gone to the back of the log house, built and shared by the three, and returned with gifts of smoked turkey and a rifle. He gave the turkey to Feather and the rifle to Scout, saying:

"These are small gifts of friendship. . . . The rifle is old, but sharp on target. It's for your son, Arrow Feather."

Astonished and joyful, Feather placed her hand over her mouth to stifle a sob while Scout turned away to hide a tear or two rolling down his cheek. Both then nodded their thanks.

Joseph repeated his question quickly and cheerfully in deference to their friends' embarrassment.

Scout answered, knowing Feather was still filled with emotion. "We must meet with our Monongahela leaders to see how they feel. I believe they will approve Feather's plan."

Feather said simply, "Our plan."

"Here's what we could do," Scout said. "While you are back home, or with your militia, we will continue to care for your cattle . . . in hidden meadows. . . . We will make diversion, build Indian sheds to fool troops, who come to inspect area. Troops will think you have gone."

"That's very good of you, my friends," Henry said, "but we haven't decided to leave, not yet anyway."

Scout then asked, "Why does your 'Gov' Penn want you to leave? How does he know which are squatters here about?"

Henry responded, "Gov Penn wrote a decree to all pioneers that don't own their land. He said we must leave so our friendly Indians can use these lands for huntin'. He's a good friend of yours. . . . He knows we are here 'cause of the road tax we have to pay."

"He didn't ask us about your leavin'," Scout responded.

"No, he didn't, Feather agreed. "I talk to Indian women. Most want you stay. They say you are friends. . . . Would pioneers let us use land to hunt? Would you?"

"That's a good question, Feather," Isaac said. "But braves would have to stick to the woods. They would have to take care and not kill our stock," he added with a smile.

"It would be good to ask around," Isaac continued, "to find out how tribal leaders feel toward us stayin' or leavin'. But I don't believe Gov Penn will change or cancel his decree. At least, I never heard of such a thing happenin' afore."

Before leaving, Scout and Feather agreed to visit Indian friends to get a better understanding of how they felt toward pioneers. At the same time, Joseph, Henry and John said they would survey pioneers to see if they would allow the Indians to hunt farm lands. They held doubts, however, about fooling the troops with diversionary tactics.

On their way back to their village, Scout and Feather spoke to braves at length about relationships between pioneers and braves. Scout took somewhat of a negative but realistic tact.

He told Feather that, "Our Indian warriors laughed at the English way of fighting out in the open in straight lines, like at Fort Duquesne in seventeen fifty-five.[12] That was when I was learning to be a scout under Braddock.

"At Fort Duquesne," Scout continued, "General Braddock's forces could not see anything to shoot at because the enemy fought from behind trees. He thought that was cowardly to be fighting that way. He was mightily wrong. He was killed and most of his army was killed or wounded.

"That kind of past fighting still works against support of us. Our Indians and pioneer friends know that well. They have seen it and their troops suffered sorely from it."

"You are right, mostly," Feather agreed, in her language, "But you are mixing turkeys with doves. We are talking about farming, not militia fighting. We know pioneers are good farmers."

Feather then said to her husband, "As scout for many, many moons with the English, you know strategies. How can we win stronger Indian support for squatters?"

"By reminding them that our worst enemies, the Cherokees, are in bed with the French," Scout answered promptly. "Menongahela know most farmers here about are militiamen, too. So as you say, they are good farmers and by that, good men, squatters or not."

"That's our strategy in talking to Indian leaders and wives."

"That good fishing," Feather said with a grin.

Did they squat it, own it or lose it?

Henry, Joseph and Isaac, frequently called "the three," held a strategy session, too, arriving somewhat at the same approach to their pioneer farmers. They were aware, however, that some pioneers would reject that reasoning, largely those who sorted all Indians into the same bag with their enemy Cherokees. In ignorance, they hated all Indians.

The three had stressed the point that "all possible farmers, squatters and militiamen, must agree and sign, or put their marks on, our petition sheets," as Joseph put it. They also stressed the need to enlist another nine more men to help scour the countryside within a 50-mile radius of Three Forks, formed by the Youghiogheny, Laurel and Casselman Rivers.[13]

As good military strategists, under Ensign Joseph, they drew a map and circled their area, then divided it like a pie into 12 cuts, each numbered one to twelve. Henry was to oversee cuts one through four; Joseph, five through eight; Isaac, the remaining cuts.

"Petitioning will begin at dawn tomorrow morning," Joseph asserted, adding with authority, "Report back here in 10 days with petitions completed."

Henry and Isaac, both sergeants, responded in dead-serious manner. "Yes sir, Ensign Plowman."

Joseph served under Captain Cresap's command, Cumberland, Maryland,[14] about 60 miles south and a bit east of Three Forks. He was on leave visiting and working with his brother and cousin clearing land and doing other squatters' chores on their 600 acres. Each squatted 200.

Joseph knew full well as did his brother and cousin that they were skirting close to violating codes of ethics for militiamen, particularly Ensign Joseph Workman. They discussed this at length, arriving at two reasoned solutions which Joseph wrote out:

(1) Reassure Governor Tom Penn that Indians in this area of Penn Province want pioneers to stay, largely because of friendships, but also . . because:

(2) The Indians rely on us for protection and for gifts (or barters) of vegetables and other produce grown by farmers.

A precautionary change was made cancelling their previous agreement on the method of soliciting petition signatures. Instead of 12 solicitors doing the complete job they would select solicitors on a relay basis, "Like mail riders or Greek relay runners of old."

The three would go to the outer reaches of the solicitation area, "the pie" as Henry called it, and select nine trusted squatters to join the three Plowman men. Each of the 12 then would move inward on their cuts of pie toward Three River forks, until they obtained signatures from four squatters, each of whom would be asked to continue the relay system until the pie was consumed.

"No mention will be made of who concocted the idea and who came up with names," Joseph had commanded. "The key to all of this is the selection of trustworthy workers."

"Ensign, why don't we just keep our seats and come up with names we know to be most reliable?" Henry asked. "Then we can tell each worker who he should contact. . . . and don't forget the women. I can tick off at least three who'd be good riders and more trustworthy and experienced than us men at gettin' petition signatures.

"Fine, let's do it," Joseph said.

The three set about offering and selecting names, four men and five women besides themselves. The very next day, they were on the trails by dawn.

On their way home, Scout and Bright Feather had discussed in Iroquois their plan of approach, beginning with a question by Feather: "What way should we talk with our friends?"

"We now must speak in our tongue," Scout said, "and without the pioneer, back-country words." The two laughed, although both intermingled back-country words when using English.

"First, we must make them see that pioneer farmers are our friends. Second, we must say they protect us from Cherokees. Third, we say we must help them save their farms."

Continuing, Scout said he was worried over how their Indian friends feel about how some of the English fought — in the open and in lines. "They are now mostly using our way, but Indians here still remember the past. . . how the French and Cherokee shot them down in rows. Braves think that is how pioneers fight because they were trained by early English here."

Feather countered, "That is like mixing apples with turnips. Militia fighting has nothing to do with farming. Pioneers good at farming we know, and good men, too.

"Yes, they are, but folks are remembered mostly for mistakes." . "It would be wise if talked with our Chief Light Bear. He has memory better than any other. He can tell us much about friendships in the past between his tribe and pioneers. He fought side by side with English."

Scout and Feather, mostly listeners, met late into the night with their Chief, who was receptive and proud of Feather's way of helping pioneers save their land. He told them how General Washington fought the French with mediocre subordinate officers and poorly trained troops, sometimes short of gunpowder.

"That's the real problem. Pioneers are having to take orders from inexperienced officers," the Chief emphasized. He then scoured the past for examples of known, strong relationships. Even though he was nearing 75 years, his memory was indelible.

Chief Bear, as he was commonly called, cited friends of Indians. . . General George Washington, Governor Thomas Penn and Indian leaders, too, like Pisquetomen.

Grinning broadly, he said, "I like to think of that man as 'Pisquet Amen.' He calls it right and true, no matter which side he is on. He then told a story.

"One cold, wet day back many years, the sixth day of November, I remem-

Did they squat it, own it or lose it?

ber, Cherokee Indians stole 20 horses from local farmers and militia. The English retaliated by killing thirty of them.

"My friend Pisquetomen heard that one of the horses had been stolen from a widow, Jenny Frazer.[15] It was her only steed. She used it for plowing and for such errands as helping Indian women with birthings," Chief Bear said. "On a visit, he told Jenny he was sorry she had lost her only horse, and that he would give her one back."

As Chief Bear continued, the tale came alive.

Gratefully thanking Pisquetomen, Jenny reached for the reins of a spare horse the chief had trailed with him.

'No. You should have better. Take my steed, Star Bright. . He is faster and sure footed, gentle and powerful. He could pull two plows and be happy. I ride home on second horse.'

Jenny was embarrassed by such a noble gesture, attempting to persuade against the gift, but to no avail. Pisquetomen insisted, almost demanded, she take his steed. She had no choice but to accept Star Bright graciously, or insult him.

In return, Jenny gave Pisquetomen two smoked turkeys.

He then thanked her and said, 'I give you my Star Bright for strong reasons: one, for help you give our women in child birthing; two, even more important, for my family and family roots here in the earth.

'Many pioneers think we not settle in one place. That not true. We go hunting for three or four moons. Return home each time after hunt. Need place to rest and see friends, have children and cure and store meat from hunt. Thank spirit for our good times and good lives.

'I have other reason for giving you horse,' Pisquetomen . . . continued. 'Time will come soon when deer and bear and fish will be hard find. Our people will have stay and raise meat and grain and fruit, like settlers.

'We need help to farm. We need learn how choose best stock. How build log houses. How plant, grow. How make linen, wool. . . Settlers help us learn, be friends, stop killings.'

By now, tears were trickling down Jenny's face, no matter how weathered her cheeks and how tough her resolve.

'My good and solid friend,' she said, 'I thank you. I thank you for what you say and what you give. I will feed and care for Star with love. I thank you even more for what you said. Your words have made us friends for our lifetimes.'

Jenny assured Pisquetomen that pioneers would help train Indians in farming, then saying, 'This can be a two-way trail. You braves know much about finding and storing fruits and vegetables from woods and meadows. You can help us in many Indian ways.'

Each then placed a right hand on the other's shoulder, stood quietly face to face, eyes to eyes, in a seal of faith and friendship, and parted silently.

Did they squat it, own it or lose it?

* * *

Bear Chief continued his stories well into the night, providing examples of friendships and meeting mutual needs. In closing, he said, "You, Scout, have one of the best stories to tell. . . . The one about how Joseph and you saved each lives. You must tell my warriors about that, case they forgot."

"Lucky we both were not killed," Scout said.

The story went like this: About five years ago, Joseph was returning from his family farm near Baltimore Town, where he had been with his wife and family for six months. As he got within a short distance of Turkey Foot, and home, close rifle shots bludgeoned the silence.

One struck Joseph in the fleshy part of his upper left leg. He immediately dug his heels into his horse, "Steedy," and raced to the cover of woods. There he crouched and coaxed Steedy to lie down. Then more shots echoed through the dense woods. Rising slightly and peering through a break in the underbrush he saw Scout at a distance riding speedily and skillfully, bent low over his horse. What a brave but foolhardy thing to do, Joseph thought, realizing that Scout was purposely using his body as a diversion to save whomever was under attack.

Shots bore in around Scout from both sides of the trail, one grazing him in the shoulder.

Joseph gave a crow call of distress, held his rifle tighter and squinted for sharper vision as the sun edged closer to setting. He was sure Scout had heard his call but he wasn't sure he would make it through.

Unknown to Joseph, Scout was riding out front of a squad of mixed militia and local braves, eight in all. They were hunting a group of six marauding Cherokees when they heard the round of shots, one of which had struck Joseph.

Scout did hear the crow call, then another. So did his pony, Snort, responding with a whinny answered immediately by Steedy. Without command, Snort reared, wheeled and took to the woods.

Joseph and Scout joined in a quick greeting and led their horses deeper into the dense forest where they waited. No sooner had they knelt down than rifle fire broke out again.

Scout examined his shoulder wound quickly. It was superficial but paining severely.

Suddenly, a friendly voice called out. "Jake! Will! Harold! Intercept at the creek! At the big oak overhang."

Then galloping horses and riders raced by, followed by more rifle shots. Acrid smoke wafted into the woods and nostrils of the combatants. All birds remained silent.

Jake, Will and Harold meanwhile had taken a shortcut they knew to intercept the marauders.

Seeing that Joseph was wounded in the leg, Scout asked, "Can you walk? Can you shoot gun, fight?"

Did they squat it, own it or lose it?

WHETSTONES

"I b'lieve I'm fit," Joseph said, rising as a slight moan escaped between clenched teeth. "Not bleedin' so's I'll run out of blood. It hurts like blazes, but thank the good Lord no bones were damaged."

"How 'bout you, Scout?"

"Not serious wound. Bullet shallowed through clean."

Scout then retrieved his aid kit from a saddle bag and treated Joseph's leg. Joseph, in turn, gave aid to Scout's shoulder. Both wounds were wrapped with long strips of linen.

The two mounted their horses and moved quickly through the woods toward Branch Creek, Scout in the lead.

They took the shortcut, crossed Branch Creek and followed it near to where it intersected the trail. As they moved forward, every snap, of a twig caused anticipation of enemy approach. Pain creased their faces. Another moan escaped from Joseph; Scout searched his face to determine his condition and reserve.

On reaching Branch Creek, the two led their horses into clear, cool water, stopping briefly to dip their wounds and let their horses drink. The water eased pain and refreshed them.

Across the creek, red oaks, red maples and green ash formed such dense stands that little underbrush could survive to hinder progress on horseback.

The two mounted and trotted their steeds rapidly along close to the creek banks, as the cadence of woods' crickets slowed and temperatures dropped. Frogs croaked and hoot owls exchanged calls and swished and stirred the late afternoon air with their giant wings.

Without speaking, Joseph and Scout rode the route to where the stream crossed the trail. They dismounted and walked their horses into a thick grove, out of sight and away from impending gunfire along the trail. On their return, they saw that Jake, Will and Harold were fanned out and positioned between trees. Joseph and Scout selected frontal positions lying behind logs.

Their guns were cocked and ready; but deep down, they hoped killing would not be necessary.

As senior officer, Joseph called out commands as he heard approaching horses: "Hold your fire 'till they reach that oak overhangin' the trail. Then on my command, fire a volley above their heads. If they don't reign in, lower your sights and bore in on lamin' their horses first. Lastly, aim to kill."

The Cherokees speedily approached, closing in rapidly.

Joseph eased his leg to a more comfortable position; Jake, Will and Harold nervously regripped their rifles, awaiting Joseph's command.

"Get ready! . . . . On mark! . . . . Fire!"

Bullets slammed high into the overhanging oak. Roosting owls and crows fanned the air, as they escaped the unexpected.

Thunder echoed from distant clouds.

The Cherokee reigned in their horses; the animals reared and pranced impatiently, nervously.

Did they squat it, own it or lose it?

"Hold your fire, men!" Joseph barked out, then said in a quieter voice, "Jake . . . Harold . . . Steal over and mount your horses. Jake, you cross the creek to the north; Harold, you to the south. . . Flank them from both directions. . . The three of us will cover for you."

The two stole away undetected, climbed their mounts and rode quietly across north and south, as instructed. Then they moved unseen into flank positions.

Meantime, the Cherokees sat their steeds nervously, knowing enemy troops were closing from behind. One of the Indians called out in broken English:

"Sir! We not braves shoot you in leg. We want no fight. We hunt meat for wives an chil'en. We find meat, we go home."

"How you know I was shot in leg?" Joseph asked, then spoke in slow, simple language. "You not dressed for hunting. You dressed as warriors. . . Stay where your are! Stay!"

"We aim rifles from flanks. . . from front. . . from back. Do not try escape. . . We shoot to kill," Joseph said in a strong but tired voice. "Sit your horses."

All but one warrior obeyed. He dug his heels and reigned his horse sharply in the direction of his village. He was still in sight when Harold's rifle cracked and felled the warrior from his horse. He was dead before hitting the ground.

The other Cherokees sat their horses, as ordered.

The remaining five renegade Indians were captured and taken to the fort after they built a mound and buried their fellow warrior. They then were forced to work for 30 days throwing up earthen bunkers for defensive needs, a punishment considered demeaning to Indians.

* * *

At the end of the story, Bear Chief yawned and dismissed Scout and Feather, saying, "Land is most important, most valuable to all of us, except for family. Visit and get support from many tribal members. I will talk with my leaders."

Meantime, the three Plowman men and their helpers completed their petition drive in good spirits. They obtained signatures from nearly eight of every ten farmers for a total of 47 favoring Indian hunting on their lands, based on conditions of safety agreed upon previously.

Two weeks later, Captain Cresap arrived at the Plowman farms where he confronted the two brothers and their cousin. He knew, but could not prove, that the three were responsible for collecting signatures on petitions to influence Tom Penn about revoking his decree.

Only the three would have the savvy to do it, he judged correctly. The Captain actually sided with them against Penn's mandate. He saw no need to return their land to the Indians for hunting, regardless of whether they squatted it or owned it. . . . But he could not admit it.

Did they squat it, own it or lose it?

Joseph, Henry and Isaac made a strong case for their position, citing facts and friendship ties backed up by actual happenings. When they told the story about "Pisquet Amen," Cresap laughed heartily at the newly given name but was quiet and touched over how Pisquetomen had helped Jenny Frazer. He had heard about Scout and Josh saving each others' lives but listened as though he hadn't.

The captain had known and respected Scout for many years for his adeptness in scouting out enemy locations, numbers of troops and amounts of food and munitions. He knew also how supportive and intuitive was Scout's wife, Bright Feather.

Henry suggested, "Sir, you should visit and speak with Chief Bear. You know him well. He says time will come when his tribe will have to turn to farmin', as wild meat animals are killed off. He also knows that we can help them learn our ways. Then our good friends, the Indians, can help, us with theirs."

The captain did meet with Chief Bear and with other tribal leaders, selected carefully by the Chief. In balance, their comments did support what the Captain's subordinants had said. Still later, Captain Cresap met alone with Joseph whom he had pegged as the prime organizer and mover of their plan and actions. He did know, however, that Scout and Feather acted independently.

"Joseph, you know my feelings about this situation, but feelings and actions are butting heads. My superiors are angry . . . . demanding action against what's been going on here."

Interrupting, Joseph asked, "Why don't you just demote me to sergeant or corp'ral?"

"Thanks, Joseph. I had somethin' like that in mind. . ."

"As you know," Cresap said, "I've been pushing for your promotion. Fact is, papers have gone forward to my superiors requesting your upgrade to lieutenant. What if I withdraw my recommendations? Such action would placate my superiors, without doubt, and without lowering your grade. . . What do you think?"

Joseph extended his hand to shake the Captain's, then Joseph said, "I've admired your prompt decisiveness and judgment for years. You know that. . . I agree with your decision fully. I'll do my best to keep out of trouble. . . and you can bet I'll climb to captaincy, at least."

Cresap laughed, saying, "You'll not push me out of my command. I'll bet on that. And I'll bet with you, on your bet, too."

They shook hands again and parted.

* * *

Louicie moved to the Workman farm at Turkey Foot, Penn Province, from

Baltimore Town where a nephew made it possible for her parents to keep their farm. She moved there to be with Henry at the same time as Isaac's wife, Bell, who was childless. So was Louicie, except for adult children. Joseph and his wife, Sarah, had grown children and two younger ones. Sarah would visit Turkey Foot as frequently as she could.

"Farming's been good, for our men," Louicie wrote in May, 1775, but they often do not know which way to turn. Land still was not secure, during the Dunmore War.

"It was a wrong war, sad for Indians, mostly Shawnee and Mingo," she continued. "Henry and I talked of moving again, maybe in 1775. I didn't want to cry, but I did. Things are so upsy and downsy. . . Reminds me of a shortest story about a neighbor girl, only six, named Marsha Annie who woke up crying. When her mamma stroked her head and asked her why, she burst out and said, "I dreamed I woked up and was dead."

"Now let me tell you about when our three Workman husbands were discussing . . . and probably cussing . . . that land maybe was not ours. They were talkin' and askin' (to use their words) questions, then worryin' if they had broken militia regulations.

* * *

. . . . "What in hell ever happened to Governor Tom Penn's decree," Henry asked. "You think he backed offen it?"

"Think he's taking our survey seriously?" Isaac asked.

"Damned if I know," Joseph said. "There's lots of talk goin' on . . . some good, some bad. Captain Cresap said the governor may decide to ignore his mandate, partly because of our survey activity, yes.

"Top of that, word's out that Penn is figurin' on buying back land the Province deeded over to Indians. Can we believe that? . . . . It's not likely we can plan ahead on it, that's certain. "Were we wrong to have our wives come here with things so unstable?" Henry wanted to know.

The men were aware that quite a few absentee squatters had returned from previous locations, many without their families.

Isaac had become very successful at farming in Penn Province; Henry held his own but talked about moving; Joseph, the perpetual soldier, spent more and more time in militia activities, letting his farm out to Isaac and his hired men. As Louicie said before, "Times were topsy-turvy."

Dunmore's war began over the land, then called "the dark country"[16] and to the north, also. Settlers wanted land for farming, Indians for hunting.

At the behest of Captain Cresap, Joseph mustered five of his key militiamen for a briefing, including seasoned fighters Henry, Isaac, Scout, John Miller and Peter Jones. They met at Isaac's place, first for supper, then for briefing.

"Men, there's no doubt we are facin' difficult times," Joseph began. "It's the same old story, a fight over land, over who's to farm it or who's to hunt it. . . Up to now, our troops here have been able to dodge bein' drawn into battle. . . But not now. . . Let me give you some background."

Joseph told the men that they could be facing Shawnee and Mingo warriors. "They'll be seasoned fighters and well organized good fellows. This time we'll be the bad ones."

Continuing, Joseph said the Shawnee and Mingo had raided some white settlements in recent years, but nothing of consequence. While pioneers and militia have been the aggressors, the Indians have shown some great restraint. . . that is, until early this spring.

"Joseph . . . Sir. . . I'm willin' to fight for our families and our land. Nothin' more than that," Miller said bluntly. Others agreed.

Miller's statement stirred a hot debate, near fisticuffs at one point, when all but one stood with scowled face and clenched fist.

Even Henry sided with Miller against his brother.

"Joseph, don't you recognize we've got our land here, and now our women? I agree with John. I'm confused, too. We're tired of fightin'; the Indians is tired of fightin'. If it don't stop, families will head back to where they came from."

"What in hell's fire do you want, Sergeant Henry Plowman, don't you have the sense to see what we're aheadin' for? French are tryin' to move us out; the Indians, excepting our Monongahelas, are rampaging. . . Now you and Miller want to drive a wedge between us and the English. You . . . "

"Brothers! All of you! Sit and let us reason!" Scout shouted firmly. . . . "Strangely, both sides are right.

"True . . . We Indians are tired of fightin'. Our wives are risin' up. . . We are losing many sons, some daughters. . . . We have no Baltimore Towns to go back to.

"If we Indians had formed a nation of tribes, not all breakin' up into chips of a log that float without direction, we would own this great and beautiful, rich land."

As Scout spoke, his voice remained firm but progressively quieter. He looked each individual in the eye. He remained seated, hands imaging words, as chips floating hither and yon. His presence, hypnotic, quieted emotions, stimulated reasoning, "We fail to see big forest spotted with meadow and deer. are blind to clear bubblin' streams and fish that struggle, flash up rivers with direction. . . don't sigh at beauty of scattered clouds, breath deeply after a gentle rain or see plants grow as rains freshen lands. . . too busy to wander woods. . . We don't even look up to stars and wonder at twinkles and order."

Scout then melded for a moment into the quietness, stillness of the cabin, as the men marveled his poetic depth of feeling, a side of him that none had seen or heard before.

"We need vision to scout ahead for what's in store . . . not spoiled meat, fruit, grain . . . not men always cleanin' and polishin' guns, sharpenin' knives

Did they squat it, own it or lose it?

and arrows . . . not killin's and woundin's or weepin's . . . not children who wander and tremble as lost.

"We must unite all forests and meadows, scout and map streams, rivers as trails. . . Watch loving care and teachin's given by bear and deer and raccoon to their young. . . Be wary of cunning and shifty and selfish, those who think only of self first. . . Look to moon and stars and heavens for true and lasting guidance. The heavens and the spirit god will tell where we go from here."

After an extended silence, Joseph remained seated and spoke calmly, saying, "Scout is right. He has described what is happening now in true parables and what is best for our futures, and those of our families.

"In the past three years or so, we pioneers have not been the peace makers. The Shawnee and Mungo have cut back on raids. They want to fish and hunt like most Indians.

"The Indians hoped the Penn Quakers would find peace. They tried hard but failed. We fought on, like at big forks at Fort Duquesne . . . instead of negotiating, just last spring.

"Fact is, since I've been crippled, for now, from another leg wound, I've heard that one of my superiors has set out to kill Indians for no special cause . . . killings for whose sake?"

Various others then shared more sad happenings.

"I've heard about a man called Greathouse who came across a group of Indians, some drunk, some not. His men killed nine of 'em," John Miller chipped in.

"Yes, and one of those killed was a sister of Chief Logan, a Mingo,"[17] Isaac added. "That killin' sure failed at peace."

"Joseph," Isaac continued, "what about Major Angus McDonald? I hear tell he was instructed to take 100 men up the Muskingum Valley . . . on orders to destroy any Indian villages they find."

"Is that true?" . . . . Joseph nodded, shrugged.

Isaac then questioned actions by the man, Dunmore, whose name was given to the war. "What of Colonel Dunmore? He's maybe done as much to rout out Indians as anyone. Word is out that he and eleven hundred men drifted down the Ohio . . . then went across land, and the Hocking River, to strike down villages."

Joseph answered Isaac's what-of question, "Yes. Far as I've heard. It's all true about Dunmore and others you men have told about.

"But there's a bit of moonlight shining through all of this madness . . . for those looking for land to settle by children of us Penn folks."

Henry perked up on hearing of that possibility.

"I've heard officially," Joseph continued, "that the Indians sued for peace at some sort of treaty camp, they called it, at Charlotte in Virginia. The treaty gave settlers the right to settle and farm land that is called 'the dark country'. . . . without trouble from Indians. It's the western-most third of Virginia."

Did they squat it, own it or lose it?

WHETSTONES

Six months later, Joseph sold his farm and returned to Baltimore Town where he could be with his family and where he was named a lieutenant (later captain) as a provincial advisor on military strategy. Henry decided to go to western Virginia, selling or renting his farm to Isaac, still expanding. Louicie would go to Baltimore Town until Henry wrote that it was safe for her to come.

Next day Louicie asked Henry, "Why are you so all fired up about going to the dark country? Scares me just to hear it."

"Oh dung. That just means it's dark 'cause of thick timber."

"Henry, don't you try to cornball me. I know what's been going on down there. You should know that, what with my scribblin' so much in letters and my diary. I get to read letters from down there when I'm back in Baltimore Town."

"Well . . . my lady noselong . . . why don't you wanta go? You afraid of huge ugly shadows in the forests and devil animals stalking at midnight?"

"I ain't said. I have not said I would or would not go." . . . "And, I ain't said you is, and I ain't said you ain't."

"All right. All right. You know I'll go wherever you go, as long as it's safe. Ain't that so?"

Both then laughed heartily and felt warm and comfortably in love after nearly 20 years of married life.

Henry refused to believe that peace was present in the dark country. He knew Lord Dunmore said it was so, but Henry was wary of the lord, spelled with a small 'l', he'd always add.

The next day, he told Louicie he would visit his friend, Isaac Cox to volunteer and make plans for a trip down the Ohio River to the dark country. Isaac was getting up a cadre of 18 or 20 men who wanted land to squat for themselves and their children.

Cox and his two brothers had for many years built forts along the Monongahela River where he lived and was well known as an Indian fighter.[18]

Henry began his 35-mile trip the next day on horseback. He traveled west and a bit north from Three Rivers, better known than Turkey Foot, where Henry and Louicie lived and farmed.

They both wanted to help their tenant sons find land to squat and own, if they chose, but doubted if their sons would leave Baltimore. Their children were either tenants or farmers, or wives of farmers, back on Middle River, near Baltimore Town.

Louicie naturally was concerned for Henry's safety during the arduous and risky journey and arrival in the dark country. She knew, however, that the team of men would plan and implement carefully during the next six months.

As Henry was leaving for his 3-week visit, Louicie gave him a pair of woolen gloves made of fiber she had sheared, combed, spun and knitted. Henry then gave Louicie a silver necklace adorned with finely cut and polished gemstone inserts. He had intended to present her with his gift on his departure for western Virginia, but decided he wanted to see her wear and enjoy it before leaving.

Did they squat it, own it or lose it?

Henry placed the necklace lovingly around his wife's neck, stood back admiringly, then took her in his arms. They embraced emotionally, tears flowing down their cheeks, and warm hearts throbbing their lengthy love affair.

Henry pulled on his gloves proudly, patted and rubbed his gloves together, placed and secured his saddle bag, mounted Starlight gently and set out on his journey, waving and throwing kisses as he left.

His journey soon found him swimming Starlight across Juchio Geni stream, later called Youghioghany, then riding up Laurel Hills. From there, he peered southerly at "The Great Meadows," where Fort Necessity had been located and where George Washington suffered a costly and embarrassing defeat against the French on July 4, 1754.[19]

Henry tried to visualize the "fort," nothing more then than crude embankments, and the positioning and tactics of the French, who killed and wounded two-thirds of Washington's men. He then skirted an area called Stewart's Riff but couldn't for the life of him pull from his memory what historic event such a riff represented. He thought harder and decided it must have been something to do with politics.

Now a day and a half away from Louicie, Henry gazed at the great Monongahela River, chuckling over the translation of the Indian river's name, as he recalled, "High banks, breaking off and falling down in places."[20]

He then spotted a group of men in a dry bog area next to the river. Among them was Isaac Cox with five others who had positioned huge yellow poplar logs in parallel pairs and were cinching them together with planks across paired blunt ends.

Henry knew at a glance that they were building flatboats for transporting the men to and down the Ohio River to western Virginia. He knew also that boats had to be finished by spring flooding to float them out of the bog and onto the Monongahela.

* * *

Scout and Isaac, meanwhile, were pinned down fighting marauders who had stolen a dozen or so horses, vitally needed next spring for plowing and dragging land for planting. Other pioneers were grouped strategically along the same trail, not knowing that Scout and Isaac were cornered.

It was the same trail where Scout and Joseph had been wounded. . . . The leader of the well-known marauding band, nicknamed "Twitch," because of a facial affliction, had ordered four of his ten men into the underbrush to find and kill Scout and Isaac. The four braves were slinking skillfully through the brush when one tripped, grabbed and broke a dead limb.

The snap of the limb alerted Scout and Isaac, who immediately rose and fired, killing the marauding brave, and another at his side. The snap also alerted Peter Jones who then shouted out a command in code words: "Climb! . . .

Scoot! . . . Pepper heart!" . . . which meant to mount, charge and shoot to kill."

The pioneer farmers, angry and mightily motivated, ferreted out the marauders and captured all of them, after wounding three and killing one. During the turmoil, Scout and Isaac captured the two remaining men who also sought to kill them.

To Peter's astonishment and chagrin the marauders weren't Indians at all. They were white men dressed authentically as Cherokees. Peter realized, on seeing Twitch, that it was the same group that attacked, slaughtered and maimed farmers and other tribal braves to the north, after stealing horses for sale to the French.

As a trademark, they mutilated victims by scalping with ears attached. One of Twitch's men had such a scalp, dried and stuffed in his small duffel bag cinched to his horse. All of their horses were confiscated on being found hidden deep in the woods.

The dead marauders were buried in the woods; the wounded, treated and cared for; and all survivors were tried and imprisoned. Twitch died of his wounds.

* * *

Henry meanwhile had pitched in to help build the flatboats. He worked side by side with Isaac Cox securing planks vertically across the huge pairs of poplar logs. While working, Isaac told Henry about the boats and plans for travel.

Each of the flatboats was to be 20 to 25 feet wide and 85 to 95 feet long[21] with rough shed cabins on each for cooking, eating, sleeping and storing supplies. Cabins were to be roughly 40 to 45 feet long and 12 to 15 feet wide, centered on the deck allowing walkways from bow to stern along both starboard and port sides.

The boats would be large enough to transport the horses of the 18 men, Isaac said, adding, "We'll tether them to the cabins at the bow and stern, where they'll have enough slack for movin' around some and to eat and drink from troughs and tanks."

A colonel and a wealthy landowner, Isaac was direct, determined and assured, the type who instilled confidence and savvy in those who worked for and with him. These attributes were necessary particularly on a journey of this type and settlement in the dark country. He demanded dedication from his men, partly because he and his brothers were funding the project.

Their goal, of course, was ownership of land, lots of it.

"Flood waters, floating logs, boulders and sand bars will challenge us at every rapids, narrows and bend of the Monongahela and the Ohio," Cox said. "Hidden stumps and logs, trapped in unsuspected spots, will be among our biggest concerns — besides Indians along the way.

Did they squat it, own it or lose it?

"But we'll be prepared with an excellent pilot, Tom Stearman, and a top flight crew on our sturdy flatboats."

Henry smiled and chuckled over the pilots name, asking Isaac, "I'd bet Tom chose a stage surname to match his trade."

"No, his family name originated in Holland, where it was common to take trade names as surnames. Piloting water crafts goes back in his family for hundreds of years."

Unknown to Henry, the colonel and his brothers held preemptions for 2,000 acres of land granted him by Virginia officials. Half of the land would go to Isaac and the remainder divided between his brothers.

The land was assured only on condition that Cox establish a permanent station, and eventually a thriving community, within five years of arrival. Then he was to establish a militia unit in western Virginia among his group and build on the unit by attracting others down the Ohio.

The colonel then told Henry, "I've briefed the others on all of these points. They all know it's still a time when only armed men can set foot on western Virginia soil."

Continuing, he then said, "Henry I've known you for a long spell. No question in my mind that you are at the top calibre of men I need in order to succeed, and we will succeed. But I must ask you, as with the others, three specific questions:

"First, are you in good health? . . . Second, what does Louicie say about you signing on? . . . Third, where do you want your roots to grow? Here? Western Virginia? Or both?"

Henry responded, not nearly as directly, but with tinges of humor and philosophy:

"One, I'm in real good health, so good I may need to share some with others in the crew.

"Two, Louicie has said 'yes.' She thrives on challenges. and she'll have more to scribble about in her letters and diaries on our journey that's ahead.

"Three, our family roots are where our love nests . . . in our hearts, in our minds and in our bodies . . . even when some are back east, some here and some at journey's end."

He went on to say that Louicie will go back to Baltimore Town to be with their sons and daughters and families, and to "cuddle up" to her only grandchild.

"We'll sell our farm at Turkey Foot to my cousin, Isaac. He's makin' a good country run out of his herds of cattle, sheep and hogs, usin' help from returning squatters — even local Indians," Henry said. "Fact is, he and his foreman are startin' up 'prenticeship programs in land and livestock."

Henry and Isaac then shook hands and slapped each other on the back, thus sealing the agreement. The two and the others finished nailing down poplar planks and were ready to build flatboat sheds, also of poplar, early the next day. While working steadily as a team, they melded closer together in both acceptance and confidence in one another.

Each evening after supper, the group gathered in front of Isaac's huge hearth to discuss and plan the following day's work. They also reviewed and memorized their duties and responsibilities for the forthcoming trip. It was serious business, they all knew.

Isaac told of Pilot Stearman's talents, experience and expected duties and responsibilities to build the confidence of the men making the trip. He then announced the names of pilot assistants who would be briefed and trained by Stearman.

Isaac's choices were Henry Plowman and Peter Jones, both of Turkey Foot and both experienced militia and rifle men.

"It's true, neither has even a minute of piloting time, but don't you men worry. Tom will guide the lead boat and Henry and Peter will follow the leader's actions and commands.

"Tom, meanwhile, will drill Henry and Peter in pilot commands and duties. Others will be instructed on using long poles for rudders . . . and for leveraging us around bars and through shallows." Stearman then showed the men two types of poles, both about 20 feet long. One was flanged at the end like a canoe paddle for use as a rudder, the other without the flange, for leveraging through shallows.

"We'll finish these boats in another three weeks, before snow falls," Cox said. "Then by next spring, most probably the middle of April, the river will be high enough then to float our boats and we'll be on our way."

The three remaining weeks went by rapidly. Cabins were built, bunks installed and horses "quarters" made ready. As a final action, the men augered holes in strategic points around the walls of each shed to be able to see and fire their rifles should they be attacked by would-be river bandits or by Indians.

* * *

Once back in Turkey Foot, Henry told Loucie all about the flatboats and plans for their journey, assuring her of the many safety precautions and the supportive crews. . . "We melded and welded together like a group of ponies kicken' off wolves." Loucie was to leave for Baltimore in two days as part of a caravan returning for visits. Before leaving the two had a farewell picnic at the crook of Branch Creek. They ate quietly listening to woods birds and watching a doe and her twins munch colorful fall foliage. They laughed as one of the overgrown twins nosed and butted the doe's udder for milk that had ceased flowing. They cried as they spoke of their departure.

They then made passionate love before leaving for home.

After Loucie departed, Henry leased their farm to Cousin Isaac, for buying later. He then spent most of the next five months helping Isaac and his foreman,

Jed, with farming and organizing their apprenticeship programs. Even though busy, time dragged on.

Springtime finally arrived and, as Henry approached Cox's farm, he saw the flatboats floating the flooded bog as the men loaded supplies. The sight sent shivers of enthusiasm sprinkling through his body.

On riding close to the bog lake, Henry bellowed, "All aboard! . . . New land, ahoy! Shouts of agreement responded quickly and echoed in both directions along the river.

Isaac Cox beamed at the enthusiasm shown by the men, particularly a man like Henry, in his early forties. Isaac knew him as a man of trust and determination, a man with a sense of humor who also knew when to be dead serious.

With horses, supplies and 18 men aboard, the journey began.

* * *

Dear children and other loved ones, Louicie wrote from Baltimore Town. "I can hardly believe so many land problems just keep on and on. You know that's why we left Turkey Foot. . . First the mean Indians, then Tom Penn and then land grabbing by 'fat landowners'. Even a church.

"My story begins with a short tale in a letter from my Henry, probably written by Isaac Cox. It was mailed from Parker's Station on the Ohio River from on board his flatboat. Isaac was talking hard to the cook, Bill Baker, aboard one of the flatboats heading for western Virginia. The flatboats were anchored next to a sandbar as Cox was asking questions, that Henry probably put him up to. Cox called out loudly so all three crews could hear[22]:

"Mr. Baker. Is your stove workin' well enough?" . . . "Yes sir!". . .Did you remember to stoke it for the night?". . . "Yes sir!" . ."You got enough grease for cookin'?". . "Yes sir!" . . . . "Did you grease the anchors before we left?"

"Did you, or did you not, grease the anchors?"

"Uhhh, no sir!"

At that a gale of laughter exploded from each of the flatboats, then echoed up and down the Ohio. Even Baker joined in with spontaneous laughter forced upward and outward from deep within his protruding belly.

The men then heard turkeys calling out to one another close by, as mouths immediately began to water.

"They're sure talkin' turkey," Stearman called out. "Tellin' us what's gonna roast for supper. How 'bout that, Cookie?"

"Comin' right up," Cookie responded. "Browned and tender, as roasted chestnuts."

Isaac called out to his brother, nicknamed "Target," to "gather up Henry and Tom Stearman," both crackshots, "and fetch us a couple of gobblers."

Henry joined the others wondering if the calls were real, but dismissed the notion quickly on the remoteness of the impenetrable woods.

Did they squat it, own it or lose it?

While the trio was hunting other men were busily inspecting for damage to the flatboats caused by the submerged and floating logs. To their pride in craftsmanship, they found only minor damage, most needing no repair despite thunderous pounding.

Three men were assigned an unpleasant chore, that of dumping overboard the horse belonging to Bill Chenoweth, who was asked by Cox to join the crew. His horse, called "Staunch," was killed by a tree that was dislodged by the flooded river and fell across the stern of one of the boats causing negligible damage. Even though Cox had promised a replacement soon after journey's end, Chenoweth continued to grieve his loss.

"Where's Chenoweth," Cox bellowed suddenly, his voice again echoing up and down the Ohio.

"Bill musta joined the hunters," came a reply. "Prob'ly didn't wanna see Staunch dropped from the boat." Then a volley of shots rang out.

Peter Jones asked the colonel, "Would marauding Indians fire such a volley at two, even three birds? Turkeys don't gather in flocks, particularly in this kind of woods."

"We'd have heard return fire if our men were being attacked," Cox responded quickly, an edge to his voice. "It's that simple."

Cox remained silent, then recognizing his possible blunder, ordered, "Peter! Pick five men and reconnoiter the area. On second thought, all men grab your rifles.

"Peter, you take men from the far boat and pick half of the men in the middle boat. You and your men reconnoiter to the north; I'll take the others to the south."

As the two units moved into position, only the tittering and scolding of squirrels, the rushing of the Ohio and a twig snap now and then could be heard. All men suppressed breathing, hopelessly trying to raise their declining spirits.

Then a moan was heard.

Henry raised up on an elbow only to see a feathered end of an arrow protruding from his side. He tried to remove it but fainted instead.

Then Peter Jones appeared with his men, including Chenoweth, at the same time Cox did. They had found two corpses. Target's dead arms were tugging at a tree trunk in an obvious attempt to rise; Tom Stearman had hold of his aid kit to no avail.

Squirrels had silenced their scolding, the river swirled on.

Cox immediately snapped off the point end of the arrow in Henry's side, tugged the other end to free the staff from his body, followed by a little bleeding. He then shook herbal powder on the wounds and pressed it in lightly into the openings with wads of cotton to seal both entrance and exit. He then bandaged both openings.

"Peter, you've had medical experience. See that Henry is cared for properly. Immediately when you get back, splash some whisky into each wound open-

Did they squat it, own it or lose it?

ing and change the cotton plugs and wrapping. Do that once a day."

By this time, Henry had regained consciousness, cringing at the thought of whiskey being splashed in his wound, but he knew it was proper and necessary. He thanked Isaac with his eyes and a nod of the head, then said falteringly, "Damn it Colonel . . . I shoulda followed my first gut feelings . . . that those birds wasn't the flying kind."

The Colonel tried to quiet Henry, but he talked on.

"I've heard . . . I've heard turkey gobbles . . . hundreds of times . . . since I was a kid. There ain't no sound like it. . . . from any animal or human. . . Scarcely few can talk straight turkey. I shoulda known it was Indians."

"Be quiet and rest, Henry. You just don't know . . . " the Colonel said, as his voice fell off to silence. He felt guilt rising up in his body and mind like bitter gall rising from his stomach. He then rose quickly and went to his dead brother's side.[23]

As Isaac knelt beside Target, his whole body shuddered and shook from silent sobs. He then rose slightly to a prayer position and remained there without sound or movement.

All of the men drifted away, some to the body of Tom Stearman, whose left arm, the one not gripping his aid kit, was pointing north, one finger aimed directly that way.

Even in death, Tom Stearman was pointing the way.

Half of the group headed in that direction. Enroute, they found two dead Indians and one wounded. They treated the wounded just as gently and expertly as Isaac had treated Henry. They then buried the dead in shallow graves so that the Indians could readily retrieve them, along with the wounded, whose injured leg prevented him from moving.

One of Cox's men, called "Thatch", angrily said, "These Indians prob'ly are renegades, not belongin' to any tribe. Why in hell is we treatin 'em likes they was royalty?"

"You may be right, Thatch," Peter Jones said. "I hope so . . . though we don't know that to be true. Anyway, they may have wives and children waitin' for them at home."

Most others in the group murmured in agreement.

On returning, Peter found Colonel Cox back in command, even though much subdued. Peter explained their find and asked, "Should we track and bring the Indians back to justice?"

Cox hesitated thoughtfully and said, "No. Our trip south takes priority." He then named Peter Jones as head pilot and Brandon Acker, called "Soda", as with cracker, to replace the injured Henry as assistant to Jones.

The remaining trip to the mouth of the Kentucky River, where it runs into the Ohio, was without serious problem, if one doesn't count the following: They lost one flatboat, without loss or injury of men; they thought they had lost a man, who fell overboard, but was saved, and they worried over another who

Did they squat it, own it or lose it?

was bitten by a snake, a deadly water moccasin, they thought, but was not.

Cox got lucky and sold the two remaining boats to a trader who shipped pork, corn and maple sugar down the Ohio and Mississippi to New Orleans.

* * *

"Louicie here in Baltimore Town with a short letter from Henry saying that he arrived safely at Cox's Creek, as they are calling it. His letter is in good hand, probably written by one of the crew. Henry said they got there in late April, sometime, with arrow holes in his sides — just one arrow in, and partly out. He's healing well, and is up and around.

"Now for a strange and sad story of how a big church full of powerful people took land from the rightful owners. Trinity church on Manhattan Island first leased the land. Then over a period of time, they took possession of it.

"How do I know that? My Uncle Zach gave me an official document detailing the land take-over, involving the Anneke Bogardus estate.[24] (We've known a few Bogards here and there, like our Nelly. Wonder if they came from the same line.) I have kept that statement for many years. It was written by the corresponding secretary, Bogardus estate, the document says.

"To be sure I'm factual, I'll quote from the official document leaving out only the unimportant parts. Then because it is legalistic, I'll clarify a few points you'll read between paren's. The following is quoted directly:

"'On about the years of 1637 there was a grant (of land) made to Roelof Jans and wife of the Dominies Bowery, by Governor Van Twiller, containing 67 acres. The grant was confirmed on (by) a ground brief (survey) dated July 4th, 1654 from Peter Stuyvesant, The Dutch Governor, and confirmed to Heirs by the English Governor Nicholls, March 27th, 1667.

"'The record parcel of land called Dominie's Hook containing 130 acres was granted by Peter Stuyvesant the 26th of November 1652, and confirmed unto her Heirs by Governor Nicholls (13 years later)' . . .

"It goes on to say it was recorded in a patent book, likely still there this day.[25]

"Did you laugh over the "Hook" farm name? I sure like best the way my earliest Enloes named their farms: Dutch Neck, Tryangle Neck and Enloes Rest, if one can rest on a farm. I like most the farm called "Expetation," the way it was spelled in court house records. It promises hope of good things to come on a journey of farming. Most all of these farms were along the Middle River, Baltimore Town. Just think what they'd be worth today. . . . Now back to unpuzzling the document.

"Ten years after the confirmation, The English Government made the said lease of property of one David Snedecker for 20 years. The document then said, 'The English Government made the said lease for the benefit of Heirs and to hold the said property in trust for them. . . . The property at that time was of lit-

Did they squat it, own it or lose it?

tle value and the heirs occasionally returned to assert their rights.' (I believe they went to Delaware Bay where some of my earliest family settled first.)

"At the expiration of the lease to David Snedecker," Louicie wrote that, "a lease was made to Trinity Corporation for 20 years upon the payment of 20 bushels of wheat per year. The English Government reckoned the last lease was 'extravagant' and 'revoked it.' So, then Trinity Church had a lease by grant that was supposed to come from Governor Conley, under Queen Ann. Then in true words, 'The grant was signed by said Government' but had 'no government Seal.' Then the Queen called the grant 'null and void.' . . . . Can all this be true?

"You should know that the rightful owners had followed squatting ways properly," Louicie continued. "They built cabins and fences, probably hog and bull strong and horse high. Some of those Trinity wild ones then tore down fences and fired buildings to blot out all evidence of true ownership and that's an indirect quote.

"That's all I know for now, except that I believe some of our Enlow people were in the Bogardus line. Later on, I'll tell you of even more land problems, about a fat landowner trying to steal 100 acres. Oh, I forgot to tell you that some of the Trinity folks have started calling themselves Episcos, for short, because I'm not certain how to spell it. I guess you know that our Benjamin Plowman does some preaching at the Episco-Methodist church. Your Louicie is part of that same mix.

"I love you all . . . Louicie (Enlow) Plowman."

Did they squat it, own it or lose it?

What came of Chiefson, heir apparent?

Little happens in a 50-mile radius of Cox's Creek that Louicie Plowman doesn't know about, largely due to her extensive friendships with her patients. In this letter, dated only Spring, 1776, she writes about everything but her midwifery experiences.

"I'll get back to present time and begin with the scariest first," she wrote. "It's a lot about Honey Bear and Wolne, our lab dog who is called 'Beardog' by our Indian friends. The people in the story are Joseph, Jr., my nephew, and his friend, Chiefson, true-name Fleetfeather[26].

"Then I'll tell about the woman in the moon, next about my husband, Henry, who was promoted at a big military gathering here, then on how Isaac Cox saved Henry from being killed by another bear, back a spell."

Louicie's tale begins with Chiefson, up and down a tree.

* * *

Joseph Plowman tilted his head and listened intently; his dog, Wolne, simultaneously sniffed the air and growled menacingly.

"Wolne, that's sure enough your bear growl, but your ears ain't laid back, liken when a bear is closest."

Wolne, a black Labrador, wagged his tail momentarily, then rushed into the wooded area snarling and barking. Joseph, 17, trailed quickly for a short distance, longbow and arrow up and ready, but no protection against a bear.

Then he heard moaning from behind a mature sugar maple that he recognized immediately as a honey bee tree, one of several land markings for the Plowman 300-acre "Hope" farm. A lower limb had been bent downward and grafted in a slash and secured with pine tar. It appeared to Joseph that the graft had taken.

Edging closer, Joseph saw a pair of moccasinned feet, a bit smaller than his own. He realized after a few more steps in his own moccasins that the feet belonged to a friend, Chiefson, an Indian youth about his own age, the eldest son of Chief Tallfeathers.

Joseph thought his friend was dead. But the youth's eyes flicked open momentarily, reflecting fear and pain. He found on inspection that his deerskin sleeve was torn and his left arm swollen. His forehead was gashed to the bone and bleeding.

Chiefson was in bad shape, probably from a fall out of the honey tree.

Joseph was doubtful that the bear had attacked Chiefson. He had suspected it was "Honey Bear," that frequented the area and that had a pronounced limp from an injury to her left hind leg, probably occurring as a cub falling out of a tree. This caused him to speculate further. Maybe Chiefson was collecting honey and fell from the tree trying to flee from the bear. He wasn't bleeding from clawing and no bear slashes were found in his deerskin clothing.

Joseph wanted to cry but he dared not in front of his friend under such critical conditions. He didn't want to throw up either, but he couldn't avoid gagging. Once that ceased he said aloud: "Dear God, don't let my friend die. Please give me strength." . . . His fears and doubts immediately were washed away from head to toe. He felt strength surging into his body; he knew exactly what he had to do."

Wolne knew, too, what he would do.

He spotted Honey Bear in the woods, eyes glaring out and fixed on him. As soon as the bear looked away, perhaps hearing her cub, Wolne crept low through tall grass and into the wooded area. Once in the woods, he spotted the bear and flushed the large female into the open with her cub scrambling after her.

"It's sure enough Honey Bear, just as right as rain," Joseph said.

Wolne then circled around until he was positioned about five poles midway between the bear and Joseph and Chiefson, to let Honey Bear know his position, and why.

Joseph then started to lift Chiefson, but his friend was now partially alert, shook his head, then signalled with his good right arm to get down.

"Wait! Bear go way with cub," he said.

Ears erect, Wolne's eyes moved in rhythm with the bear swaying and shifting weight from left to right, back and forth. Then, after what seemed a long five minutes, Honey Bear reared up, bellowed an angry, deep growl, and charged full weight and speed at Wolne.

Wolne stood his ground.

The very instant the bear reared up, Joseph stammered out, "We better ru... ru... run!"

"No! Down! Bear no bluff."

She wasn't bluffing one bit. She charged, bellowing and bounding up the slope like a huge bull after a wildcat.

Wolne trembled slightly and waited to the last moment, hair along his back standing straight up. He remained quiet. . . Wolne knew he was no match against Honey Bear in head-on battle, against the bear's forearms tipped with deadly-sharp claws.

What came of Chiefson, heir apparent?

But Wolne knew also that his power, coupled with his agility, matched or exceeded that of the bear's — if for no other purpose than to maneuver out of danger's reach.

Then at the critical moment, he feigned slightly to the left, then leaped to the right, snarling angrily as Honey Bear slashed at his head. On landing Wolne rebounded to the right — like a tightly coiled spring releasing pent up energy. He caught Honey Bear off balance and off guard, just for an instant, but long enough to sink his teeth into the bear's lame hind leg. Wolne then rebounded out of reach and speedily feigned interest in Honey Bear's cub, an action that distracted the bear and caused her to sit and reflect.

Wolne sat also, growling softly but alertly on guard.

Both animals eyed each other warily for several minutes.

Honey Bear had stopped roaring and barking.

"Could be a standoff," Joseph said, and Chiefson agreed, as they watched Honey Bear lumber off to her cub.

With that Joseph rose quickly to his feet, removed his shirt and arranged a sling for Chiefson's left arm. His head was still oozing blood. Once the sling was in place, he took Chiefson by his good arm, pulled him up and ducked under Chiefson's body to lift the injured friend upon his back.

Although the action was done quickly, in one continuous motion, Chiefson cried out as his injured arm bumped against Joseph, who then moved quickly in a gliding motion toward home, maybe 100 poles away. He thought of their bows and arrows but decided to leave them there for now.

Moving toward home, they saw Wolne racing to catch up.

"Good dog!" the two called out.

"Good Wolne. That good dog, Wolne," Chiefson said, through clenched teeth. "You saved lives. Wolne fooled bear, made Honey Bear take eyes off, like soldiers and our braves do. What you call that? Division?"

"No. Called diversion. Means what you say, 'Take eyes off.'"

Without reason Joseph suddenly felt homesick for his mother, Sarah, and his sisters and brothers back in Maryland, where he was born. He worried about his father, Joseph Sr., now a lieutenant in Captain Cresap's company serving out of Cumberland, Maryland. Perhaps it was a reaction to the tension and to Chiefson's injury.

He hadn't felt like this all summer, since his father brought him to learn farming from his uncle Henry. He wondered where his father was and if he was in battle, maybe fighting as an ensign, against the French in Pennsylvania Province. At least that's what his aunt and uncle said was possible. They didn't know his father was now a lieutenant.

Joseph wanted to join the militia at Cox's Station, but both Henry and Louicie needed him and wouldn't allow it, but he couldn't join up for even a stronger reason. Col. Isaac Cox, a friend and neighbor headed up the militia unit.

What came of Chiefson, heir apparent?

On arriving at the cabin, Joseph's Aunt Louicie, saw them coming and dropped the wet laundry she was hanging to dry. She scurried to help Chiefson into the kitchen area of the small but tidy log cabin where they layed him out on a bunk and covered him with a blanket.

"His arm's broke, I think," Joseph said, then quickly explained what happened to Chiefson while gathering honey. He told them that Honey Bear got angry when she saw Chiefson in the tree after honey, got angry and climbed up and cuffed Chiefson who fell to the ground.

Later, Joseph told them about the standoff between Wolne and the bear and that he was sure Wolne didn't want to hurt her.

"He could have ripped her leg when he took hold of it, ifen he just twisted his head," Joseph said. "I'm happy he didn't." "Wolne very brave, very smart, very strong and fast." Chiefson said proudly, and jestingly added, "You should change Wolne name to 'Brave', like my Pa Chief."

"Oh, my God in heaven," Loucie responded, "It's a wonder you're both still alive. That's a deep cut in your forehead, Chiefson, and your arm does look like it's broken. And you ain't . . . you haven't even called out in pain."

She took command immediately. Both Louicie and her husband, Henry, were experienced in medical emergencies and first aid treatment, Louicie as a midwife, Henry as an ensign in the local militia unit, "protectin' against rowdy whites and Indians," as Henry put it.

"Joseph, bring the other blanket and cover Chiefson. He's shiverin' fierce. Then kindle the fire under the kettle at the hearth.

"After you've kindled, go fetch your uncle. He's pickin' corn back of the pig lot. Tell him what happened and fetch splints for Chiefson's arm. Tell him to chisel holes in the ends, so's I can thread linen strips through and tie the splints in place. And tell 'im to uh . . . tell 'im to bring his jug he's got hidden over in the woods."

Louicie proceeded then to swab Chiefson's head wound gently with warm, soapy water. She removed bits of dirt and bark from the wound and again swabbed it before applying a poultice of herb to stop the bleeding.

"Did you hit yo're head . . . your head on a limb when you fell from the tree?" she asked.

Louicie and Joseph had been teaching Chiefson and his younger brother, Beaver, to speak the pioneer tongue without back-country colloquialisms. But Henry enjoyed their use, 'specially when puffin' up a story.

"Hit arm and head on stump. Tried to soften blow with arm."

"Does your head hurt? Can you see like yesterd'y?"

"Yessum. . . Arm hurt strongest. . . Have hard head," Chiefson said, smiling slightly.

The front door opened just then, and in walked Henry, a tall, stocky man of 43, and nephew, Joseph, a thin rail of a youth. They carried the splints, the jug of home mixings and an oak bucket of icy-cold spring water.

What came of Chiefson, heir apparent?

WHETSTONES

Louicie quickly folded a bunch of linen strips, sloshed them in spring water and placed them on Chiefson's injured forehead. She then applied a fresh herb poultice and held her hand firmly in place to help stop the bleeding.

Henry smiled and nodded a greeting, then said, "Chiefson, don't you know none better than to wrestle Honey Bee — 'specially up a tree? Let me take a look at that arm, and then yo're head. This'll hurt some 'cause I gotta feel if you've a clean break or not."

Henry then took up his jug, glanced guiltily at Louicie and said, "Take a swig or two, Chiefson. You'll need it."

Chiefson refused. "I no drink firewater . . . see too many young men go wild, even one time my Pa Chief. He tangle with three braves in village. They try to get bottle away from Chief. He like cornered wild boar 'til one brave club him down with stick of firewood. Among us kids, we called him Chief Firewater," which prompted laughter.

Henry shrugged, nodded in assent, and set the jug back on the floor. He took the youth's arm in both hands and probed the inside arm bone around the point of swelling.

Chiefson screamed in pain and involuntarily shuddered and twisted away. He was close to passing out. Louicie sponged his forehead with the cold linen cloth, as she'd done repeatedly, then pulled his blankets up around his shoulders. His forehead had stopped bleeding, thanks to the poultice.

"We best wait 'til he stops tremblin'," Louicie warned. He's wore . . . He's plumb worn out. Will you have to probe his arm again?"

"No, I'm sure he has a saplin' break, liken when you bend a small green limb. It breaks maybe half way, then bends," Henry explained.

Chiefson heard and asked, "That mean I get crooked arm?"

"We'll straighten the bone back in place with the splints and pressure, such as we can. Then we'll stretch your arm to help set the bone proper," Henry said.

Chiefson remembered only the phrase, 'such as we can.'

Turning to Joseph, Henry told him, "Go bridle Whinny and ride over to Chief Tallfeather's village. Tell his squaw, I mean, Moondove, what happened here. Tell her he's gonna be all right and that we'll keep Chiefson here for a few days 'til he's able to travel, or 'til the chief gets back, at least. Moondove may want to send a brave on horseback to fetch the chief home."

"Yes sir. . . I'll take Wolne with me."

"No. He'll keep Chiefson company and he's apt to get into a row with the tribe's dogs."

Before Joseph closed the cabin door, Chiefson turned his head to him and said, "Thank you and Wolne for savin' life."

"Not me. Wolne saved both of us," came the reply.

Wolne wagged his tail and layed back down by Chiefson's bunk. "Time to look at your head and for puttin' on splints," Henry said as he removed the linen poultice. "Not bleedin' a bit, but it needs some of Doc's stitchin'."

What came of Chiefson, heir apparent?

Henry then placed the splints, one on one side of the arm and the second on the other, next to the swelling.

Louicie had threaded strips of linen through the ends of the splints and then spaced others along and under the arm. She then inserted a thick fold of linen over the arm swelling, under the splint, and placed a stick in Chiefson's mouth on which to "bite down on, and fight the pain."

"Now, I'm gonna bring pressure," Henry said, "to force the linen fold against the break. That should straighten it some. You sure you don't wanna swig first?"

Chiefson shook his head vigorously, tensed rigidly as Henry brought pressure, moaned loudly and clamped his teeth sharply into the stick.

While Henry kept the pressure on, Louicie tied the linen securely along the length of the cast, then wound a long length of the cloth tightly, from wrist to elbow and back again. She then tied it firmly in place.

Henry tied a small rope to a quilting hook in the ceiling, stretched it tautly and tied it to Chiefson's hand, "to help stretch the bone back in place. The doc will be here tomorrow to see that we done it proper'," Henry continued. . "You can bet he'll stitch your head up once he gets here."

Chiefson reached, patted and scratched Wolne's back, and asked, "Why his name, Wolne?"

Henry and Louicie laughed.

"He was stubborn as a young dog," Henry answered. "If we told him to sit, he'd still be astandin', tell him to lie down and he'd sit up. If you threw a stick and told him to 'fetch,' he'd run the other way and fetch a different stick or a rock, most likely."

Chiefson chuckled quietly.

"That's not all," Louicie joined in. "If I called him to come, he'd edge backward a few steps, cock his head and stare to see if his trick went over. One time he backed smack off an embankment into swift spring waters of Cox's Creek. He liked to drowned."

Chiefson laughed again, then moaned from pain and asked, "What name Wolne mean?"

"Wolne is backward for Enlow, my maiden name, to fit dog's early ways," Loucie said. "Name means people living on a hill."

"As an Enlow, you must go down hill," Chiefson said with a grin, "'cause you don't live on a hill, now." This brought laughter again from his "adopted" grandparents.

"Thank you Chiefson for being a brave, cheerful and bright young one," Louicie said, "and for agreeing to be our adopted son. We're powerfully proud of you for today and for how fast you have learned our tongue in only, let's see, in only about 15 moons. But you should rest now. Sleep a full moon." . . . .
Chiefson smiled, knowing a full moon lasts about three sunsets. He dropped into a deep, sleep almost immediately where he envisioned the biggest, bright-

What came of Chiefson, heir apparent?

est moon he'd ever imagined. The face on the moon was that of his late grand-mother, smiling happily down upon her grandson on earth. Her name was Moonsmile.

Chiefson awakened nearly 10 hours later when Louicie placed another cold pack on his forehead and served up a meal of wheat muffins and honey, a cut of venison and a serving of hominy. He was famished, a good sign, but still weak. He awakened just in time for Doc Stitchler to examine his head and arm and to proclaim the treatment as "first rate." Doc then closed Beaver's injury with 8 stitches.

Before Doc left, he turned to Henry and Louicie and said, "I hope you two don't decide to open an office here around. My family's having trouble enough with stretchin' and fittin' bartered goods to meet our needs."

Joseph had returned from Pa Chief's village just in time to give a hello to the Doc and announce that Moondove sent for the Chief. He then left to do chores, departing with Doc Stitchler, a name Joseph was afraid to use for fear he'd "bust out laughin'."

This troubled Joseph. He had been raised to address most adults as mister, reverend and captain, as such.

Chiefson later told of his dream, wherein his Gramma Moonsmile beamed down upon him. "She was sorta sparkly, like foggy, ripplin' waters in Cox's Creek with a misty circle around her head. She talked Indian tongue loud so I could hear."

My grandson, Chiefson, you will heal and be better for your injuries. Now, put your mind to learning farming. Mix with neighbors and be good friends of both white and red skin. Listen to Louicie and Henry and Joseph. They have taught you their tongue and how to farm . . . and they will help you get land. I know your thoughts. They are right ones. But life isn't all straight arrows. Keep faith in yourself and trust in a much higher being. Don't pay attention to those who claim you go to church just to meet the warrior chiefs and the land chiefs. Those who make these claims aren't all good doers like the dutiful beaver and a proud pony. Neither are chiefs. They need help too, in keeping the peace in villages and towns, and on farms."

The small cabin was silent. Tears flooded Louicie's eyes; a lump grew in Henry's throat; a stutter, but no words, came from Joseph who'd returned with Wolne.

Louicie finally broke the silence. "What a beautiful dream. How wonderful of Moonsmile. Her words spoke truth about such sweet meanings. I feel like I should cry, but also like a bubbling spring."

Henry and Joseph lacked words. Wolne's tail was still.

What came of Chiefson, heir apparent?

* * *

"Louicie back again, with quill in hand after a glass of cider and more to write about. Did you know our Henry talks to our horse, Whinny? Well, he does, mostly when there isn't another person around. Did I write about how Henry is pushing to get an apprenticeship program going with volunteers? I've been working on that, too, with Jacob and Isaac and Henry, whom I call 'the three'.

"Now hold your breath for what is coming: Chief Tallfeathers still is against his two sons being farmers. Looks more and more like the tribe will go west. I forgot to tell you that at the military ceremony General George Washington sent his praises and $25 to each man! Now, here's what Henry had to say to Chiefson about 'prenticeships, as he calls them.'"

* * *

Henry cleared his throat and questioned Chiefson, "Have you talked with Pa Chief 'bout yore 'prenticeship here on Hope farm? We need you, and I b'lieve yore needin' us. This would start you off right, on your own land. But it's a matter of a short time afore land is all taken up, so you best move quickly."

"Yes, I talk to Pa Chief. He angry for reasons. He want Cheifson to be hunter-warrior, not farmer. He against Chiefson speaking yore tongue. He say Indian here long, long time before white man. White man not speak Indian tongue. Pa Chief mad, too, 'cause fat land owners steal land. He ask how could Chiefson, a Shawnee boy, keep land?"

"My Chief like bull stuck in place, sad to say. He walk into deep mud with eyes open, has horns too long, need cuttin' back."

"A bull is a strong animal," Louicie interjected, "but we can spread much clean straw on top of mud patch. Then Chief can walk free, to green meadows."

"Plowman people more like beavers," Chiefson persists. "They no get stuck in mud. Joseph and his 'Ma' and 'Pa' not fear starting new when river washes out old dam. . . Pa Chief work on new dam on stream that trickles, even when he hear rush of waters in next valley. . .

"Sorry I talk of Chief like this, but true talk. He good hunter; strong, brave warrior; leads tribe, treats well."

Louicie pressed her point. "What kind of straw should we spread, Chiefson, to get Chief Tallfeathers to walk on solid, green meadows?"

"I not sure. Could be gifts. Could be treaty and gift of land as home for whole tribe." Then he said, "Could be peace and brothergood. Not that. What say preacher? Oh yes, brotherhood. It even could be like preacher say, 'Heaven on land,' or even. . ." Chiefson chuckled, "Could be like heaven on reservation."

Louicie laughed hilariously. Henry laughed so hard he fell off his stool.

What came of Chiefson, heir apparent?

Joseph, joining in the fun, said, "You best pick yourself up, Uncle, just like fallin' out of a honey tree."

"We best be gettin' serious. You know Chief will return home from his council meetin' in just two days," Loucie reminded.

"Chief loves his sons very much. Don't you remember how Pa Chief saved Chiefson's life when they were huntin' coon along Salt River? He dove into raggin' flood waters and swam down stream a hundred poles or so to reach and save Chiefson. The Chief was in bed for days 'cause of serious cuts and bruises. He could of drowned with his son. Isn't that right Chiefson?"

Sidestepping an answer, Chiefson said, "I'd rather hear what brother, Joseph, wants to say."

Choosing his words carefully, Joseph said, "Chief prob'ly will come to see Chiefson, if it's true what Moondove told me. She said Chief wants best for his son, 'though he's still struggling over Chiefson farming here with us. He's even madder, too, 'cause Beaver has been working on our 'Hope' farm, now and again, and taking talking lessons from us.

"Moondove said too that Chief wants a four holer for a family of five when only two, at most, sit at a time." Joseph usually a subdued sort, knew he'd get laughter with this one. He did.

"If true, we must keep this story to ourselves," Louicie said, "else it gets back to the Chief. Then he'd never come over to our side."

Henry planned to leave the next morning to go over to talk with Jacob Plowman, his first cousin, a justice of the peace at Salem, nearly a half-day's ride away. Henry thought highly of Jacob as one of the savviest and most fair-minded men he knew on Indian affairs. Jacob and Isaac Cox would be a big help in polishing up and adding to the plan.

As officers of Col. Cox's company of militia, the three were most dedicated and proud of their record of peace between Indians and pioneers in their area. All members of the company were honored at a military ceremony last July, including inspection and marching to drums and bugles. All were presented honorable mention certificates, signed by none other than General George Washington, commander-in-chief of the armies.

As names were called out each militiaman strode forward to the review stand where, at the roll of drums, they received their certificates in sealed envelopes from Col. Cox. A crowd of relatives and friends of more than 200 applauded and whooped and hollered as each exchanged snappy salutes with the colonel.

The checks and the final recognition would come as a complete surprise to all but the colonel. After the crowd settled down, he called out: "Ensign Henry Plowman! Step forward!"

Henry was startled but did as commanded.

"Not a single individual in this company has contributed more to the peace and security of this community than Henry Plowman," the colonel said, fol-

What came of Chiefson, heir apparent?

lowed by a spontaneous and vigorous cheer from the crowd. "I wish to give special honor to this man for his dedication and his plan to develop community relationships amongst all. As you don't know, Ensign Plowman, from now on, will be called Lieutenant Plowman."

The crowd roared its approval, then roared again continuously as Henry walked awkwardly to the stand. Drums rolled in salute to an embarrassed winner; smiles stretched weathered faces beyond normal grins; scores of hats sailed upward without known ownership. Many wiped away tears, including the tough and ready colonel. Louicie, however, led them all in love and tears.

It was a tribute unequaled anywhere; all was in loving thanks to their close friend and neighbor.

Once at the stand, a red-faced and embarrassed Henry shifted from one foot to another, folded his arms and unfolded them, then put his hands in his pockets, then took them out to dangle nervously at his sides.

While his eyes shed tears, his spun-funnery and grit-logical mind and mouth, for once, were numbed and quiet. Henry spoke in his usual and curious way, but only after staying his tears and calming his emotions.

"Thank you! Thank you! Thank you! What else can I say, except I love and respect you all as neighbors and friends. But I ain't really . . . I'm not the one for you to be abellerin' for, like I had sired triplet heifer calves.

"Anyway, I'm faced with two problems. I'm not the hero you sound like you think I am. Then, I'm worried. . . I'm worried over how you men are ever gonna match your hats with your tousled heads, and you with hair-free heads.

"Seriously, 'though, often I am not, most of you here know my Louicie. . ." (The crowd cheered affirmatively.) "Louicie's the one that shoulda been promoted to lieutenant and got all this hootin and hollerin'. Why? 'Cause our community bondin' program has always been her idea.

"I just trudged along and followed her dream. . . . Louicie! Louicie Enlow Plowman, you come up here and take yore bows."

At that, many in the crowd began shouting out, "We want Louicie! . . . We want Lieutenant Louicie! . . . Louicie, take your bows! Take your bows with yore sire of triplets."

Louicie was in a state of emotional shock. She tried to hide behind Joseph, who with Chiefson, hoisted her wiry, short body up on their shoulders and carried her to the review stand. Mixed tears of joy and disbelief flowed down her cheeks. She sobbed quietly.

Once on the review stand, Joseph and Chiefson lowered Louicie into Henry's arms where the two clung to each other in moods blended between joy and embarrassment. Then Louicie got hold of her emotions, turned to Henry and cuffed him playfully on the side of his head, causing laughter all around.

"You big overgrown cub," she shouted at Henry. "How do you expect to grow to be a general, if you give away all the credit?" . . . . Colonel Cox led the laughter following that one.

What came of Chiefson, heir apparent?

Back in the crowd, the men began opening their envelopes following instructions to wait until the ceremony was over. When they did, a roar rose from the crowd of jubilant men, women and children. Each received $25 in pounds, still the legal tender, and still an undreamed amount of money for the times.

As Louicie and Henry strolled home, arm in arm, to the cadence of the crickets, not a word was spoken. Their thoughts ran the same trails, as usual, almost as though they were carrying on a conversation sharing minds. Louicie broke the silence:

"Henry, you know good and well the idea about community bonding wasn't mine any more than it wasn't yours. We've been living together so long we've started to think alike."

"All I know, Louicie, is you spoke about it first. And that's a lot like filin' first for land, ain't it? . . . Isn't it? You can't just keep an eye on the land, you gotta mark it, sit on it and claim it."

"Oh well, let's just be happy about how it turned out," Louicie responded. "Who cares who was first? I don't, and knowin' you, I'm certain you don't either."

As they continued to stroll along, arm in arm, Henry and Louicie discussed ways to extend and strengthen community bonding, paying particular attention to apprenticeships in farming. Many questions were posed and many went unanswered. Then, from the blue, Nelly changed the subject to Isaac Cox. . . . "What sort of feelings do you suppose our neighbors have toward Isaac? Is he really strong on peace? Or is he strong on soldiering?"

"You heard all the cheerin', didn't you?" Henry asked.

"Yes, but . . .

"No buts about the colonel, Louicie. He's loyal to the community. . . And he's first rate in everything he does."

"Could it be you feel that way because you hunt with him, soldier with him, and do a bit of drinking with him?"

"I s'pose that might lean me toward the colonel, but let's talk about my huntin' with him. I wouldn't be here if it wasn't . . . if it weren't for his bravery and his experience as a hunter and a soldier."

"What are you talking about, Henry?"

"Before you came west, the Colonel and I were out huntin' along the Salt River and ran across the biggest bear prints I ever saw. It was an injured bear, one mean and ornery enough to turn and track us.

"I was walkin' ahead a bit to the east of Isaac, not knowin' the bear had doubled back, not knowin' it was hurtin' and not knowin' I was right in the bear's path.

"But Isaac knew, thank the good Lord. Somehow, he sensed or smelled the critter.

"Instead of circlin' around to the back, as would be normal, Isaac circled to

What came of Chiefson, heir apparent?

the front and stood rigidly without movin' a hair . . . somethin' like a combination of Wolne and a redcoat soldier standin' and challengin' right out in the open.

"About then, I spotted Isaac and the bear.

"Isaac stood dead still with eyes starin' right into the eyes of the bear. It was one of the most courageous standoffs I ever seen. . . I ever saw. The bear stood and Isaac stood, like Wolne between Chiefson and Joseph, scarcely six poles apart.

"Isaac couldn't shoot 'cause I was in the line of fire. He just kept aglarin' for what seemed like eternity. Soon, the bear just turned around and walked away.

"We had to hunt him down, his bein' wounded, sos he wouldn't attack and kill or injure anyone. This all happened close to a village, where we saw Indian children playin' in the woods," Henry said. "We gave the carcass to Chief Butterfly Wing."

"Henry Plowman, why didn't you tell me this before? Not that it has anything to do with the colonel protecting the peace, as we were talking about."

"I didn't want to scare you off from comin' west."

Louicie and Henry walked on in silence, arriving home in time to find that Joseph, Chiefson and his brother, Beaver, had fed and watered the stock, and were then picking corn.

That night Henry told Louicie he was going to Salem to talk with Cousin Jacob and Isaac Cox.

The Coxes farmed 1,000 acres along their namesake creek, not too far from the Plowman's Hope farm, made up of 300 acres along the same creek. Isaac was well off financially, the result of building forts for 25 years with his two brothers to protect against Indian attacks along the Monongahela River, then in Virginia province.[27]

Henry reminded Louicie of this as evidence that the colonel was a solid citizen. He also reminded her that the colonel had built Fort Salem (later Bardstown, Kentucky). "We spent many a safe night at the fort along with other families, as you know. If that isn't protectin', I don't know what is."

Henry didn't remind Louicie that Isaac and his two brothers were also well known Indian fighters during those 25 years. Still, Henry believed firmly that, as time passed, Isaac converted to a devoted peacemaker.

Early the next morning, Henry was cornering Whinny to bridle her for his ride to see Jacob, while his thoughts flashed back to ways farm families could help Indian youth get started on granted lands. But he knew that providing land to all needing help would be like hand feeding every deer in a 5-day radius of Hope farmstead.

"What about a widespread 'prenticeship? At least we could get 'em ready for farmin'," Henry said, prompting Whinny to neigh softly and move her head as if she were in full agreement. Henry grinned while stroking the horses muzzle.

When alone, Henry enjoyed talking to himself, and to Whinny. He was of the opinion that, if you hear your thoughts, you can analyze them better — and

What came of Chiefson, heir apparent?

not make a clownin' fool of himself. Also, he knew his family got a lift out of it. "You bonny broodmare, sometimes I think you understand what I say. So smart yo're prob'ly gonna tell me when your apt to foal." Whinny shook here head vigorously, objecting to being bridled. At that, Henry guffawed so loudly that Louicie, Joseph and Chiefson heard and laughed heartily back at the cabin.

"Wonder what tickled Uncle so," Joseph said.

"I reckon Whinny played some sort of trick on Henry, like usual," Louicie said, still chuckling.

Chiefson smiled, and said, "Yo're man's happy, full of hope." . Enroute to see Jacob on the trail to Hodgenville, Henry skirted "humpback" hill country, an area he had ridden through many times before, but was still awed by what he saw. Forest growth was so thick, "it'd be hard for a coon to get through," he thought, then wondered how nature, or the Lord, built the knobs.

To pass the time, Henry let his mind slip back in Louicie's family history more than a century ago when her family was called Enloes, way back in 1657. Decades before that, he had heard, but wasn't sure, that they lived in Westmorland County, England, same as Henry's forbearers, in what was called lake country. The Enloes were a small clan; Plowman was a large one.

Louicie often pondered the change in the name, from Enloes to Enloe and then Enlow, and often said, "Hell, I'd be happy if my name was Enloes." Then she'd say, half jokingly in back country language: "Oh shaw, I figur' we'd still be Enloes if more of us had taken readin' and scribblin', sos we could spell out our names for clerks akeepin' records."

* * *

Louicie here again with more happenings, after having another glass of cider. I declare, tastes a bit on the hard side. . . . Ha ha and a ho ho. Just jokin, I guess. . . Anyway, I hope this letter doesn't wear you out or put you to sleep. Mostly what you will read now is sad and scary but with a bit of sunshine peeking through, now and again.

Oh yes, by the way, all of us Plowman people have been takin' speech lessons from the local teacher. I gotta admit that I frequently slip into backcountry talk, 'cause I hear it daily from my midwife patients. Though Henry's a love, he's the worst and most purposeful back-country talker in this part of north central Kentucky, I do believe. . .

* * *

Truth is, Henry knew, Louicie taught him to read and write. She and Nephew Joseph then taught Chiefson, who in turn, taught his younger brother, Beaver. Henry also knew that schools often didn't exist for earliest settler families, so the women had no other choice but to practice teachin'."

What came of Chiefson, heir apparent?

"I shore credit the women," Henry said aloud. "As a filly, don't you agree, Whinny?" He got a whinny in response.

Henry also remembered jokes told about him, mostly by the women folk and educated gents. The jokes rankled him a bit: "You know Henry, don't ya. He's a reader. When he goes ahuntin' he reads the sites on his rifle." Or: "I saw Henry out in the pen sloppin' one of his sows. The sow was readin' and understandin' Revelations."

Those jokes were about a man who didn't learn to read and "do a bit of scribblin'," until he was 39 — just 4 years ago. Nephew Joseph could read and write at 9 years, a fact that pestered Henry in times past. It forced him to go to Louicie, then 35, hat in hand, and learn reading and writing, to which he adapted slowly but astutely.

He was very proud to be reading.

On arriving at Jacob's cabin and office home and farm, Henry found him refereeing disputes among farmers who lost — or said they lost — horses, cattle and pigs.

"I've said a hundred times that you farmers gotta brand your stock and fix your fences. I'm gettin damn tired of settlin' whose horses or cows belong behind whose fences and whose pigs belong in whose pens.

"Do I have to butcher the poor, lost critters and give the meat to the hungry folk? They need it more than you, I guess. Then the Indians could sure use horses, " Jacob threatened.

Henry sat in on the hearings, waiting patiently until Jacob was finished and the farmers had left.

"You sure told 'em right Cousin Jacob," Henry said elatedly. "That part about butcherin' and given meat to the poor and horses to the Indians was arrow straight to the gut."

"Thanks, Henry, I hope you're right. I just don't have time to farm and hold court with a bunch of farmers that ain't school kids no more. But what brings you here?"

"It has to do with Indians and then Isaac, too. Let's take the Indians first, then lump Isaac with them," bringing laughter from both Jacob and Henry.

"Jacob, Indians face a dim future here, as you know, what with much of the land bein' taken up and farmed. They'll soon scarcely have land to hunt, and they ain't lookin' to bein' farmers. We're just damn lucky times ain't so warsome now, and how good our militia are . . . at keepin' the peace.

"That likely means trouble not far down the trail for both Indians and us farmers," Henry emphasized.

"You're a binful right, Henry. But you didn't come here to talk about the problem. I suspect you have an idea for a solution. Let's hear it."

"I hope I do. It has to do with farmin' 'prenticeships like for Chiefson. He wants to farm, and so does his brother, Beaver; they're both eager and take hold fast. Chiefson bein' a year or so older than his brother, is teachin' us things like

What came of Chiefson, heir apparent?

findin' bee trees for honey and doin' maple sapin'.

"Beaver's been teaching young pioneer boys and girls how to build canoes and measurin' a tree before it's cut."

"How's Chiefson find honey trees?" Jacob asked.

"It's plain simple, but smart. You'd think us farmers would've come up with the idea, but we can't even know about brandin'. . . . . "Here's how it works. Chiefson takes a chunk of honeycomb into the woods and builds a small fire. Then he puts a rock on the coals and heats it good and puts a chunk of the comb on the hot rock. The breeze then comes along and picks up the honey smell and floats it to where the bees are feedin' and collectin' pollen. Soon as the bees get the smell, they make a line direct to the comb, near where Chiefson is ahidin'.

"When the bees get their fill," Henry continues, "they bee line it to their hive, and Chiefson follows. Ifen he loses the line afore he finds the hive, he goes a short ways off that line and heats another one, then puts on more honey comb and starts the hunt again, like before.

"Where the two bee lines cross, he finds the hive."

"Henry, that should cure a lot of sweet tooth, here about," Jacob said chuckling as he spoke. "But go on with your idea."

"I figure Indians can help us improve on farmin' ways to grow and harvest and store things, like berries and veggies growin' wild in the woods and meadows. Beaver has showed us whilst we been teachin' him.

"This bein' good and neighborly . . . even more than that . . . we could match boys and girls with the right men and women, those who are short on children, to school them in farmin' and homemakin'. Teachin' like that most likely would make better friendships.

"Lookin' even farther down the trail, we might want to start the same program for pioneer children from largest families."

"Henry," Jacob interrupted, "where would we put Indian and pioneer youngens to work at farming and homemaking? We can't go and run farmers away to make room for youngens.

"You've bee lined to the hot rock. But look at it this way. When Chief Tallfeathers and his tribe move west for better huntin' grounds, and I think we agree that'll happen, Indians will be both hunters and farmers. Meantime, Indians and farmers gain from the 'prenticeship program."

"So far, so good, but what then?" Jacob asked.

"I'll wager more Indians hanker to get in the program than we can handle. That'll be our first problem, unless Chief decides to leave a lot earlier than we figure. If the tribe doesn't leave, we could solve the problem with some sort of cullin', like with horses — for strength, health and keenness.   First,   we'd need to pick leaders, both Indians and farmers, men and women, to face up to a fair way of cullin'

"But I ain't prepared to say how at this branch of the stream."

What came of Chiefson, heir apparent?

Jacob and Henry talked then about Isaac Cox and whether he was now a peacemaker, for true, or still interested in waring. Henry took Louicie's flank, not because he felt that way, but for his respect of Loucie's judgment and because he was sure Jacob would choose the other side of the river. Jacob did take the opposite bank.

They argued front to back and all around the subject. Then:

"Dang it, Henry, you know fair-thee-well Isaac is true to his word. You sure you aren't polishin' someone else's Sunday shoes?"

"Jacob, damn it, I ain't polishin' nobody's boots and never will. But you're right again. I don't like to admit it, but Loucie is so on target, so often, I gotta cogitate careful like, else I get winged. I don't know how she always figures out the right breeze to flow with, but she does.

"I'm with you. I wanted to hear you spell out your feelins." "What say we close out our meeting?" Jacob asked. "I'm bushed. Shall we meet over your way, say a week from today. . . . to go through some names for the cullin' committee?"

"Yes to both questions. . . . By the way, I guess I didn't tell you, Isaac's gonna join us."

"That's good. He'll be a big help. . . Did Louicie agree to help pick women for the culling committee and to take some notes on our selections and action?"

"She agreed," Henry said, "but she won't be able to come for an hour or so late. Doc Stitchler asked her to help with what sounded like a difficult resettin' of a broken leg."

"That's a good sign for relationships . . . between doctors and midwives," Jacob said, as they shook hands and parted.

Henry, Jacob and Isaac met at Salem to compile a list of nominees for their culling committee of farmers and homemakers. They then fleshed out the apprenticeship details and started to select three men and three women from their list. Just as they began, Louicie arrived and heard Isaac say, "Well, I guess we're ready to narrow down to three men and three women."

"Hold on, you three," Louicie said pleasantly, but unsmilingly. "I'm happy to hear you want an equal number of women and men; but if I'm to help out here, I want some say in which women are selected, and maybe men, too."

Louicie did more than take notes, a duty Henry asked her to take on. She pulled out a slip of paper from her handbag and handed it to Jacob, saying, "Got these names on your list?" . . . . The three, as Louicie called them, eyed each other guiltily and shook their heads. Then Louicie said:

"Why don't you three pick the bulls and I'll pick the heifers. Let me see your list of candidates."

She then scanned the list, selected one woman and one man, whose names she wrote on her slip. She then crossed off one of her women choices and handed the slip of paper to Jacob with: "These are as fair minded and dedicated to the community as any I know.

What came of Chiefson, heir apparent?

"Now gentlemen, I gotta get back to helping Doc Stitchler," she said as she rose, kissed Henry on the cheek, then said before leaving: "Don't you dare leave Indian women out of your upcoming leadership powwow. They gotta have a say about whether or not the tribe moves west. The two are tied together like a dove and her mate she said before leaving."

"That's what I call a right, rapid filly," Jacob remarked enthusiastically. Henry agreed. Isaac gave a mild nod.

The three continued the meeting, voting two to one in favor of the women and man that Louicie had recommended. Isaac voted no, and changed the subject to the planned powwow.

"Jacob. . . Henry . . . You know how Indian tribal leaders dominate their women. I think Louicie's off track of her midwifery domain. Don't you agree, Henry?"

Henry stiffened and said, "Hell no! I don't agree one speck." . . . "But we ain't got a chance in a windstorm of makin' any headway in drawin' injun leaders here . . . ifen we ask for their women to come," Isaac grumbled in backcountry language, which he frequently used increasingly as his anger grew.

Jacob noted that Isaac's reasons for use of back-country words differed totally from that voiced by Henry, who went back-country with humor — not with anger. But Jacob knew also, that men tended to use the language more when with other men. But as the peace keeper, he said quietly, but forcefully:

"Isaac, we've got a choice of streams to fish in, one's near dryin' up, the others flowing with a sparkle; one has boney fish, the other has fleshy ones. Which do you choose? You got to know the stream and the fish.

"How well do you know Indian families? Better than Louicie? I doubt it. She's with Indian families frequently, as a midwife."

Continuing, Jacob said, "I have to agree with her. I've visited a crowd of Indians over the past year, many individual couples in my post as a justice of the peace. . . and many more, since you two asked me to head up our friendly neighborhood phase of the community program. It's been an eye-opener for me. I believe . . ."

"You've a right to believe what you want, Jacob," Isaac interrupted. "But I don't believe tribal leaders would like invitin' women to a leadership meetin'. The women likely would sit there without sayin' a word."

"This is a tough one, even leavin' Louicie out, and I'd like you to do that," Henry said. "I've gotta agree with Isaac, unfortunately, in this case."

"What say we suggest an auxiliary meeting of Indian and pioneer leaders of women — at the same place and time?" Jacob proposed. "That way, they could attend and meld into our meeting without causing a big splash. Then if they decided to participate in the meeting, it would be up to them."

"It certainly would take the heat off of them," Isaac added. "Would it be correct if I spoke to Louicie on this idea of yours?" Jacob asked Henry. "Or would you rather do it?"

What came of Chiefson, heir apparent?

Henry responded, "You do it. I've been stoneheaded on a couple of points with Louicie of late." He then said, "Let's wind up this meeting. Can we agree now on a date for our leadership powwow? It's apt to be asnowin' in a few weeks. What about next month, say October 15, give or take a day or two?

"Meantime, I'll get in touch with Chief Tallfeathers to give him a rundown on what we plan, and let him react."

Two days later, Henry met and spoke with the chief and found him agreeable to the apprenticeship program, but wouldn't say whether or not the tribe would move west. The chief seemed to have mellowed toward his braves learning to farm, probably so that some would be better prepared to farm out west.

The next step was a meeting of the culling committee, elevated to an advisory group and overseen by Jacob and Louicie, two level-headed arbitrators. Louicie then spoke with Chiefson, who took an immediate interest in the program and offered to help. His apprenticeship experience at Hope farm would counter balance his youth, Louicie knew.

* * *

Sheriff Noble visited Jacob Plowman's office and inquired of him, "Did you know your nephew, Brutus, is being accused of stealin' a pig from Bill DeCur's place yesterd'y? He claims it's his, but it's awearin' DeCur's ear notches, I guess."

"Oh hell! What's that youngun gonna be up to next?" Jacob exclaimed angrily, then asked: "Did you check the notches against the records?"

"Just now. They match, all right," the sheriff said. "But I'm sure they were clipped next to somebody else's notches."

"Sheriff, are you suggestin' that Brutus stole a pig that DeCur stole first?"

"Looks that way to me," Sheriff Noble said. "Could you double check me? I think there's a couple of extra notches in the left ear. I drew a sketch for the file. Together, the notches match DeCur's, but the new ones ain't fully healed.

"DeCur has brought charges agin Brutus, but they'll not stick."

"I'll look into it and get back to you as soon as I can," Jacob said with a sigh. "Thanks for tellin' me about it."

After the sheriff had gone, Jacob recalled that Brutus, 17, had been in more trouble than three his age could muster up together. To some, Brutus was as mean and sassy as pure horse radish, topped with redhot peppers; to others, he was loving and helpful.

Jacob's sister-in-law, Tilly, had farmed him out about a month ago at the Smithson's place, he recalled, hoping that would do some good. "If that doesn't work," Tilly told Jacob, "Brutus is gonna wind up on Sheriff Noble's work crew."

Jacob then visited Sheriff Noble and agreed with his analysis that the pig had been stolen twice.

What came of Chiefson, heir apparent?

WHETSTONES

Sheriff Noble had heard from another farmer who had reported the loss and gave evidence to support his claim. Charges were brought later against both Brutus and Smithson. Because it was Brutus's first scrape with the law, he got a month with the work gang. But Smithson had served time for other charges, so he pleaded guilty and went to jail for 6 months.

Changing the subject, Jacob told the sheriff that he would go before the county board the next day to request authority to hire part-time help. He needed someone who could manage the registration of livestock and the branding and county's notching identification system. He later got approval.

Jacob wondered, then, if his nephew, Brutus, would fit the part-time job. He felt good about the possibility, but he knew he'd have to set firm guidelines, enforce them and be a good father figure for the young man who could stay at his place and help with farm chores.

Brutus's father died and had been gone half of his son's life.

Jacob knew his plan would match everyone's needs, starting with Brutus' mother, Tilly; then Jacob's wife, Martha, who would enjoy mothering Brutus; and himself, in avoiding most of the headaches of lost stock, registering animals, and long hours of bickering.

Jacob's and Martha's children were grown, married and off on their own, all farming or keeping homes.

* * *

Henry and Jacob met again with Chief Tallfeathers who had decided once again to oppose the apprenticeship program and who still wouldn't say if his tribe was moving west. After long negotiations, the proposals were deadlocked to the point of failure, largely because the chief maintained iron-fist control over his tribal council.

Following the meeting, Isaac not attending, Henry and Jacob commiserated their failure:

Henry: How could we be so wrong about Indians takin' part?

Jacob: We didn't judge Chief's anger and his almighty power, just as simple as that.

Henry: Why don't we go ahead an open the program for pioneers and Indians, anyway? We could start with Chiefson and Beaver, maybe as junior leaders, if they don't move.

Jacob: How much time does Chiefson have farming?

Henry: Two crop seasons with Beaver helpin'. But they're among the brightest, finest young men I ever met, solid workers and loyal friends.

Jacob: Are they friends enough to quit the tribe, considerin' Pa Chief's anger and power?

Henry: I b'lieve so. We'd need to feel them out. . . But I've got some good news

What came of Chiefson, heir apparent?

that'll tilt Chiefson and maybe Beaver, too, to our point of view. . . Isaac .
sent word he'd leased 50 acres to Chiefson for purchase later if he
choses. To start, Chiefson can pay with corn, pigs and honey, and with . . .
out payin' interest.
Jacob: Best news we've had — a good note to wind up on.

* * *

Not surprisingly, Chiefson was out on his "gift" acreage with Beaver the
very day after he signed a contract with Isaac. Chiefson felt strongly toward a
partner relationship of learning and building shoulder to shoulder with his
brother. They were plotting in their minds and on paper what areas could be
cleared for crops where the log cabin and barn would best be located and where
a pig lot and feed storage would fit best.

Suddenly, Beaver grabbed Chiefson's arm and tugged him behind a clump
of shrubs. He wished for Wolne, who had gone hunting with Henry and Jacob.
They then spoke in pioneer tongue:

"You didn't see those make-b'lieve Indians yonder?"

"No, but why make believe?" Chiefson wanted to know.

"Make-b'lieve 'cause they don't wear their feathers right, and 'cause one of
them is 'Fatlandowner', I'm certain. He walks with a limp and sticks way out
in front."

"Beaver, you wait here. I'll move in closer to hear them talk."

Beaver didn't stay hidden. Instead, he circled the other direction and
dropped to the ground behind a tree that looked like it had been axed and felled
very close to the ground that very day. . . It was the honey tree from which
Chiefson had fallen three moons ago. Why, he wondered, had a land marker
been cut down.

He listened intently, close enough to hear Fatlandowner's labored breathing, and peered through the dusk for his brother.

He then heard Fatlandowner, first-named Boulder, growl out in a near
whisper to one of his men: "I ordered you to go after Chiefson. Do it now! Or
I'll sight you down for good."

All was silent for a moment.

Then, a rifle shot shattered the silence, followed by a long gasping moan.
Beaver sobbed quietly, and knelt:

> My spirit, on high, I kneel to thee in fear that Chiefson has been
> shot. What treasures can I heap at your thrown? I promise good
> and true living, friendships and loyalty to all beings, including
> those wild, and I promise fresh fruit and meat to the hungry — in
> prayer and hope it is not Chiefson, or that he is only wounded.
> Thank you, God of the high heaven.

What came of Chiefson, heir apparent?

Beaver then heard Boulder bragging over what his men had just done. He heard him say: "Cover him with dirt, leaves and a log or two and some limbs. Make it look good and natur'l."

Beaver knew Chiefson was dead, then broke into quiet sobbing.

Boulder gathered his henchmen saying, "We got this land in the bag. Isaac Cox don't know that a hundred acres of his land ain't mapped and recorded proper in the county records. I seen them with my own eyes. Soon as we finish changin' the land markers, I'll rewrite the description and file my . . . our claim . . . on the hundred."

As a result of information from Beaver, Isaac later corrected his map and description to prevent Boulder from rustling his land.

Chiefson's body was recovered and buried on a small hill on his 50 acres of land by his father, mother and Beaver. Nearly all of the Plowman people were present as were many Indian and pioneer friends.

A week after that, Chief Tallfeathers gathered his warrior leaders together and told them of a rumor some of his men had spread widely, at Chief's request. It was about a group of eleven buffalo grazing Bighills country near Thinline Gap.

"I've good word that Fatlandowner has heard of the buffalo and is set to go after them the day after next two sunsets. We will go early that day and be waiting among rocks above the Gap. Bring only your, bows, knives and spears. Want no gunfire. Bring shovels, too. We wake you much before sunrise.

"Be ready! Don't let any get away," the chief ordered. All knew Fatlandowner and crew were the same men who masqueraded as Indians that killed Chiefson. Some of the men were believed to be remnants of marauders who stole horses, and killed and scalped pioneers up in Penn Province, but it was never proven.

Chief and his warriors arrived at Thinline Gap in moods of combined anger and high spirits. All were keenly alert and tightly strung, as the bows they carried.

At sunrise, the chief selected men — 18 in all — for critical positioning among the huge boulders.

"Do not attack until the killers have reached Biggest Rock," which all knew was located half way through the gap. "Ten of you will be hidden near Biggest Rock, two will be at the entrance and six will be after the big rock to watch for any who may be escaping. Chief then will call out names and positions."

After all were positioned, Chief and his warriors waited. One hour went by, then another and another. A fiercely hot sun roasted down on them, very unusual for the time of the year. Stinging flies circled and bit them time and again. Welts rose abundantly.

Buzzards circled above, as though they knew carcasses would soon be available, burned side up from rays of the sun.

A dove call, however ironic, signaled the Chief and his men who tensed and made ready for a massacre.

What came of Chiefson, heir apparent?

And a very bloody massacre it was.

Not only did Chief's warriors kill them . . . .

Boulder, the fat landowner, was knocked from his horse with a large rock. No sooner had he hit the ground than two demons were upon him.

One speared him several times in the groin. . . He screamed.

A second warrior cried in Boulder's face, then thrust his spear through his heart. . . . Others were killed in like manner.

Several of Chief's warriors vomited throughout the melee, one of whom asked of another in their tongue, "Why are we so angry to kill all, when only one killed Chief's son and another gave the order?"

The response: "You know why. . . We killed Boulder first for Chiefson. We had to kill them all. They pretended to be Indians. In past they killed and scalped many for horses."

At that point, the chief screamed, "You didn't follow orders! We count only eleven bodies. One of the killers got away."

"All of you will suffer for this."

The chief was raging like the maniac he had become, regardless of not losing a single of his men or himself — not even one wounded. His actions were unlike him, one of his warriors said. "He's gone over the edge of his mind," another whispered.

On his return, the chief rode hunched over. Then he was unable to stay his steed and was tied in place . . . and led home.

Moondove, chief's wife, had suffered terribly over her son's death, and was still suffering. She had an omen that something just as terrible was beginning. She was a mix of fear, dread and morbidness . . . She couldn't dry up a steady flow of tears.

Lovedove could not cheer her up, even by flying around Moondove with her cooing song turned on brightly, even when Lovedove landed on her shoulder to coo in her ear, even when she brushed her bill across Moondove's lips.

Lovedove was so frantic that Moondove asked of the bird, "You have your reasons, but why so franticly? It is like you are trying to tell me something, or console me for bigger reason than Chiefson's death. Is the Chief in danger? Has he been wounded or killed? Is it something worse?"

Chief came home late that same evening looking as down and remorseful as Moondove had ever seen him. He stumbled, blundered and stuttered. . . He stared blindly at Moondove. . . . He jumped at every sound, even the very smallest.

The council was to meet with the chief the next day but, of course, he did not appear. Knowing his condition, the council voted unanimously to move west. They did not tell Moondove about the massacre or how he had to eat crow before his men for threatening them after the Thinline Gap killings.

Those who participated in the Gap killings, except for the chief, returned and buried the dead.

What came of Chiefson, heir apparent?

The tribe left a week later, without Beaver, who said no, as a young man who meant business — farming business. In fact, Beaver was not told about the killings and his Pa Chief's illness; none of the council members had the heart to do so. Beaver learned of it a year or two later.

Lovedove flew along with the tribe and soon was joined by her mate, Earlybird. At night, they found a niche in Moondove's baggage. During the day, they ate hoppers and flew circles, arcs and waves or perched on the manes or rumps of the horses, cooing to their hearts content.

They made tribal members laugh and sing . . . but only after the third day out.

What came of Chiefson, heir apparent?

Where is Beaver agoin', anyway?

Louicie wrote a lot about Beaver in a diary-type letter on September 11, 1778, saying, "Beaver, 17, lived with us and has been as much of a son as our own nephew, Joseph Plowman, now 18, who was sent by his parents to live here with us for two years. Joseph was interested in farming and wanted to learn the trade from my Henry.". . . Louicie then wrote how Beaver, brother of the late Chiefson, taught a group of pioneer youngsters and adults how to build a canoe.

Louicie wanted to be sure that today's Plowman people, as well as descendants, know "how hard we try to be friendly with Indians, mostly because they are friendly to us." She then wrote:

"You youngsters, particularly, have to get a good education and a trade, and to learn how to treat people well. Then you must provide for yourselves and your families and help the needy who can't face up to hardships and dangers. Then, stand up with family and neighbors in the worst and the best of times."

She then recounted the story of teachings by Beaver, whose father, Chief Tallfeathers, planned to leave with his tribe for happier hunting grounds to the west. He was angry because he had lost his first son, Chiefson, and the other was taking on settler ways, just like his first. Louicie then wrote that one night, not long ago . . .

* * *

Beaver bolted upright in bed, sat quietly a moment to clear his mind, then grinned happily about his dream. It was so real he tried to convince himself that it wasn't, but he couldn't. Actually, he had a dream within a dream:

He rose and dressed, in his dream, then left his small cabin and walked into his 50 acres of mostly wooded land. He wanted to figure out how best to enlarge his garden and his pigpen; then he fed his hogs and his pinto pony, Snort.

Once these chores were completed, he returned to the woods, sat down on a moss-covered mound, listened in his dream to the sounds of the woods and gazed up to the moon. Only the crickets could be heard. He felt chilled, yet warm, as he determined the cadence of the crickets. It had slowed down. He knew this meant that the temperature was dropping as fall approached.

Beaver shivered, not from the cold, but as though eyes were fixed upon him from the woods. He knew, somehow, they weren't the eyes of a wolf, some of which prowled the area.

Was it the eyes of one of Fatlandowner's men who had killed his brother very close by? Could it be one who may know that Beaver witnessed the killing and was afraid Beaver would identify him?. . . Nonsense, he thought. Fatlandowner and his men were hunted down and killed by his Pa Chief and some of his braves, Beaver believed. Just the same, he held his rifle tighter and searched the surroundings, but saw only the woods and the moon. . . . Beaver gazed at the moon, blinked and then closed his eyes tightly to be sure they were in focus. Chills again slithered through his body. He couldn't believe what he saw, but the large image was sure.

"Could it be true?" he asked so loud that the crickets stopped chirping. "Is it really your face I see on the moon?"

"Yes, brother Beaver of the woods. It is Chiefson you are squinting at," came the voice from above. "I am here with our Gramma Moonbeam in our happy huntin' grounds, a place that reaches throughout the heavens.

"Gramma Moonbeam knows your thoughts and wants to speak to you about them. I send my love to you on the back of a spirited and speedy Indian pony, one like your pinto, Snort," Chiefson said, as he faded from Beaver's sight.

Beaver then visualized Snort, foaled by Whinny, and given to him by Henry and Louicie, dashing through space carrying bundles of love strapped to his brown and white back.

Gramma Moonbeam's face appeared gradually. She wore a sparkling circle over her head, just as she had in Chiefson's dream. Her smile radiated so brightly that the crickets again were chirpless. Her presence was misty.

Gramma Moonbeam spoke to Beaver, "My dear grandson, Beaver, how I do love and miss you. I wish I could take you in my arms and hug you, like a mamma bear hugs her cub. It is true that I know your thoughts and see your actions. They are good; they are lasting.

"You have shared Indian skills with pioneers; but of late, you have spent nearly all of your time becoming a farmer. That's good, too, but you should never forget how Henry and Joseph taught you to farm . . . and how Isaac gave you your land. I know you will grow even better in your farming and in your values toward helping others.

"Your father, Chief Tallfeathers, has mellowed. His rigid dislike of your being a farmer and speaking the pioneers' tongue, has melted as his blood warms to loving thoughts of you . . . I know this as a fact; I can read his mind.

"Chief now wants to return home to be close to you, but he is still too

Where is Beaver agoin', anyway?

proud. Your Mamma Moondove never wanted to leave, as you know. . . You need now to send a message of love and respect to your parents, particularly your stubborn Pa Chief. Invite them to return soon. "As one last wish for you, I ask that you do as Chiefson did. Teach neighbors how to work the woods for food, how to break and train horses and how children can build a canoe. It will be fun for you, and you will make many more friends for Indians. . . . . "Good moonbyes to you from your brother, Chiefson, and your Gramma Moonbeam. We love you," she said, gradually fading into their moon heaven for a time of eternity." Her last words were: "We hope your crickets soon chirp more rapidly."

Beaver laughed aloud at Gramma Moonbeam's joke, and the crickets chirped more rapidly for a moment.

* * *

On awakening, he wondered if the spirit had prevented his gramma from knowing who killed Fatlandowner. He wondered, also, how he could have had a dream within a dream. Did it happen? he asked himself. Or did my own thoughts make such a mystic meeting possible. Whichever, Beaver would write a letter to Pa Chief and Ma Moondove tomorrow, caringly inviting them to come home and carefully assuaging Pa Chief's pride.

After writing his letter, he gave it to the mail rider, Isaac Walker, who would saddle up and track westward as the first of a chain of horsemen carrying Beaver's letter. Each spent three days or so on his route, delivering mail to every little hamlet along the way and return.

Isaac assured Beaver, "Yore letter'll go through, you can bet on that; but it'll take a spell to get there."

The next day, Beaver was in the woods early where he located the birch tree he wanted, growing near the bank of Cox's Creek bordering his land. He had contacted farmers during the past week to invite their children, and adults, who wanted to see how a canoe is crafted. Before leaving the woods, he cut several saplings to build a wooden frame for the canoe before his visitors arrived. On returning to his cabin, he checked and found he had enough pine tar and deerhide lacings for the job.

Beaver would begin by showing his visitors how to measure a tree's height from its shadow, "if the sun is still out," he had said aloud. He had the tree in mind, a tall cottonwood located in a rare open area, allowing it to display its shadow.

Two days later, the sun was shining warmly as a group of twelve showed up, including five boys and three girls, along with four adults: Henry and his nephews, Joseph and Mordecai; cousin Jacob; and, of course, Wolne, Joseph's black lab, always a tag-along. Beaver introduced himself and shook hands with each youngster, then acknowledged his friends, the Plowman adults. Realizing

Where is Beaver agoin', anyway?

he had not met Mordecai formally, he exchanged handshakes and a few friendly words.

Beaver viewed the group of youngsters with interest, as they examined the canoe frame, particularly Felicia, whom he'd met beforehand and took a likin' to right off, as he had acknowledged previously. The children varied in ages from 8 to 17, Felicia being the eldest.

"I'm happy to see so many of you could come," Beaver said. "We'll start by showing you a way to tell how tall a tree is by measuring its shadow and without cutting it down. Loggers and farmers need to know that. See that tree yonder, pointing to a tall one. What kind is it? Anyone know?"

"That's one of them that blows cotton all about," one said.

"Yep," said another, "that cotton has seeds in it sos to blow it hither and yon to start seedlin's."

A third youngster called out, "That there's a cottonwood. My ma says it's the messiest tree there are."

"All three of you are right, Beaver responded. "It's a dirty one, true, and it's one of the tallest-growin' trees in this whole area. Shall we guess how tall it is before we measure its shadow?"

"'Bout eighty foot, I'd say," one offered.

"I'd make it like ninety-five foot," another called out.

"I reckon two hundred and twenty-five," said a third.

At that point, Beaver raised a wooden pole and said, "All of you should know what this is."

Several youngsters answered. All knew what it was. One said it was for measuring between posts, another, for measuring and plotting land.

The group was silent for a moment. Then Felicia spoke up. "A pole is sixteen and one-half feet long, same as a rod is long. The word rod is from the Middle English period and equates to a bar or a beam. Some crude folks call a rod a 'punishing stick' for ornery livestock, and sometimes for kids."

That prompted some moans and tittering.

Henry turned to Joseph, asking, "Who's the bright young lady?"

"Uncle? You don't recognize her?" Mordecai asked. "She's the daughter of Fatlandowner, whose men killed Chiefson. She's the smart one in her family, and all over this territory, for her age anyway . . . I think Beaver's stuck on her."

"Felicia, you get an A-plus on that report, and you win the honor of being my first assistant. Come forward for your trophy," Beaver offered jokingly, "and receive this sixteen and one-half foot pole or rod or stick from Middle England."

Felicia flushed, tossed her head and took the pole amid laughter that sounded friendly toward her.

"Hold the pole straight up from the ground while I measure its shadow," Beaver said. He then took his measuring string, knotted every foot of its length, and stretched it out to the tip of the shadow. "You prob'ly notice I got the string

Where is Beaver agoin', anyway?

color coded at every five feet, so you don't have to count every knot as you go. It's a whole lot easier than using a pole."

"How long's the shadow?" a youthful voice called out.

"Ten feet, right at the blue knot, about an inch short," Beaver responded. "Now you two over there take this measuring string and find out the length of the tree's shadow. They did, and found it to be 70 feet, minus two to three inches.

"Now," Beaver asked, "anyone had algebra?"

A few groaned. Felicia answered promptly and proudly, "I have."

"Good, Felicia. Can you put down a formula that'll tell us the height of the cottonwood?" Beaver asked, followed by groans from the youngsters.

Felicia took a sharp stick and scratched out the formula in the dirt: 10:70=16.5.:X. A groan rose from the boys and girls. "Wait!" Felicia responded. "It's really quite simple. What we're doin' . . . what we are doing is matching and comparing the shadows at the left, and the heights at the right," followed by a groan from the crowd. "Don't let the X bother you. It merely stands for an unknown height of the tree. Let me work it out and you'll see for yourself."

Felicia pointed the stick to the parts of the formula. "We know that ten is the measure of the pole's shadow and seventy is the shadow of the cottonwood. They provide you with a proportion," . . . interrupted by more groans . . . "that is equal to that on the right side."

Felicia tossed her head and continued unperturbed, saying, "Let me work the formula and you'll see the process." She then scratched arching arrows from 70 to 16.5 and from 10 to X, and said, "Now you multiply ten times X and you get what?"

"Ten X,"' came the response.

"Right, but what do you do next?"

"You multiply seventy times sixteen and a half and you get one thousand, one hundred and fifty five," shouted an impatient but quick-minded youth who continued confidently. "Then you divide the ten X into one thousand, one hundred and fifty five and you get your answer. The cottonwood tree is one hundred and fifteen feet tall."

The youths cheered and applauded loudly.

"Correct! Good job," Felicia said with a sincere smile.

"Thank you, too, Felicia. You did a good job yourself by putting algebra to words and dirt sketching," Beaver emphasized.

"Now, let's see about buildin' . . . about building a real Indian canoe. To save time, I removed the bark from around this birch log . . . all in one piece, you can see. Then I used this pattern to cut it to shape.

"But let's go back to the log sos you . . . so you can learn how to peel the bark back. Take note of how heavy and strong it is. . . I'll demonstrate."

First, Beaver measured the canoe length to the log. He then drew his sharp hunting knife straight as an arrow down through the bark along the top of the

Where is Beaver agoin', anyway?

log, "carefully so you don't cut yourself," he said. Next, he made a start with his knife at peeling the bark along both edges of the cut. "This is so you can wedge this heavy duty paddle-like tool into the cut, and pry the bark away from the log.

"See how it peels back in one piece, as easy as eatin bread from the hearth, topped with honey."

Once the bark had been removed, Beaver put two of the youngsters to work with hoe-tools scraping away the bark's soft inside, "the growing area," he called it. "And don't have your hoe too sharp, less you slash into the hard part of the bark."

Beaver then asked of Joseph, "Would you and Wolne go fetch my canoe, which I forgot, so everyone can see what I'm saying from here out?"

Joseph responded quickly, his black lab at his heels, and returned on the run carrying the canoe overhead.

* * *

Joseph, 18, and Beaver, 17, had been buddies for several years, particularly since Chiefson was killed. Joseph's aunt and uncle, Louicie and Henry, thought of both Chiefson and Beaver as sons, all the more since their father, Chief Tallfeathers, and mother, Moondove, left with the tribe to go west.

Both of their sons had always refused to go because of their love for the land, and for farming.

Louicie and Henry had more or less adopted the Indian lads and began teaching them to speak the pioneer tongue, with help from Joseph. Henry's input added a speech problem, however, considering his backcountry talk. That was a major reason that Chiefson, before his death, and Beaver began taking speech lessons from the school master on a barter basis, pork for lessons twice a week.

* * *

Once the canoe was in view, Joseph described its construction, beginning with the frame and pointing out each feature as seen in the frame and the completed canoe. "The way you attach the bark to the frame is simple, but hard work," he allowed. "You gotta . . . you have to bend it in place, then stitch and tar it to seal it tight against water leaking into the craft.

"You've seen and probably used a hand auger like I have here. Trade off using it, or bring one from home, and drill three holes an inch apart. Then you will skip about six inches and drill three more and repeat doing that along the whole edge of the bark. Take a good look at my canoe to be sure you understand what I'm saying.

"Now then, you will have to tip the frame on its side so you can stitch the

Where is Beaver agoin', anyway?

bark to the top edge of the frame. And while you are at it, dab a goodly amount of pine tar between the edge of the bark and the sapplings along the top of the frame, to seal the seams.

"Next comes the muscle part. It takes two strong men or two strong women. Tilt the frame to its other side and force the bark up and lace and tar it to the sapling. Take another look at my canoe so you'll know what I'm describing."

After the group had examined the finished canoe more carefully, Beaver said, "I reckon we've taken enough time from your chores. If we stay longer, your mammas and your pappas are apt to send their hound dogs to bring you home," at which the youths groaned.

"Tell you what. You arrange with your parents to come here every day in late afternoon, by five o'clock, if you can. Stay an hour or so every evening, except Sunday, until you finish your canoe. I'll oversee and help where needed."

The group cheered loudly, clapped their hands, then gleefully danced around in circles.

Once Beaver had their attention, he instructed them to pick a partner to work with and bring leather lacing, pine tar, a hoe and auger, or share one. "I'll fell the trees and you can use my pattern. We'll begin again the day after tomorrow."

They whooped and danced around Beaver and cheered mightily while two of the boys hoisted him onto their shoulders like he was a warrior hero. All of this attention embarrassed Beaver, but he had never known such joy. Finally, the youths said their goodbyes for now, as did the adults, except for Joseph who stayed the night to work with Beaver the next day.

Wolne placed his forepaws on Beaver's chest and lapped his face with his tongue.

All of the young people showed up every evening and Saturday (after chores) to start and finish their canoes.

Beaver had to chop down four more birch trees from his grove along the creek, but that suited him fine. He was needing to clear an area for another holding pen for his hogs and for finishing them off with corn. From there, he'd boat them to market or to the militia.

He now had five acres of good corn crop to harvest and was to clear another five for planting, hopefully next spring following plowing. His hogs had good pickings in that part of the woods he'd railed off as, "pig proof, bull strong and horse high," but he knew he'd need more corn soon. Thanks to his "brother," Joseph, land-clearing went well and faster.

On top of that, Isaac Cox had offered, on a barter basis, to sell him another 50 acres bordering Beaver's property, an offer he took up on the spot.

Beaver was overjoyed with his thoughts and the dedication of the boys and girls in building their canoes, which number had grown from eight to thirteen.

Where is Beaver agoin', anyway?

"We'll have a whole navy on Cox's Creek, if we aren't careful," he mused.

He also was in high spirits because Felicia couldn't find a partner to join in building her canoe. "Guess you and I will hafta . . . will have to join up," flushing at the possible second meaning. As they worked on her canoe, their eyes met frequently from shy but radiant faces.

On their way home, Henry and his adult relatives were in great spirits, too, over how well Beaver's teaching went.

"Ya know," Henry said, "Beaver should take charge of the 'prenticeship program. He's good with children, without doubt, and he knows more about farmin' than most farmers here about, even them . . . even those that's been at it for twenty or thirty years, both here and back east."

The others agreed most enthusiastically.

By this time, all but Henry and Mordecai had branched off to their farm homes and families. The two walked along giving mute attention to their surroundings. Then Mordecai broke the silence briefly, "Beautiful evening for walkin' without talkin'."

Their thoughts then wafted back into the woods.

An owl hooted loudly close by, another responded from a distance. Beaver's crickets were chirping slower and slower; a breeze rose up and branches were bending and leaves dancing. In the distance, a wolf howled but heard no response.

Mordecai thought immediately of Katrie, his love, wondering if the single howl was an omen. Then Henry broke the silence.

"Yo're gettin' close to 30 years. Ain't that right?"

"Two years down the road," Mordacai said, and sighed. "But don't you start frettin' about me not gettin' hitched before this. I've heard too much of that from my aunties already."

"Yo're plumb right. It isn't any of my business. But what of you and Katrie? You been seein' a lot of her sos other bachelors think yo're agoin' steady. Is that fair to Katrie? Such a healthy filly shouldn't wind up with no husband and without children. And you should know how scarce women of marrying age are here abouts."

Mordecai flushed and stared angrily at his uncle, then cooled down and said, "Henry, if anybody but you said that, I'd have flattened him. But I do need to talk to someone about Katrie and me, and you're prob'ly as good or better than the rest. Yes, we're deeply in love, over our heads in it; but damn it all, she's my first cousin, and her last name is Workman. It puts me to walkin' the floor nights.

"We're fearful our children would be born idiots."

"That's plain and simple foolish," Henry snapped back. "Look at my cattle and hogs. We been back-breedin' 'em for years. Not an idiot in the bunch, exceptin' that horse, Whinny, who thinks she can read my mind. Ain't so sure she can't."

Where is Beaver agoin', anyway?

Mordecai grinned and chuckled.

"You know what Whinny did the other day? I was out hoein' weeds in the pasture, and I layed out to rest a bit. I reached to pull my hat over my eyes, and my hat was missin'. I thought and thought hard, but I couldn't figure where I left it.

"I got up and started hoein' again, really leanin' into it.

"Then comes Whinny. She nudges me hard in the rump and lifted me head over foot to the ground. Then, as I rose up, I see my hat alyin' at my feet. That horse dropped it there, then stood agrinnin' and agloatin' like a cow that dropped twins."

By now, Mordecai was laughing so hard he could scarcely stop.

Henry gloried at the sight, even though he knew that Mordecai figured out a long time ago that Henry was one of the very best at "puffin' up a story." He knew also that for Louicie's sake he had to stop using so many back-country words.

"Uncle Henry, you do know how to steal away my anger and feelin' sorry for myself, but don't you think for one minute I can't recognize when you're puffin' up a story. You're a dead give away what with your ahoein', agrinnin' and agloatin'."

Henry laughed, then got serious. "You're right, But ain't you . . . aren't you about ready to build your own canoe, one that you and Katrie can float together to happy times."

"Wish it were that simple. . . What people say and do, can be mighty active poisonin', I'm sad to say. But thanks Uncle Henry, for being so thoughtful," Mordecai said, while shaking his uncle's hand.

"I'll think on what you said," as they parted for home.

Henry thought about throwing out most of his back-country language so Louicie wouldn't take him for a clown. Then, he switched abruptly to thoughts of cousin marrying cousin and man of red skin marrying a woman of white. He hadn't missed the warm glow that hovered around Beaver and Felicia at canoe making time.

"Somethin's blossomin' there and it could become a beautiful red rose fringed with yellow," Henry said to himself. "Then again there's them damn beetles that could chew on the buds before they could burst into blooms."

He still had reservations, but couldn't come up with anything solid as to why both couples shouldn't marry. Finally, he said aloud, "To hell with them beetles."

He then quickened his long steps home to Louicie and the warmth of the hearth. Yes, the crickets were chirping slower.

* * *

Louicie took up her quill and wrote, "Dearest children, grandchildren, nieces and nephews and those yet to come. Sorry I am late in writing, but I just

Where is Beaver agoin', anyway?

don't have time to write often, what with my midwife work. . . If you read my last letter, you will recall I told how Beaver taught youngsters to build a canoe and to measure the height of a tree. Wasn't that a good way to teach a bit of algebra?

"At this writing, I'll tell you a story about something sad and something scary. You need such a mix to balance out your characters as you grow to adults. The story has to do with Beaver and Felicia. After the last day of building her canoe, Beaver asked Felicia if he could walk her home. . . "

* * *

. . . Felicia said yes, but, "I'd rather you not stop by my house. There's too much sadness in my mamma's heart about what my father's men did to Chiefson . . . and then my father's death," she said, tears welling up in her eyes. "My mother hasn't been herself since, and I'm not sure 'bout . . . I'm not sure what to say to you. How can you stand to look at me?" she asked, breaking into sobs.

Beaver lowered his head and looked at his feet to hide his own tears flowing down his cheeks. Unable to speak, he took Felicia by the arm and began walking her home. Wolne walked behind with head lowered. He sensed and felt sadness, too.

Following a few minutes of silence, a slight breeze cooled their backs and Wolne stood motionless. All was quiet in the woods, except for the crickets. Wolne raised his head to sniff the air, then growled menacingly.

"Somethin's following us," Beaver said quietly.

"You mean an animal, like a bear?"

"Not sure. It's just that Wolne never growls like that unless he smells trouble. We best leave the trail and go into the woods a short ways." . . . Beaver then put his arm around Felicia's waist to make her feel secure, and walked with her into the woods. Wolne followed protectively.

Once in the woods, Beaver knelt down beside Wolne, hugged him and stroked his back, which was tense and bristled at the shoulders. Wolne continued to growl, but softly, as his fill-in master whispered in his ear.

"Can you go see? Go fetch, Wolne! Go fetch and no tricks!" . . . "What a beautiful, bright lab dog," Felicia said. "He's magnificent. But what did you mean by 'no tricks'?"

"I'll tell you later. Now I gotta be alert and listen."

Then followed a rifle shot, a yelp and a tangle of snarls.

A man screamed.

"Wolne got hit, I guess, but he sure enough got the varmint pinned down. We best see what's happened," he said, while sprinting toward the sound. Within two paces, Beaver had snatched his hunting knife from his scabbard and quickly moved back along the trail. Felicia followed within reach behind.

Where is Beaver agoin', anyway?

Wolne's snarls led them north of the trail through thick brush and up a steep slope. Beaver stopped short to view the scene for a moment, as Felicia, a deer at running, joined him.

"Wolne's got him by the leg, that's sure," Beaver said.

Instantly, the 'varmint' twisted free and grabbed his rifle.

Felicia screamed, just as Wolne let go of the man's leg, leaped and clamped down sharply on his wrist. The man screamed again and dropped the rifle as Wolne's teeth ground to the bone.

Felicia bolted forward up the hill, grabbed the rifle, then pointed it directly at the man's head. Beaver arrived a step behind. On command, Wolne released the man's wrist.

"I know this man," Felicia exclaimed angrily.

Looking him straight in the eye, she said, "You're Will Hanger. You used to work for my father. You're the one that got away . . . when Chief Tallfeathers and his braves trapped and killed . . . and killed my father and his men for killing Chiefson. Isn't that so?"

Hanger remained silent, except for groans from pain.

Beaver told Felicia to hold the rifle near Hanger's head while he examined the wounds and said, "Pull the trigger if he moves the slightest." Felicia knew Beaver couldn't mean for her to kill him. But Hanger didn't.

Felicia held the rifle steadily at Hanger's head.

"Nothin' serious about these bites," Beaver said, after examining them. "Hanger's just lucky Wolne got only a shallow bullet wound."

"Why don't we leave Hanger off at Sheriff Nobles? He farms near our place," Felicia said, then continued, "That would kill two birds with one stone, doctoring and sheriffing."

"I'd like it a whole lot better if it was three birds," Beaver said. "Could be Hanger will try to escape."

Beaver tied Hanger's hands with twine from his pocket.

As they walked along, Hanger in front, Wolne alert at his heels, Felicia asked Beaver what he meant by saying, 'No tricks'. Beaver then told about Wolne when he was a young dog full of tricks, like he'd sit when told to stand, stand when told to sit and fetch a rock when we'd throw a stick.

"Now when I mean business, and I say, 'no tricks', Wolne knows I mean serious business."

Beaver then asked Felicia, "I'm still not sure your father and his men were killed by my Pa Chief and his braves? Did Hanger show any facial guilt back there that you could detect?"

"No. I hoped to read something in his face, but it was blank. He didn't give anything away."

Fortunately, Sheriff Noble was home picking corn when they arrived with their prisoner. "What you doin' with my friend Hanger, all tied up," he demanded to know.

Where is Beaver agoin', anyway?

"Well, he's no friend of ours, particularly my dog, Wolne."   "What   you talkin' about?" the sheriff fired back.

"Hanger, here, trailed us and was out to kill me, I believe. He thought I'd recognize him as being at Chiefson's killing. He'd of killed us both if Wolne hadn't got his scent on the trail . . and held him down 'till we took him pris'ner."

"We'll bring charges and testify against him, you can count on that," Beaver said. "Meantime, Hanger'll need doctorin' for his bites on his leg and wrist."

Before leaving the sheriff, Beaver and Felicia doctored Wolne and then filed and signed charges against Hanger, asking to be contacted to testify against him in court. Then they left for Felicia's home where her mother, Mary Matthers, graciously shook Beaver's hand and hugged Wolne, saying, "That's for savin' my onliest child from another killin'."

Felicia walked Beaver down the farm lane on his way back to his farm. Hand in hand, they strolled without a word spoken but with closeness of body and heart. When they reached the end of the lane, Felicia said, "I don't know when I've been so scared and yet so happy, all in just an hour or so."

"It was a great pleasure to me," Beaver responded, "one I hope we can repeat time and again, without any Hanger, of course. I don't know how to explain my feelins, but I'll say this:

"You were very alert, quick and brave to grasp the rifle away from Hanger. He surely would have killed us both."

"May I kiss you?" Beaver asked.

"Yes," Felicia responded, throughout her whole body and mind. "I do believe I'm in love with you Beaver."

"I'm in love with you, too, Felicia. But we have to be prepared for how folks will react to our courtin'. . . . You know, the color of my skin."

They embraced for a long moment, then kissed excitedly and strolled into the woods, where they consummated their love pact.

* * *

"Here's Louicie again, writing on September 30, 1778, about two years after the revolution began. Hard to believe it is still going on. How I worry about my ensign brother-in-law, Joseph, Senior, off fighting in his unit against who knows who and where, at this point in time. He must be lonely for his wife, Sarah, and their children in Maryland and Joseph, Junior, here with us.

"I'm lonely for all of them, too. But they don't write often, and I worry about sickness or death, which reminds me of a spat I had the other day with Felicia, a good Baptist, and me an Episco-Methodist. Guess it was kinda silly on both of our parts, but I got tired of her saying this one 'passed away' and that one 'passed away.'

Where is Beaver agoin', anyway?

"Bible says that Jesus DIED and rose again. But I had to admit that He did pass on to Heaven. To me, though, when one DIES, he or she has the opportunity to rise again, IF they lived a good life. It's an option, as part of a gifted free will.

"You know me, though, I usually find something to worry or fret about. Now, I'm wondering how the neighbors will act about our Indian grandson courting a pioneer lass. . . Last I heard, they faced some real troubled times . . ."

* * *

Beaver laid in his bunk pondering and unable to sleep. It wasn't just plain ribbing that got to him. How could some of his neighbors, whom he counted as friends, be so cruel to Felicia and him? And how come they don't have the stomach to speak directly to him about planning to "mix skin colors," as some were saying.

Beaver had tangled with words, and two times with fists, taking a beating once and winning the other.

"Winning?" Beaver questioned. "No winning for Felicia and me, even if I beat the tar out of 'em." The fight took place after Beaver heard about what Brutus Plowman said:

"Felicia's got a full belly so bad she craps red and white."

Beaver bridled his pinto, Snort, and rode to the Smithson farm where Brutus was working as a hand picking corn. His work was more like picking and scratching and picking and dreaming, Beaver observed.

Faking friendliness, in case what he heard was wrong, Beaver asked, "How's it goin', Brutus?"

"What you got on your mind, redman?" he asked in a surly tone. Getting right to the point, Beaver said, "I got it second hand that you said Felicia 'craps red and white.' Did you say that about my good friend?"

"What if I did? You plannin' on doin' somethin' about it?"

"Yes, if you said it. Did you?"

"I said it. Felicia craps red and white!"

Beaver dug his heels into Snort's flanks and smacked hard on her rump. Snort reared and charged toward Brutus who stepped aside, but not before Beaver flung his foot and caught Brutus in the throat. . . Lying on the ground, Brutus drew his hunting knife and was staggering to his feet as Beaver wheeled Snort sharply and rode down on Brutus.

"I shoulda brought my knife," Beaver thought instantly.

Snort tromped Brutus in the groin as he charged, just as Beaver leaped from Snort's back landing feet first on his adversary, knocking the wind out of him and loosening the knife that dropped from his hand.

Once Brutus had righted himself, Beaver kneed him in the groin with all his might.

Where is Beaver agoin', anyway?

Brutus screamed and nearly fainted from pain.

"If you say such horse shit about Felicia again, I'll kill ya. You listenin' to me?"

"Yeah. Yeah. I hear ya. I won't say no bad words about Felicia again," he said staggering once again to his feet.

Just to make certain, Beaver threw a right into his face, knocking him flat again, then climbed on Snort's back and rode away praying and thinking hard on what had happened. He was remorseful for what he did, but he knew he had no choice but to play dirty in a fight with Brutus.

"God on high. Spirit all around. I am frightened to think . . of what I just done . . . of what I just did. Protect me from myself. I wanted to kill that man. Send your spirit through my body to drive out the darkness and fill me with the light of your heavens."

Beaver was still frightened by his anger as he rode on wondering how far he would go if Brutus went bad on his word. As Snort trotted along, Beaver's thoughts became words.

"I've never thought of killing a man. I don't even like a deer or a bear in my rifle sights, except when I'm hungry or need protection. . . . I sure wish I could talk to my Grandmother Moonbeam's face. She's a comfort of my life," he said elatedly, as he realized a full moon was due in a week.   . . .   But difficult questions were still whirling in Beaver's mind. What should he say to Felicia if she hears what Brutus said? Will she decide our relationship isn't worth the gossip, nasty stories and even threats that come from an Indian courting a white woman? What council could Mordecai Plowman come up with, seeing he's in somewhat the same situation — courting his cousin, Katrie Plowman?"

As Henry would say and Beaver recalled, "Them beetles are in Katrie's and Mordecai's flower bed chewin up them buds before they can blossom."

Beaver decided to stop and talk with Mordecai on his way home. . . Katrie and Mordecai were in the flower garden hoeing weeds and bedding their roses for the winter. They made such a handsome and happy couple that Beaver almost turned back to avoid interrupting them. Should he speak to them now, both together, or Mordecai alone? They're both reasonable and logical people, he thought, and they sure are in the same fix, cousin wantin' to marry cousin', as Felicia and me. So why not stop and talk?

Beaver recalled a visit last spring when Katrie and Mordecai were picking beetles in their rose garden, and the discussion they had then. So he picked up, where they left off.

After greeting his "cousins," Beaver said, "Beetles are gone from your garden, but there's still a lot around, just the same."

"What are you getting at, Beaver?" Katrie asked.

"Well you know Henry's story. The one that's like a parable in the bible. He likened Felicia to a rose bud and me, too, of all things. . . I'm prob'ly more like a horse nettle bud, if there's such a thing," drawing a laugh from Mordecai.

Where is Beaver agoin', anyway?

"Anyway, Henry saw a warm glow between Felicia and me at canoe-buildin' time. He doesn't miss much, even when no words are spoken. That's prob'ly one reason why he is such a good story-teller.

"As nearly as I can recall, Henry said he thought somethin' was blossomin' between Felicia and me. Then he said, and I'll never forget this part. Then he said, 'There'd be them damn beetles that would chew on the buds, sos Felicia and you would never blossom out.'

"Felicia and me . . .and I . . . have a problem like you cousins exceptin' that we're too young, some folks say. But we're just as much in love as you are, and we're gonna marry up one of these days before long, even with all the gossip goin' around.

"I don't mind them gossipin against me, but I sure do against Felicia. She's got enough sad thoughts, what with her pa and one of his men killin' my brother. I get so mad I lose all reason when I hear bad words against her." He then told what he did to their cousin, Brutus, omitting the knee in the groin, and ending his story with:

"I could've killed Brutus for what he said, and I know that is terrible wrong. . . But I'm talkin' too much."

The three then were silent for an awkward time.

"Beaver," Mordecai said, "I'm pleased at what you said about how you treated Brutus. He's got some big problems, and so does his mama. She does her best with Brutus, you know, but both parents went too light on him. Then after his pa died, about 10 years ago, things went even worse."

"Back to our subject," Mordecai said, "you're right about difficulties in our marrying, and times won't get any better." . . Katrie then told Beaver that she had to threaten Mordecai several times with her rolling pin to keep him from fights "with the beetles, as Henry calls them.

"Mordecai and I have spoken often about our situations. Our's is even worse, prob'ly, because we are livin' here without wedlock. Don't take me wrong. We're very happy together, and we plan on marriage before long."

Continuing, Katrie said spontaneously, "Maybe we could have a double wedding. That would surely raise some scornful eyebrows . . . and it'd show those beetles a thing or two."

"Katrie, love, you put your finger right in the thimble," Mordecai exclaimed excitedly. "We should have a double weddin'. Let's show those chompin beetles we'll bloom on our own terms, not theirs. . . What about that, Beaver?"

With tears in his eyes, Beaver answered, "Felicia would dance a jig in my arms, if that's possible. . . Maybe she could jig whilst I turn a few slow country, square-steps. It'd fill us both full of happiness . . . and her mamma, too, I hope."

"Mrs. Matthers against you marryin' Felicia?" Mordecai asked. "She's not said, but she's friendly to me in a cool sort of way. I hope she isn't bein' friendly to me because of Chiefson. Then, she's still worryin' about what her hus-

Where is Beaver agoin', anyway?

band, Fatlandowner . . . what part her husband had in my brother's death."
"Beaver, I'm fairly close to Felicia," Katrie said. "What would you say if I
proposed to her . . ." All three laughed.
"Let me say that another way. What would you say if I suggest to Felicia
that we have a double wedding when the time comes? Have you talked of marriage."
"We've not talked out loud about it, but it's kinda understood in our hearts
and minds. I'd be grateful if you brought it up, about a double wedding ceremony, once we vow to marry."
"Good. Meantime, I'll be seeing more of her like I should have before. She's
a friendly, attractive young woman. Both Mordecai and I have agreed on that,
and I'm sure you agree, without saying."
After his farewell to Katrie, Beaver joined Mordecai in walking over his
farmstead and land, all planned and built by him. Beaver was impressed and
deeply interested in what he thought Mordecai called a grass "water-a-way." It
channeled water off land during heavy rainstorms so as to avoid the runoff
from cutting gullies into a field. Mordacai agreed to show him how to build
one. Beaver beamed and thanked his friend enthusiastically.
On his way home, he crossed paths with Sheriff Noble also on horseback
headed in the opposite direction.
"Beaver, curious we should meet here. I been to your place to tell you
about Will Hanger. He cinched his belt around his neck, tied a rope to the belt
and hung himself in his cell. Sad way to go, but maybe it's for the best. Save him
from trial and our hangin' him."
"Did he have anything to say before he died?" Beaver asked, wondering if
Hanger had told the sheriff who killed Chiefson. "Yes. He asked for his Baptist
minister and told him he wanted to get something off his chest. Said that he
'couldn't go without clearin' up his conscience.' Then, after talking to the min-
ister, damned if he didn't go and hang himself."
Anything else, before he died?" Beaver quizzed.
"No. Should there be?" Sheriff Noble wanted to know. "I guess he felt it
best to die without mentioning Thinline Gap."
"You've known all along about the Thinline massacre? . . . And why they
killed Boulder and all of his men?"
"Yes, I've known. It wasn't right what your Pa Chief and his braves did. . .
But by my way athinkin', it was just."
"Thanks, Sheriff Noble, for telling me and for keeping quiet." . After shaking hands, they parted, the sheriff going about his business and beaver heading
home with head held high. He felt like he wanted to skip like a child. . . It was
a relief to know that Pa Chief would never be hunted down and imprisoned, or
worse, and Mamma Moondove would be so happy.

* * *

Where is Beaver agoin', anyway?

"Here's Louicie, continuing. . . I hope you youngsters won't tire of my rambling; but, if you are half as excited as I am to hear what I am going to say, you'll surely stay awake until I'm finished.

"Firstly, our Joseph Senior wrote and says he'll be at our Hope farm in about a month or two. He's been serviced out of his militia unit and has been with his grown up family in Baltimore Town. . . . Ain't that . . .(sorry) . . . Isn't that just dandy? I think he'll stay here for a spell before he goes and locates land for him and Nelly to settle. Near Hope farm, I hope.

"Finally, I'm going to tell Beaver to write his Ma and Pa about coming home, next time I see him. I'm sure he will. . . . just as sure as a hen won't leave her nest. He'll write them asking them to return. . . We'll see. Meantime, I have a funny story of Henry's to tell, about using 'ain'ts':

"It seems a young boy's mamma asked him to go down the road a piece and borrow a cup of sugar from friends. When he got there, Billy knocked on the door and a little girl his age, name of Josie, answered. The talk went like this . . .

"'Ain't got no suga, is ya?' . . . 'Ain't said I ain't, is ah?' . . . 'Ain't ax ya ain't ya ain't. Ah ax ya ain't ya is. Ya ain't is ya?'"

* * *

"On his way home from visiting with Katrie and Mordecai, Beaver stopped at Hope farm to see his "Mamma" Louicie. After a warm and loving hug, Louicie said, "Have I ever got an excitingly good word for you.

"Sheriff Noble stopped by and said he had followed up on all the facts and claims about your Pa Chief and his braves killing that fatlandman and his men. He said, and I'll say it exactly, 'I searched and studied this case 'till my eyes near went blurry and my head went numb. I couldn't pin it on nobody and make it stick — even in a hearin'.'

"When you write your parents next, Beaver, tell them just what Sheriff Noble said."

"Mamma . . . Is it right for me to call you that?"

"Just as right as a cub nuzzling his ma," Louicie said, tears running down her cheeks. "I'd be mighty unhappy if you didn't."

"Well, Mamma, I just spoke with the sheriff. He told me what you just said. Guess he didn't tell you about Hanger hangin' himself in his cell, soon after he talked with his preacher."

"Oh my, how sad! How contrary, right after seeing his preacher. Oh my!"

"You know, Mamma, I didn't feel comfortable around Sheriff Noble before today. When Felicia and I took Will Hanger to the sheriff for trying to kill us, he said, and I'll repeat it exactly as he said it, 'What are you doin' with my friend Hanger, all tied up?'"

"Sheriff Noble plays games with people," Loucie said, "like when he isn't sure

Where is Beaver agoin', anyway?

about a man's guilt. He's all right when it comes to something big, particularly with friends. But you are right to measure people before you get to know them."

"Well, that may be, but I shouldn't be so doubting, I guess," Beaver continued. "I was fearing that Sheriff Noble might just be tryin' . . . trying to bait a hook to get my Pa Chief back here and put him in jail.

"Until today, I wasn't sure if Pa Chief had a hand in the killings, or not. Now I know, and I don't blame him. He was in a rage because they killed Chiefson . . . my only brother," Beaver said, as tears began to flow.

Louicie stood, walked over to Beaver, took him in her arms and smothered him with love, like a mamma bird snuggles her newly hatched to her breast and under her wing. As she did, she said to herself, "This one's going to the top."

She didn't tell Beaver about Joseph Senior coming home. She wanted Joseph Junior to hear it first.

"You be sure to write your parents soon, Son, and let them know about Will Hanger and Sheriff Noble not finding any evidence about the Thinline Gap massacre."

Beaver agreed to write, hugged his adopted mother, and returned to his cabin where he wrote to his parents. Among other subjects, he invited them home and told them about Hanger's death. But he didn't go into how he died or what Sheriff Noble said about not finding any evidence. He wasn't certain what his Mamma Moondove knew about the Thinline episode; but he was certain that his Pa Chief would know that the only witness at the Thinline massacre was gone, and therefore could not testify against him. He then posted the letter with Isaac Walker.

* * *

A week later, Beaver had been invited to demonstrate "How to measure the height of a tree" and "How to build a grass water-a-way to stop gullying" at a day-long "Student Extender" event. He meant to point out that Mordecai had shown him how to do it.

Even though he was surprised and pleased to see Brutus Workman there, he couldn't decide how to react. Beaver asked himself, "Will my anger and hate of six months ago still be within me and ready to bust out? Would Brutus react angrily for the vicious beating he took from me?"

To his amazement, Brutus smiled guiltily and came forward before the event, put his hand out and gave a firm shake, saying, "I knew you'd be here, Beaver, and I'm glad you are. I deserved that beatin', the worst I ever had. It made me see how low I had sunk."

"Thanks, Brutus, but I sunk pretty low myself by using my horse, Sprint, in the fight. I hope you didn't suffer any continuin' problem from those blows to the groin."

"No, I'm all right now. Took about a month to get over it, though. . . I

Where is Beaver agoin', anyway?

should never have drawn my knife on ya. When I did, you had every right to wheel and charge Sprint at me."

At that point, Beaver put his hand forward, the two shook again and then began chatting about farming and the day's program. Beaver chuckled to hear the title of Brutus' presentation, about a new hog identification method: "Clippin' won't do, not in a hog's ear. Tatoos will, true."

It was both humorous and novel, Beaver thought, and told Brutus so. Beaver noticed happily later that the same humor and novelty came through clearly in Brutus' presentation.

Henry, Joseph and Louicie attended the evening program among 250 or so students and adults as part of the biggest crowd to gather at Salem, even larger than the militia awards ceremony. They wanted to see and hear John Fitch, who was called by locals "the inventor of the steamboat."

"Mr. Fitch," as most called him, was an off-and-on resident on his farm close to Henry and Louicie on Cox's Creek. Lately, he had been more on than off, neighbors were pleased to observe. They didn't much like most absentee owners, who let their lands go back mainly to brambles and wild vines. But Fitch was different, he saw to it that all weeds were cut back, and he was friendly, even though intense and moody.

Louicie attributed Fitch's moods to his difficulty of raising money for his studies and for building steamboats; she learned later how his moods had grown worse, causing him to start thinking about selling his farm.

Louicie and Henry saw this as an opportunity for Joseph who would soon leave his Maryland militia and return to farming in Kentucky.

In his presentation, John Fitch described the race between himself and Robert Fulton to build and successfully operate a boat powered by steam. "It was nip and tuck for years," he said, "but I'm steaming ahead of him now."[29 a-b]

In support of that statement, he said, "The state of New Jersey just recently gave me the sole rights and privileges to use fire and steam to propel my skiff on the Delaware River."

That statement drew the crowd to its feet to applaud and cheer.

"But I'll have to be honest with you," Fitch continued. "I'm having sore times raising pounds and dollars in my endeavors to do research and build steamboats. I've appealed to Congress and several of the Colonies back east to pitch in and help me out. Hopefully, they will."

He then said, "I'll stick around after this gathering in case some of you folks care to pitch in a few dollars or pounds should you want to help me out."

A few of the larger landowners, and at least one small farmer, did just that. Beaver gave him ten dollars.

In a short discussion with John Fitch, Beaver and others learned that their hometown hero had propelled a small steam-driven skiff on the Delaware in 1786. Later that same year he successfully constructed and tested a larger steamcraft, also on the Delaware.

Where is Beaver agoin', anyway?

Beaver and others found out several years later that Robert Fulton tested an experimental model in 1803 and a larger steam vessel in 1807 — 12 years after John Fitch. [29 a-b]

As the crowd broke up, one youth of eight years was heard asking his father, "Pa, Mr. Fitch said he used to pitch more coal on the fire to make his boat go faster. Could we pitch more hay to our cows to get them to let down more milk faster?"

Three days later, while Louicie, Henry and Beaver were seated around the supper table they heard Whinny neigh. That neigh was followed by others of different pitches. . . "Sounds like we got company," Louicie said.

They did. It was Joseph, Senior, and Sarah, his wife, who arrived driving a covered wagon with sons, Jacob, 9, and Benjamin, 7. They were a bit behind a nephew, Hank, 18, on horseback. Hank came to learn farming, hopefully as an apprentice to his uncle, once Joseph had his farm.

Joseph Junior, thereafter called Josh, reminisced late into the night with his parents and brothers, all happily transplanted in Kentucky. The next day the adults, with Josh and Hank, began planning their future, including 300 acres Henry and Louicie expected to be up for sale by steamboat developer and inventor, John Fitch. The 300 acres accounted for less than a third of Fitch's total holdings.

"It's good land situated along Cox's Creek," Henry said, adding, "Mr Fitch said a while back he might want to sell it. . . Would you be int'rested, Joseph?"

Both Joseph and Sarah responded enthusiastically to the idea and began immediately making further plans, including apprenticeships for their two sons and nephew.

In a matter of days after examining the farm, Joseph and Sarah signed an agreement to rent for up to 10 years with an option to buy. Then on November 8, 1796, Joseph bought the farm from John Fitch[30] in fractional partnership with Jacob, Benjamin and Hank. Hank eventually became manager, then owner.

Where is Beaver agoin', anyway?

She goes ahealin'; no blood lettin'

Louicie writes in March 1811 about the busiest time of her life, "even when I'm pushing 70+ years." She was involved in midwifery work with one patient worrying and thinking she faced a breech birth. Then a doctor-type took after her hide for the way she handled the "breech."

"Whew!" Louicie wrote, "good for me that Beaver, my attorney, took my side.

"I forgot to tell you, last time I wrote, that we had a triple wedding here. Cousins Mordicai and Katrie got married. Some folks raised tarnation over that. Then, ta boot, Beaver, who's my adopted son, married a pioneer girl, Felicia. That fired up a kettle of bees, believe me. The cousins had been settled down for years on Mordicai's farm where they adopted three children. Beaver and Felicia did the same, except they have been living and farming Felicia's mamma's place. They have three children and are expecting another.

"Then, 'Cap' Plowman and his wife, Joanne, came down from Indiana Territory with our Benjamin, an Episco-Methodist preacher, who tied all three knots. Cap John and Joanne were the third couple to get married. (Actually, they repeated their wedding vows.) Wasn't that grand? . . . It was a stormy day, and just as Benjamin ended the service with a prayer and 'Thanks be to God,' a clap of thunder boomed and rattled the church to its base. Benjamin smiled big-like, and said: "I sure hope I can get the Lord's attention like that often."

"Now, Felicia's birthing has my fullest attention. . . "

* * *

Felicia's whole body, taut as a bow string, squirmed in pain as she pushed and groaned at birthing time. Her gown and hair were drenched with sweat, as Louicie tried to calm Felicia and bring her back to reality.

"Louicie, I know it's a breech. I've birthed three children before this and never had a problem. . . This time no matter how hard I push, nothing happens, except hellish pain."

Felicia wished Beaver was with her, but he was in court defending a small farmer in an extremely important case. It again involved land, an illegal takeover by a big landowner. . Louicie had examined Felicia twice during the past three weeks without finding any abnormal position of the fetus. But Felicia kept bringing up the subject of a breech, time and again, no matter what Louicie said.

"Try hard to be calm and still. Don't push, for now," Louicie said quietly while wiping Felicia's brow, then stroking her arm soothingly. "You're gonna be fine. So is your baby.

"I'm just as sure as chickens have feathers that you ain't . . . that your baby is not in a breech position. Fact is, you told me two days ago you could feel your baby kicking you high up in your belly region. That tells me the head is down and the rump is up, the way it's s'posed to be. You sure you haven't had a bad dream . . . or still worrying about what a few are saying about you marrying Beaver?"

Felicia creased her forehead, looked to the side and remained silent, except for groaning and grimacing with each new contraction, even though not as tense as she had been. But she still wore doubt and worry in her face, Louicie noted.

"Felicia, my dear one, you are having false contractions as I told you before. For some reason, they pain a lot more, I guess, because they don't open up your birthing channel like the real contractions do. . . Let me show you how to tell the difference between real ones and false ones."[31]

Louicie waited until Felicia's next contraction peaked, then pressed her fingers into her belly and uterine wall below.

"See how far into the belly I've pressed? If this was a real contraction, it'd be so strong I wouldn't be able to dent the wall of your uterus, even a little bit. And as I said before, without strong contractions the birthing channel doesn't open up, doesn't go through dilation."

"Is my baby all right? Is its head showing yet?" Felicia asked, as though she hadn't heard a word Louicie said.

"The baby's fine, but no, its head isn't showing because your channel is still closed and. . . "

"Louicie! Are you sure? Are you just trying to comfort me? . . . I'm really faced with a breech birth. . . Isn't that the truth?" Felicia asked in a fearful, agonized voice.

Realizing then that Felicia was not her usual self, that she was obsessed with fear for her child, Louicie knew that she had to relax and calm her patient. Reason and logic wouldn't bring her back into the real world.

At the last moment, she saw that Mary, Felicia's mother, had slipped into the room unnoticed and seated herself on a bench out of direct vision. Mary looked sickly from worry.

Louicie placed her hand on Felicia's abdomen, lowered her head as if to concentrate, then said to herself, "Dear Lord God and Holy Spirit, hear my prayer. Help me calm Felicia and protect her baby from injury, I ask, through thy spirit. Thank you, Lord. Thank you. . . May thy will be done. Amen."

"Mary, would you please fetch a vessel of warm water," Louicie said promptly to Felicia's mother, "And fetch a pad of linen so you can wash your daughter down and help relax her some? After you've bathed her, then give her a light rubdown, 'specially some strokes in the lower back area."

Louicie then pulled up a stool close to Felicia's head where she stroked her hair and forehead lovingly.

She spoke softly to Felicia about her young children, under care of neighbors, and how Henry puffed up stories for them. Among other tales, she told her about Henry "alosin' his hat" and Whinny, his horse, "afindin' it by the haystack" and about Louicie's dog, Wolne, and his backward ways.

Felicia actually smiled over the hat trick and at Wolne's fetching a rock when he was told to fetch a stick.

"Now, I wanna tell you a story about Henry's left foot and a worn, old boot. . . Henry's got a bad ankle, one he can't straighten out much when he goes to put on his boot. It's a real tussle for him, kinda like the reverse of your baby trying to come out.

"One might say, 'Henry, try pushing your foot in harder and you'll get that boot on.' Another might say, 'Bend yore foot a bit.' A third might decide, 'The boot's too small.'"

"Felicia, you know what I'm aiming at. You pushed hard enough, your baby doesn't need to bend and your channel isn't too small. It's just still laced shut."

At that moment, Felicia took a deep breath, arched her back a bit and groaned as she pushed. Louicie then quickly pressed her finger on Felicia's abdomen, and said: "Nothing faulty about that contraction. It's a real one."

Within 15 minutes, the top of the baby's head appeared, face down as was normal. Louicie checked immediately to be sure the baby's air passage was clear, received the infant as it wormed its way out gradually and slid into the palms of Louicie's hands and then into a warm blanket.

Once the cord was tied and snipped, the infant was bathed and cleansed by Felicia; Louicie then placed the infant in her mother's arms where it snuggled and tried to nurse the breast of a smiling but exhausted mother who said to her child:

"You are a true wonder."

Wonder, from then on, was her given name.

Louicie was a bit shaken as she drove home in her two-wheel buggy pulled by her aging roan. "Perk, you do step out proud like," she said to her 14-year-old mare. "You're high-stepping gait reminds me of your gramma mare, Whinny."

Perk responded with a whinny on hearing her name.

"You even talk back to me like Whinny used to do with Henry and me. I just wish I felt more like talking and like doing some high stepping, myself."

She goes ahealin'; no blood lettin'

WHETSTONES

Drifting back in thought to Felicia's birthing of Wonder, Loucie asked aloud, like Henry does, "Should I have had more sessions with Felicia before delivery time? If I had, maybe I could have figured out her real need in advance."

Louicie knew that Felicia was troubled emotionally from talk by crazies over racial matters. She wished Felicia would ignore it like Katrie has done, since living with and marrying her cousin, Mordicai.

Her thoughts then transferred to Beaver, contrasting him with Mordicai. She was aware that Beaver was so busy that he didn't have time to spend with Felicia. She decided she would have a talk with him.

Her thoughts next turned to Felicia's mother, Mary Matthers, a friendly person, but one who is prone to be a bit of a gossip, now and then . . . Louicie then hoped intensely that Mary wouldn't gab around about Felicia's birthing.

Then forcing herself to think on the positive side, Louicie knew she had done well under the circumstances.

"I just hope Doc Turnly doesn't get word of my failure to give proper 'afore nursing' treatment. . . And here I go again, talking out loud to myself."

Louicie was well aware of controversy brewing between midwives and a few doctors, particularly Dr. Turnly. Actually, she had concluded, the disagreements were being fueled by a group of barbers who still believed in bleeding patients[32] as part of healing, but it also involved other ancient techniques.

She then began sorting through some of the potential issues of conflict that might arise between doctors and midwives.

She ticked off in her mind several of the most troublesome situations, like fees, birthing deaths and doctor and midwife rights. Then, of course, there were several extremes, one being so far out that it was unbelievable: The use of a black cat's blood in healing.[33]

Louicie knew all responsible midwives and doctors in north central Kentucky and she was sure none of them used cats' blood in their practices. Nearly all had discontinued blood letting, except in cases of high blood pressure.

But Louicie was certain of one thing. Barbers were hell bent toward fighting for their outlandish and outdated rights.

She then made up her mind to meet with her midwife role model and distant cousin by marriage, Mary (Brooks) LaRue Enlow, to discuss the situation. Louicie Plowman's maiden name was Enlow, and that meant some important things to her, like fairness, dedication and devotion to all who needed doctoring.

As she turned into her Hope farm lane, she was in a positive and determined mood, a mood that would remain strong and lasting.

Henry greeted her at the barn door, helping her out of her carriage and hugged her sinuous, five-foot-four body off her feet, acting like a newly wedded husband of thirty or so. Even Perk was greeted . . . by whinnies from Snort II, sire of Perk, and Whinny II, Perk's dam.

She goes ahealin'; no blood lettin'

Louicie had messages, either told to Henry or delivered in writing by Isaac Walker on horseback, a contradiction that always made Louicie and Henry laugh. Their laughter subsided some when Henry told Louicie that Doc Stitchler had stopped by to say he had sewed Brutus Plowman's toe back after their nephew nearly cut it off chopping wood.

The third message, also from the Doc, was unexpected bad news stemming from an indignant statement Louicie had made about blood letting at a meeting of church women. Apparently a sister-in-law of Doc Turnly was in the audience and reported to Turnly what Louicie had said at the meeting.

"'Turnly was mad as a trapped bear,'" Henry quoted Stichler saying about Turnly.

"Turnly's a dang fool on blood lettin'. He believes in that old, outworn theory of humours," Louicie said, "and I'm not talking about jokes."

"What's humors if it's not about funny things?" Henry asked.

The word is spelled h-u-m-o-u-r. It has to do with body fluids . . . like blood, yellow or black bile, and phlegm, or yellow spit, as most call it. Turnly believes strong-like that there has to be some sort of balance of fluids in the body.

"Anyway," Louicie continued, "sounds to me like trouble ahead. That Turnly is whole mean and reckless, more like a barber-medicineman than a doc."

"You figure Turnly will single you out?" Henry asked.

"I'll bet my floral bonnet on it," Louicie said with a sigh.

Two weeks later, Louicie got a note from Mary Enlow, her role model midwife, asking Louicie to attend a meeting at her farm home northeast of Hodgen's Mill. She asked Louicie to join Doc Stitchler and her "to talk over some problems we midwives are facing."

Henry objected to Louicie taking such a long ride alone, regardless of how important the meeting would be.

"Well, there's a simple solution," Louicie said. "You ride along and keep me company."

"I'd enjoy courtin' you," Henry said, a gleam in his eye.

Shortly after leaving on the 10-mile ride, Louicie on Perk, Henry aboard Starlight, Louicie talked about Mary and Isom Enlow. Mary wed Isom after the death of her husband, John La Rue. . . . Isom was 20 years senior to Mary when they married in the early 1780s.[34]

"Mary was born the same year as our Josh, in 1766 in Fredrick County, Virginia. She was a Brooks, the family that built Brooks Fort, not too far south of Louisville."

Henry was proud, and marvelled, over Louicie's knowledge and recall, asking, "Did Mary and John LaRue have many children? I recall one was tabbed, Squire."

"They had four, counting Squire. Rebecca was born on May one, seventeen hundred and eighty-four. I remember, because that's the day our Trixie dropped twin calves — on Mayday. Then there was Squire, Pheobe and Margaret, all born the last half of the seventeen eighties."

Henry knew that Isom and Mary had seven children[35]: Abe, Tom, Mary, Lydia, Malvina, Elizabeth and Lorena, who died young. Louicie said they would attend bible and nursery school during the meeting at the Enlow farm home.

At this time, the Plowman couple stopped to let their steeds rest and drink of Knob Hill Creek. As usual they were awed by the narrow valley with its swift, shallow stream, bordered by flowing meadow grass, and backdropped by "Knob Hill Country," as locals called it. They both pondered over the beauty without a word of exchange for several minutes.

The two walked down to the stream, joined by their horses, drank of the spring-fed rivulet, then removed their shoes and socks and waded into shallows like overgrown kids.

Henry broke the blissful silence, "This is beautiful country, but it sure isn't for farming, like along Cox's Creek. That's why I can't understand why Tom Lincoln says he wants to move here and farm on land called Knob Creek farm, even if his South Fork farm[36] on Nolynn Creek is most clay and rock.

"His stock wouldn't get through that tangle of brambles and woods coverin' the humpbacks. Fact is, even if they was all in grass, the hills is too steep for any cattle to climb. If they could, they'd use up so much energy they'd lose pounds faster than they could gain 'em."

"Henry, that's Tom's business, don't you reckon? And I reckon there is something else I need to talk to you about. . . . It's your constant use of backcountry words when you are out in the open like this, or with men friends, even if I do use ain'ts and other backcountry words here and there."

Henry mocked seriousness for a moment, then leaned over, put a finger to his nose and quickly blew snot from one nostril to the ground, peered closely at it, and said:

"I reckon my snot looks healthy enough. You spose I'ma commin' down with 'hume-hour' disease. . . that my black bile and my blue blood is afighten it out for balance and control?"

Louicie couldn't help but laugh over Henry's response. But all the same, she knew he got her message.

With their steeds rested and quenched, they trotted Perk and Starlight for several miles before resting again. By middle afternoon they rode onto the Enlow farm where they were greeted by Isom who was stacking hay on sloping valley land.

Isom had been justice of the peace for several years and a month ago was elected sheriff of Hardin County. He replaced Robert Hodgin, owner of Hodgin's Mill.

"Isom, congratulations on bein' elected sheriff," Henry said. "Yes, Cousin Sheriff Isom, congratulations. . . Our church group talked a good bit about your election, even though we all live and farm in Nelson County," Louicie added, "We agreed that you are strong minded, some said a bit bull headed, but we know you're fair and just."

"You'll make a good match with our Sheriff Noble," Henry said. "He's matured a lot down through the years."

Isom thanked the Plowman couple, long-time friends of the Enlow family, and said, "Sometimes a man has to be bull headed, but I can't think of any elected official that needs more local support than sheriffs do. . . I'll do my best to be worthy of your opinions, even bein' bull headed."

Mary LaRue Enlow then came walking briskly up to them, hugged Louicie first, then Henry, saying to him. "You big bear, why don't you shave once in an age? You growing a beard or did you lose your straight razor?"

Henry flushed and said, "I think a man of my age deserves time off from shavin' and nickin' his face. And I reckon as how I need somethin' to hide my smiles when Louicie bawls me out for atalkin' backcountry ways."

They all laughed, then Mary turned the talk to a serious note. . "Louicie, I invited Doc Stitchler, Beaver, and Felicia here for our meeting. They'll be here in the morning. I think they'll add facts and strong reasoning to our defense, if that's needed, and I believe it is.

"Henry, we'll need you and Isom as observers and reactors to whatever actions we propose and agree upon. That Doc Turnly believes he has the citizens at heart, but he's terribly behind the times, as you well know."

Louicie then added, "Have you heard that barber Billy has teamed up with Turnly? Fact is, I b'lieve Billy is at the bottom of all this mud slingin'. Word's out that the two of them plan to bring charges against me for my statement against blood lettin' and prob'ly others."

"It's not just against you; it's all midwives," Mary said.

That evening, the four spent most of their time talking family and community needs in general. They purposely ignored the impending midwifery challenges so that all could have fresh minds and an equal start. Beaver and Felicia had arrived that afternoon, but Doc Stitchler couldn't attend. His brother, Tom, fell out of his barn loft and was under Doc's care.

Once dinner was over, Mary took charge as chairman to be sure the meeting moved along and participants kept on track:

"First, I appoint Louicie as secretary, largely because of her experience writing her diary letters. Any objections?

. . . . Being none, I now ask those present to tell us why they are here. In plainer terms, what background do you have that will contribute to our cause? This will stimulate ideas among all of us. Once we have done that we'll talk about issues. We'll narrow down to those issues we, as a group, feel may be charges brought against midwives, not just Louicie.

"As our attorney, Beaver, will this procedure stimulate and lead to information you need? By the way, I feel awkward calling an attorney by his nickname."

She goes ahealin'; no blood lettin'

"Well, you could call me "Your Eminence," Beaver said, while grinning and rolling his eyes upward, "but the judge wouldn't like that, even a little bit. Call me Beaver, here; counselor, in court.

"I'd like to include one more approach procedure," Beaver continued. "What do you think could be the prosecution's strongest and weakest positions? I'd like to have you state them as you see them; then I'll add to and decide which in preparing my case . . . our case . . . should it go to court."

"That's an excellent addition," Mary said. "Now Felicia, you tell us why you are here and what are important issues."

Felicia pondered a moment, then said, "I don't know why I'm here, aside from the fact that I enjoy the company very much. I do know one important issue, one my mamma may have stirred up without meaning to or without knowing it.

"Because I was so sure my baby was bottom down for birthing, Mamma believed me instead of Louicie. Then she happened to mention it to a group of ladies at her quiltin . . . at her quilting party. One of the quilters is a close friend of Doc Turnly's wife, May Belle.

"Since then, I've heard a rumor floating around," Felicia said. "I'm so sorry all of this had to happen."

Henry then spoke up, saying, "Felicia, you brought somethin' up that had to surface: the overall dispute among midwives and the doctors and barbers. Don't you all agree?" They did, unanimously.

"Louicie, we know why you are here," Mary asked, "so what charge do you think will be most important?"

"Well, aside from breech birth, which it wasn't, I'd say our opponents will tell the court that it ain't . . . that it isn't likely that I could stop false contractions, just with talk. Doctors are bound to stick a needle into women, 'stead of trying to calm them down natural like."

"By the way, I agree it's Doc Turnly and barber, Billy, who are stirring up the fuss," Mary said.

Beaver interrupted, "Let's talk about them at a later meeting. . . . Louicie, have you stopped false contractions by telling stories to calm, say in recent times, and more than Felicia?"

Louicie paused to think and answered, "Several times, at least a half dozen, in the past year and a half. I can name each of the patients later, if you like. But a lot depends on the nature of the women, their willingness to listen and accept something as simple as telling stories.

"On the other hand, doctors don't know their patients well enough because they make short calls and not very often. We midwives call them "short stops" and "quick peeks."

After a short silence, Henry asked, "What about death rates?"

Isom then asked, "How about fees of midwives and docs?"

The discussion continued throughout the afternoon, then broke for supper

She goes ahealin'; no blood lettin'

followed by a barn dance at a neighbors. Louicie and Henry won the waltz contest, and Beaver and Felicia took top honors in the "barn trot," a popular new dance step.

Henry likened the barn trot to a "fast race to the outhouse."

The next morning, they agreed upon calming of birthing mothers, versus needle shots, as the number one issue, and as a defense. They chose it also because it offered a way, Beaver said, "to counter attack and take the initiative away from the opposition."

Second choice was infant death rates, stressing fewer deaths in midwifery, and third, blood letting. The latter, Beaver said, probably wouldn't be allowed for lack of verification.

"Next," Beaver said, "we should be prepared to present facts on fees, if the opposition raises the issue, or if we find it to our advantage to introduce the subject." Finally, he judged two more potential issues as being so irrelevant and so unbelievable that "the judge surely would throw them out on first mention." He referred to the use of cat's blood in plasters and the use of forceps and knives in removing dead infants.

The group agreed and ended the exchange of ideas just in time for a hearty noon meal of roast beef, mashed potatoes and gravy, corn bread and a mixed fruit salad, followed by apple pie.

Louicie pondered over how Mary could make such delicious salad and pie from dried fruit and told her so.

While others talked farming, the two midwives then reviewed difficulties they had in finding backup midwives in their absences. They discussed and selected names, divided them by areas and agreed to make contacts and develop a small group of fill-ins, including themselves, to substitute for midwives on short notice.

The others, who had been listening, drifted over and joined Mary and Louicie, realizing the input this activity could have on the possible court hearings and trial. Beaver put the group thoughts into words, when he said:

"Mary, you and Louicie have hit upon a remarkable idea. Have you looked beyond your small group of fill-ins? Your idea could develop into a local association, even Kentucky-wide, if you stress these same points. Your idea could improve your standings as midwives and help professionalize medical procedures, both for midwives and doctors. It might even make it possible to eliminate doctoring by the few remaining barbers."

Louicie listened to every word, every syllable Beaver spoke. She could scarcely believe how Beaver, now 32, had matured, how confident he had become and how well he enunciated. . . not a hint of backcountry, not a hint of excessive pride and not hint of doubt.

She remembered how, at the age of 17, he taught a group of youngsters to build canoes, and later saying to Henry, "That young man is going to take the high road. He's one to watch."

She goes ahealin'; no blood lettin'

Continuing, Beaver said, "I'd like to flesh this out a bit, on my own, if you are willing. Then Mary, Louicie and I should meet, if that's agreeable to all. What about meeting in a week and a half, say Saturday at my place at one o'clock sharp?" . . . . They all agreed.

"This could be a positive action in support of a public hearing," Beaver continued. "If properly handled, it could even prevent us having to go before a judge and jury."

Felicia then changed the subject and suggested a name for a midwives association. "What about 'Midwives for Lives' as a name for our group, as the first such affiliation in the State of Kentucky." All applauded in support.

Just before they bid farewell, Louicie and Mary agreed to start calls on midwives as part of their usual rounds of the countryside. They would enlist midwife friends to call on midwives they knew best; both groups would visit men and women of farm families, as well as businessmen, county officials and whoever might be interested and supportive.

Felicia, who had been making calls with Louicie, said she would like to help promote "Midwives for Lives," whenever her mother was willing to take care of her children. Felicia previously had expressed to Louicie a burning desire to become a midwife once her children had grown up. Her offer was accepted gratefully.

Over a period of weeks, following the meeting of Mary, Louicie and Beaver, their campaign became the major subject of discussion throughout the area. It was of particular interest around towns like Bardstown and Hodgenville where Midwives Louicie and Mary were best known and highly respected.

But not all was rosy. An outspoken group of doctors and their families and friends organized and actively campaigned against what they generally called, a bunch of granny women interfering with doctoring by men of medicine.

* * *

"Louicie, again. . . . Hard to believe it is June, already. Kinda hard, too, to believe Henry and Beaver are so worried over me that they even want me to see Judge Bartlett. . . Can one beat that? . . . Then there's going to be a public hearing. Over me? Who am I but a little mite, only five feet four!

"I reckon I brought trouble on myself, like my blabbing before the Baptist women. . . Heavens to Betsy! Would you believe that the hearing likely will bring out everything from black cats to rabble-rousing. . . I just hope Judge Bartlett can control the crowd, so it won't drag out too long.

"And I hope my poor Henry will stop worrying over me. Kinda nice and loving of him, but . . . "

* * *

She goes ahealin'; no blood lettin'

94

. . . Henry was still concerned over the grueling pace and the amount of time Louicie was devoting to "the midwiferey cause", as he called it.

"Louicie, my darlin', you know I'm highly proud of what you are adoin'. It's a good and mighty cause. But what about your health? You know you're seventy years of age and actin' like you're still in your forties."

"Now Henry, you know how fired up I get. It's like someone putting more and more logs on the hearth, and the flame sends out heat that warms my heart and body. . . I love the challenge; I've never felt better. You're just having guilt pains. You shouldn't, you know, 'cause farming keeps you so busy.

"You just keep on making hay, fixing fences and chopping wood. I'll keep on chucking logs on the fire."

Henry understood, but he was still worried, and said, "You just be careful you don't get too close to the fire. Some of the logs might be greenish and spit fire on you."

"Henry, you know full well that you split and store up wood long enough to dry and be ready for the hearth. . . that kind wouldn't dare spark or spit on me."

Yes, Beaver was concerned about Louicie the past weeks, to the extent that he made an informal call on Judge William Bartlett, a former senior law partner of Beaver's before being elected judge. His visit to the judge's chambers involved an idea he wanted to try out on the judge.

Visits to his chambers stimulated Beaver, nearly took his breath away, and redoubled his dream of becoming a judge.

Beaver related the effort by midwives to bring their case before the public, a move known by Judge Bartlett who, in fact, was well informed of the situation. That pleased Beaver who then could concentrate on his idea for a simple solution.

"Judge Bill, you've held hearings in the past to lessen your court docket, what with land challenges still a large problem. I believe such a public hearing would be most suitable in our case."

"Give me your reasoning, counselor," the judge said.

"Number one, we can prove without doubt that only a handful of doctors, and a few barbers, are behind all of this, although I know I'd have to bring this out in court on cross examination.

"Number two, we have strong arguments to show that their attacks are not truthfully . . . . not factually based.

"Number three, we can show that their attacks are selfishly motivated. Some doctors have joined the opposition only because they oppose organizing into groups, including their own medical society and Midwives for Lives.

"However, I won't pull any punches if our opposition attorney gets too far out of line . . . too unreasonable in his charges against us."

Judge Bartlett remained silent for a time while reading through his notes on Beaver's reasoning. He believed in Beaver's sincerity, honesty and integrity; he was not the type, however, to let friendship color his decision making. . . But he had, in fact, been thinking of a public hearing for this case.

The judge then told Beaver that informal charges had been made by Attorney Jack Upton, selected as representation by Doc Emil Turnly and barber, Billy Watts. Beaver knew Upton as an aggressive, sometimes arrogant court battler, one that he had faced in past cases. He knew also that he would have to prepare his case even more carefully and thoroughly than normal.

"Beaver . . . Counselor . . . As you showed in your reasoning, you are correct. I will follow rules of court in whatever evidence I allow in the the hearing. In other words, your number one would not be allowed."

"Sorry, I tripped on that one," Beaver responded quickly. "I'll turn it around and prove the large backing of our side. That should force Counselor Upton to remain silent to the extent of their backing . . . or to hedge his response."

The judge was pleased with Beaver's quick recovery and showed it with a slight smile that faded into his normal stern facade.

"Counselor, I'm sure you know I will allow you to enter your item two if you present the issue factually and have witnesses and conclusive evidence to back it up. The same applies to item three, if you peg it exclusively on Doc Turnly and Billy Watts, and back it up. . . Judge Bartlett then shook Beaver's hand and dismissed him with a pat on the back and a smile.

Beaver then rode immediately to let Louicie and Henry know the outcome of his meeting with the judge. He later wrote to Mary Enlow and had the letter delivered by horseback the next day by his law clerk. He was very excited over the outcome, particularly the pat on the back and the smile Judge Bartlett gave him on parting. . . That told him a lot.

Judge Bartlett later called in Counselor Upton, who arrived with Doc Turnly and Billy Watts, requesting them to give their reasonings for court action. Upton and Turnly did all of the talking, frowning Watts down whenever he attempted to speak, the judge noticed; they were not as objective as Beaver, plus a bit too pushy, the judge also noted.

At the end of the short session, the judge told them that he did not feel they had a case and that he decided to hold a hearing that would be open to the public. "There's been too much talk and activity over these issues to not be aired.

"Our public and our medical community deserve a hearing. I'm setting the date for June 15, at nine o'clock sharp."

The crowd began gathering in clusters an hour earlier, anticipating an action-packed hearing. Action began before the courthouse door was open in the form of loud arguments and two fistfights that almost broke into a riot. It would have, had it not been for Sheriff Noble and his deputies who had been prepared for possible physical disturbances.

Judge Bartlett and the two counselors, Beaver and Upton, were being briefed in the judge's chambers as the raucous crowd grew in size and emotional intensity. Beaver had estimated his supporters outnumbered the opposi-

She goes ahealin'; no blood lettin'

tion, perhaps by ten to one. It would become a standing room only crowd, he was certain.

Among instructions, the judged warned them against "any sort of rabble-rousing talk in my courtroom."

Robed in black and mirroring dignity and confidence, Judge Bartlett gaveled the crowd to silence, rose imposingly to his full six-foot-three and said in a strong baritone:

"Neighbors and friends, ladies and gentlemen, I assume you are all adults. . . But, I will not tolerate any more barroom outbreaks the likes of which took place outside. This is not, and never will be, a circus court. You will conduct yourselves as citizens faced with serious issues and, eventually, a few vital decisions.

"I called this public hearing to give you the opportunity to evaluate the issues presented and discussed here today. They are serious issues, as most of you know, affecting all of us and our growing medical profession. We are not here to argue or disrupt, in any way."

Judge Bartlett then outlined the procedure to be followed: "Each attorney will have fifteen minutes to discuss what they see as issues, their benefits or detriments. Questions and answers will follow the presentations, beginning with possible observations from the bench, then comments and answers by counselors.

"Following that, I will allow questions and reactions from the courthouse floor. I will, however, gavel down remarks that are irrelevant and in poor taste. If my gavel fails, I will motion for the sheriff to assist offenders out of this court of justice.

"You may begin, Counselor Upton."

"Your honor, Beaver, citizens of north central Kentucky. "

"Your honor, I object," Felicia Workman interrupted. Would it not be more fitting for Counselor Upton to call our attorney by his chosen, legal title and surname, as 'Counselor Workman'?"

As the crowd stirred and murmured, largely in agreement with Felicia, the judge hammered his bench for silence, then said, "Misses Felicia Workman, you are correct, but out of order. In the future, allow the bench to respond to such outlandish recognition of a fellow barrister.

"From now on, Counselor Upton, you will address Mister Beaver as Counselor Workman. Is that understood?"

Louicie started to applaud, but knowing better, plus a squeeze of her knee by Henry, reluctantly confined her glee to herself.

"Counselor Upton, continue," Judge Bartlett said sternly.

"Your honor, COUNSELOR Workman. . . ."

The crowd again objected, with murmurs and catcalls, resulting from Upton's sarcastic inflection of Beaver's title.

The majority of those present held Beaver in high esteem, honoring him as a man who worked and clawed his way up from a destitute Indian boy to become a noted attorney. They even accepted his marriage to Felicia, an Irish woman.

"That will be enough, Counselor. Continue your presentation . . . minus any inflections," the judge demanded and pondered over whether the hearing was a good idea or not.

"Your honor, Counselor Workman, citizens. . . I welcome this opportunity to tell a story. It's about a woman and witchcraft, in my viewpoint. Her name is Louicie Enlow Plowman."

At that, many in the crowd jumped to their feet, objecting boisterously by waving arms and shaking fists.

Judge Bartlett called for silence while pounding his gavel angrily and vigorously, so vigorously that he broke the handle.

Some tittered, some guffawed, most sat quietly embarrassed.

"This is my last warning," the judge said. "I absolutely will not tolerate such reactions. One more like it and I will clear this courtroom and discontinue this hearing. He then reached and retrieved another gavel.

"You may continue, Counselor."

"As I was about to say, Louicie Workman is well meaning and dedicated to helping the sick. We all know that. But she is not a psychologist, as she apparently claims. . . ."

"Objection, your honor," Beaver said. "Midwife Workman said nothing of the sort. I was at the Baptist church gathering and heard every word she is claimed to have said."

"So did I," one called out. . . "I, too," another responded.

"Objection sustained. . .Be specific, Counselor, and continue."

"At the birthing, Felicia had been in pain and in labor for nearly two hours without success. Felicia told Midwife Workman several times that she was certain her unborn was in a bottom down, breech position.

"That raises a question," Upton continued. "As a midwife, how could she determine, without any doubt, that Felicia did not face a breech?"

Beaver squirmed and thought of objecting, but held off. He didn't want to overuse that right; and, furthermore, his instinct told him that Upton was digging his own grave, that questioning Louicie's judgment would work against him later.

Continuing, Upton said, "I'm willing to give Louicie Workman the benefit of the doubt. She's delivered babies for decades.

"Her next decision gets to the core of this hearing. She told the Baptist group that Felicia was suffering from false contractions. That her pain was caused by them as a result of the failure of the contractions to open the birthing channel.

"Now, I know little about birthing, but this decision raises two more questions. Is it appropriate for a midwife to make such a decision? Shouldn't that call be made by a doctor?

She goes ahealin'; no blood lettin'

"I say it should, without the slightest doubt," Upton said, ending his presentation on that note.

As Beaver took the stand, supporters of Louicie stood and applauded; Judge Bartlett hammered the bench for silence.

"Friends and opponents, let's examine Counselor Upton's last question: 'Shouldn't that call be made by a doctor?'

"Most doctors would have made the identical decision, and correctly so. They make judgments based on education, training and experience. Misses Plowman makes the same judgments, based on comparable background in birthing education and particularly in experience. She holds a remarkable and enviable record in birthing, one I'm certain would match or exceed that of most doctors. . . "

"Objection, your honor. Such a statement demands proof," Upton said with emotion and an edge of anger.

"Objection sustained. Counselor Workman, cite your proof."

"I have no proof, your honor, except the record made during the past year by Felicia's midwife, Louicie Plowman . . . She brought sixty-three infants into this world during a single year ending last December thirty-one."

"How many birthings did she handle in total that year?" Beaver asked of the crowd. "Sixty four. . . Only one baby died."

Most of the crowd stood, applauded and cheered. Judge Bartlett once again hammered for silence.

Continuing, Beaver again attacked Counselor Upton's questions, arguing that, "Decisions have to be made by midwives, frequently in emergency situations. In Felicia's case, Louicie Workman chose not to give a sedative to calm her and stop the false contractions. She did this based on sound reasoning and knowledge about Felicia, herself.

"As Louicie told the Baptist women, she knows Felicia's nature . . . has known her since she was in her early teens. She also reminded the women of the harassment Felicia went through during her courtship and marriage to a 'Redskin,' . . . as some still insist on calling me. . ."

"Objection, your honor," Counselor Upton interrupted. "Beaver. . . . sorry . . . I mean Counselor Workman naturally is a bit biased, being an adoptee of the Workman family. And he's playing on sympathy by bringing up heritage."

"Objection overruled, providing Counselor Workman can provide convincing reasoning. BUT, we are NOT going to get involved in interracial courting or marriage. . . in any way, shape or form. . . Is that understood by both counselors?"

Both agreed; Beaver continued his presentation, saying:

"My reasoning is based on three points, the same points Louicie made before the Baptist women. One, Louicie knows Felicia well, as I stated previously. Two, Felicia is reluctant, as is Louicie, to take some new medicines into her body. Three, Louicie knew Felicia so well that she was confident she could calm Felicia with backrubs, bathings and soothing stories.[37] She was one hundred percent right.

"With these calming strokes and stories, pain greatly subsided; within an hour, the false contractions became real. Fifteen minutes later, Wonder, as the child is named, was born."

All in the courtroom cheered and applauded the arrival, and cheered again, after Beaver told how Wonder nestled in Felicia's arms, sighed happily and immediately began nuzzling Felicia's breast. Some present at court hid tears, including a few men.

Beaver also told them why Wonder was named Wonder, receiving a light rap of the gavel and a mild reprimand from Judge Bartlett, who turned his head and wiped his eyes under the guise of blowing his nose. He then announced that the court would adjourn for the noon meal, resuming again at one o'clock sharp.

But the hearing did not resume as announced.

One of Beaver's assistants appeared with two black cats in a crate and set them down in front of Beaver, saying, "Sorry I'm late. I corralled them at Billy the barber's place. He must have had more than a dozen like these.

"Not a white hair on 'em."

Hearing and seeing this action, Billy drew his knife, charged Beaver, screaming out, "What in hell you doin' with my cats?"

Judge Bartlett stepped quickly in front of Beaver, as did Brutus, Henry's nephew, to intercept the charge. They succeeded in deflecting him, causing Billy to miss a vital target. The knife slashed through Beaver's sleeve penetrating deeply into his left forearm, thrown up to protect himself.

The judge immediately grabbed Billy's right arm and forced it powerfully across his own knee, causing the blade to tumble down the courthouse steps. Brutus then grabbed Billy from behind in a bear hug and, along with the judge, held him until a sheriff's deputy tied him securely and took him to jail.

During the noon recess, Doc Stitchler treated, sewed up and bandaged Beaver's arm then ordered him home. Beaver refused and entered the courtroom where most had returned.

Judge Bartlett said from the bench:

"Calling this public hearing was a mistake. . . I misjudged the moods of a few of the participants; I'll not reopen the hearing and face more fist fights and possibly more knifings. This hearing is cancelled.

"In its place, I will call together the leaders of the Midwives for Lives and Medical Doctors, North Central. They will meet here two weeks from today, at nine a.m. sharp. I will instruct them to come up with plans for positive actions . . . and to resolve their differences. We will then meet back here one month from today."

"Your Honor," asked an angular man, nicknamed Clipper. "What about us Barbers for Health. Ain't we included?"

She goes ahealin'; no blood lettin'

ROBERT E. ENLOW

"You may be part of the problem, but by no measure are you part of the medical team," the judge said. "You are not invited and will not participate. "Thank most of you for coming. This hearing is closed."

Then turning to Beaver, he instructed him to report to his chambers for a short meeting.

Once there, Judge Bartlett showed concern over Beaver's arm and told him he should go home following their short discussion. Beaver, feeling a bit weak, agreed.

"Beaver, I don't like bringing this up now, but I will. Whose damn fool notion was it to bring black cats to the courthouse? What in hell's tarnation did they have to do with this hearing?"

"Sorry, sir, it was my action and my fault. I told Lawton to pick them up and hold them as possible evidence. Apparently, I did not make it clear to him . . . that he was not to bring them here today."

"You didn't get a warrant?"

"No sir. I judged wrongly, I see now . . . even though we did not have time to get a warrant and bring the evidence here. I was mistaken."

"But black cats, without a single white hair?" the judged asked, trying unsuccessfully not to laugh. "What's your need for these special feline? What are their medical specialities?" the judge asked in mixed scorn, disbelief and uncontrolled laughter.

"Do these cats have urgently needed legal or medical skills? Tell me before I die of curiosity."

"Your honor, sir . . . One's a male and one's a female, obviously for breeding. Both Billy and Doc Turnly raise them for drawing blood," Beaver tried to explain, while visualizing his career as a judge sinking into a deep mire of cat dung.

Continuing, Beaver said, "It's hard to believe, but Billy and five or six other barbers think blood from totally black cats has some healing property . . . that it heals as part of a plaster, maybe for chest sicknesses and wounds.

"It's my guess, sir, that Billy and Doc sell it at a good price to barbers. I can't believe that Doc uses it in his practice. But who knows?"

"I know this," the judge said. "I'll set the sheriff and their deputies on their tails . . . their trails . . . yet this day. Meantime, I'll back-time a warrant in your name to cover your mistake. No word to anyone about this.

"I'm disappointed in your judgment in this case, but your past record justifies my help. Fact is, I still see a great future for you and I wouldn't want a small stumble flawing your career growth. . . What you need now, is to get away from lawyering for a while. Go fishing. Better still, take Felicia on a vacation."

Beaver started to refuse the judge's back-timing of the warrant but decided otherwise. He would not breathe a word about the warrant to anyone, even family. He was confident that his progress and achievements outweighed his blunder. Instead he merely said, "Thanks, Judge Bartlet, I will honor your request. . . And, thanks also for protecting me against Billy. You and Brutus saved my life, I'm certain."

Beaver took the judge's advice and went fishing with Brutus, even though they knew little about catching fish. The two relaxed at Beaver's farm at a bend in Cox's Creek where a massive red oak stretched out across the water. A long rope dangled down a half a pole's distance from the water. Attached was a wooden handle, old and shiny with wear.

Brutus immediately snared the rope with a pole and hook, handy from past days, swung out over the water and flipped and plunged, clothes and all, into the cool depth. Because of his arm, Beaver sat and watched with envy, and happiness, as Brutus swung and plunged. Meantime, Beaver had removed his shoes, rolled up his trousers and waded into shallows.

Soon they sat and dried on the bank.

"I guess I succeeded in scaring the fish away," Brutus said.

"Who wants to fish, anyway," Beaver asked. "Do you?"

"No. I haven't had so much fun in a coon's age."

Beaver agreed, then said, "Brutus, I want to thank you for helping Judge Bartlett keep Billy from killing me. Sorry I didn't before this. Billy went wild; he intended to kill me."

Brutus grinned, shrugged and said, "No need. I still owed you one for bad-talkin' your Felicia."

Lying on their backs, they peered up at the sky and watched the clouds form various images, including one that looked like a huge fish. . . On seeing the image, they laughed until their cheeks and sides ached.

"Guess we're supposed to fish," Beaver said, and they did.

Meanwhile, Felicia, busy with keeping house, had stepped outside to shake dust from her cloth. She heard and saw her eldest son, Jedd, yell and bolt toward her.

"Mamma! Mamma! Marvette's not breathin'!" he screamed. . . "I think she choked on a seed of corn."

Felicia raced to her daughter, hoisted her up by the feet and directed Jedd to pound her back. He did, but to no avail. Her body was limp and her face was blue, especially the lips. Felicia then ordered Jedd to, "Fetch a flat piece of firewood."

She then hoisted Marvette up by the feet, belly outward, and shoved her daughter's lower legs over her shoulders, one on each side of her neck. As Jedd pulled downward on his sister's ankles, to hold her in position. Felicia took the firewood, grasped it firmly on each end and pulled it forcefully and abruptly against Marvette's belly. She then repeated the action.

Marvette coughed, gasped for air and began crying.

"Mamma! Marvette's breathin'! She's alive!"

Tears streaming down her cheeks, Felicia said quietly, "Yes, thank the good

She goes ahealin'; no blood lettin'

Lord, she's alive and breathing. . . Dear God, thank you! Thank you for allowing Marvette to remain with us!"

When Beaver returned home, carrying a string of trout, he heard the story about his daughter, Marvette, and took Felicia in his arms, holding her tightly, with teary eyes and not a word. Finally, he said, "Felicia, my true and only love. Thank you! Thanks be to our almighty spirit!"

* * *

"Dear loved ones and those yet to come.

"Louicie again: Thank God for Felicia's fast thinking. How she knew to use a piece of kindling the way she did is beyond me. She said she learned it by watching her father's belly go in and out as he breathed. . . Marvette's fine. . . So is Beaver. His arm healed, but I expect he'll remember that knife attack for years to come. . . But I have some sad news.

"Shortly after Beaver got home, he got a letter from his Mamma Moondove out west that took his mind off his arm, pronto. It was a terribly sad letter about sickness and deaths.

"I'll tell about that later, after giving you some good news, and a funny happening. You remember me talking about the Thompson family at Salem. . . Oh, shaw. . . I mean, it's Bardstown, now. The Thompsons had six children until just three weeks ago. Now they have eight. Yes, you guessed it. They had twins, a little boy and a little girl, named Thana and Sven. And I had the honor of bringing them into this world. . . . . "Their brother, Lars, 10, was wiggling their toes the other day, and asked, 'Is they 'dentical twins, Mamma?' His mother responded saying, 'Lars, I guess you ain't changed their "dydies", just yet.'

Now for the saddest story. Some of you may have heard about Chief's tribe moving west to the rocky mountain area. They found happier times, good hunting and fishing. . . Chief's wife, Moondove, writes in her letter to Beaver that. . .

* * *

Chief Tallfeathers went to his "happiest hunting ground" where he joined his son, Chiefson. Chief and nearly the whole tribe caught scarlet fever, a deadly disease that spread rapidly and killed many of the tribe.

Moondove, now able to write in English, said that, "A trader stopped by our camp to swap goods for fish and deer meat. After the trading was done, the men sat around the campfire and talked and shared Chief's peace pipe. As is the custom, the guest smoked first, followed by my Chief and his men."

Continuing in her letter Moondove said that a few days later the men started getting bad headaches, then raw, sore throats. They felt tired out and weak, so that they couldn't even fish or hunt. Wasn't long after that the men began

She goes ahealin'; no blood lettin'

dying, and women came down with symptoms. For some reason, many of the younger children and some wives were spared.

Altogether, 33 adult Indians and six children died.

With super human effort, Chief buried the last of his tribe, then dug his own grave, before dying himself. With help from women and children, Moondove then placed his body in the earth, covered it over with dirt and put large stones on his grave. Later that evening, Moondove prayed over the grave to her spirit god, as a full moon rose from behind a rocky mountain.

Beaver and his cousin, Brutus, each drove wagon-teams west and returned with Moondove, 11 children and 3 women who survived, as did a few families that had moved south earlier for better hunting.

Louicie grieved for weeks over the deaths believing she might have been able to nurse some of them through their sicknesses.

She goes ahealin'; no blood lettin'

Lincoln was a Linchorn! . . . Tain't so! . . . Tis so! . . .

"April 10, 1810: Here I go back in time to the Lincolns' baby boy, Abraham. And don't you tell me I told you this story before, because I didn't. It begins on February 12, 1809, more than a year ago.

Abraham Enlow plays a big part.

"So do all of the Lincolns: Tom and Nancy, Sarah, their first child, and little Abe. Then there's the midwife, called the "granny woman." She's my good friend, Mary (Brooks) Larue Enlow[38]. She plays a big part. So do her son Abraham, a distant cousin of mine, and his horse, "Span," named for his long legs. Young Abe Enlow was riding toward Hodgenville from the home of his parents, Midwife Mary and Sheriff Isom, whose farm is located on the road to Bardstown. . .

* * *

. . . Young Abe, then 16, was riding Span to the Hodgenville mill with a sack of shelled corn to be ground into flour[39]. On the way, he met Tom Lincoln who was walking to the Enlow farm to fetch the granny woman. Tom was taking longer strides than usual, young Abe observed and wondered if he needed a ride.

"Mornin', Mister Tom. It looks like yore in a big hurry this mornin'. Can I give you a ride?"

Tom nodded and said, "I'm on my way to fetch your mamma."

Abe knew that Nancy Hanks Lincoln was about to birth her second child so he offered to ride back to his home and tell his mother that she was needed. Tom accepted gratefully and began retracing his steps to be with his Nancy.

When Abe arrived home, he found his mother picking herbs from her garden.

"Mamma, Mister Linchorn says you best be goin' to his cabin. Misses Linchorn's time is about to come."

Mary, then 46, set out her herbs to dry and quickly hitched her horse to the buggy and drove to the Lincoln farm. It was a drive of only three miles to the farm, located on the south fork of Nolynn Creek, about two miles south of Hodgenville.[40]

She drove her horse gently but with urgency into her "home territory" where she had lived as Mrs. John LaRue and bore two of her three children. Enroute, she picked up close neighbors of the Lincoln's, Rebecca Hodgen Keith and Mary's daughter, Margaret "Peggy" Walters, who often helped Mary with her deliveries. Rebecca was a cousin of Peggy's. . .

Both admired and emulated Mary, each aspiring to be a midwife.

On arrival, Mary found Tom kneeling beside his wife and nervously swabbing her face with a linen towel soaked in cool water from their "sinking spring." Nancy appeared tense, obviously in labor, but she relaxed and smiled as Mary and her helpers walked into the cabin.

Mary observed that Tom had hot water steaming at the hearth and linen towels handy on a nearby table. Their younger daughter, Sarah, 2, was visiting neighbors before and during the delivery. She also observed that Tom, like many fathers to be, was stroking his thighs, then walking, then sitting.

Mary smiled broadly and knowingly said;, "Tom Lincoln, one would think you were about to have this baby yourself. You can't sit still for even a moment. You must be three times as nervous as the mother to be.

"Why don't you take a stroll? Or chop some wood? One of the girls will fetch you once the baby is birthed."

Tom grinned sheepishly, donned his coat and walked outside.

After Mary had scrubbed her hands, she became all business, tersely instructing "Becky" and Peggy to wash quickly and to be ready with warm water, a bathing cloth and a quilt for the baby. She then told Peggy, "Have the shears handy, and be quick to tie the cord, then cut it."

Turning to Nancy, she asked, "How long have you had your pains? Are they severe?"

"They started close to twelve hours ago, faint and weak then, strong and more painful now. . . You s'pose I have false labor, like Felicia's?"

Mary reached out and pressed her thumb hard against Nancy's abdomen at the same time Nancy tensed in unison with a contraction. "You see my thumb leaves no dent in your belly. That means your contractions are real."

Mary heard Tom chopping firewood, steadily and at a good pace, to warm the cabin against cold February days. She also heard a dove call, returned by its mate, as she kept a close watch on Nancy. The top of the baby's head had not shown yet.

Within an hour, she told Nancy to breath deeply and push hard each time she pained; then relax until the next pain begins and to push hard again. Nancy knew this from Sarah's birthing; but she followed instructions even more intensely, grunting and groaning at each push. Perspiration soaked her hair and flowed off her forehead, yet she remained in good spirit.

Again, Nancy groaned, grunted and pushed harder as another contraction began. Mary watched closely.

"There's the top of the head!" Mary exclaimed. "All covered with longish dark hair. . . Good! The baby's coming face down, like it should."

Within minutes, the baby was born followed by the placenta immediately thereafter. Once the cord was tied and clipped, and Nancy was cleansed, the baby was washed and wrapped in a hearth-warmed quilt. Becky then placed him in Nancy's arms where he cuddled contentedly.

Nancy searched the baby over, looked into its face and said tearfully, but joyfully, "Praise God, a healthy, sturdy boy. Tom will be mightily happy."

Responding to Peggy's call, Tom entered just in time to hear his wife say, 'a healthy, sturdy boy.' He beamed down on his son, saying, "Welcome! Abraham! . . . Welcome into our home and into our family," then asked quickly, "What do you reckon he might weigh? How long be him?"

"Wish we had a scale here," Nancy said, "but I'd guess a bit over seven pounds."

Mary lifted Abraham, saying, "I've hoisted a lot of them. I agree with you, Nancy. Close to seven pounds. Tom, you measure him." . . . He did, and found him to be 22 inches long.

"Mister Tom, did you name Abraham after Mary's Abraham[41] 'cause he fetched Mary to deliver your baby?" Peggy asked.

Tom laughed and said, "No, but maybe he can be named for two Abrahams: my father and Mary's son. That's not a bad idea," he added laughing heartily and not believing anyone would take his statement seriously.

But a few neighbors, on hearing Abraham Lincoln was named after Abraham Enlow, accepted the story willingly as fact. Hadn't the son of Mary and Isom lived under the same roof with Nancy who worked there as a live-in maid?

It didn't matter that Abraham Enlow was away in Indiana Territory working for cousins Josh and Nelly. He was gone the whole time Nancy worked for Mary and Isom.

* * *

"Dear children and other loved ones: Here's Louicie again, and I'm angry. Not at you. . . I'm angry that people are saying that our Abraham is the father of Abraham Lincoln. I say tain't so, but some few are saying the opposite, 'Tis so!' It goes back and forth: Tain't so. . . Tis so . . . The 'Tis-so' ones don't even know the working end of a pitchfork.

"Tom Lincoln came from good stock, beginning with his grandfather, Samuel Lincoln, who immigrated to this country where Samuel's son, Abraham, became a captain in the militia. Then when Tom's father and mother, Bathsheba, got to Springfield, they bought 2,000 acres of land and were gentleman and lady farmers to the end.

"Some day doctors are going to find a substance in blood of man and woman mates that matches that in their baby. Then they'll be able to compare blood and find who is mamma and pappa.

"Now, Tom couldn't help it if he's having land trouble. Or could he? He's friendly and treats his wife and other people well. Quite a few, however, do call him a wanderer."[42]

* * *

Tom Lincoln got permission to go before the Nelson County Community Bonding Council to present his land problems. He hoped it would carry some weight with his home court in Larue County. After explaining his predicament, the Council peppered him with questions and he replied as best he could:

"What did you do after leaving your mamma's homestead farm?"

"I reckon I sorta lost direction, prob'ly had it soft at home. Then I worked for some farmers, maybe six or seven of 'em, on a bit of carpentry work and handy jobs.

"Did you have proper paper when you bought Mill Creek farm?"

"Prob'ly didn't 'cause I lost my farm. But that's why I'm here. Top of that, when I went to buy the land at the South Branch of Nolynn Creek, I found out I didn't own my Mill Creek land, either.[43] I'll prob'ly move up Knob Creek way sooner or later."

"You believe Knob Creek would be better than South Fork?"

"South Fork is most clay and rock, good bet for livestock, but not for corn, and I can't afford to buy any stock."

"What acreages did you have at Mill Creek and South Fork?"

"Two hundred and forty acres at Mill Creek, three fifty at South Fork. . . Oh, I should tell you I'm just about certain I got bad papers that go back even before the man I bought South Fork from. I can't recollect his name at the moment. . . . Let me think. . . Oh, yes, it was a Doctor Slater, Doctor John Slater. Guess he lost his money, too."

"Is it possible the papers were bad because of incorrect geographic locations and overlapping lines drawn?" another asked. "We've found common causes in a lots of these court challenges."

"Yes, sir. I recall that being the reason. That's the same reason my good friend, Dan Boone, lost some land."

"Your daddy and mamma owned a large acreage and a lot of livestock. Where'd your inheritance go after your daddy died?"

"Well, a lot went to mamma, and some to my brothers, Mordecai and Josiah. Most of mine went for the Mill Creek farm, except some that dwindled the years I farmed out."

Further questions from the Council members brought out that Tom's parents paid $400 for 2,000 acres about 5 miles north of Springfield and near 10 miles west of then Salem. A council member then asked what happened to his elder brother, Mordecai, who saved the lives of Tom and Josiah.

"No question he saved our lives. It happened two years after we come here . . . after we came here from Virginia in 1782. Four of us were working in a field when our pa was killed by an Indian that fired on us.

"Mordecai raced to the cabin and grabbed a rifle. He fired through a peep-hole, killed the Indian with one bullet that plunged into the brave's chest.[44] . . By the way, I guess my good friend Mordecai Workman was named for my hero brother."

Interrupting, a council member asked of Tom: "Did warring Indians play any part in your land problems?"

"No, sir. You prob'ly know that Indian raids were rare by sometime around the middle seventeen eighties. As I recollect, there mighta been a few attacks after that. But I bought my first farm in 1803. That was the acreage I lost from bad papers. You know, the land jest north of Elizabethtown.

Tom also told the council that he and his family had lived only a very short time at South Fork. "We didn't feel right about it, our not owning the land, and we would have had to pay rent for staying there. The council can check this with neighbors, Thorp and Betsell."

The questioning ended with the Council voting unanimously to contact the Larue County Court officials about Tom's Elizabethtown farm to see if it would take on his case. They did. But after reviewing it, they rejected help on the basis of it being "too many years after the purchase of the land."

The council continued its land confirmation depositions on numerous individuals over a period of days, the most noteworthy being "the inventor of the steamboat," John Fitch. They verified that he had taken a patent on 1,000 acres on Cox's Creek on October 15, 1779 and arrived in 1780 in Kentucky, then still called "the dark country" of western most Virginia.

One witness, Bill Larkillson, said that he recalled, but "wasn't sure" that John Fitch "suffered a bad case of darkness sickness in 1789, just before he died." On hearing later about the Larkillson statement on Fitch's death, Louicie looked back in one of her 1789 diary letters to be sure she knew how he had died.

"Just as I remembered," she told Henry, "John Fitch died by his own hand.[45] It was only two years after we bought our farm from him. Sure was decent of Bill not to mention in public how he died. That would have brought back sad, sad memories. I recall his darkness of the mind being caused by his shortage of money to build a larger steamboat."

"Yes," Henry agreed, "but I reckon history'll show he was first over Robert Fulton, even though he exper'mented with small skiffs. After all, a boat's a boat, ain't it?"

* * *

A week later, midwife Mary and Felicia arrived at the Lincolns' cabin, hurriedly examined Nancy and her baby and declared them fine. She was all worked up over the group of "tis-sos," as Louicie now called them. She had great difficulty understanding how so many people could be so mean and so wrong.

"How could they believe my teenage son is the father of the infant Abraham? That's evil, even more so."

"Yes," Nancy followed. "How could I dirty up your household by havin' time with your Abraham? . . . Right under your noses. Your Abraham is too young . . . Makes me wildly mad. Makes me wanna cry," and she did.

Louicie interrupted to tell them of Will Hanger calling for his preacher, then hanging himself.

Mary looked shocked but kept to her subject: "The 'tis-sos' are kinda like that ornery wild boar we've seen now and again in our woods. He calls for young mates, does his thing, then nips off part of the mate's ear. Some say that's to identify his girl friends and to frighten off other boars."

The women then discussed Will Hanger's death before shifting to their planned subject of midwives and what they had accomplished toward meeting Judge Bartlett's orders after the hearing. They knew Midwives for Lives were far ahead of schedule over Medical Doctors, N.C.

Discussion began with the survey on practices unacceptable to midwives. Doctors were doing the same.

"Most of the questionnaires are in," Mary said, "and I'm very pleased with the results so far. Midwives voted nearly a hundred percent against the use of blood from black cats . . . for any kind of healing . . . and were against using black wool to treat humours, even though most weren't sure of what they were."

"I'm not sure," Felicia said. "Fact is I never heard of them." "Not sure myself," Mary said. "It's an ancient and outdated notion of some doctors and midwives. They thought our health requires a certain balance of all fluids in the body."

"You mean like blood?" Felicia asked.

"Yes, but also phlegm, bile, mother's milk, fat and serums," Mary responded. "But, as I said, humour is just a notion."

Louicie then told them Henry's joke about humours, when he put his finger to his nose and blew snot on the ground, then said, 'Looks all right to me. I reckon my humour is balanced'.

The women all laughed heartily; Louicie then wondered if it was right to have told the story, in fear it would reflect badly on Henry. . . making him into a "carny clown."

Mary returned to the survey, saying, "Midwives voted strongly in favor of cathartics or purges. They should be continued, of course. Some used to call them 'pukes.' But they thought wrongly that all parts of the body were tied together, and that a cathartic would treat the whole body, not just the digestive tract."

Louicie then said, "Practically all voted that birthing children is our primary function. It takes up most of my time. Have you heard what doctors are saying about that Mary?"

Lincoln was a Linchorn! . . . Tain't so! . . . Tis so! . . .

"Nothing official. But I believe most support that position.

"We all know certain conditions require doctors to be called in, time permitting, when serious birthing and other problems crop up. As you know, these can cause friction. And that's where the Midwives for Lives association can play a big part. We need to discuss these potential frictions and make our recommendations. . . and to defend our domains, like birthing."

To make a point, Louicie then told a story about one of her patients who literally whistled while she labored.

"At first, I thought Ellie had been nipping hard cider. She'd change positions, suck in air and whistle out a tune with each contraction. It didn't matter that I couldn't tell what tune she was whistling. . . Then I saw how relaxed Ellie was, even during contractions."

Felicia laughed with the others while taking notes as elected secretary of the association. Mary was elected president and director, Louicie, as a director. Felicia grinned, wrote down the elected officials, then grinned again and wrote, "Whistle while you labor."

The group of three, and Nancy as an interested listener, then discussed infant death rates among midwives. Mary summarized the survey results in one terse statement: "Our midwives' notes show just under two deaths for every hundred births.

"That's not bad. But it can be reduced to one per hundred."

"I expect it can," Louicie said. "It can if we have closer relationships with doctors. A few deaths were from breech positions, mostly babies with bottoms down. Some others were strangled by umbilical cords.

"Too many midwives have to rely on the old hearing horn, 'stead of that new stetoscop."

"You mean stethoscope, Louicie," Mary corrected. "But you have a good point. Felicia, jot down an item on our needing a survey to find out how many stethoscopes, hearing horns, or neither, that our midwives have."

"I've cut birthing deaths since I began using my stethoscope, mainly because of early detection of the baby's faulty heart beats and lung congestion. That allows more time for doctors to meet emergencies, not that they can always save a child."

Discussion then turned to callbacks, time spent with patients and amount of fees. They were aware that midwives made far more calls and spent more time with patients than doctors. They also knew doctor's fees were more than twice what midwives asked for or charged their patients. Felicia then asked:

"Do we need guidelines on how to determine fees for the poorer families? I realize we have to judge them as individual families and how much they can afford in money or barter; but as a new midwife, I would need some sort of blueprint."

"Felicia, make a note of that for the future," Mary said.

Lincoln was a Linchorn! . . . Tain't so! . . . Tis so! . . .

"That's a good suggestion. Our survey is accurate, but it doesn't include or consider the poor. Yes, we should at least come up with general guidelines that are fair to all.

"But to get back to the survey on fees. It shows that we all ask two to three dollars per patient for each illness. It's accurate. I know that... Doctors charge at least five or six dollars, and they spend much less time with their patients. But, if for some reason we were to challenge doctors on fees and time, we definitely would need accurate records, including those for the poor."

Next, Mary said that the survey showed a high degree of satisfaction in how midwives view their work, except for duplication of barter goods as pay.

"Many cited, 'Too much corn; too little coin,' as I recall from the survey forms we read and tallied," Louicie said. "But, dang it all, nearly all midwives we interviewed had nothing but 'good patients', not that they wouldn't like small raises."

My son, Beaver, suggested a way to make bartered corn worth our while," Louicie said. "His idea is as simple and clear as most bubbling springs. He said we should pool our corn and hold it until we get a wagonful, then sell it to the militia or to well-off farmers who often run out of corn in late winter.

"Henry has offered to collect corn once a month and haul it to market. He advises us to sell it in late winter when bins are pretty near empty."

All three accepted the idea enthusiastically.

Before adjourning, they put their decisions in priority order and asked Felicia to write the report. She agreed, happy to be trusted with the responsibility. After review by Mary and Louicie, the report was sent to and approved by both the board and Judge Bartlett. It was six months later, however, that the Medical Doctors, North Central, submitted the report to Judge Bartlett, who angrily accepted the long-overdue document.

* * *

Louicie again: "We got some fast reaction from Judge Bartlett. After reading and studying the reports, he wrote a plan for leaders at the state capitol. It passed through pronto.

"First, barbers were ordered to 'Stop any and all doctoring.' Second, doctors were ordered to make more callbacks on patients, then to inform midwives if more treatment was called for on those patients needing appropriate midwife treatment.

"Third, on the judge's advice, the capitol folks ordered a study to 'find and eliminate any and all ancient treatments not appropriate in today's medical practices.' Those included were: using black cats' blood, letting blood to treat humours and most all of those we midwives asked to be eliminated.

"That's the good news, now for the bad, I'm sorry to say. The Tom Lincolns moved again, and mud tossers kept throwing at them. Some folks say it's best to get things out in the open. Louicie says it isn't so good when its dirty laundry.

"Before I let go of my quill, I want to end on a happy note by telling you a story about a 'picunic', as one of our French friends calls it. She spells it 'piquenique'. My, isn't that interesting? Anyway, Henry and I love piqueniqueing on a small meadow, midst our tall oaks, where we can be ourselves and enjoy the quietness and the birds. On one of our outings, Henry was pouring us another glass of wine and said . . ."

* * *

. . . "I reckon we can handle a second mug. You deserve it, my darlin', what with all you been adoin' lately. I run out of breath just watchin' you come and go," he said, as he snuggled up close to Louicie. "Just to keep warm," he said with a gleam in his eyes. (Louicie didn't write of the following details.)

Louicie moved in even closer as Henry put his arm around her shoulder and caressed her face with his hand, then with his lips. His lips then found her neck, an act of love that caused Louicie to shiver in delight.

Responding to her shiver, Henry took her in both arms and kissed her hard on the mouth; Louicie opened her lips slightly as an incentive to Henry.

Louicie then opened her blouse to expose her large and shapely breasts, remarkably youthful for a woman her age. She nudged Henry's head down toward her breasts, inviting him to caress and kiss and mouth them. Her breasts pulsed, her body trembled and tensed, as did Henry's.

A slight breeze carried wildflower scent wafting upon them. A dove called and was answered. Crickets were chirping, first slowly, then rapidly. It was as though they sensed the heightening emotions rising from Henry and Louicie, who slowed to prolong their love actions.

Slowly and more slowly, gently and more gently, they moved to the harmony of love . . . a deep, very deep emotional love, a love that came from their hearts, their bodies and minds. They grasped each other tighter as the peak moment neared. Tremors of joy continued to throb their bodies, repeatedly sending ecstatic sensations through them.

Louicie cried out, then sighed; Henry moaned and gasped, as the big moment arrived. Tremors of joy continued to throb them, repeatedly spreading ecstatic sensations, like lightning snapping and cracking from above.

"You are a lot of woman, Louicie! . . . A whole lot of woman!" . "And you, my love and lover, are a whole lot of man!"

They lay quietly in each others arms, until Henry rose on one elbow and said, "Louicie, I wonder what it'll be like ten years from now, when we're in our eighties. We better practice up on as many moves and positions as possible, before then."

Louicie screeched with laughter, then punched him in the belly, saying,

"That long from now, Henry, you'll not be able to rise to the occasion."

Henry roared in glee so loudly that the birds fluttered and flew away. But not to be topped, he responded, "The hell I won't. If I have'ta, I'll stiffen up by drinking a glass of your cornstarch mix."

Henry and Louicie called it a draw, after laughing until their cheeks and bellies hurt.

* * *

Nancy Lincoln hurt even more, what with the rumors continuing to bounce around here and there. She told Tom she wanted to move, maybe up to Indiana Territory. They did move eventually, but only a few miles away.

"What sort of rumors are you hearing now?" Tom asked.

"It's about dates. Has to do with Sarah and Abraham, both bein' born February twelve, two years apart. I gotta admit that odds against that are pretty high, but you'd think people would give us the benefit of the doubt."

"Nancy, you best not fret over a few buzzards circlin' around with smelly messages, like dead animals. You'll soon get sick."

"That's easy for you ta say, Tom... Seems like it's always the women that are the loose ones... Next, they'll be sayin' we didn't marry 'cause it was on the twelfth of June, instead of the tenth or the eleventh... Just maybe they don't know we take a liking to the number twelve," Nancy said jokingly.

"Bad enough they keep gossipin' over my so-called affair with young Abraham Enlow."

* * *

Louicie, the worrier and fixer, got wind of the recent chatter, too. She was so worked up that she contacted local preachers and asked if lay leaders could meet and figure out ways to "stifle the mean talk." They agreed, if they could attend.

Louicie didn't like that, and told each of them so... The preachers compromised, agreeing to attend as observers.

Henry, meanwhile, grumbled at Louicie for fear she'd wear herself down. Louicie just smiled and said with a gleam in her eyes, "Henry, you know how to perk me up now and then."

The lay leaders did meet and most agreed on what should be done. Louicie attended and told Henry later that only a few disagreed. Henry then asked if Louicie looked the refusers over carefully "to see if their noses had turned to beaks and their fingers to talons."

"What sort of leaders will they come up with?" Henry asked.

"If they do what they say, they'll pick those most fair minded and eager to help. They're willing partly 'cause there's an ecu... ecumental... Oh shaw!..

Lincoln was a Linchorn! ... Tain't so! ... Tis so! ...

. an ecu-men-i-cal movement going on that's working well . . . Even the Baptists and the Catholics are talking again.

"They agreed to select two lay persons from each church. Those selected would be willing to come up with a plan, mostly to listen first, then to counter soft-like with the truth. I believe it will work."

* * *

On midwife Mary's most recent call-back to evaluate Abraham and Nancy, she found them both healthy and cooing. . . Abraham cooed at his mother, and his mother cooed back. But all was not cooing time.

The mail carrier arrived by horseback carrying a letter for Nancy from a former North Carolina neighbor. The neighbor wrote that she had read or heard a rumor about Nancy's birthing of Abraham and expressed indignation and concern.

The former neighbor hoped to soothe Nancy by telling her she knew it wasn't so . . . that she knew that teenage Abraham Enlow wasn't the baby's father. She then said she tracked down the rumor and found that the story was told in some sort of news sheet that claimed an Abraham Enloe of North Carolina was really the father[46a-b].

Nancy's immediate response to the letter came in the form of a question to Mary, "How in God's name could a Mr. Enloe of North Carolina have fathered Abraham? It's been several years since we moved here to Kentucky. . . Mary was very angry over Nancy's treatment. She didn't believe for a moment that anyone but Tom Lincoln had fathered infant Abraham. She was relieved, however, that Nancy could coo with her baby in spite of her problems.

* * *

Beaver was happiest when strolling about his 100 acres. It gave him time to relax and think and plan. He felt concern about Tom and Nancy Lincoln, who had moved to a 30-acre farm bordering Knob Creek, and was immediately immersed in conflict. It had nothing to do with the claims against Nancy.

In fact, he now lived close to some of his best friends, including both Mary and Isom.

The Lincolns' problem, once again had to do with land.

Beaver knew of the new land problem and relaxed his lawyer mind before puzzling a way he might help the Lincolns. He hummed a familiar tune, then said aloud, "Beautiful sunshine; beautiful day. . . There oughta be a song for a day like today."

He traced long-erased footprints to a grove of birch trees, adjacent to where he had taught pioneer children to build a canoe and to measure a giant cottonwood tree. He recalled how their faces shined so brightly and eagerly. He remembered Felicia's quick mind and loveliness as she stood before the group and demonstrated how to solve an algebra problem related to measuring the cottonwood.

He remembered, too, walking Felicia, his only love, home in the face of danger, and how Felicia and Wolne helped save their lives. He then felt guilt about sneaking off onto the woods with Felicia. They did consummate their love affair, but it was a costly experience to a virgin like Felicia who, willing and happy as she was, felt guilt then and still does.

Beaver's mind then wandered up into a long-gone tree, a landmarker on his property cut down by "Fatlandowner" as a means of confusing boundaries. He could hear the honey bees buzzing and stinging angrily about Chiefson's face, how he fell from the tree when "Honey" bear objected to Chiefson's presence in a honey tree and how his brother then fell from the tree. Most vividly, he recalled how Josh and Wolne saved him from the angry bear that wanted honey, and protected her cub.

Then he saw and heard the killing of his brother at the hands of land robbers dressed as Indians. The fatal shot still echoed through his mind.

He then perched himself on a moss-covered mound, leaned back against a red oak and reluctantly erased his mind of the past and its joys. He was faced with today's problems, including that of Tom Lincoln. He said a prayer to his heavenly spirit, speaking through his granny, his risen angel and guardian:

* * *

"Granny Moonsmile, I feel you are there and listening, even without your face showing on the moon. . . I feel your presence as a good spirit, always. This time, I speak mostly of happiness and joy that Pa Chief and so many of our tribal loved ones have been with you since the scarlet fever attack. I know you must be happy for this . . . and for my Mamma Moondove now living with a close, loving neighbor of mine.

"Moondove is very happy for the tribal children, those whose parents were killed by the fever. If you don't already know, please tell the parents who died of fever that Moondove found loving homes for all of their children and that she spends much time teaching them new and old ways. . . My only problem is how to help Tom and Nancy survive their newest challenge, that of their 30 acres of land bordering knob country.

"I feel your presence and believe you will respond, perhaps later. . . I love you, and all of those with you. Please tell of our gratitude to the tallest spirit. Thanks be to you and to the chief of all. Love from your grandson, Beaver."

* * *

Relaxed and clear of mind, Beaver knew immediately that his Gramma Moonface wanted him to help himself, just as she had said before. He then began placing his thoughts in order. He knew Tom Lincoln had been accused of being a trespasser and was behind in land taxes on his 30-acre farm. He wondered how one man could stumble into so many land problems. Then saying aloud, "He's snakebit without doubt."

Beaver decided to ride over Knob Creek way and talk with Tom. He had heard Tom say he had paid his land taxes, but "a few days late" was totally confused over why he was being called a "trespasser". Beaver was confused, too, unless another boundary mistake had been made.

Finding Tom hoeing weeds, Beaver greeted him and said, "Tom, I'll stop by the courthouse and check on why you are being called a trespasser. It could be you were late enough in meeting your payment, or it could be boundaries were incorrectly drawn and registered. I hope it's late payment.

"Anyway, I can't check your records unless you hire me in writing to take your case, without pay, of course. Things official and personal, in a manner, are held in secrecy now days, ever since the last big hearing on land problems."

Tom agreed, and after a brief discussion about Tom's farming plans, Beaver left for the courthouse with Tom's written authority. He found the newly-elected county clerk at his desk, piled high with documents and two thick ledgers of regulations. Most of the documents appeared to be tax complaints and land challenges, Beaver noted and scowled.

He frowned, then smiled, on seeing the young clerk's name, Clem Clerick. "Must be some sort of spun-funnery," he thought. "Surely Clem is a pet name, hopefully not short for Clementine."

"Yes, what can I do for you?" Clem asked with slight arrogance. . "I want to see the land tax record on Tom Lincoln. He's authorized me to represent him on his taxes and being accused as a trespasser. I've not got a lot of time, so I'd like an answer when I get back in about an . . . "

"What's your name? Are you an attorney?" Clem snapped.

"Name's Plowman. Yes, I'm an attorney."

"What's your first name?"

"Just call me Attorney Plowman. I'm the only attorney in this county with the name Plowman. Most others are farmers."

"Mister! I must have your first name before serving you. It says right here in rule number two five five that I must have a man's full name."

Just at that moment, in walked Sheriff Noble who hailed Beaver with a greeting and a pat on the back, saying, "Well, if it isn't my good friend Counselor Plowman. What you been doing these past months? How's your arm?"

At that moment, Clem Clerick hurriedly left his desk and headed toward what Beaver assumed was the file room.

"Arms fine; like new," Beaver said.

Beaver was annoyed over Clem's treatment of him and mildly so over the sheriff asking an attorney such a question about his work. Beaver worked at lawyering "too long and too hard," Felicia often was prone to say, strongly but

WHETSTONES

kindly ... Beaver then dismissed Sheriff Noble politely and said he'd be by his office shortly.

Clementine, as Beaver would hereafter call him, returned in a matter of minutes, appearing shy and guilty, with papers in hand. Beaver took Tom's papers aside and sat down to study them. All but one were dated, then marked, "Received and Reviewed; Action Pending" and initialed, "CC".

Nothing was marked on Tom's tax payment form, which included an envelope that was unopened. It was marked, "Payment of Taxes, Thomas Lincoln," and "Handed to Clem." Tom had dated it March 23, 1811, nearly 6 months ago. The envelope contained bills, Beaver knew by feel and shape.

Realizing the new county clerk was rightfully elected and relatively new at his job, Beaver bit his tongue and said quietly, "Clementine, I assume you sign in documents."

"Yes sir, Attorney Plowman. Though I guess I missed Mister Lincoln's submission. It's not in my log, sorry to say."

"Have you any notion what mental pain your omission caused Mister and Misses Lincoln?" Beaver asked quietly, recognizing that Clementine freely admitted his mistake.

"I have no excuse, sir. I'm sorry if I caused the Lincolns unnecessary grief."

Beaver felt good about Clementine's response, yet he would continue to call him Clementine, for a while, to be sure he remembered his mistake. He was even more pleased because he had solved one problem for Tom Lincoln, that of land taxes. Now he faced the difficulty of Tom being accused as a trespasser. He wondered if Sheriff Noble could provide any help, particularly if it involved illegal activity.

Surely Tom would have been alerted about false or mistaken boundaries, considering problems he had faced, and lost, previously. Or would he? Beaver asked of himself and sighed.

Sheriff Nobel was polite and wanting to help, but he said he didn't even know the land, nor was he aware of others in that immediate area facing problems on boundaries. Beaver then visited the office responsible for land assessment and sales. He asked Manager George Levey, if he knew of Tom Lincoln's 30-acre holding. He said yes, but he knew of no problems. On checking, Levey found it was a very small parcel of a 10,000 acre holding patented in 1784 by Thomas Middleton.

"What's Mister Lincoln's concern? Is he 'cused of farmin' someone else's land?"

"He's accused of trespassing, yes... I'm representing him."

"To my knowing," Levey said, "we have no reports ag'in Middleton or 'Linchorn'. I b'lieve they both stand up straight as a tall oak. Maybe there's some kinda poor understandin'."

"But let me check on who sold Linchorn his thirty," Levey suggested. He did, and found Lincoln didn't buy his land from Middleton at all. He bought instead from Roger Lester of Virginia, unknown to Levey.

Lincoln was a Linchorn! ... Tain't so! ... Tis so! ...

"I know the man," Beaver said. "He stands tall; but isn't from Virginia anymore. He lives in a county south of here, not sure of which, but I've done legal business for him."

Nearly a month later, Beaver met cousin Brutus in Bardstown. He recently had been named as an assistant justice of the peace for Larue County. He complimented Brutus on his new job, then asked, "You had any luck finding anything about Tom Lincoln's trespassing charge?"

"Yes, I have. Though I'd rather not tell you who give it to me. One of my former friends was drunk at a loghouse tavern last Saturday night, where he talked Tom Lincoln apart arm by arm, foot by foot. I heard 'im say, time and ag'in, that Tom was no better than a trespasser, and had no son."

"Brutus, where's your cousin from? Down North Carolina way?" "Right. He moved up here a year ago. How'd you know?"

"I've heard it from the same source. I believe now it's the beginning of a rumor caused by a dislike of Tom Lincoln."

They parted, Brutus in search of owners or thieves of lost livestock, and Beaver to ponder his naevity. He shrugged to himself, knowing he'd rather not judge a man too quickly.

He and Felicia soon took a two-week holiday to Boone Forest, where they recreated, made love often and seeded a fourth child.

* * *

"Louicie again, with a story about riches that starts back in the 1500s on Manhattan Island, New Amsterdam, and comes home to Enlow people in Maryland Colony in the 1700s. I just learned from my Uncle Zach in Maryland that a somewhat distant cousin of mine, John Enlow, married Elizabeth Frazee in 1790 in the western most part of Maryland.[47] I was about 50 then and had known about John but had never met him then or since.

"And guess what? Elizabeth Frazee is a direct-line relative of the Bogardus family that lost their land to Trinity church on Manhattan Island. Today, Uncle Zach, pushing 91, is fully involved in tracking ancestors, including Bogardus people. He wants me to get involved, too. But even if I had four hands, I'd not have the time to spare. I wrote to Uncle Zach and said no, but maybe, when I retire from midwifery, if ever.

"The estate amounts to 67 acres which may some day be named Kings' Park, bought originally from the Indians for a box of glass beads. Now it's impossible to fathom what the land is worth. It'd be more than the several hundred acres once owned by Enloes families on Baltimore's Middle River.

"Here's the important part what Uncle Zach wrote to Elizabeth and sent a copy to me.

"Elizabeth's father, Elisha Frazee, wed Polly Bogardus. Polly is said to be the great granddaughter of William Bogardus, son of Reverend Everardus

Bogardus, first Dutch Minister of Manhattan.[48] He was the second husband of Anneke Webber, the traditional daughter of William the Third, also known to history as William of Orange of Holland. His father was the King of Holland, the founder of the Dutch Republic, then known as Prince of Nassau . . . (That's sure a quill full!)

"I still wonder what relationship there might be between these Bogardus families and our Nelly Bogard, who married Josh in Kentucky and now lives in Indiana Territory. The fact that many people Anglicized their names — or clerks misspelled them — on arriving in this country makes it difficult to track back. As an example, my maiden name changed from Enloes to Enloe, and then Enlows and Enlow.

"A few think McEnroe might have been a predecessor. That's a wild one to knock around. . . Then there is the Enelow family, originating from Russia, whose son became a noted rabbi in this country[49]. . . Then there's Abraham Enloes known to have asked his wife in his will to free their slaves[50], who may have taken their holders surnames as sometimes happened.

"It's like mixing fruit squeezings together. Usually you get a good or interesting flavor, but at times they won't mix, or aren't, because of fear of flavor or unacceptable color. But everyone to their own taste, said a neighbor woman who kissed her cow. . . We were all given free choice, I believe, to do right or wrong, or nothing.

"Now, back to Uncle Zach. He wrote a short letter to me about earliest apprenticeship programs, like the ones Henry started here several years ago for our 'adopted' Indian youths, Chiefson and Beaver. They were the first to go through the program. Now Uncle Zach reminded me that the earliest of our settlers in this united country went through 'prenticeships, as Henry calls them, to learn farming as a trade, like carpentry.

"'In June 1714,' Uncle Zach wrote, 'Abraham Enlow, 13, and his brother, Henry, 10, were bound to serve farming. Abraham served Charles Simmons, and Henry served William Wright. They were sons of John, who died in 1706, and grandsons of Hendricks, the first of my clan in this country.' . . . Well, enough of my quill, for now. Love to all, Louicie."

* * *

"Your Uncle Zach makes it sound a bit like they were bound to serve as slaves," Henry said with a chuckle. "I'm glad we didn't use 'bound to serve' in our program. Folks around here likely would have thought we were starting up slave camps."

"Reminds me," Louicie responded, "of what Nelly wrote in one of her last letters. She's all fired up and working hard to get anti-slavery passed by the legislature for all of their Indiana Territory. That would be a blessing, there and here."

"Our Beaver believes it will pass, but not 'til that territory becomes a state,"

Henry recalled. . . "As you know, our Kentucky legislature failed to see that opportunity when we won statehood. . . What year was that?"

Louicie answered, "It was eighteen years ago in seventeen and ninety-two," then added:

"You know, reading Uncle Zach's letter about Abraham's bonding gives me an idea. . . Henry, do you recall reading Abraham's will and what he said about their slaves?"

"I reckon I do, but you're gonna have to set me straight on just which Abraham you mean. Is it he that was bound to serve? If he is, I can understand his wanting slaves to be freed."

"Henry, it's no time for spun-funnery. . . This Abraham Enlow was the uncle of the two apprentices Zach wrote about. I have a copy in our sea chest, I believe. Hold on a minute and I'll get it."

On returning, Louicie and Henry read the part of Abraham's will on freeing the slaves. The will stated:

"I give and bequeath unto my Loving Wife all my negroes to wit, Negroes Joshua, Sarah, Thomas, and Ann with their increases to her, her heirs and assigns forever, as was my Intention to have Manumitted my negroes aforesaid, but my present Indisposition hinders the same.

"I have given them to my wife to do with them as she pleases, yet having confidence in her that she will, by sufficient deed of manumission, make them free after my decease."

Both Louicie and Henry remained quiet, mulling over the words and their meanings. Henry then said, "I remember puzzlin' over the words 'manumitted' and 'manumission'. They mean freeing the slaves, I recall."

"Correct, Henry. The base word is manumit, meaning to free from slavery. . . Their words back then copied middle or king's English, to a degree."

"Sounds kinda stuffy to me," Henry said.

"It troubles me" Louicie said, "that the will doesn't ever name Abraham's wife. I recall from Uncle Zach it was Eliza."

"And that raises the main question," Henry said. "Did Eliza ever free the slaves? It's kinda like Moses and his people. He got them out of Egypt, but where did they go? Into a dry desert with little or no food. Is that being freed?"

"Henry, we're getting way off the subject, but I believe that people are not free until they are tried and hardened, like a blacksmith's iron. They're then better able to face decisions and challenges of the deserts of this world. Once they do that, they can enjoy their freedoms. If not, their free wills will be at the mercy of desert bandits and wild animals."

"Maybe all that's part of the problems of slavery," Henry responded. "Slaves don't want to be slaves, I'm certain. But how do they face freedom if not prepared? They know farming, but where's their land? Deserts usually don't grow much grain."

"Henry, you should know the answer to that. We need to expand more into apprenticeships in other trades."

Changing the subject slightly, Louicie said, "Let's get down home about this discussion. I believe we have two tools that we can use to sway landowners and their families toward freedom for their slaves.

"First, we have a successful apprenticeship program that can be adapted to Negroes. It already includes effective placement; that should answer questions about the desert. Second, we have before us a mechanism called a will and testimony.

"Churches have been big on helping apprentices. I believe that preachers and church leaders would help people decide to release their slaves through their wills. Many preachers write out wills for those who ask, as does Beaver, as a lawyer."

Later, on hearing Louicie's idea, Beaver was quick to respond. Because of serving both as an associate judge and a lawyer, he didn't have time to write wills. It usually meant writing and rewriting them for older people who found it difficult to make up their minds. For another reason, Beaver knew that Negroes most often were down trodden and without opportunities to advance. Beaver knew what that meant. . . As an Indian, himself, he had seen many failed attempts by fellow tribesmen to make a living once free of their tribes.

First, Beaver borrowed Abraham's will from Louicie, read it carefully and wrote down the relevant facts and parts of the will about releasing the slaves. Later, he drafted and redrafted sample wills that could be used by preachers and lay leaders working with elderly members of their churches.

Like Henry, he puzzled over whether Abraham's wife, Eliza, had actually freed their slaves. He decided to assume so, even though lawyers should never assume anything. This, he felt, was a just cause.

The idea of enlisting lawyers in the cause immediately came to mind. . . Most big landowners held slaves, and lawyers represented most big landowners. The pieces all fit together.

Then, much to Beaver's joy, he read an unusual story about Mary (Brooks) LaRue, later Enlow, that was very fitting to his present need.[51] It was written by the Hardin County Historical Society, a fledgling group of older pioneers, mostly women who wanted to document historical developments in their county. It had to do with a Baptist preacher at Mary's church:

* * *

"A remarkable incident occurred in the old Nolin church. Rev. David Thurman was pastor. He was a strong Calvinistic and an ardent defender of the doctrines in which he believed.

"On this day, he was noticeably despondent and remarked his dissatisfaction with the response that had been given to his zeal and efforts, and even suggested that the church call another pastor. As he paused for reply, Mrs. LaRue spoke up in steady tones:

"Brother Thurman, I'll tell you what the matter is — stop preaching John Calvin and James Arminius and preach Jesus Christ."

After a moment's pause, the pastor, with tear-streaming eyes, repeated the passage from First Corinthians 2:2, "For I determined not to know anything among you, save Jesus Christ, and Him crucified," and burst into a fervent and powerful discourse which launched a revival that began with that day, and in which were one hundred additions to the church.

"The tide swept from church to church until there were more than a thousand conversions in the association".[52]

* * *

Beaver felt blessed with such information, particularly at this critical time. After a discussion with his boss, Judge Bartlett, on the overall ideas and developments, he would solicit help from Louicie in enlisting Mary LaRue Enlow on church leadership calls on the slavery issue.

The only problem, Beaver recognized, was that Mary at one time held a slave named Nancy, who was willed to Mary by her late husband, John LaRue, in 1792.[53]

Beaver puzzled over this contradiction because he knew Mary was a remarkable and fair-minded individual who was educated in schools in Virginia and Philadelphia. Even Kentucky Governor Helm had given her a highest tribute, saying she "was the best granny in Kentucky in her day."

Continuing his thought pattern, Beaver asked of himself, "Why worry? Louicie knows Mary much better than I do."

Following his appointment with Judge Bartlett, Beaver knew he was on the right track. The judge, his mentor, had accepted and agreed wholeheartedly to plans made by Louicie and Beaver. But he worried still over what the pesky gossipers would say about Mary helping to free the slaves, as a slave holder herself. Louicie didn't worry at all, telling Beaver later, "Heavens to Betsy, Beaver, Nancy may be a slave, but she is, and always has been, a close and helpful member of the LaRue and Enlow families. Mary offered freedom to Nancy several times; Nancy, in turn, asked to stay on each time."

Beaver wondered if insecurity caused Nancy to refuse freedom, but he accepted Louicie's conclusions. Why shouldn't he? He trusted Louicie's judgment, and Louicie and Henry had "adopted" him. He even took the Workman name, legally and rightfully as a member of the family.

Beaver then pondered another incident: He recognized how unusual it was that Nancy Hanks, now Lincoln, once lived at the Enlow home at the same time as the slave, Nancy. That might explain why some people refuse to believe the claim that Nancy Lincoln was working for Josh and Nelly

Workman in Indiana Territory at the time she reportedly conceived Abraham.[54]

Beaver had difficulty accepting that Nancy Hanks was in Indiana Territory at the time of conception. Now he thought of contacting Josh, Louicie's nephew, who could verify Nancy's presence, true or not.

He then decided to leave well enough alone, asking himself: Why make more trouble for Tom and Nancy Lincoln? What effect would it have on Mary's credibility and stature? Why do I weave myself into a briar patch of tangles? he pondered, while turning thoughts back to ways to get lawyers and wills to help free Kentucky slaves. Beaver went back to talk more with Judge Bartlett. "Sorry to bother you, but my mind is wandering into extra-thorny bramble patches."

He then told Judge Bartlett about the plan and asked his opinion on the direction to go.

"It won't be easy, and it would be as slow," Bartlett said, then paused. "But I believe it best to present the idea before church, community and county organization like our Bonding Council. You'd have to start at the grass roots and build strong support. Something like that might prepare the way for lawyers and the State legislature to take a hand in it. But they wouldn't unless strong public pressure is brought to bear.

"On second thought, Beaver, my advice to you is to leave this project alone. It's explosively emotional. Leave it to community and church leaders.

"If you will put Louicie's and your ideas down on paper, however, I will refine a plan in writing and present an official plan to our local Bonding Council and to leaders in the State legislature.

"As your supervisor, I direct you to drop the idea completely, not because I don't agree with the need, but because you don't have the time to get involved. Let's leave it that way."

Beaver felt deflated, but in a way relieved. . . On receiving Beaver's written plan, Judge Bartlett did as he said he would. He refined it and submitted a plan. It was received thoughtfully by the church leaders and the Nelson County Bonding Council, but rejected vehemently by State legislative leaders, most of whom were large landowners and holders of slaves.

Local churches united in writing wills that made it possible for owners to "free," not 'manumit', their slaves.

The next week, Beaver and Tom Lincoln, met unexpectedly enroute to Salem on horseback. Without dismounting, the two discussed the accusation made against Tom for trespassing.

"Beaver, you told me I shoudn't worry over being called a trespasser. How do you know I shouldn't worry?"

"As far as I know," Beaver said, "Clem Clerick made a mistake. He failed to register your first payment. That mistake led to your being in default and without rightful use of the land, then caused rumors about you being a trespasser."

Lincoln was a Linchorn! . . . Tain't so! . . . Tis so! . . .

"Just the same," Tom said, "I'm still plannin' on movin' north. A man can't compete here in Kentucky, so long as big farmers have slave labor."

"That's your choice, Tom. But holding slaves in Indiana Territory is still legal," Beaver said, "until it becomes a state and if the new legislature outlaws slave holdings."

Are they takin' the high road or the low road?

"Dear children, grandchildren and those yet to come:
"I don't know whether to be sad or joyful, maybe both," Louicie wrote in her letter of August 7, 1810 from Cox's Creek, Kentucky. "They thought she was dead but couldn't find her body. I'm writing about Betsy Plowman, 10, my great niece, who was out in the woods gathering acorns for their pigs with her brother Benjamin, 5, when she was attacked by a wild boar. Benjie wasn't hurt, thank the Lord. He ran for help, crying out . . . ."

* * *

"Mamma! . . . Daddy! . . . Betsy's hurt by a wild boar. She's in the woods near our spring. She's bleedin' bad like."

The woods, dense and deep, were well known by Benjamin, Sr. and Fanny, his wife. He scooped up Benjie and held him close before asking, "How near the spring?"

"Right aside it. We was gettin' thirsty and was kneelin' down to get a drink when the boar charged Betsy. Knocked her into the spring. I pulled her out."

"Fanny, you and Benjie, get some linen towels and strips. Hurry! I'll go ahead and see to her."

With that, Benjamin got his rifle and raced off across his pasture and into the woods, calling out for their dog, Kent, as he ran. He wondered where Kent could be and if the boar was the same one he shot and wounded a week ago. When he arrived at the spring, Betsy was nowhere to be seen. Only droplets of blood and a basket of acorns remained.

Benjamin tracked Betsy for a short distance but soon lost the trace, almost as though she disappeared in space. Again, Benjamin called for Kent, but to no avail.

"Did you see anything of Kent?" Benjamin asked as Fanny and Benjie arrived.

"Kent was wif us at the spring," Benjie responded. "Last I saw him, he was chasin' after that mean ole boar. Daddy, you think that boar turned on Kent and kilt him, too?"

"No, Benjie, I don't. Kent can take care of himself. It's Betsy, we're worried about. I tracked Betsy a short way, but her footprints soon disappeared, like she took to the air like a bird."

Fanny also tracked Betsy, finding droplets of blood here and there, then came to the same dead end. "Looks to me like she was reeling and stumbling along," Fanny said, choking back sobs, "like she might be in a stupor."

"Mamma, don't cry," Benjie said, man-like. "Betsy can take care of herself. She always has."

The three fanned out in different directions, calling out again and again for Betsy but without response. Finally, they returned to the spring to rest and think and plan what they should do next. Tears flowed freely.

"We need help," Fanny said. "I'll take Benjie and go home and see first if I can find Kent. Then Benjie and I'll go see if Jacob will ride out and ask neighbors to join a search party. You best stay here, Benjamin, and keep looking."

Benjamin agreed, knowing that his brother, Jacob, and sister-in-law, Elizabeth, would be hurt if not asked to help. Benjamin searched the area thoroughly along paths and through dense underbrush for more than an hour. He found no signs beyond what they had already seen. Then about two dozen neighbors — men, women and grown children — began entering the Workman woods, led by Jacob. They came by horseback, in buggies and on foot — to help find their young neighbor.

Fanny and Elizabeth took responsibility for caring for younger children, their own and those of neighbors, at the Benjamin Plowman farmstead.

A sudden and prolonged downpour soaked everyone and washed away whatever remained of Betsy's trail that might have been scented out by neighbors' dogs. Kent still had not been found.

But Benjamin had found the boar, and quickly shot and killed the animal. On checking, he found to his gloom that it was the boar he wounded previously; he knew he was indirectly responsible for the attack on Betsy. He then made the sign of the cross, dropped to his knees and sobbed out a prayer, pleading for help in finding Betsy alive.

"Lord God, hear my prayer. . . Help us in our time of tribulation. Let us find Betsy alive, if that be thy will. I ask this for her sake but also ours, and particularly for Benjie." He then ended the prayer, again crossing himself as he said, "Thank you Lord God on high. I know and believe that all things are possible through Ye that strengtheneth us."

Benjamin immediately felt washed, invigorated and confident that Betsy would be found alive, but he was still depressed over allowing an injured, dangerous boar to run loose.

In the meantime, the search continued as the sun set and darkness was at hand. Many close neighbors were seen with tears flowing down their cheeks, wiping eyes and blowing noses. They knew Betsy as a loving youngster who helped other children with their homework, planned after-chore games and

Are they takin' the high road or the low road?

carved willow whistles and hand-stitched rag dolls for the neediest.

Benjamin knew too that Fanny would want the wild boar skinned, butchered and given to needy families, and that none of the Workman people or neighbors would feast on a beast that had attacked his daughter. Unknown to Benjamin, Dr. Aron McCrillus and James Pitch stood by quietly and respectfully while Benjamin prayed. Dr. McCrillus shared the pulpit with Benjamin at their Methodist-Episcopal Church services,[55] held alternately at their homes. Jim Pitch was a hard-working farmer, one who seemed plagued with difficulties of making a living and one who suffered seriously from periodic dark moods. Benjamin had an eye on Jim as a potential member of the church and hoped to have private counseling with him over his moodiness. Benjamin believed strongly that he or Doc McCrillus could help Jim.

Dr. McCrillus, 42, a well-loved country doctor, stepped forward and said, as though he had read Benjamin's mind, "Ben, Jim and I have agreed to skin and butcher the boar later tonight at my place; then we'll divide it up and give it to the needy. Is that all right with you, my friend?"

Benjamin choked back a sentimental sob then thanked them. . . Fanny and Elizabeth had food prepared and ready on tables for the neighbors who had searched, unsuccessfully, for Betsy. The mood was quiet, loving and respectful, but awkward to some, as guests served themselves silently, then seated themselves on the lawn under a full moon. Crickets were chirping rapidly in keeping with the warm summer night; a breeze carried voices of a wolf and it's mate exchanging their haunting and mournful messages.

The group represented a rainbow of protestants, mostly Baptists and Methodists, a few Methodist-Episcopalians, and two Catholic families, a "vanguard" of many to come from Germany. It was an unusual group of people, some of whom would never have believed they would share a meal with "Romans."

Nevertheless, a union was in the making as Dr. McCrillus stood and said, "Let us all bow our heads in silent prayer, thanking our God for this food and for a healing of Betsy, in God's given way."

After the prayer, Benjie wandered over to the knoll of a hill, sat down and cried silently in a deep mood of gloom. He loved and emulated Betsy deeply; she was his ideal, in many ways. He pulled his willow whistle from his pocket, carved and given to him by Betsy; he toyed with it lovingly and put it to his lips, but couldn't bring himself to blow it because it didn't seem right. Instead, he broke into mournful sobs for Betsy, and also for Kent.

His mother stood out of sight watching and listening. She didn't dare let him know she had heard him sobbing. Benjie, although only five, had the pride of a 5-year-old stallion. She waited until his sobbing ceased, then walked to and sat close by him, snuggling an arm around his waist.

Benjie couldn't stifle a sob that broke loose from his proud, tense body. His mother remained silent but drew him even closer to her side. Benjie composed himself, sighed and asked, "Mamma, do you s'pose Betsy is lyin' out there in the woods, still alive and bleedin'. . . Or is she lyin' out there dead? "

After a moment, Fanny said, through tears, "I don't know, Benjie. She wasn't bleeding so badly. She's prob'ly dazed and has wandered off without knowing where or who she is. We just have to pray and wait, no matter how hard that is to do.

"We'll find her in the morning. Just you wait and see."

They remained silent, still snuggled closely. Fanny then asked, "Aren't you hungry?" Benjie shook his head. "Would you rather wait here?" He nodded and hugged his mother tightly with both arms, shaking and sobbing for a moment.

Benjie jumped to his feet, on hearing a whimpering in the distance. Both listened intently.

Benjie raced in the direction of the sound. He found Kent, glassy eyed, trembling, and still whimpering. As Benjie stroked the Labrador's back and hugged him, Kent licked Benjie on the hand, then on the face.

Benjie saw blood on his hand and Kent's left hind leg that was bent back grotesquely against its thigh. As Benjie gasped and screamed, his mother picked him up lovingly and called out loudly as she raced to the house, "Benjamin! Come quickly! We've found Kent! He's hurt badly."

Benjamin and "Doc Mac", as most called him, arrived together, examined the dog's condition, then hoisted Kent gingerly and took him to the barn, where they examined Kent in more detail. . . . They found shattered bones in his left hind leg and a gored right shoulder, plus other minor injuries.

"We have two choices," Doc Mac told Ben. "We can put him out of his misery or amputate the lower left leg. That's vital. But first, I'll treat the gore in his shoulder against infection, to be sure the wound will heal properly.

"What's your decision, Ben? If we amputate, you'll have a crippled dog, one that probably won't re-adapt to cattle herding or protect your sheep against wolves."

"True, but then, there's Benjie and Betsy to consider," Ben responded. "They love that dog something fierce. So do we all. Kent's got a bundle of spirit, is dedicated to us Plowmans and takes his chores seriously.

"In short, I vote for amputation."

After retrieving his medical satchel from his buggy, he first clipped and shaved the areas of Kent's wounds. Then, as Ben held Kent, Doc Mac cleansed, treated and bandaged the shoulder injury. This was followed by cleansing and amputating Kent's lower left leg at the joint and stitching a flap of skin and flesh over the stump. The leg was so numb that pain was at a minimum; most nerves to the lower leg had been severed.

Ben continued holding Kent and watched closely as Doc Mac rigged and fitted Kent with a holster-like bandage and strapped it securely in place. He then reviewed with Ben how to clean, construct and apply the leg and shoulder bandages, saying that it must be changed at least weekly. The procedures took nearly two hours.

In the meantime, the guests had left, promising to return early in the morning to continue the search for Betsy and to learn how Kent was getting along.

With help from Benjie, largely in fetching tools and boards, Ben then rigged a small holding pen for Kent, built a raised "bunk" and instructed his son on keeping a watchful eye and caring for their Lab dog.

At midnight, by lantern light, Doc Mac and Jim Pitch skinned and butchered the boar into portions. They then salted the meat to preserve it, and packaged and stored it temporarily for delivery to the needy by volunteers who had agreed to pick it up and distribute it within a day.

At dawn, following two hours of sleep, the two joined the search for Betsy, already well underway. All neighbors, and more, had returned for the hunt. In fact, Doc and Jim arrived just in time to see and hear a group of neighbors cheer loudly on finding Betsy in a cave in the bank of the Patoka River.

Their cheering, however, turned to quiet dismay over her condition. Betsy seemed friendly but stared blankly at neighbors she had known since she was a toddler, including family members and Doc Mac, who delivered and was now examining her.

He found and treated a minor tusk puncture on her rump, undoubtedly inflicted by the boar when Betsy was bending over for a drink at the spring. Otherwise, she was in good physical condition. Her memory loss, Doc Mac figured, could result from fear and shock.

But a big question rose among all searchers. How did Betsy get from the spring to the cave without leaving a trail beyond her initial footprints? The heavy downpour could have wiped out her prints, but it didn't rain until after her father, an expert tracker, was able to trail her only a short distance — to a dead end.

Some of the searchers, including Fanny and Elizabeth, Benjamin and Jacob and their parents, believed Betsy's guardian angel may have raised her up and placed her safely in the cave. Many were simply perplexed; others laughed at the possibility of an angel being involved, or that angels even existed.

Betsy, of course, couldn't throw any light on the subject, because she couldn't remember. After a week, she still didn't recognize her parents, even though they spent hours of loving time and counseling with her.

She did, however, know Benjie and Kent, possibly because they were with her when the boar attacked, her parents surmised.

The angel issue became a community-wide topic of debate, particularly at church functions. The issue then spread to include such traditions as genuflecting, crossing one's self, wine at communions and addressing ministers as "father".

Some called it high church against low church.

Benjamin said in a sermon, "People should be allowed to stand on their

Are they takin' the high road or the low road?

heads if it would help instill or strengthen faith." He was one of the ministers criticized, as a result of crossing himself before and after praying in the woods when searching for Betsy.

His sermon was entitled, "To believe and belong," in which he stressed the positives of church membership and attendance, starting with individual benefits.

"Most of you know what I'm gonna say, but it helps to get down to the basic question: Why do you go to church? Is it to meet influential people? Is it to show off a new bonnet or a new tie? Is it to sing in the choir or help with a bazaar to raise money for a new steeple?

"There's nothing sinful about these actions; but as I hope you know, they are not the basics of church involvement. If a new bonnet makes you feel better and puts you in a receptive frame of mind, then that's good. If you enjoy bazaars, and make close friends, then that's good, too. If you sing off key in church, that's fine. At least you are singing.

"Yes, it's even good to want to meet influential people. It gives the influentials an opportunity to know those in need, and what their needs are. But more important yet is to meet and get to know the poor and downtrodden, whether in church or through its activities. This will lead you to go out in the community and find and help the needy.

"Remember, your friends are where your heart is.

"But you cannot and will not help the downtrodden, unless your heart is involved, and unless you enjoy it, which brings up a vital aspect of religion.

"Christ wants us to be happy, to be joyous with and about the Lord who resides within us through his holy spirit — if we make a place for the spirit in our heart, mind and body. Making a place means prayer, reading and studying the bible and doing good deeds. Spread light, not darkness. Light drives away the darkness and brings joy to people and to the Lord.

"Now, let's turn to angels. Do they exist, and if so, what part do they play in our lives and those of our children? I'm sorry to say that I do not recall any time in my life that I have known or been helped by a guardian angel. But in my mind, that does not mean there are no angels. It doesn't mean also that I have not been helped by an angel or two or three.

"My daughter, Betsy, believes in angels, and because of Betsy, all of our immediate Plowman family here about, including myself, believe in angels. So do thousands and thousands of people throughout this good earth, particularly those in need, those who have faced trials and tribulations. Here's how I know, if you will pardon additional personal experiences of my family.

"Our daughter, Betsy, has met and been saved or helped by angels four times, prob'ly more. The latest meeting is known perhaps throughout this area. The other three went unknown outside of the family:

"When she was three, she fell in deep water of the Patoka River, just below the mill. She couldn't swim, but she reached shore safely. How? . . . When she was five she was chased by a raging bull and faced by a tall bull-proof fence. She flew up and over the fence. How? . . . At six, I saw her standing under a tall oak during a thunderstorm when lightning struck the tree and split it top to bottom. Half of the tree fell where Betsy had been standing. She was not injured, let alone being killed. Why wasn't she?

"The answer in my mind, without doubt, was angels.

"Now, let me conclude with a short reminder of human spirit between loved ones and in relation to Jesus Christ and angels.

"Have you ever watched a mother and one of her toddlers exchange loving glances? The mother looks at her child at play to see if she or he is safe and having fun. Without a word from the mother, the daughter looks up and smiles.

"Have you ever noticed how elderly couples speak of the same thing at the same time? Or just look at each other with understanding and silent communication as a reaction to a grandchild's antics or actions?

"Have you watched a fawn receive silent instructions from her mamma, in the face of danger? Or a hunting dog obeying and reacting to his master's thoughts?

"It's human and animal exchange of spirit, in action.

"So, don't you accept the fact that our all-powerful and all-loving God the Father communicates, in the same way, with us and with angels He has selected as helpers? True, many people do not receive His messages because they have not prepared themselves for His word, even when the word is God. . . . . "Now, let us rejoice with a hymn about angels."

* * *

Betsy, Benjie and Kent were inseparable during the weeks following the attack by the wounded boar for their shared experience and for reasons of spirit. The two youngsters, who took care of Kent, had heard their father's sermon and asked of him and their mother many questions, which were answered patiently.

The youngsters then became aware of silent exchanges of their own. When one occurred between them, and with Kent, they laughed spiritedly while rolling over and over on the ground. When talking about Kent's amputation, and without mentioning his name, their Labrador would show off by running (or hopping) circles around the two, then sit up in near-perfect balance.

As their father had said, "That Kent has spirit, lots of it. He'll be back herding cattle soon. You just watch him." Kent heard and apparently understood Benjamin, because he then raced to the hilltop to gaze down eagerly at the grazing cattle.

This caused Betsy and Benjie to go into stitches of laughter.

Her parents knew that Betsy, and Kent, were nearly healed.

Are they takin' the high road or the low road?

* * *

Louicie Plowman again on September 15, 1810. Wasn't that a splendid sermon? I love to hear about guardian angels. One I've called on at times was at
my side when I had a patient with multiple fractures of the leg and no doctor
to help me out. My angel assisted me (or I assisted her) in stretching the leg
straight and putting on a temporary splint. When the doctor arrived, he could-
n't believe I did it by myself, so I told him my guardian angel helped me. He
just laughed.

"This time I'm writing about 'Doc Mac' to tell how he helped out Jim Pitch,
a distant neighbor of ours. Then, if I have enough paper and time, I'll tell about
how warriors of The Prophet have been stirring up our Indian friends, the
Piankishaws, who are part of the big Delaware family.[56]

* * *

As a result of Benjamin's sermon, Jim Pitch, troubled by relationships with
a neighbor, Karl Stien, contacted Doc Mac in his capacity of co-preacher with
Benjamin at their church. Jim, who had black moods, was acquainted with the
doctor and had heard about the sermon from Stien, whose farm bordered that
of Jim's.

Doc Mac asked Jim to tell about his problem. Jim did so, elaborating on
what he had told the doctor-minister earlier.

Pitch: I've been praying now and then even though I don't belong to no
church, to help mend my fences with Stien. His farm borders mine, and he
claims he owns a half-acre that, by God . . . excuse me . . . that is mine.

I prayed, 'Lord I don't b'lieve you are pitchin' troubles at me. Could it be
that devil, Lucifer, that's doin' it?' Then, a big shiver went from my head to toe
and back, several times. . . Preacher, what does that mean?

Doc Mac: Did you feel washed and cleansed, as a result?

Pitch: Not till I bathed off my field dust, I didn't.

Doc Mac: No, I mean washed within yourself.

Pitch: Yes, and I felt better. My black mood mostly melted away. . . You
think it was that Lucifer fellow?

Doc Mac: No, I don't think Lucifer caused your shivers; it was the Lord
who gave you that message. He answered your question, letting you know that,
yes, you should take Lucifer seriously. He's a fallen angel, who for some reason
keeps some of his powers. Maybe it's because we all have free will, gifted to us
by the Lord. That way, we have choices between good and bad, between Jesus
and Lucifer, in what we do and say. Jim, does prayer help you with your black
moods?

Pitch: Sometimes, but not when I need help the most.

Doc Mac: You need to strengthen your prayer life. . . When something

Are they takin' the high road or the low road?

good happens to you, say a prayer of thanksgiving; when something bad occurs, pray for help. Keep God in your mind as much as possible. And pray positively, believing that good will be the result.

Pitch: But how will I find the time from farming?

Doc Mac: You don't have to stop what you're doing. Use a breath prayer. As you exhale, say to your maker, 'Dear Lord, drive away the darkness.' Then when you inhale, say, 'And fill me with the light of your Spirit.' Then thank the Lord.

Say it many times a day. . . Keep the faith. Know that the spirit is present and good will come of it. And always remember what Benjamin said, 'The Lord wants us to be joyful.'

Jim used the breath prayer, to the extent that he made friends with Karl Stien, accepting the fact that the half-acre of land did belong to his neighbor. His dark moods diminished in time, and, he joined the Methodist-Episcopal church. He knew he had a guardian angel when he and others were saved from The Profit's marauding warriors, who were trying to win over the peaceful Piankishaw Indians near his farm.

* * *

"Louicie back again. . . My Henry has made up his mind to take time off from farming for a spell, and do some soldiering up in Indiana Territory. Can you imagine that, at age 70. As a militiaman much of his life, he's going north to be an advisor to Henry's nephew, John. Two other nephews of Henry's, Mordicai and Brutus, will share overseeing and running our Kentucky farm, while he's gone. Henry promised me he wouldn't get into actual fighting.

"I told him he better not, believe me, or I'll take away his favorite pastime at picnics with me in our woods' meadow."

Louicie continued telling a story about a "string of Henrys", leading up to her husband, who "hates to be called 'Hank' or — and even worse, he dislikes being called . . . "

* * *

"Henry the Third, you old war horse, we've been anxious to see you," his cousin, John Workman, called out so that all could hear.

"Hello Captain John, you scoundrel. You want a broken arm? I can still out-arm wrestle you with either one. . . And I ain't old, and I ain't no such royalty as Henry the Third."

Henry had arrived at Plowman Hill, where a group of men, mostly Plowman, were meeting as their wives prepared dinner in the kitchen. He always magnified his prowess and back-country language when with a group of men. Even so, he was proud, still in good health and powerful as a lifetime farmer and soldier. He also had abnormally long forearms which gave him an advantage in arm wrestling.

Henry came from a British line, but he was sensitive to being mingled into English royalty, of which he was not. His forebearers left England for Holland because of the state run church and its power of bishops. His grandfather was a Henry, called Hank the First, and his father was Henry, middle named, Young,[57] known as Henry the Second.

Henry was expected to name one of his sons, Henry, back in Baltimore Town, but he refused, for reasons obvious to himself.

"Tell me, Cap John, did you plan this gatherin' jest for my arrival — sos you could spin tales of funnery about me? I challenge you right hear and now to an arm wrestle, John, before this group of 'king's men'."

"I accept the challenge. Call out the 'queen's women,' as added witness to the outcome of this 'King's Court Contest.'" . . Out came Nellie, in the lead, followed by Fanny, Elizabeth and Joanne, wives of Joseph, Benjamin, Jacob and John. Then came Benjie, Jr. and his sister, Betsy, appearing a bit insecure, followed by a three-legged Kent, who guarded the two children wherever they went. The others present were Doc Mac, Jim Pitch and Karl Stien.

Henry and Benjamin seated themselves at a picnic table, took off their shirts, puffed up their chests and arm muscles, eyed each other as antagonists and positioned right elbows and forearms on the table for the tussle.

Doc Mac served as starter and judge for the combatants. He saw to it that elbows were positioned fairly and hands gripped properly. The group gathered in more closely, all eyes on straining arms and hands. Satisfied that the combatants were properly positioned, he barked: "Let the tussle begin!"

As Henry and Benjamin tensed, muscles in arms and backs bulging, the viewers pressed in even tighter. The two arms bulged and strained in their upward positions, neither gaining an advantage. Sweat flowed freely, eyes penetrated deeply, faces grimaced and muscles strained and bulged to the maximum.

For the first few minutes, it was a standoff.

But Benjamin gradually and slowly pressed Henry's arm backward, shifted his legs for better leverage and found a sudden burst of energy and strength.

The first bout was over. Benjamin quickly had flattened Henry's arm on the table to the delight of some, but to the disappointment of others who rooted for the elder of the two. Nevertheless, they all cheered and applauded; some slapped the backs of both contestants.

After a short rest, Henry challenged his nephew, "Now you young whippersnapper, I'll take you on in a lefthanded grapple. And to make it more interestin', I'll wager a full day of choppin' kindling that, this time, I'll pin yore arm to this here table before you know what's ahappenin'!"

The two positioned themselves and Doc Mac said, "Let the tussle begin, again!"

Are they takin' the high road or the low road?

WHETSTONES

This time, Henry had positioned his left elbow more snugly against Benjamin's to take fuller advantage of his more elder but longer forearm. The two again strained, bulged and sweated.

Henry then positioned and pressed his left foot against a surface root of a tree for more leverage. He then dug deeply and found a reserve of energy and strength. In a flash, he pinned Benjamin's arm to the table.

They then flipped a coin to determine which arms to use in the third round. The coin landed in Benjamin's favor, as did Henry's right arm — flat on the table — in the final and decisive match.

After congratulating both contestants, they all feasted picnic style on the lawn, enjoying beef roast, carrots, cabbage salad, potatoes and gravy, cornmeal bread and apple pie.

The men teamed up and alternated chopping kindling wood while the women cleared the table, washed and dried dishes and tidied the kitchen. The men then turned to talk about stirrings among Indians, headed by Tecumseh and his brother, "The Prophet." All were aware they were attempting to intimidate local friendly Piankishaws into siding with them against pioneers near the community of Ireland, a few miles south and a bit west, and up north on Hill Creek.

Cap. John Plowman, who had retired from the Kentucky militia and moved north near Plowman Hill, had volunteered as a community advisor on Indian affairs, now assisted by his Uncle Henry. From previous military experience, Cap. John was backgrounded on Tecumseh and The Prophet.

"You should know about these two leaders. First, don't underestimate them. Tecumseh is the smart one; The Profit is cunning. Both are from triplets, born of a Creek mother and a Shawnee warrior in 1768."

Continuing, Cap. John said, "The Prophet, who has only one good eye, is the most dangerous of the two because he's convinced their warriors that he has mystic powers that will protect them against our guns. He claims he has charmed white men's bullets so they won't injure or kill any of the tribe."

"What's stirred them up." Jacob asked.

"It's the same old story. They're angry over loss of lands to pioneers," John responded. "Tecumseh believes all lands belong to all tribes in common; therefore, no tribe can sell land. He has much influence within his and other tribes."[58]

Doc Mac added, "Indians are doing more than just trying to win over our Piankashaws. I have reliable information that Profit's men have killed settlers while stealing their horses, including four from John McDonald's farm. As you know, that's not too far north of here, at the intersection of Hill Creek and Buffalo Trace, close to the buffalo wallows.[59]

"Farmers up that way don't go into their fields without their pistols and placing their rifles close at hand, marked with a stick stuck in the ground."

Changing the subject, Henry suggested that they get back to the fact that Profit, given name, Elkswatawa, has mystic powers. "Why don't we use Profit's tactics? If his warriors believe he can make our bullets harmless to them, then why don't we use a similar kind of mystic powers?

"With all the talk about them angels, why don't we call on them? We might just throw enough terror into Shawnee Profit's warriors, with carefully planned rumors, so that they'll stay away from settlers' land."

That brought a burst of laughter from the other men.

"No, I'm dead serious," Henry continued. "Just think if we convinced them that swarms of pigeons would take over their land if they didn't stop killin' and stealin' from us pioneers. If we planned carefully, maybe we could convince our Piankishaw friends to spread the rumors.

"Fact is, I heard flocks of pigeons were swarmin' up from the south, just before I left home. They could land on Indian land up north at Profit's Town on Tippecanoe Creek."[60]

"Let's be careful about using angels," Benjamin warned. "It might work, but it could fail us for miscalling sacred beings."

"It'd be for the good of us settlers, the Piankishaws and the Shawnees," Henry insisted. "I'm for tryin' it."

"What if we was to use liquor on Shawnees?" Jim Pitch asked. "I hear tell that Profit is a drunkard."

"No! That wouldn't work. He's changed," John exclaimed. "When Profit established his town on Tippecanoe, he demanded that his warriors would not drink. His decree has held."

The men then returned to the subject of angels, agreeing that it would be for a good cause.

"Luke two, verse ten says angels were used as messengers," Doc Mac said. "If I can recall correctly, that passage reads, 'And the angel said to them. Fear not: for behold, I bring you good tidings of great joy, which shall be to all people.'

"The angel referred to the coming of the Jesus Christ, the Lord, when speaking to shepherds keeping watch over their flocks. But of course the primary duties of the armies and legions of angels is to tell of the glory and power of God."

Continuing, Doc Mac said, "Benjamin, I believe our Lord and Savior would agree to us calling upon angels for the cause of peace, particularly if we can convince the Piankashaws to call upon their Indian spirit-angels. In fact, it would be best if we did not call upon angels of our race."

Benjamin agreed, but added a precaution: "Some people around here, including a few in our congregation, hold to a belief that it is sacrilegious to view angels as intermediaries to God. They're viewpoints are honest and just, but unreasonable.

"All people can pray directly to God the Father, or His Son or to the Holy Ghost. Angels help the almighty to serve and keep in touch with his flocks. Let's make our prayers real, asking God to send Indian spirit-angels to talk with the Shawnee leaders, and to us. We must believe, and keep the faith."

Are they takin' the high road or the low road?

Pitch then asked, "How are angels chosen."

"For their good and lasting works in helping to further the Kingdom of God," Doc Mac answered.

* * *

"Here's Louicie, back again. When my niece by marriage, Nelly Plowman, heard about the religious campaign calling on angels, she spoke out strongly, saying:

"'First, we best find ways to help Indians. For example, why are Indian men judged by whites for killing whites? Shouldn't whites then be judged by Indians for killing Indians? It's not fair. Not fair at all.'

"Nelly successfully used her influence with women, and a surprising number of men, to call for a public referendum on the issue. She and her supporters, of her unsuccessful campaign for councilwoman earlier, remained potent backers and supporters of Nelly's ideas and effort to help the Piankashaws and Shawnees. In fact, she was looked upon by Indians as a 'she chief', ever since she saved the small group of Indians from trial in an unjust Kentucky court.

"I should add, too, that all of the Plowman people helped in her campaign, only two weeks long, for signatures and support for trials of Indians by Indians. Ninety percent of women voted in favor of the issue as did nearly 50 percent of the men. Nelly and her key campaign leaders then filed a petition with the Pioneer Council and campaigned vigorously with each councilman, who voted five to two in favor of the issue.

"Her son, Jacob, still a councilman, did a fine job of swaying councilmen, judges and lawyers in support of the issue. Local lawyers and a judge then formed a committee that placed the issue before Indiana Territory officials, who jumped at the opportunity to pacify Shawnee leaders and warriors.

"Local and territorial leaders then met with Shawnee leaders and negotiated a court procedure for trying Indians by Indians."

Louicie then changed the subject and told of efforts by her 10-year-old niece, Betsy Plowman, in support of calling on Indian spirit-angels. She had fully recovered her memory.

* * *

Betsy, and Benjie, along with three neighbor girls, were finishing Indian cornhusk dolls, designed and made as spirit angels. Betsy, now 11, had taken an immediate interest in calling upon angels, her own and those of Indians. She and her neighbor friends had met twice to develop a way of helping further the effort of contacting angels.

Their plan sought out the neediest Indian youths and presented the dolls at a "Youth Peace Camp." To avoid calling attention to the needy, they had concocted a lottery, "fixed" in advance, to be sure the dolls went to the chosen individu-

Are they takin' the high road or the low road?

als. The Camp meeting was organized by teachers and parents, both of pioneers and Indians, none of whom knew that the lottery winners were chosen in advance.

Betsy prayed to her guardian angel to be sure that they were not sinning by fixing the lottery. Her guardian told Betsy it was for a good cause and therefore not sinful.

On the day of the event, a crowd of more than 100 gathered for games and a picnic, followed by the lottery draw. Betsy called out the five winners, pronouncing the names with help from an Indian teacher. As the youth came forward, the crowd applauded each. Betsy and her friends gave out the dolls. . . Tears and smiles of joy flooded the faces of the winners and of their parents and friends. In fact, every face in the crowd beamed over the presentations as the Indian youth hugged their spirit dolls tightly.

Benjamin then, as planned, gave a short homily, about spirits and angels. He repeated in part his church homily, the part on Betsy's curious disappearance from the woods to the cave, saying to the crowd, "I stake my reputation as a minister of God that Betsy did not walk out of those woods. Nelly and I both tracked her to a dead end, as did others. There were no signs of grass or bushes being bent or broken, and there should have been, even after the heavy rain.

"As an adult of forty-plus years, I believe in my mind, heart and body that Betsy was saved by her guardian angel."

A doubting Thomas then shouted, "Let Betsy tell it!"

"Betsy's not said and does not recall how she was saved from the boar," Benjamin answered back.

At that point, Betsy tugged at her father's sleeve and whispered to him, "Daddy, I just now recall my experience with my angel. I'd like to speak to our friends about it."

Benjamin hoisted her up and hugged her lovingly, then said to the crowd, "Betsy would like to speak to you."

The crowd applauded; one youth called out, "Good girl, Betsy." Benjamin raised Betsy to his shoulders from where she spoke: . . . . "It is hard for me to believe, but my guardian angel has come to mind. He is not what we think of as an angel. His face is wrinkled; he has a long tangled beard, is badly crippled and without wings. He looks to be as old as Methuselah.

"But, when he first showed his face to me, his smile was big and grand. When he touched my head, I was sprinkled all over, like chills throughout my body. He didn't speak, but somehow I knew his thoughts and his name. It is Saint Joyous."

"What was that boar adoin' then?" a gravely voice called out.

"The boar just stood dead still, and when my angel put up his hand, the boar was gone."

Another voice asked loudly, "What happened to your footprints?" "There were none, from that point on.

"I was whisked up into the air by the wind and carried to the mouth of the

Are they takin' the high road or the low road?

cave. When I went inside, Saint Joyous was waitin' for me, his smile even brighter and more beautiful, even though he had no front teeth.

"I had to laugh when he was thinking thoughts for me. His ears twitched back and forth like our cow, Tucky, when she's tryin' to get rid of flies. Saint Joyous laughed along with me, without making a sound."

The crowd guffawed, particularly Benjamin, who laughed so hard he nearly lost hold of Betsy, who had finished her talk.

Still laughing, Benjamin lowered Betsy, then said, "I won't try to top that. I do want to add one short and final message of thanks to Betsy and her friends and brother, Benjie, who dreamed up this glorious affair. I also want to recognize the many fine deeds ours teachers and parents, many of them Piankashaws, did in support of the children's plan. Now I have a short story about spirits.

"I want our many Indian friends to know that your spirits are the same as our angels. I believe it's in the Old Testament, Isaiah, that says that God's attendants are spirits, which leads to the teaching that God is himself a spirit."

Once Betsy and family were home, she went to her mamma and daddy and said, "There's one thing I didn't say about Saint Joyous, 'cause I just wasn't sure. He looked like he had very real Indian features, but he wore no feathers or braided hair. His clothes were of skin, the same as ours and the Piankashaw.

"Oh, yes, another thing," Betsy continued, "my guardian angel told me through his thoughts that he would be present more often to call on me and some of the Indian leaders. Then, Saint Joyous disappeared, in a puff of air."

A wide-eyed Benjie, who had been listening, said. "When I grow up, I'm gonna be a spirit angel."

This brought laughter to his parents and sister, and prompted his mother to pick him up, hug him lovingly and say, "You don't have to wait until then. You and Betsy are already our spirit angels." Benjamin and Fanny then tucked Betsy and Benjie in bed and congratulated them again for their efforts to help the needy Indian children. They also told them they did much toward making stronger friendships with the Piankashaws.

Within two weeks, Saint Joyous appeared to Betsy and Benjie in their barn where they were feeding Tucky some hay. Tucky's ears were flapping away flies as she munched the hay. Saint Joyous saw Tucky's ears and laughed silently, shaking from his head to his waist. He then smiled broadly down upon the youngsters, his own ears flapping, and let them know he wanted them to go on an angel mission with him.

His thoughts then told them they would be safe from any danger and that no time would pass, so that their parents wouldn't worry. He then picked them up, tucked each under an arm, and was away in a puff of cloudy air.

In an instant they were at Prophet Town, standing before The Prophet, himself, who was frightened by their sudden visit and who stood up suddenly and called for one of his Indian guards. Somehow, Saint Joyous intercepted the call, placed his hand on Prophet's shoulder and spoke to him through his thoughts, calmness and his beaming smile.

This quieted The Prophet but also frightened him.

Saint Joyous knew that Prophet was proud of all Indian children and loved them dearly. He also knew that the Prophet should see the "Youth Peace Camp" in retrospect, so he drew a picture in his mind and took Prophet through the event, step by step. .... When Prophet saw the needy Indian youth awarded their angel dolls, tears of joy flowed down his face. He even cheered and applauded with the crowd. So did Betsy and Benjie, who were also drawn into the event by the strong mind pictures being projected by Saint Joyous.

When the mind pictures were over, The Prophet, Betsy and Benjie were smiling as broadly as was Saint Joyous, who winked at them and placed his hand on Prophet's shoulder, saying through thoughts, "Peace be with all Indians, particularly the Piankashaws, who want to continue living their lives joyously. And may the peace of the almighty father be with you and yours."

Instantly, Betsy and Benjie were back in their barn; Tucky was still eating hay and twitching her ears; and Saint Joyous had left in his cloud of air. Then Kent appeared, sat whining and sniffing the air suspiciously, barked three times, wagged his tail vigorously and smiled broadly.

Betsy and Benjie smiled in return, grinned at each other and began laughing so hard that Benjie peed his pants. Even Tucky smiled and swished her tail.

The two youngsters, accompanied by Kent, then ran and told their parents what happened. Benjamin and Bessie were at first shocked, then stunned and finally at ease, seeing that both youngsters were smiling happily and were unharmed.

Both parents, nevertheless, sat in wonder, somewhat dazed. Bessie broke the silence saying, "I pray that you youngsters understand how important this is to you — and to all of us. You became one of God's messengers, along with Saint Joyous, on a mission that will be of great help toward peace. It must make you both feel very warm and happy."

"It does!" Betsy exclaimed. "It makes me very happy and full of wonder." Then with great amazement in her eyes, she turned to her father and said, "It's like what you preached from Isaiah at our peace camp . . . that Indian spirits are the same as our angels, and that God's attendants are spirits.

"Benjie and I WERE attendants and spirits, along with Saint Joyous. We may even have helped build God's kingdom."

All sat quietly smiling and wondering. Then Benjamin spoke: . . . "You are correct, Betsy, very correct. . . Now, we will not have to call on our angels and spirits to bring flocks of pigeons into our skies, and down into our forests and fields." He then told Betsy and Benjamin about the pigeons, emphasizing that he had felt uncomfortable about such a plan.

When Doc Mac and the others heard about the experiences of Betsy and

Benjie, they all agreed with Benjamin that calling on angels and spirits for pigeons would be unnecessary.

* * *

"Louicie Plowman again with my last round-robin letter, unless my guardian angel takes up where I left off. I've got to slow down on my writing and social activities. That's sure, or else my midwifery patients will leave me for another. I so enjoy the contacts with my patients that I'll probably treat my last one the day before I meet my maker.

"My Henry wrote and said he would stay a while longer with Joseph and Nelly. He told me about how Saint Joyous took Betsy and Benjie to see The Prophet and Saint Joyous scared The Prophet into making peace with the Piankishaw Indians. That's something to remember, always. But Henry wrote, too, that it still looked like there could be warfare between Tecumseh's and The Prophet's warriors against Indiana and Kentucky militiamen on Tippecanoe Creek. He said he guessed it would be at Prophet's Town. Henry better not get involved, or else . . . or else, you know what.

"Oh, yes, I nearly forgot the thousands of pigeons that flew north over our farm. There were so many that they blocked out the sun. It was so dark, we had to light lanterns in the middle of the day. . .

* * *

Henry was the first to awaken. He listened intently to a strange noise and the frantic barking of Kent. It sounded like a tornado overhead. He jumped out of bed, pulled on his trousers and raced outside in the dim early light. He saw thousands of pigeons circling and landing in woods nearby; he couldn't believe what he saw.[61]

Just then, Henry was joined by Josh and Nelly who also were awakened by the birds. They stood in silent awe as they listened to the snap of limbs as the pigeons overloaded the trees. Kent whined strangely and hobbled speedily from yard to woods and back again, barking and snarling incessantly.

"These must be the same birds that Louicie wrote about in her last letter," Henry said.

Scratching his head, Josh then posed a question. "Do you suppose some locals have been praying to their angels for the birds to come because of what we had planned?"

Ignoring the question, Henry reasoned, "Strange the birds would come north in late summer. If The Prophet and his Delaware warriors heard that we was plannin' on prayer vigils for pigeons to come, all bets are off on their peace with the Piankishaws."

Nelly then added, "Yes, particularly since Prophet will know birds always

Are they takin' the high road or the low road?

migrate north in the spring. Because he's a mystic, he'll think you men went ahead with the vigil."

Just then, a large oak limb snapped and thundered to the ground, causing hundreds of the birds to squawk loudly and flutter upward, only to drift back again into the same trees. . . . . . Kent continued to bark and snarl.

As morning light brightened more, batteries of rifleshots broke out from many directions, sounding like an army of soldiers battling several tribes of Indians.

Betsy and Benjie, staying overnight with their grandparents, sauntered out rubbing their eyes and yawning widely. They stared at the birds in wonder and amazement, then peppered their grandparents and grand uncle with questions:

"What's all the gunfire about? What are all those pigeons doing here? Do they migrate in the summer? Where did they come from? What caused that big oak limb to fall? Should we all go huntin' pigeons?"

Henry answered the questions. "Betsy, you're right, pigeons migrate in the spring. They're here 'cause they're hungry, prob'ly 'cause of a bad drought I heard of in areas of the south. Those are hunters' guns you hear, Benjie; and yes, we will go huntin'." The one question left unanswered needed no explanation as another oak limb cracked sharply, broke off and fell to the ground scattering the birds.

"Lucky we got our oats harvested and stored," Josh said, "and that our corn is still in tight green husks."

"Yes, but we're gonna be short on jams and jellies come winter. Just look how the pigeons are going after those blackberry and raspberry vines."

Nelly then noticed that Betsy was missing. She asked Benjie if he knew where she went and was told, "I reckon she went in the house. She's mightily sad over what the birds are doing to the trees and where they will get their next meals."

Nelly noticed also that Kent was missing, but she knew why immediately. Kent loves and trails after both of the youngsters, but the Labrador is partial to Betsy because of the attack on her by the wild boar.

On entering the house, Nelly tiptoed to the youngsters' room, where she saw and heard Betsy on her knees by her bed and Kent at her side. Nelly caught only the last part of her prayer: "And, Saint Joyous, I promise to help more of the needy Indian youngsters if . . . if you will chase the pigeons farther north where there's no farming goin' on. Thank you, and Aaamen."

As soon as Nelly, Betsy and Kent arrived outside, a powerful southerly wind blew in at tree-top level. The birds were flushed from their roosts, faced south as one and tried vainly to fly in that direction. The wind blew so hard that the powerful birds lost ground or flew in place, then turned north and sailed with the winds to where there was no farming.

A great and prolonged cheer rose from all woods in the area and Henry said, "Well, Benjie, there goes our huntin'," causing Benjie to grin and laugh

Are they takin' the high road or the low road?

with his great uncle. Benjie then said with a straight face, "Well, there's still wild boars; the wind won't blow them away."

Everyone laughed heartily, but partly because of Kent's growl on hearing the words, wild boar.

The Piankishaws were angry, largely because the pigeons scared away the Carolina paraquets that had migrated north. The Indians were fond of the paraquets because of their brilliant plumage, used by Piankishaws for ornamental purposes.[62]

Then the Piankishaws laughed and were happy to learn later that the pigeons stopped by for a week at Prophet's Town on Tippecanoe Creek at the Wabash, more than 100 miles north. Winds then blew them even farther north, amid silent laughter.

* * *

But war was to be inevitable a month later after Indiana Territory Governor Harrison at Vincennes completed a treaty with the Delawares, Kickapoos, Miamis, Pottawattomies, and the Wea and Eel River Indians, obtaining 3,000,000 acres of the finest hunting grounds on the Wabash. The price was $8,200 in cash and $2,350 in salt annuities.

"Naturally, this made us settlers happy, but . . . " Cap. John Plowman told a gathering of 20 local community and military leaders that . . . "Tecumseh and The Prophet vehemently protested the purchase, even though only a small part of the land belonged to his tribe.

"In an attempt to change Tecumseh's mind," Cap. John continued, "the Governor invited Tecumseh to come alone and meet with him. Instead, Tecumseh showed up with 300 armed warriors, a deed that frightened most settlers and angered the Governor. In response, the Governor paraded two companies of militia in view of Tecumseh and his warriors."

John then said, "Admiring the Governor's courage, Tecumseh softened his attitude and agreed to meet, but Tecumseh took a hard line. He agreed to ally his warriors with our militia ONLY IF the 3,000,000 acres be returned to the Indians."

Interrupting, Henry reminded, "John, you missed an important point. . . After parading the militia, Governor Harrison ordered Tecumseh to withdraw."

"Oh, yes. Thanks Henry. You're correct. All you folks know my Uncle Henry, I'm sure. He's a battle-experienced militia officer in both Pennsylvania and Kentucky who volunteered to provide advice and training of a group of select horsemen. Lieutenant Henry Workman will discuss that in a minute or two. . .

"Now, one or two more developments. . . Governor Harrison wrote a complaint to our President Madison telling him what Tecumseh had done. The President then gave the Governor power to order Kentucky troops as support for our Indiana militia."

Are they takin' the high road or the low road?

"How many troops will we have, Cap. John?" Josh Plowman asked. . . .

"Henry has the numbers and types of troops in mind. I'll let him tell you," Cap. John said, as he took his seat. "That will lead into a plan Henry has come up with."

Standing tall at more than six feet, Henry selected proper words and phrases, mostly and carefully, "To pick up on what Cap. John just said, the Governor then received a broad order from the Secretary of War. He instructed Governor Harrison to attack the Indians at their home camp on the Tippecanoe, if he thought that was necessary.

"He did, and ordered up eleven hundred or so troops. That number includes two hundred and fifty U. S. Fourth Infantry, sixty Kentucky volunteers, six hundred Indiana militia and two hundred and seventy mounted dragoons and riflemen. . . As you can see, the Governor feels war is close at hand and I can guarantee that most Kentucky military and community leaders agree and favor this action.

"Now," Henry continued, "let me get to the main point. I'm told that this area has some very fine horsemen who took top honors in dragoon exercises last year in the whole territory."

This was followed by cheers and applause.

"With very little added training, I b'lieve we can come up with our own unit of dragoons and raise the total to three hundred. When I say 'we', I'm includin' the top dragoon, Captain Spier Spencer, who leads what he calls the 'Yellow Jackets'."[63]

"What might that name mean?" Bill Flute asked. "That they wear yellow jackets? Or they have stingers?"

"Well, I guess it's 'cause of the jackets," Henry answered. "But, you can bet they do some serious stingin'. After all, yellow jackets belong to the pesky hornet family."

Henry told the group that he had discussed his plans with Captains' Spencer and Workman, both of whom supported the idea.

* * *

Henry gathered the 24 local dragoon members, along with ten other experienced horsemen, at an isolated location for training two miles from the Workman farm. Both Captains Spencer and Workman provided official support and recognition of organizing and training the local unit of horsemen.

Captain Spencer chose Cap. John as leader of the group and confirmed the fact that Henry was well qualified as a training master. He told the men also that once they got to know each other they would vote on other leaders of the unit. He then suggested they select a surgeon and chaplain when they liked.

Jim Pitch immediately nominated Doc Mac as their unit's doctor, and Bill Flute recommended Benjamin Workman, as chaplain.

Are they takin' the high road or the low road?

The group cheered the selections and voted unanimously for the two men. Then unexpectedly, Karl Stien nominated Lieutenant Henry Workman as third in charge.

Henry immediately rejected the nomination, saying, "In the first place, I'm here to train you horsemen as dragoons. Second, I'm in my seventies. And third, my dear wife, Louicie, surely would skin me alive if I accepted."

But most of the men didn't want to accept Henry's rejection. . Down deep, Henry, like his horse, Whinny II, was chomping at the bit to join the fray. "Maybe," he thought to himself, "I could agree without Louicie ever knowing about it."

Henry knew that all of the 10 horsemen who volunteered, plus the local dragoon team, were seasoned riders and fighters. He felt certain and told them that he could train them adequately as a fit dragoon unit in two weeks, "if each of you work hard and put in long hours every day."

They all were experienced in fundamentals of handling their steeds, all could live in the wild, all were crack shots and both men and their horses could function well under fire. But he wasn't sure how the 10 volunteers would function in drill team maneuvers in unseating enemy horsemen and in keeping their horses from whinnying at other steeds. Then there was the question of concealing themselves and their horses.

Training began with teaching horses to lie down on command and remain silent, processes that took all of the first three days and into the next. Many of the horses were already trained to meet both requirements because of hunting and previous skirmishes with outlaw Indians and the trained horses were valuable aides in teaching the learners.

For example, Henry's aging Whinny, who normally whinnied frequently, was silent when Henry had nothing to say. Although she was smaller than most, she had a dominant nature. When other horses whinnied or snorted, she'd lay her ears back and nip the guilty ones in their flanks. This action served as a bit of entertainment for the riders who laughed but couldn't understand why their steeds didn't nip back or kick out.

For meals, all of the men cooked and ate hoecakes made of corn ground at the Workman grist mill. They cooked corn as patties on hoes held over an open fire then sat down to a meal also including dried beef and spring water.

Next, the learners watched closely as the local team of 24 went through relatively simple maneuvers. Then learning riders and horses gradually filtered into the team of the experienced. This took the remaining days of the first week.

Following that, they trained in hand signals, use of guns as lances in unseating the enemy in close contact, fast and simple methods of capture and emergency medical aid, the latter being taught by Doc Mac. Fortunately, all knew what and how to pack needed gear and how to survive on wild vegetation.

After nearly three weeks and a day, a bit longer than planned, they were ready to put on drill review before Captain's Spencer and Workman, in addition to a crowd of neighbors. The Captains were amazed at how well the men went through the maneuvers, except for a horse that whinnied once, but quickly was nipped hard in the flank by Whinny close by. After that, except for the noise of horses hooves and breathing, all was quiet.

Blacksmith "Sledge" Hammler, a scout member of the original team, had stitched padded leather socks for his horse, "Anvil," to wear when scouting behind enemy lines. He was detailed to the unit by Colonel Toussaint Dubois selected for duty by the Governor to be in charge of scouts and spies, [64] then was sent ahead of the troops to try to make peace with the Indians.

After a commendatory talk, Captain Spier Spencer, sometimes called "Lance," asked Henry Workman to step forward and be presented with a commendation certificate and a $20 bill for training the men well in such a short time. Then, as Henry began bidding farewells to return to Kentucky, the men began chanting, "We want Henry! We want Henry! We want Henry!"

Sledge Hammler then came forward, saluted the two captains and presented a formal nomination of Lieutenant Henry Workman as third in charged of the Indiana Dragoons, Squad Unit D, Yellow Jackets. All 34 men had signed their names or put down their marks at the bottom of the petition.

Captain Spencer studied the petition, handed it to Cap. John who smiled broadly and then handed it to Henry whose face flushed and words failed to come out of his mouth. He shifted from one leg to the other, folded and unfolded his arms, then let them dangle awkwardly at this sides. All of the men laughed and cheered and resumed the chant, "We need Henry! We need Henry! We need Henry!"

Henry stammered, took off his hat and wiped his brow, dabbed his eyes with his blue bandanna, then was able to say, "Men, you make it mightily difficult for me. I don't know what to say, except that I'm honored by this commendation and your support. I just . . . ."

The chanting of the men began again, "We need you! We need you! We need you, Henry!"

"Tell you what," Henry responded. "If you'll all keep it quiet, I'll agree to stay on as a backseat buggy rider and as a spyglass observer."

That brought on gales of laughter and loud, prolonged cheering from the men and the crowd until Captain Spencer hailed their attention and said, "Congratulations, Lieutenant Workman, third in charge. We'll be happy to have you in any capacity you like."

The men then cheered again and milled around Henry patting and slapping him on the back and wringing each of his huge hands.

* * *

"Louicie back with a final note. . .   That Henry should know by now he

Are they takin' the high road or the low road?

can't keep a secret from me. I heard third hand from a neighbor of our black-smith who is a brother of Sledge Hammler that Henry will stay on for the bat-tle of Tippecanoe, backseat buggy or not. I'll skin him good once he gets home You can bet on that! But I do hope he takes care of himself in the meanwhile."

* * *

"Tecumseh has gone south to convince the Creeks, Choctaws and Chickasaws to join his troops," Cap. John told Squad D, gathered and ready to move west to Vincennes on September 23. "Farmers and townspeople got word that Tecumseh was gone and urged the Governor to attack while The Prophet, a poor strategist, was in charge at Tippecanoe. Then the Governor got permis-sion from the secretary of war to attack Tippecanoe.

"Thanks to Captain Toussaint Dubois, while on his scouting trip, he learned that Prophet was gathering warriors at Tippecanoe."

Continuing, Captain Plowman informed the dragoons, "Captain Spencer left for Vincennes three days ago for a staff strategy session. We'll leave at six sharp tomorrow to join the expedition at Vincennes. We'll walk our steeds slow-ly and let them graze now and then to save and build energy."

Led by Governor Harrison, the expedition of nearly 1,000 troops left Vincennes early in October and moved up the Wabash Valley to a location 100 miles north. There the troops made camp, built a stronghold and named it Fort Harrison, thus honoring their commander.

The expedition lost first blood October 10 when a sentinel was wounded by a Shawnee warrior. Commander Harrison then sent a message to Prophet demanding that he return horses and other property stolen from pioneer families.

Harrison then moved troops forward within a few miles from Tippecanoe. The troops were divided into two columns, guarded at the flanks and rear by dragoon units as an extra defense against the enemy that was now appearing frequently. Captain Spencer's unit, that was at the right flank of the east col-umn, had split his horsemen into two segments, both followed immediately by foot soldiers.

Lieutenant Henry rode behind and a bit at the side of his nephew, Captain Plowman.

Ensign Hammler had been reconnoitering cautiously ahead of the east col-umn where he encountered some of Prophet's warriors riding south and wav-ing a white peace flag. The lead warrior, who spoke broken English, told Hammler that Prophet did not want war. He then suggested a camp sight where Commander Harrison's troops could pitch tents and rest during a pro-posed peace party requested by The Prophet.

Ensign Hammler earlier had ridden around the sight, a bluff overlooking Profit Town. On riding up to Captain Plowman, he told what had happened and recommended against the bluff, explaining his reasoning.

Are they takin' the high road or the low road?

"Cap. John, the bluff looks safe from here, but not on the sides and rear. They're heavily wooded and marked by paths leadin' to the top. From what I saw, it looks like ceremonial grounds where Prophet and his warriors would be mightily familiar with the 'proaches and possible plans of attack."

Cap. John and Henry agreed and immediately rode over to where Captain Spencer and his troops had mounted and were beginning to move toward the bluff.

"John, you're a bit late," the Captain said. "Most of our troops are moving up to the bluff now. But the news is vital to our defense. I'll report it to Commander Harrison. Meantime, send Ensign Hammler to meet us at the south side of Sliver Lake as soon as possible. Captain Dubois and the Commander will want to get the information direct from Sledge."

On arrival at the bluff and after Sledge had reported to the Commander, he was assigned under Henry to position guards and be in charge of strategic points along the several paths leading to the top. After positioning the guards in heavy underbrush, just off turns of paths and a flowing creek, the two split and rode the paths periodically to monitor each guard position. Both horses were equipped with padded hoof socks, thanks to Hammler who outfitted other scouts as well.

The night went quietly, but just before dawn arrived on November 7, a rifle shot pierced the silence. One of Prophet's warriors stepped on a dead limb while moving up one of the paths through the woods. Sledge Hammler fired at the sound, killing the intruder instantly and putting Henry and all other scouts on instant alert and rousing all in their tents on the bluff.

The militia's bugler immediately blew the call to arms and the battle was soon to be on.

Henry waited by a prone Whinny for sound of approaching enemy but heard none. He could see light through the trees but little at the floor of the forest. He decided to maintain his position. Then he heard volley after volley of rifle fire coming from the face of the bluff.

He waited impatiently pondering what should be done next. It was obvious to him that Prophet had made a frontal attack on the bluff, but would it be followed by pincer attacks through the woods? On a hunch, he hooted three owl calls, a signal for the guards to assemble immediately at Henry's location. Ensign Hammler appeared, followed by ten others.

Henry told the men, "I have a strong feeling that a diversionary attack will be in the woods, unless we can put up enough fight until help arrives."

By then, light had penetrated the woods sufficiently to view portions of the adjacent paths.

Henry devised a plan to station the guards first in groups of six along a fast-flowing creek that dissected the two most used and worn paths. Henry had scouted out the stream area and knew that the two paths had trees that had fallen at the needed strategic points. He divided the group in half, putting Ensign

Are they takin' the high road or the low road?

Hammler in charge of one , and himself, the other.

Henry instructed Ensign Hammler to give a hoot call twice in the event he sighted the enemy; Henry would do the same, and give a single hoot designating the men to go forward. They all then moved cautiously to their designated locations, nearer to the edge of the woods and in sight of the plains.

Hammler's horse, Anvil, bolted slightly on hearing close gunfire; Henry's horse, Whinny, nuzzled Forge in the neck to calm him. Once the two horses had layed down, and were quiet, the two groups waited nervously but alertly behind their logs.

A few minutes later, Hammler noticed from his position that one section of Prophet's warriors had broken off from the rest at the bluff's front and were headed directly toward the secluded guards. He immediately gave the two-hoot warning, followed by a single hoot from Henry.

All twelve of the men tensed, gripped their rifles more tightly, peered more intensely from the woods and moved forward cautiously to new locations behind tree trunks. They were positioned in an arc-like formation dissecting the two main paths. Henry and Sledge were at the outer ends of the arc to protect their flanks.

They watched as the foot warriors edged closer and closer.

Henry said quietly, but so all heard, "Hold your fire until they pass that large boulder."

They waited nervously when all of a sudden Sledge's horse reared up from his prone position and trotted out of the woods. Sledge followed immediately, grabbed Anvil by the tail and began tugging him back.

Henry quickly mounted Whinny who whirled up and galloped after Sledge and his horse. But it was too late. Enemy warriors fired a volley of shots at Sledge, killing him instantly.Anvil then galloped away toward the bluff where she inadvertently attracted attention and help.

In the meantime, Henry's horse, Whinny, stepped in a gopher hole, causing Henry to fall from his steed. He was up quickly, but several shots felled him in a heap.

Possibly wanting to make amends for her mistake, Whinny then attacked the oncoming warriors. She ferociously reared, stomped, bit and kicked the men. One warrior broke away from Whinny and headed toward Henry with a spear. Whinny then reared and turned on the warrior, stomped him down and turned her rear toward Henry who grabbed her by the tail.

Whinny then dragged a seriously injured Henry to safety, while the guards fired repeatedly, killing or wounding them all.

Alerted by Anvil and gunfire coming from the woods, fifty mounted dragoons, screaming battle cries, quickly rode down both wooded sides of the bluff, one group following the paths to Henry and his men and expecting more warriors to attack.

The two armies continued their brutal battle at the bluff and in the woods

Are they takin' the high road or the low road?

on both sides. Fortunately other dragoons, were directed to enforce counter pincers through the woods bordering the bluff.

These horsemen came galloping down the paths,also screaming and yelling battle cries of dragoons dating back many centuries. The cries had been handed down from generation to generation beginning with Anglo-Saxons battling the Vikings. They were likened to Indian calls and warhoops in that the cries bolstered morale and courage.

Prophet's warriors feared hearing and seeing these horsemen, knowing that they fought dangerously with intense bravery. Horses heads reigned high by the dragoons, the proud steeds and their riders thundered down paths on both sides of the bluff, knifing out in an arc as tong-like pincers of 50 dragoons each.

They drove their charges hard, thereby dividing Pilot's footmen and horseman in half. No sooner had they achieved this division, than another 50 dragoons poured out from paths on each side of the bluff to divide the halves into quarters.

Meanwhile, having been doctored and bandaged by Doc Mac, Henry groaned, stirred and attempted to stand. He then fell back on his blanket covering a nest of leaves, growling out: "My Louicie will skin me dead—if she don't get at me alive."

The men were encouraged by Henry's attempt at humor, but their laughter was tempered by his serious condition.

Doc responded curtly, "Henry, you're apt to be dead if you don't lie still and keep from bleeding. You're in bad shape, too bad to be tryin' to crack jokes."

Meanwhile, the battle raged on for two hours, but Harrison's troops held the upper hand as the divided warriors fought bravely but lacked leadership and organization. They also lost faith totally in Prophet and his promise that the white man's bullets were charmed and could not hurt them. Prophet, himself, was taken captive as were several of his key leaders.

The battle ended when a final direct assault, headed by Commander Harrison, routed the remaining Indians causing them to retreat in mass.

Dead and wounded were scattered over the battlefield. Commander Harrison lost thirty-seven killed and one hundred fifty-one wounded. Prophet, on the other hand, lost many more. Thirty-eight were found killed on the battlefield, and many other dead and wounded were seen carried away, as was the custom, in large but unknown numbers.[65] Wounded were estimated at more than two-hundred, bringing the total to a dramatic loss in casualties and reputation to the Indians.

The following day, after releasing the captives and burying the dead Commander Harrison and troops entered Prophet's Town and found it vacated. The troops did find firearms of British make, however, thereby confirming the suspicion that the British government was behind the Indian uprising.

Are they takin' the high road or the low road?

* * *

Louicie arrived at Plowman Hill in time for Henry to be operated on by Doc Mac, who told Louicie that Henry had a bullet next to his spinal cord and another close to his heart, found through preliminary probing. Three other wounds, serious but not critical, had been treated and bandaged.

He told her also that he found the bullet next to the spinal cord which apparently had caused some paralysis, but he felt the damage to the cord was minimal and that paralysis would go away with time.

"I won't operate on the back," Doc Mac said, "for fear I might do more harm than good. I'm quite sure the bullet can be left alone without causing any further problems."

Doc Mac then explained that the chest wound had shattered part of the rib thus saving Henry's life.

"The rib deflected and slowed down the bullet from a path that, without a doubt, would have pierced his heart," the Doc said. "I'll operate to remove splinters from the rib, but I may not remove the bullet. The operation shouldn't take more than three hours, starting early tomorrow morning."

"Can I see Henry now?" She asked, tears flowing.

"Yes, but he'll be hurting and a bit remote and groggy from the sedative I gave him before the preliminary probing."

Henry opened his eyes to see Louicie standing beside him.

He forced one of his broad grins, and said, "I reckon as how my time has come. Is my dearest here to fulfill her prophecy to skin me alive?"

Louicie broke into sobs, knelt down beside Henry's bunk, pressed her lips against his month-long , bearded cheek and gently slipped one arm over his body. She continued sobbing quietly then gradually took control of her emotions.

She raised her head and gazed down upon Henry's withered, bearded and weathered face. She couldn't remember when he had looked so poorly. She sobbed and kissed both of Henry's eyes.

Henry reacted with a sob followed by a long sigh and tender strokes of Louicie's face and hair.

They both knew it was not a time for talking. Instead, they just gazed at each other. Their love was there and known: in their eyes, in their strokes, and in their minds.

The two then kissed and exchanged their customary love sign, a wink and a pucker, and held each other as close as they could considering Henry's condition. Louicie then said, with tears overflowing her eyes, "I love you, my dearest one."

Henry forced another grin and said, "I love you too, my darling, more than you know." He then winked and puckered his lips, as did his wife for 50 years.

Next morning, Doc Mac began operating on Henry in his small clinic. It took nearly four hours because of the location of the bullet and the numbers of bone splinters that had to be removed. He did remove the bullet near the heart then stitched him up.

"Any other man his age would have died," Doc Mac told Louicie later, as he hugged her warmly to lessen her emotional state. "Henry's physical and mental conditions are remarkable for being 71 years of age. Lucky he's been a farmer."

* * *

Louicie stayed on with Josh and Nelly while Henry recuperated. Fortunately, after six weeks, he was rid of any sign of paralysis and was exercising regularly to rebuild energy and muscle tone and to regain twenty pounds he had lost. Most of his exercise came from feeding cattle, chopping kindling and walking the woods and herding cattle with Kent, the three-legged dog.

He frequently strolled over to the Benjamin and Fanny farm to visit and walk the woods with Benjie and Betsy who were happy tagalongs. He also spent time discussing land care with Benjamin who was now growing all his crops on the contour around slopes.

Benjamin had contacted Governor Harrison about an awards ceremony for the late Ensign Hammler for his invention of the spyglass transit, now widely used by farmers throughout the area in building waterways, terraces and in contour farming on hilly land. His wife, Paula Hammler, received the recognition in place of her late husband.

Unknown to Henry, the ceremony also honored him, Sledge, and the late Captain Spier Spencer and his Yellow Jackets for their heroism at the battle of Tippecanoe. Governor Harrison was invited and attended.

It was among the largest gatherings ever at the community called Plowman Hill. All close relatives of the Plowman family from Kentucky were present and practically every family locally was represented, including the Piankishaws, who were grateful for peace brought by the defeat of The Prophet and his warriors.

At the climax the audience roared a welcome to Saint Joyous who blew in from the south bringing with him the Carolina paraquets that were chased away by the throngs of pigeons. Joyous landed on the ceremonial stage, beamed and wiggled his ears, and withdrew a paraquet that had nested in his beard.

Everyone laughed and cheered, particularly the Piankishaws, who welcomed the birds for their gayly-colored feathers of green, yellow and red for Indian adornment.

Saint Joyous then drew mental pictures and transferred them to the minds of those in the crowd. He conveyed the heroism of Henry Workman, Spier Spencer and his Yellow Jackets, then depicted Sledge's spyglass transit and its conservation results.

Are they takin' the high road or the low road?

Then, Gov. Harrison presented medals in honor of the three.

"Dear children, grandchildren, and those yet to come.

"I decided to write a note as my last diary-letter to let you know we got home well and happy, and that Henry is back in shape and working Hope farm with help from Brutus Plowman, mostly, but also from our Beaver.

"Beaver's still working hard at his lawyer business, besides being an assistant to Judge Bartlett. He still wants to be a judge, himself, and I'm positive he will be some day. He's always set his goals high and worked long and hard. I hope he continues to set an example for all you children and those yet to come. Are you setting your goals high enough? Have you picked the right role models? You know that you can be what you want to be—if you plan and work at it. But enough of my preaching. I'll end my note on a funny story.

"Henry's got his sense of humor fired up again. On our way back home in our buggy he looked up at a flock of geese flying south and asked, 'Louicie, do you know why that goose gave up leading that flight formation? It's 'cause the other geese got fed up of him breaking wind.'

"Love to all of you, for ever and ever, Louicie Plowman."

Are they takin' the high road or the low road?

Did descendants ever amount to much?

Dear Great³ Aunt Louicie,

Thanks for your final note, particularly the joke by my Great³ Uncle Henry. There was no better way to let us know that he is back to normal. I'm glad, too, that you spoke about role models. You always have been strongly in favor of "those yet to come" getting a good education and planning and working hard about one's future.

I've been calling you Plowman in this book because I didn't want to sound like a braggart about the Enlow family. But now, I will do some boasting about Enlow-Enloe people. According to the late E. E. Enlow who made a survey of judges to learn if any had ever had to go before a judge for some type of crime. He never found a single one,⁶⁶ but only about 3,000 Enloe-Enlow-Inlow people lived in 40 states, as of 1940.

Numbers dropped from a peak of 16 in one family in my immediate line to an average of two to three now.

I have to admit that I was in jail for two hours one Halloween about 55 years ago. Some of us boys tied a big sign onto the top of a car; the police caught us and put us in cells until our parents picked us up. All the other parents came quickly, but mine waited to let me cool my heels in the clinker, then strolled leisurely two miles to the police station.

I'll tell you about a few of our people based on first-hand knowledge or from newspaper clips and from libraries, archives, and descendants. My youngest daughter, Shelley Enlow Scurry, is the eleventh generation to make a living in the field of agriculture, as a horticulturalist. Her great grandfather was the last full-time Enlow farmer, although her grandfather was born and raised on a farm in Kansas and I made a living as a farm and agricultural sciences reporter, writer and editor.

Some Enlow and Enloe people lived very exciting lives. I'll try to capture that, and their humor, too, in their profiles. My only reason for doing this is to point up the importance of role models to all youngsters . . . just as you always did. Some must have inherited uncle Henry's sense of humor, like a distant cousin of mine, Harold Enlow of Dogpatch, Arkansas. (Really, that's his address.) Harold travels a lot throughout the U.S. and parts of Canada conducting seminars as a woodcarver-instructor. He wrote his own profile, herein enclosed with a few other profiles.

But before that, I'll review portions from E.E. Enlow's desktop booklet about our vocations down through the years. From his home in Sebastopol, California, he wrote that in 1940 many thrifty farmers were still "active descendants of the early Enloes . . . found in nearly all States."

Louicie, as you well know, farming was basic, of course, in settling this nation, just as were such trades and professions as schoolmasters, ministers, blacksmiths, merchants, hunters, midwives and soldiers. More specifically, E.E. Enlow cited, among others, Dr. Ella M. Enlow of Washington, D.C., as a scientific writer; Justice Solon Augustus Enloe, Judge of the U.S. Appellate Court of Indiana; Dr. Newton T. Enloe who founded the Enloe Hospital, Chico, California; and Charles Bates Enlow, president of the National City Bank, Evansville, Indiana, who was also mayor of that city. The Evansville sports arena, incidentally, is named "Enlow Stadium", after Charles.

These historic facts about family remind me of a quote I read recently by Cicero, cited in Wilson's History of Dubois County, Indiana. Cicero said that "Not to know what happened before we were born is to remain always as a child, for what were the life of man did we not combine present events with the recollections of the past."

Like many families, Enloes and Enlows of more recent past were involved in politics, law, medicine, education, ministry, farming, finance and industry. Benjamin Augustine Enloe, an editor, served his district in Tennessee as a U.S. congressman; Augustus Enloe was a U.S. judge in Indiana; Charles R. Enlow, my father, was a U. S. agricultural attache, first ever to the Union of South Africa; Allen Thurman Enlow, formerly of Ohio, became a stockholder and manager of the Lysaght Dominion Sheet Metal Corporation of Hamilton, Ontario, Canada.

But now, here are profiles of Enloe-Enlow people, any of whom could be used as role models by "those yet to come," in part anyway. As you know, Louicie, patterns should be drawn from a mix of models; hardly any single individual can provide the full and necessary designs for lifetime achievements.

A woodcarver whittles out his life

by Harold Enlow, the carver, himself

I was born in Springfield, Missouri on October 13, 1939 (a Friday the 13th — Wow!) on West Division Street. My father is Harold Albert Enlow and my mother is Genevieve Frances (Billups) Enlow. I'm the oldest of 9 children. The doctor who made out my mother's birth certificate spelled her name Geneva, as shown on that certificate.

Did descendants ever amount to much?

Almost everyone in the family does roofing for a living. I have one younger brother who is police chief in the small town of Ash Grove, Missouri. Even "Beany", the policeman, roofs once in a while. At one time, I tried roofing; but, by golly, it's hard, hot work. So, to live by the old hillbilly rule of, "never stand up when you can sit down and never sit down when you can lay down", I became a woodcarver.

I've always been interested in drawing, and art in general, and have always liked knives and whittling. While in the army, I started getting interested in carving all over again. I was stationed on the island of Okinawa for 18 months without a lot to do in my spare time, and my boyhood hobby came out naturally. So, in 1959 I was busily carving wood from all the pallets and crates I could find laying around the island.

A friend checked out a woodcarving book for me from the Air Force library, and I was on my way to a future career, although I didn't know it at the time. My idea of a career was to work for Walt Disney as a cartoonist, so that's what I thought I'd be. The book title was "How to carve characters in wood" by Andy Anderson. It was full of cowpokes, Indians, etc. I guess it's true that every new generation of carver, artist or whatever, is standing on the shoulders of folks before them. Seems I'm standing on Andy's shoulders.

Hoeing weeds, cleaning smudgepots?

After the army, I married Elaine and did various things to keep her clothed and fed. I hoed weeds in lemon orchards (in California, for a while), cleaned smudgepots (dirty work), picked avacadoes, worked in a dairy, etc. During the Berlin crisis I was back in the army for a little stint and was stationed at Fort Lewis, Washington. Once during bivouac I had to be in Yakima for a whole month while my new wife was in our tiny apartment in Tacoma.

Talk about my misery! Anyhow, the only wood I could find to carve on was holding up the latrine. The two-by-sixes were much taller than the canvas that was attached to them, so I sawed off what I needed. I never did figure out what kind of wood it was, but it was great for whittling.

I still have a little horse that I carved from that wood.

Blow dryer heated shed?

Later, I worked in a typewriter factory for a while and carved late every night I could (at Springfield, Missouri)... Elaine was something of a whittler's widow in the evenings, while I carved in the lawnmower shed out back. The shed was so small that I heated it with Elaine's blowdryer in the winter. . . I'd come in long enough for Elaine to bandage my cuts, then go right back to carving (on wood, I hoped).

While I was doing all this, a future friend, Peter Engler, opened a wood carver's shop at Silver Dollar City, Missouri. It wasn't long before my uncle Al told me about Pete. Soon after I met Pete Engler, I started selling to him. It wasn't long until I quit my factory job and went to work for my friend. Pete was different than all the other bosses I'd had. He loved to play practical

Did descendants ever amount to much?

jokes on me, and was truly a good friend too.

After several years, I opened my own shop in Dogpatch, USA, a theme park near our present home. I've since become interested in writing about and teaching carving. I'm now a 30-year veteran of the craft and enjoy helping those just taking it up. I no longer have a shop but spend my time giving seminars around the country and that is how I make my living.

P.S. We have one six-year-old child, Katie. (She was six when Harold sent his profile to this author.) We live on 38 acres, three miles west of Dogpatch U.S.A.

P.S.S. from the author: Harold should have stressed his ability as an author and a publisher. He sent me all eight of his training books on wood carving. They are impressive, to say the least, thanks both to his writing and his art abilities.

P.S.S.S., also from the author: Harold has tracked back to his great[3] grandparents, John and Elizabeth (Frazee) Enlow of western-most Maryland, and also ancestors of E.E. Enlow.[10]

How did a papaw patch lead to a medical doctorate?

(NOTE: The following article was written by Sylvia Storla Clarke of Chico, California, who gave written permission to publish it here. The article was copyrighted in Clarke's name in 1973 by The National League of American Pen Women. . . The subject of this article, Dr. Newton T. Enloe, M.D., was among a line of 17 Enloe doctors of medicine or dentistry. . . Dr. Newton's daughter, Nancy Enloe Hodges, referred the following article by Sylvia Clarke to me — along with appropriate acclaim.)

By Sylvia Storla Clarke

There would seem to be no possible connection between the present day N. T. Enloe Memorial Hospital and a papaw patch in Russelville, Missouri. Yet, according to the account given by Dr. Newton Enlow, there might not have been one without the other.

One day, in a one-room schoolhouse in Missouri, the eight year-old "Newt" Enloe was absorbed in a penmanship lesson. Suddenly the words he had been practicing took on an unexpected meaning. "Where there is a will, there is a way," he wrote.

"Why shucks!" he thought. "I've got plenty of will! Now, all I need is a way, a way to get myself out of this papaw patch that I've been plowing every day." Anyway, he couldn't understand why this orchard had to be plowed so much. Must be just his father's way of keeping eleven children out of mischief, he supposed.

Did descendants ever amount to much?

Arms too short?

Nevertheless, young Newt had been told what was expected of him about the plowing. So he set about it, as he said, doing his share of work. But his arms were much too short to do a skillful job of handling the plow. Despite all his efforts, the plow lurched this way and that, batting at him when he least expected it. After a particularly hard jolt, Newt jerked the horse to a stop, tried to get his bearings as he swiped the tears of frustration from his face.

From nearby he caught the sound of a light buggy, wheeling down the road at the edge of the orchard. It was the village doctor, driving past in his fine rig, the sleek coat of his black carriage-horse glistening in the morning sun. The gentleman, unaware that he was being observed, looked neither left or right, but continued down the road. Yet because of this man, a small boy in an orchard was busy building a dream. "I want to be a doctor," he thought excitedly, "that's what I want to do!"

Plowing might be right for those who liked it but suddenly Newt felt that for him it was wrong.

At the age of fifteen, when Newt had finished his studies at the country school, the persistent dream still worried at his mind, even though the realization of it appeared nothing but impossible.

A single footer?

To add to the problems, the family home was now encumbered with a $1200 mortgage. The method of paying off that encumbrance was not exactly in Newt's plans; the solution came as a result of his boyish spirit of venture — and because of a saddle horse which the father had allowed each of the older boys to claim, but not to own until they reached the age of seventeen. When the three older boys had made their choices, Newt, being the youngest, was left with the horse that "appeared to be the sorriest of the lot."

However, in appraising his new horse, Newt noticed that the colt he'd drawn was known as "a single footer." Newt decided to make the most of that, and recalled he'd seen an advertisement in a magazine which might be of assistance. He sent for the booklet which dealt with the training of horses.

Implicity following directions, he began training the colt, working against the date of the gala day when the county fair at California, Missouri, would be held. Prior to that time, he had secured consent to attend the event; this consent, however, included the stipulation that he must do his allotted amount of work before leaving for the fair. When the anticipated morning arrived, he set off, as he related it, "like another Yankee Doodle Dandy, riding on a pony." He admitted that "the horse races were drawing me like a magnet."

The first classification had only three contestants. One of the officials indulgently suggested that he enter his horse. Hastily, Newt debated. Since rig and harness would be supplied, he decided to take a venture on that one.

According to Newt, the colt entered the race so nervous that "there wasn't a dry hair on his coat." He won the third prize of twelve dollars.

Did descendants ever amount to much?

WHETSTONES

Called paces in order?

More confident now, Newt approached the officials about entering his horse in the five-gaited competition. The prize for this was the fabulous amount of $1200. Entries were numerous, all professional. It was laughable to suppose that Newt's horse, one who so recently had been plowing the orchard, would attempt to compete with such fine material. There was a hush and then Newt heard someone say, "Aw, let's give the kid a chance!" And the next thing Newt knew, the race was on— and he was in guiding his colt around the ring in borrowed rig and harness.

The animal had been taught to respond to the mounted rider's change of position, not to calls for change of pace, as was expected in the harness competition. Rapidly, Newt decided on a desperate strategy. When his turn came, he began calling his paces in the order in which he had trained the horse, summoning his loudest voice for the calls for the benefit of the judges and audience. It worked perfectly! The kid from Russelville came away with the prize money of $1200.

Since checks were rarely given in those days, Newt stuffed the precious winnings into both pockets, rode home, and presented his astounded father with the exact amount needed for the mortgage!

When Newt was seventeen, he approached his father about studying medicine as he had done many times before. Again, he was told that it was a financial impossibility that anything to which he aspired must be through his own endeavors. The boy considered the bleak possibilities, but stubbornly kept his dream.

To begin with, he resold to his father the latter's gift of saddle horse and bridle. This netted him $70. Then, he made arrangements with his father to cut wood on the papaw patch. This labor added another $210. And since the first crop raised on the cleared land was also part of the bargain, he was ahead another sum, this time $68. Slowly the nest-egg was growing.

A bouncer as a teacher?

Being in possession of a second grade teacher's certificate, Newt became interested in the news of an opening for a teacher in California, Missouri. This fine position paid the huge sum of $32.50 per month.

It was common knowledge that the school's opening for a teacher was due to the pranks of hoodlum scholars who had evicted two of the previous teachers via the schoolroom windows. In relating the situation, Newt later said with eyes twinkling that it might have been more logical for a man his size to have paid the school to avoid that teaching position! But years of hard work, together with an accumulated knowledge of wrestling and his wood cutting experiences put him in advantageous position. During the first recess he piled up five of the obstreperous students on the ground. He stayed four months and saved $98 from his salary.

The last sum brought a total of $446 and made possible his enrollment for

Did descendants ever amount to much?

a two-year course in Hospital-Medical School in Louisville, Kentucky. During his time there, his dwindling funds were supplemented by work as an assistant janitor at the school, plus janitorial work at two saloons. During the summers, work in the grain fields paid $1.50 per day.

Hunger ups thought capacity?

Despite every effort, he was without funds and without food when the time for final examinations arrived. Somehow, the examinations were successfully completed. Later he said he often wondered if lack of food could increase one's thinking capacities.

With the medical course completed, he immediately joined another physician and they opened an office in Osage, Missouri. There the Federal Government had started one of its first flood control projects on the Gasconade River, and there the two men attended medical needs of the area.

In three months Dr. Enloe had built a substantial practice, had collected $2200 during the time, although charges for the first office call were a dollar and the ensuing calls were fifty cents per call.

Lifted floor planks?

This success only served to whet Newt's appetite for further education. When the older doctor approached Dr. Enloe about buying Newt's practice, the figure of $800 was mentioned and immediately rejected. But the older man must have given the matter further thought, for one night Dr. Enloe was asked to come down to the office. There, the older man lifted some of the planks in the office floor, and to Newt's astonishment, extracted the amount requested and the bargain was completed.

With this sum, Newt was able to enroll at St. Louis, Missouri in the Washington University Medical School, which was one of the first in those days to offer a four-year course. He graduated in 1895. Following graduation, Dr. Enloe established his practice in Jefferson, Missouri. He remained there for six years, until failing health required him to move to Pueblo, Colorado.

In 1901, he decided to move to California. With $15 from his pawned watch, he located at West Branch, a canyon logging center located between Forest Ranch and Stirling City. There logging lumber camps decided to pay Dr. Enloe a dollar a month per person for medical care. One of the companies even included board for the doctor and his horse. Actually, this arrangement turned out to be one of the first prepaid medical plans.

Rode the flume?

In that same year, by the work of his own hands and with cast-off lumber from the mills, Dr. Enloe built his first hospital, a crude building of five-bed capacity. In only a matter of seventy years, there is sharp contrast between this West Branch hospital and the doctor who "rode the flume" from West Branch with his most severely injured patients to the hospital that now bears his name. His goal was then, as always, that of improved patient care.

Did descendants ever amount to much?

It is told that when an injury occurred in West Branch when time was a factor and which required care in town, the lumbermen worked overtime, and any time, to construct a "box" in which patient and the doctor could ride the V-shaped flume in relative comfort. This flume terminated its log-carrying function in the region of East Eighth Street and Pine in Chico, California. When the logs were dumped at the lumber mill in that location, the water flowed down the present Flume Street and onto Bidwell's Flour Mill where the water provided power to turn the flour mill.

Pile upon pile of dreams

During Dr. Enloe's stay in the little known region of the canyon, dream continued to pile upon dream, his work embroidering the patterns. With a foresight that included the hospital needs of Northern California, Dr. Enloe moved to Chico in 1904. In 1913, he established a hospital on Flume Street in Chico. His staff consisted of three physicians and five nurses.

He bought land in Paradise and established the Paradise Tuberculosis Sanitarium, now no longer in existence. In 1924 it was advertised in the following manner:

"North, south, east, or west — every direction — is like a beautiful painting. Towering pines, beautifully colored shrubbery and a variety of bushes, trees, flowers — God's garden — to greet patients from every door and window."

First 50, then 82 beds

In 1937, a long-held desire for a modern hospital was realized with the building of his $100,000 fifty-bed hospital on The Esplanade at Fifth Avenue in Chico. "I appreciate what Chico has done for me," Dr. Enloe said at the time, "and I think that the institution will show my appreciation."

In 1952 the addition of a maternity wing on the north side of the original building enlarged the hospital to a capacity of eighty-two beds.

In December, 1954, the community was saddened by the death of Dr. N. T. Enloe. His acts of generosity, his ingenuity, his humor were recounted by the way many friends had gained through the years of work in the community.

His wife, Dorothy, with a confirmed diagnosis of cancer in 1945, was benefited by the treatment to the extent that she was able to pursue the management of the hospital until shortly before her death in 1956. Acutely aware of the value of deep therapy Mrs. Enloe often expressed hope that a center for care might be available to others at some future time.

Renamed as memorial

In 1956 Enloe Hospital was renamed the N. T. Enloe Memorial Hospital. It was changed from private ownership to a California non-profit organization; Thomas Enloe, M.D., the youngest son of the hospital's founder, was included in the Board of Trustees.

The new Radiation Therapy Center was opened in conjunction with the hospital on April 28, 1968. It was added to the hospital at an estimated cost of some $110,256. The center, being within a day's drive from anywhere in the northern part of the State, now serves much of northern California. From this center, vital patient data can be sent via telephone hook ups to other cities, an invaluable adjunct to the increasing and outstanding patient care.

The need for further expansion of the hospital became clear, and on August 19, 1971, the newly constructed and expanded south wing was opened for service to the community. Following closely upon that date, a new intensive care unit was put into operation on February 29, 1972. And so, as of 1972 the N. T. Enloe Memorial Hospital provides a total of 117 patient units, a modern hospital such as might well have been an unthinkable dream for the devoted "lumberman's doctor."

To this intrepid, small-statured man with his astute glance and pixie-like twinkle in his eyes, hardships seemed not to have been a barrier but a challenge. Through the years, he retained the Missourian humor and turn of phrase. Through the years, his manner retained that of a simple, humble man, filled with understanding for the foibles of his fellow men and the love of his profession.

Was he surgeon AND a comic strip prototype?

Even though Dr. Cortez F. Enloe, Jr., M.D, was one of the most decorated medical officers in the American Armed Forces during World War II, he claims that his greatest distinction was in being the prototype of the character, "Doc", in Milton Caniff's comic strip, "Terry and the Pirates."

He was chosen as prototype based on his participation in combat as a flight surgeon of the First Air Commando Force in the airborne invasion of Burma and in commando operations behind enemy lines in central Burma. He took part there in 39 combat missions. Overall during his military career, he received 13 military medals from the U.S. Army, U.S. Air Force and the U.S. Navy. Honors included the legion of merit, air medal, bronze star and the Antartic medal for polar exploration.

17th doctor in line

Dr. Enloe is the seventeenth member of his paternal family line to become a doctor of medicine or dentistry, so states his six-page curriculum vitae of 1988. Not only was he a physician during his career, he was also a photographer, writer, editor, newsman, explorer, medical consultant, lecturer, businessman, soldier and yachtsman.

As a photographer he received the 1939 National Leica Photographers Medal (second place); as a yachtsman, he was first in number of racing awards in 1964 for the Atlantic racing trophy, New York Yacht Club; as a newsman, he was a central European correspondent for the Kansas City Star; and as an explorer, he was director of the 1968 Antartic Nutrition Survey of the South Pole and chairman of the 1968-69 Scientific Advisory Committee, Staib American/Norwegian Trans-Polar Expedition to the North Pole.

Did descendants ever amount to much?

One of his many specialties included human nutrition. He created and was editor and publisher for 20 years of the internationally renowned journal, *Nutrition Today*, written to increase and disseminate sound nutrition knowledge to physicians and other health professionals.

Dr. Cortez Enloe has been a fellow in the New York Academy of Medicine, Royal Society of Medicine (London), Aerospace Medical Association, American College of Angiology, American Geriatrics Society and American College of Preventive Medicine, as well as an honorary life member of the Hollywood Academy of Medicine.

A Cum Laude graduate

An intense, dedicated and enthusiastic man, he was born in 1910 in Jefferson City, Missouri, where he was educated in public schools, then continued at Culver Military Academy, Indiana, and the University of Misssouri, where he earned his bachelor of arts degree in 1932. He graduated as a doctor of medicine (Cum Laude) in 1937 from Friedrick-Wilhelms Universitat Medical School, Berlin, Germany.

In addition, he gained medical knowledge at institutions in Heidelberg, Munich and Berlin, Germany, as well as graduating as a flight surgeon from the School of Aviation Medicine, Randolph Field, Texas.

This author (of WHETSTONES) first met Cortez Enloe, Jr., by telephone from Peoria, Illinois, in the late 1970s and later met him in person at his long-time residence in Annapolis, Maryland. There we discussed our Enloe-Enlow genealogy. Dr. Enloe is the lineal descendant of Enoch Enloe, one of three brothers, Scottish Presbyterian school teachers all, who migrated from Aberdeen County, Scotland, and arrived in the new world at Salem, New Jersey in August 1639.

As one would guess this Enloe of great note is listed in the Directory of Medical Specialists, American Men of Science and found in various annual volumes of Who's Who in the East, Who's Who in America and Who's Who in the World.

Son like father? In dedication, banking, yes.

My Dear Great³ Aunt Louicie, the roots of this father-son profile grew and flourished from newspaper articles at Evansville, Indiana. One story features the father; the other, the son. Both men were role models. Both had drive and dedication; one wound up as a bank chairman, and his son as chairman of the same bank, then publisher of the Courier. Credits go to reporters, including Joe Aaron who wrote about the father, and Ed Klinger who wrote a shorter article about the son. These two articles will begin with initial paragraphs and then resume profiles of the subjects. Love, your great³ nephew.

* * *

Did descendants ever amount to much?

ROBERT E. ENLOW

Evansville Courier: "C. B. Enlow came to town 50 years ago tomorrow and started work the following day," wrote Joe Aaron.

"He is still working — now as chairman of the board of National City Bank where he started as a cashier.''...

* * *

Evansville Press: "For the first time in more than half a century there is no one named Enlow at the executive helm of the National City bank," Ed Klinger reported.

"Bank directors yesterday regretfully accepted the resignation of Robert C. Enlow as board chairman. He is not severing his connections with the bank. He was elected honorary chairman and will continue as senior director.''...

* * *

Charles B. Enlow died in 1961 at age 83; his son, Robert C. Enlow, died seven years later at 62, following a lengthy illness.

Both left as positive role models; one left some negatives.

Joe Aaron had this to say about Charles Bates Enlow, who was born March 23, 1879, on a farm near Bridgeport, Ohio: "Few men in Evansville's history have been so often praised, so often criticized. The man on the street can assure that C. B. Enlow brought International Harvester to town, single-handedly. The man on the street also can assure you sagely that Enlow drove International Harvester from town, single-handedly.

"It is actually a tribute in his wide influence that he is so many things to so many people. And somewhere in between the good and the bad laid to him is the real C. B. Enlow, the Ohio farm boy who came (on October 11, 1909) and stayed to become one of the city's most influential citizens."

Engineer, banker, adviser

"Who is he?" Aaron asked in his news article, then answered: "He is a farm boy who became a chemical engineer who became a banker who became an adviser to political leaders — both in city and state. . . He is a real 'charmer' of a man, with the disconcerting habit of carrying a pocketful of quarters so to jingle them. . . He is a gardener of no little stature, an avid sports fan, a transportation expert, a former school board member (for 10 years), who is still remembered for his accomplishments for Evansville schools. . .

"His father, John, died when Charl — as he was called in Bridgeport — was 2. His mother, Suzanna, died 14 years later . . . The future banker worked on the family farm and attended school in Bridgeport — where he once made a 60 in grammar and a 86 in music.

No slouch as scholar

"He also made a 73 in deportment, which undoubtedly would cause many

Did descendants ever amount to much?

later political foes to crow: 'I told you so!'

"He was no slouch as a scholar, however. He was only 16 when he entered Ohio State University in 1895. He worked his way through college, at the time serving as drama critic for the Columbus (Ohio) Dispatch, receiving a degree in chemical engineering in 1899, and becoming a chemist for Carnegie Steel Company at Mingo Junction, Ohio."

Continuing, Joe Aaron wrote that Charles B. Enlow then returned home and became an assistant cashier at the Bridgeport National Bank, following a strike at Carnegie Steel. While still an assistant cashier, he married Anna Lee Cooke, a school-days sweetheart on April 15, 1903.

Later that year, he became cashier of Citizens National Bank, New Lexington, Ohio, and he and his wife, Anna, became parents of their only child, Robert Cooke Enlow, born February 28, 1905. Robert's mother died in 1958.

Knows about school affairs

His father emerged in Evansville as a community leader in 1917 when he was appointed to the City School Board. He served 10 years, part of the time as president, and was recognized as an extremely able member.

Joe Aaron then quoted Howard Roosa, former Courier editor and for years a school stalwart, who wrote:

"I don't often admit that anyone else is as good as I am, but Enlow knows as much about school affairs as I ever did and, in addition, he has the advantage of a fine business training."

Aaron then cited accomplishments: "During Enlow's tenure the board (1) devised a salary merit system for school employees, (2) eliminated sex and race discrimination from salary schedules, (3) equalized educational opportunities for all children in the city, (4) drew up the first five-year school-building plan in the city's history and (5) set up what was called the best facilities for high school sports in the entire country . . . "

Charter member of toll road

Continuing, Aaron wrote that Enlow was a wartime director of the local civil defense office receiving the Rotary Club civic award in 1942 for the job he did . . . a prime force in securing Evansville-Henderson bridge, opened in 1933 . . . a member of the State War Finance Board . . . a "charter" member of the Indiana Toll Road Commission serving with the group about six years, until the road was a reality. He handled most of the financial arrangements for the $280,000,000 job.

And he found time — or made time — for the beautiful flower gardens in the back yard of his home at 1312 Southeast Second Street. He also raised many vegetables there, possibly a throwback to Ohio when he was a little boy on the farm.

* * *

Robert Cooke Enlow, a versatile man and basically a shy person, neverthe-

Did descendants ever amount to much?

ROBERT E. ENLOW

less, was well know as a lawyer, then a publisher of the Evansville Courier and finally chairman of the board of the Evansville National Bank.

His achievements equaled those of his father, following patterns of dedication and achievement that formed a role model for future doers and leaders to mimic. But, his life highlighted differing pinnacles of success than those of his father, Charles Bates Enlow.

Broad range of interests

Enlow was a noted leader in fields of business, government and civic activities and an avid supporter of sports and hobbies, including woodworking. Here are some of his prime interests:

- He was commissioner for the Southern Indiana Federal Court District for 13 years — 1931-40 and again in 1946-50.
- He pioneered drive-in banking.
- He was an early proponent of the computer, foreseeing the need in 1963 of a GE-225 computer.
- He and his family were prominent patrons of the arts and played a leading role in support of the Evansville Philharmonic Orchestra. The family established in his wife's name, Rossanna M. Enlow, an artists award to encourage young musicians.
- He was a board member of the Southern Indiana Gas & Electric Company, the Evansville Museum and Oak Hill Cemetery.
- In addition, he was active in past Cancer Crusade campaigns, and, during World War II, served as chief of the Evansville Plant Area Board.

Like father, goes to OSU

Robert C. Enlow was born in New Lexington, Ohio, and was brought to Evansville, Indiana, by his parents in 1909, where he was graduated from Wheeler School and Central High School. He then was graduated, like his father from Ohio State University, with an A. B. degree in 1926.

After that, he studied law at Indiana University, receiving his L.L.B. degree in 1929, then established a law firm in Evansville with Bernard Frick.

First love, police beat

Workwise, Robert Cooke Enlow's first love was The Courier newspaper, particularly his stint as a police reporter in the early 1920s. Then in 1959, he "plotted" a surprise story to observe his father's fiftieth anniversary in Evansville, taking boyish delight in the intrigue that he and a Courier reporter used to gather information.

The scope of Robert's interests range widely when one considers his memberships. He belonged to the Evansville Chamber of Commerce, Union League Club of Chicago, the Columbia Club of Indianapolis, the Indiana Bankers Association, the Indiana and America Bar Association, the Petroleum Club, Lessing Lodge F. and A. M., the Scottish Rite and the Hadi Temple Shrine. He also belonged to the First Presbyterian Church, the Indianapolis

Athletic Club, the Evansville Country Club and the Indianapolis Athletic Club. In one of his lesser-known activities, he was instrumental in helping to get the first Little League baseball franchise in Evansville. That action sparked the growth of competition that brought benefits to hundreds of area youth.

Then for private time he was an ardent craftsman in woodworking who spent hours in the basement workshop in his South Willow Road home that he loved. The lectern presented to his church was crafted lovingly by him in his workshop. Robert Cook Enlow died at age 62 on January 23, 1968.

* * *

(My dear Great³ Aunt Louicie an additional note to let you know that Enloe-Enlow families have kept their faiths, as did you and your immediate families in pioneer days. That includes your Nephew Benjamin (my Great² Uncle) as a Methodist-"Episco" minister in Indiana Territory. Down through three centuries I've found records that our line includes mostly Presbyterians, Methodists, and Baptists. Oh yes, I forgot that one was a Jewish rabbi, named Enelow. Oh well, God is God, and to most of us, Trinity is Trinity because I believe that most down through the years were Baptists, I'll profile those of that faith, an Enloe man and wife and an Enlow minister of 64 years.)

Baptist ministers extend a custom

They travel, they spread the Word, they sing

Where is their pulpit? Answer: Most everywhere . . .   They travel widely and frequently: singing, preaching and worshiping. They are Reverend Phil Enloe and his wife, Jan, infrequently of East Alton, Illinois.

In fact, Rev. Phil Enloe could be called a singer and a writer — but also a world-traveling preacher. So could Jan. Together, this dedicated couple managed to give some 300 concerts per year traveling over 100,000 miles annually and crossing many denominational lines. Their resume tells us that:

"Phil Enloe, born in Illinois, comes from a large and musical family. A high school scholarship started him in a career of singing in 1964. He studied at Southern Illinois University and at Akron University in Ohio. Phil then spent seven years as a member of well-known groups as the Couriers, the Imperials and the Blackwood Brothers Organization. In 1970 he began concerts as a soloist and has maintained his evangelistic ministry since that time.

Writes 80% of material

"Phil, now in his early 50s, uses his three octave range to sing with his wife in many styles of sacred songs of which he writes 80 percent of their material.

"Phil is not only a recording artist of 28 albums but an author as well. His travels have taken him into all of the 50 United States and 38 countries around the world. His television experiences include frequent appearances on the PTL Network, CBN's 100 Club, Trinity Broadcasting Network's Praise the Lord Show and other productions there, as well as Canada's own 100 Huntley Street Program and many independent Christian Telecasts.

"Jan is a very talented lady gifted with an exceptional voice and a charisma that emulates her honest love of people. Everyone loves this Illinois pastor's daughter. She grew up in a home dedicated to helping people. Jan was skilled by her talented mother and lovingly groomed for the ministry. She learned to sing and play the piano as she learned to walk. Her ear for harmonies developed as Jan sang in church duets, trios and choirs. Though naturally and musically gifted, Jan went on to further her education at Central Bible College in Missouri."

Janus Ann married Phillip Gene Enloe on February 8, 1945. They have four children, LaShonda, Stephanie, and twins, Tuesdee and Wensdee, who now are in their 20s and 30s.

Albums, tapes sell 200,000

Phil authored, "Don't Quit Now", a book that sold over 27,000 copies; copyrighted 46 songs (published and recorded); recorded 29 long play record albums (sold 200,000 albums and tapes); was a recipient of the Southern Illinois University music education scholarship; and was a board member of The Great Commission Evangelistic Association.

In his first job, Phil was into newspaper art and advertising, public relations and sales for the Emons Printing and Publishing Company. In this capacity, he developed the major logos for the City of Alton, Illinois. In 1970 to 1972 he worked for Wood River Publishing Company as a staff artist for its Journal Newspaper. He did layout and design for commercial advertising, finish artwork, customer public relations and sales and consulting.

This Enloe couple tells their major motivations in this way: "Our deepest desire and purpose is to lift Jesus, win souls, heal the wounded, encourage the disappointed and be messengers of confirmation to what the Holy Spirit has already been saying through you."

And this author is certain that, from above, the following could be added: Joy to the world and to its people — from the Highest.

* * *

Preached his first official sermon at 16

Isham E. Enlow was a Baptist minister in Kentucky for 32 years, plus another 32 years in Florida, from 1912 to 1976. But he was an active Baptist much longer, from boyhood to 92 years of age. He preached his first formal sermon at age 16.

During those years he set exemplary records as a preacher and a manager, organizer and administrator:

Did descendants ever amount to much?

169

He became pastor of the First Baptist church at Whitesburg, Ky., where he started five other churches. There, he served as a dispensing agent for the Red Cross (in floods, mine disasters, food shortages and epidemics). Earlier, he was a pastor of Long Ridge Baptist Church; served as secretary of the Kentucky Baptist Conference at Dry Ridge; and was elected a member of the executive board, Ky. State convention, for several terms. He even coached the Overton high school basketball team while carrying out his many ministerial and civic duties.

Isham was embued at an early age with the strong Baptist background that came to him from the earliest pioneer days of his forbearers in Kentucky, so stated his son, The Reverend Eugene Isham Enlow of Louisville, Kentucky.

Both Isham and his son were among a long line of Baptist ministers in Kentucky, one of the earliest being Reverend Robert M. Enlow, born in 1827. He was the son of Abraham, born in 1793, and grandson of Isom (b. 1771-72; d. 1816) who was born to Abraham and Jemima (Elliott) Enlow in Baltimore, Maryland in 1726. This Abraham married Jemima Elliott who raised 15 children in Washington County, Pennsylvania, including Isom.

A Kentucky family founder

Actually this Isom was the founder of the Enlow families in what is now LaRue County, Kentucky. He married Mary (Brooks) LaRue, the midwife at the birth of Abraham Lincoln, born in a log house, and the former wife of John LaRue, namesake of that county.

Isom witnessed the death of John La Rue on January 3, 1792 and later that year posted bond for his marriage to Mary LaRue. Upon Enlow's death years later, Mary married Thomas W. Rathbone. Isom and Mary were married by Reverend Dodge, then pastor of Severns Valley Baptist Church, Elizabethtown, Ky., the first church of this denomination in that state.

This Enlow family line goes back to Hendricks and Christina Enloes of Holland and possibly originally from either Northwestern England or Scotland. Four Enloes families were settled in the Delaware Bay area by the middle 1650.

An indelible impression

Now back again to Isham. He experienced an indelible impression as the result of an early religious experience. When he was about seven years of age, his mother became seriously ill. He went to his bedroom across the hall from his mother's sickroom where he closed the door, then prayed for his mother promising that he would be one of God's children.

Not long after, he attended a Baptist revival at White City, Larue County, riding 3 to 4 miles across fields seated behind his father on horseback. When the preacher invited the congregation to come forward and be saved, no one came. The elderly preacher closed the service with a prayer, "Oh Lord, break down the stubborn will of the sinner part of the congregation, and may they make their will your will."

Young Isham prayed that same prayer, then rose with a feeling of utter relief from the burden he had felt for some time. He later often looked back to the incident as his conversion experience with the Lord.

Preached as eighth grader

Isham attended a revival meeting at which the preacher failed to appear. The song leader, who was the rural Sunday school superintendent, announced to Isham's surprise that the youth then in the eighth grade would be the preacher . . . Isham rose from his pew, went to the front and asked those present to sing another song. He then preached on the subject, "Be sure your sins will find you out."

Several came forward after the service to be converted, including three of his school mates who gave testimony of conversion experience that night.

Nine new missions

Motivated by religious passion, Isham as an adult preacher stressed new missions wherever he served. During twelve years as a pastorate at Whitesburg, he started nine new missions, five of which became full-fledged, active churches. His means were simple but very effective. He sent deacons and lay preachers out to the mission points from the mother church each Sunday afternoon to set the pattern for the church-centered mission program.

As a result of this success, the program was used later by the Kentucky Baptist State Mission Board and the Home Mission Board of the Southern Baptist Convention.

His zeal carried him forward in 1928 in a revival at the Walkertown Second Baptist Church, now Petry Memorial, Hazard, Ky.. More than 100 people were converted in the two-week gathering, all baptized on a Sunday afternoon in the Kentucky River. Converts were lined up along the river bank with Isham baptizing from one end and his associate and predecessor, the Rev. A. S. Petry, baptizing from the other. An estimated 1,000 spectators viewed the baptisms from banks of the river and from a new highway bridge.

Like father, like son

When Isham's son, Eugene Isham Enlow, was ordained to preach at the Dry Ridge Baptist Church in 1942, forty preachers attended the ordination, seen also by more than 400 other guests. Most of the preachers were well known Baptists, some of whom travelled from distant Kentucky churches.

An "Enlow Fund," established for potential and promising preachers, helped Eugene go to Georgetown College. The fund, established many years before at Bethel College, was then moved to Georgetown, Kentucky, when the two colleges united as one.

A stalwart partner

Marzella (Phillips) Enlow, a dedicated mother and church supporter, bore and raised three children with Isham. Besides Eugene, they include Philip and Charlotte (Mrs. William McClatchey.) A high school teacher much of her life, Marzella experienced the rigors of life and illnesses that come with age. She

Did descendants ever amount to much?

died March 4, 1982 in Florida and is buried at Red Hill Cemetery, Hodgenville, Kentucky, along with many other Enlow people, including Abraham, son of Isom and Mary (Brooks) LaRue Enlow.

Isham died June 20, 1989 at Ft. Myers, Fla., and also was buried in Red Hill Cemetery, Hodgenville, Ky.

[Note: Eugene provided the author of WHETSTONES with the information for this profile. That information came in the form of a presentation Eugene made about his father before The Kentucky Baptist Historical Society, Deer Park Baptist Church, Louisville, Kentucky, on July 23, 1982. The facts in the presentation largely were from writings by Reverend Isham Enlow and from diaries written by his wife, Marzella (Phillips) Enlow.]

"Chas" Ranger Enlow: from farm boy to U.S. diplomat?

Pilot's leaflet reads, "Fly, Fly."
Explorer finds plants that vie.
Diplomat: "He's my son, no lie."
Did you hear music? Not goodbye!

Naturally, as author of WHETSTONES, I must include a profile of my father, who is deserving of it and who was my role model, mostly in work ethics and achievements.

"Chas," as he was called in his early days, lived a full and rich career from birth to death (1895-1975). He was an explorer-diplomat who pioneered worldwide in seed improvement and soil conservation as a government official.

Early careerwise, he was a plant explorer in Russia, Russian Turkistan and Turkey in the early 1930s. Much later, when 72, he was the oldest man assigned to Vietnam including the period when the North Vietnamese initiated their Tet offense against South Vietnam. He headed a seed improvement team for both the U.S. State Department and the Agricultural Research Service, U. S. Department of Agriculture.

Earns international medal

For these and other achievements he was nominated and awarded the Frank N. Meyer Memorial Medal, an international recognition. . This medal is awarded to the top plant explorer periodically for international achievements in plant exploration and introduction. The medal was presented to him by the American Genetic Association for his distinguished service and, in addition, was presented a personal citation from the President of the United States.

"Chas" was the thirtieth recipient of the medal awarded since 1920. In general, the medal is awarded for finding and developing improved food and feed crops on four continents and in many nations. His citation for his varied achievements reads, in part:

" . . . for your distinguished service to the United States and world agri-

172

culture through leadership in the collection, introduction and establishment of plants for agriculture and conservation. In particular, special tribute is paid you for your successful introduction of grasses that have proven to be outstanding in the dryland areas of the Unites States, your successful efforts to assist countries of Africa and the Near East ... and especially for your recent leadership of the USDA Plant and Seed Multiplication Team in Vietnam, wherein this eventual success of the improved rice varieties in Vietnam is largely credited to the initial introduction and testing program developed by you and your associates."

During the Tet offense, an annual 3-day celebration, the Viet Cong attacked the Palace grounds at Seoul. Charles Ranger Enlow's team had planted various crops there for testing under Vietnam conditions.

The rest of the story? Those grounds were destroyed by mortar fire, as were the test plots. Fortunately, however, the plots were replicated elsewhere near Seoul.

A ring-around bell

But, let's go back a spell, when Chas was a teen, to make a point about his determination and zeal — and his youthful sense of humor. It happened in a small, Kansas country school.

Chas and another youth slipped into their high school one weekend and redid some wiring — namely, controlling the school bell. They, in fact, installed contact points, readily available to them in a classroom and the assembly hall.

What then? Well, as Chas told the story, he and his chum would sit attentively in class, naturally absorbing every word teacher said. However, whenever the teacher stepped on a specific spot, Chas or his chum would touch two wires together, and the dismissal bell would ring.

This non-scheduled ringing occurred off and on all day sorely puzzling the teachers and principal.

The ringing continued the next day in assembly called expressly to solve the riddle of the bell. The school principal was prone to walk back and forth in front of his podium. Each time he stepped on a specific board, the bell rang.

"This bell ringing is going to stop," he said most emphatically. "It's terribly disruptive of your education, and I intend to get to the bottom of it."

At that moment, the bell rang again as he paced back and forth. On the third ring, he studied the floor closely and pressed his foot on the suspected spot. The bell rang. He pressed it again and again and each time the bell rang.

"This assembly is dismissed," he said angrily, his eyes still glued to the floor.

Chas and his friend slipped into the school in the wee hours that night and removed all evidence of their wiring. The bell ringers were never found out, and the principal never said what he didn't find under the board by his podium.

A star student, athlete

Did descendants ever amount to much?

WHETSTONES

Chas went to Kansas State College, Manhattan (now KSU), where he triple-lettered in sports and where he received his bachelor's and master's degrees in agronomy.

While at Kansas State, he lettered in football, basketball and track. He played end and captained the football team and was center on the basketball team. He also sailed the discus and polevaulted in track. In fact, at one time, he held the Kansas polevault record at 11 feet, 5 inches.

That was back when they used bamboo poles for vaulting. During one vault, the pole split and a portion of bamboo pierced the skin of his chest. Someone had left the pole out in the sun and rain which dried it out and caused it to splinter.

Up, up and away

A Manhattan (Kansas) Mercury sports account of the 1917 Kansas State football team reads:

"Enlow enlisted for aviation while in attendance at the officers' training camp at Fort Riley this summer . . .

"Enlow's play has shown enough improvement . . . that Coaches Clevenger and Schulz have ceased to worry about right end. Charlie tackles fiercely, always gets his man; his speed makes him invaluable in running down under punts.

"He has shown an almost uncanny ability to go away (sic) up in the air after Johnny Clark's punts (passes?) and return to terra firma with the ball tucked away in his arms."

He took to the air in yet another way, so his 1918 pilot's logbook relates. It cites solos, rolls and spirals in his JN4B, a Jenny biplane, powered by a Curtiss OX engine. His logbook also says, in his own hand, that he was five feet, eleven inches. He must have grown another inch or two in later years; he certainly towered in achievements.

Chas' first solo, at the School of Military Aeronautics, University of California, was March 12, 1918, flying "eights and landings." On his second solo he added spirals and did more eights, moved on to spot landings and then to cross country. By April 1, he had logged 38 hours and 47 minutes and was graduated as a pursuit pilot (called a fighter pilot, now). Then came another challenge to be faced.

Death of a friend

At advanced training at Payne Field, West Point, Mississippi, he continued cross country flights and hurdles (sounds scary), stunts, spirals and formation flying. One formation flight included a "23 min. jazz." (What's jazz, Chas?)

His June 10, 1918 entry stated: "Stunts and sideslipping," and ended somberly, " . . . Bowen, C.G., Killed."

The 176 hours of flight training at Payne Field included extensive formation flying (9 ships, and "ships on circus day"); reconnaissance work (photography and sketching, wireless and panneaux (trapping?); releasing pigeons, among other jazz. Combat work came as the finale. He practiced maneuvering for blind spots and tail positions, zooming, camera gun work, camouflage, aerial combat and cross country flights to Tupelo, Mississippi.

On graduation, Chas requested aerial combat. "I told them I wanted to fight, not teach," he was quoted in a modern-day feature in the Lafayette Journal Courier, "but they said, 'the last fellow who told us that isn't flying anymore.'" He was assigned in France as a flight instructor, unhappily for him, joyously for his descendants.

Brevetted as such

I hold in my hand a family heirloom, a three-by-four-inch, leather-bound, aviator's certificate. On opening it, I see a handsome officer in a WW I, U.S. dress uniform adorned with silver braid wings above the left breast pocket. His pompadour combed hair and high-buttoned military collar frame a youthful but intense face of 23.

The certificate was issued to Second Lieutenant Enlow, U.S. Air Service, on September 25, 1918 at Paris, France. It declares he became a member of the Aero Club of America, Federation Aeronautique Internationale, number 2349. It could be 2849, because the ink has faded in three quarters of a century.

Examining the document further, I discovered that the French Federation recognized that Lt. Enlow fulfilled all French conditions for an aviator pilot, "and is brevetted as such." That means no more pay and no more authority, Webster says.

I discovered also that Lt. Enlow penned his birth date as June 25, 1895 just below his signature. Sorry to bring it up, Chas, but the actual date was June 28 of that year. I know because I inherited one of your leather suitcases with a combination lock set for 6-2-8, for June 28, not 25.

Fly with an "Old Bird"

After World War I, pilot instructor Charles R. Enlow returned to Kansas from France, bought a Curtiss Jenny biplane, and set himself up as a barnstormer. He'd buzz low over a town a day or so ahead and toss out flyers that read, "Fly! Fly ... He's coming again ... That old bird Enlow ... Saturday and Sunday, June 5 and 6 (1919) ... Your chance to fly with the best aviator in the country ... Book your rides early and be sure of a trip ... Watch for him!"

Then on return, the "old bird" took passengers up for 20-minute spins at $5 per head.

Man who hunts grass

Fourteen years later, Enlow spent half of 1933 in Russia, Russian Turkistan and Turkey as a plant explorer for the U.S. government, a unit now known as the Soil Conservation Service, U. S. Department of Agriculture. He and H. L. Westover collected seeds of 2,500 plant strains, mainly grasses from dryland areas of Russian Turkistan and Turkey.

One of those seed species, designated Plant Introduction No. 98568, became the basis for five domesticated wheatgrasses largely still grown widely in the plains and intermountain areas of the central and western United States.

As his son, when a child, I thought he had discovered an alfalfa that was called Ranger, named for Chas' middle name. He didn't. I believe, however, he was middle-named Ranger because of the Kansas terrain where he was born and grew up.

Shortly after Chas returned to the United States, he was interviewed by the late Ernie Pyle, world-renowned war correspondent who identified him in his feature article as "a different kind of hunter, a grass hunter." Pyle also pegged Chas as a man "with big ears." (Like father, like son.)

Then came varmints, vipers

Plant explorers Chas and Hal found more in Russia than just useful plants growing in their natural habitat. Much to their displeasure, they found a barbed wire border, a poverty-stricken youth of 12, scoundrels who rob trains, plagues of fleas and bedbugs, disabling strains of flu, cobras that sing at night and one dead cat in Chas' bed, under his pillow. As he recounted in portions of his diary:

May 19, 1934: In the evening about 6 p.m., we reached the Russian border, where we were again briefly examined by the Polish authorities. Then we crossed into Russia. A barb wire entanglement is on the border line between the two countries. Four decks of playing cards were taken from us as they are barred in Russia. Odd, barbed wire but no decks of cards.

May 20: I found an interesting diversion in watching an 11 or 12 year old boy bum a ride on our train. He was very dirty, barefooted, with long trousers and a heavy coat like a mackinaw. As soon as the train would start, he would climb aboard somewhere underneath. At the next stop he would be strolling along beside the train all unconcerned. Couldn't help but think how glad it wasn't my son, Bob (then 11), and I felt very sorry for him (the Russian youth, he meant).

June 11: This has been a gloomy day. Someone got in our compartment last night and stole my passport and $15 in cash, also my fountain pen — lucky I have another; also Westover's watch, knife, keys and fountain pen; Alexiv's watch and 2000 rubles. (Their tea had been drugged, and the thieves were never apprehended.)

June 21: Had the "trots" last night — something I ate didn't agree. I spent part of the night chasing up and down the path to the nearby great out doors. And, it didn't help to know I was in cobra infested country. Two have been killed in the door of the kibitki. We heard the song of the cobra last night, a throaty guttural sound coming from rock ledges not far away.

August 1: . . . Slept in a small shack. Flees were terrible, bit me all night long. Bedbugs were even worse at other lodgings.

You're his father

Besides being a plant explorer, Dad became the first chief agronomist of USDA's Soil Conservation Service which he helped form in the early 1930s with

Did descendants ever amount to much?

ROBERT E. ENLOW

H. H. Bennett, that agencies first director. He also was the first agricultural attache to the Union of South Africa, later holding that same position in Kenya and then in Turkey where he also was acting first secretary of the embassy.

In my travels as a journalist I frequently was greeted by the statement, "Oh, you're Charlie Enlow's son." But when he was at the American Embassy, Ankara Turkey, the tables were turned, a happenstance over which Dad and I often chortled.

It came about this way: Dad was replaced on completion of his tour of duty as attache in Turkey by a former county agent, Gordon Schlubatus, Hillsdale County, Michigan. On meeting Charlie, Gordon said: "Oh, you must be Bob Enlow's father. I knew him in the 1950s when he was a reporter for the Battle Creek Enquirer and News."

On top of that, you'll remember that he was the oldest American assigned in South Vietnam as head of a seed improvement team for the U.S. State Department. He and the team were very successful, but they made one wrong choice. They chose the palace grounds at Seoul as a safe haven to grow test plots.

You may know the rest of the story: Those grounds were destroyed by the North Vietnamese during the Tet offense. Fortunately, they had replicated the plots elsewhere.

What music, Dad?

Following a half a century of career service to mankind, Charlie Enlow died on March 28, 1977 at Lafayette, Indiana. He underwent an operation 7 months before his death of a bulbous aneurysm of his aorta. (Later complications from the operation are believed to have killed him.) After the operation his family was with him in the hospital visitors' lounge. He asked:

"Did you hear all that music?"

"What music, Dad?" I asked in response.

"You didn't hear any music? . . . I'm not ready to go just yet," he said quietly and solemnly.

But it wasn't long until he left for those bountiful rangelands beyond
. . . to a place where he might just be found gleaning better plants for our fields of the future.

An Enloe teaches children peace by peace

By Jack El-Hai

Get to know Walter Enloe for any length of time and he'll give you a crane. Folded origami-style from a single sheet of paper, the bird is an elegant, simple reminder that people working together can learn peace-making skills.

Enloe, the 45-year-old director of outreach in the Institute of International Studies and Programs at the University of Minnesota, can fold a crane with his eyes closed. Since 1985 he has been involved in international efforts to help children create birds by the thousands and present them as peace-signifying gifts to people in need. His office is tangled with wreaths of paper cranes that school children around the region have made and sent to him.

Enloe's past as an American boy growing up abroad and as the principal of an international school in Japan led him to his current role as promoter of international education and peace skills. The son of Presbyterian missionaries who moved to Japan, he quickly learned how to see things through the eyes of others. To commute to school at a U.S. military base near Hiroshima, "I took a bus at 6:30 a.m. and walked through a mile of bars and bordellos," he recalls. "I was living in several worlds every day. The popular image of Americans was schizophrenic — we were both the hero and the Ugly American, and the A in 'A-bomb' stood for 'American.'"

After earning a Ph. D. in liberal arts at Emory University in Atlanta, Enloe embarked on a teaching career in 1980 and returned to Japan as principal of Hiroshima Inernational School. Five years later, during the 40th-anniversary observance of the atomic bombing, Enloe and his students began folding cranes. Reporters had flooded the city. "TV crews came to interview our kids all the time," he says. "They asked them questions like, "As Americans, what do you do for peace? Do you feel guilty living in Hiroshima?" These were questions adults couldn't answer. But the kids expanded on those questions and asked themselves, 'What can we do for peace?'"

Thirty years earlier a Hiroshima girl named Sadako Sasaki, ill from leukemia contracted from atomic radiation, set out to fold a thousand cranes based on the folkloric belief that doing so guarantees long life and grants wishes. After Sadako's death, her classmates founded the Paper Crane Club in her honor and helped build a monument to Hiroshima for all the children who had died in the bombing. Enloe's students invited children around the world to fold 1,000 cranes and send them as a gift to the mayor of Hiroshima.

"Folding cranes is a constructive activity, and it can be a model for something larger," Enloe says. "It takes persistence. Sometimes a younger person has to show you how to do it. And it results in a peaceful act of giving." With pride he talks about students in Redwood Falls, Minn., who have folded thousands of cranes for a child sick with leukemia and residents of a retirement home. "I taught three third-graders there how to fold cranes, and when I came back six weeks later the whole school knew how," he says.

The program is now called Birds of Peace Project. It's cosponsored by the United Nations Association of Minnesota and Enloe's department at the U. of M. Uncountable cranes have since arrived in Hiroshima.

Enloe left Japan for Minnesota in 1968, settling in Golden Valley with his wife, Kitty, a teacher, and their two teenaged children. He serves as a consultant and partner in Building a New World, a program that teaches children how to erect the giant globe that filled the sky last year in front of Northrop Auditorium at the university and at the Minnesota State Fair. Soon the globe will travel to Russia and Israel.

Did descendants ever amount to much?

ROBERT E. ENLOW

In addition to teaching, Enloe writes teacher's guides for human rights and conflict-resolution workshops for children, including a future session planned for Palestinian and Jewish children in Israel. "It is very important to devote our resources to children 10 and younger," Enloe says. "I don't believe schools should be merely preparing kids for adulthood. To do that doesn't aid them in their life right now."

CREDIT: The article by Mr. El-Hai was published in a truly excellent magazine, "MplsStPaul," the magazine of the Twin Cities, Minnesota, issued August 1994 under the editorship of Brian E. Anderson. Jack El-Hai, a freelance writer, gave permission to publish his article; so did Dr. Enlow and Mr. Anderson.

* * *

Dear Great³ Aunt Louicie, still another note: I want to be sure that you and other readers realize that no scientific study was followed to pick the role models included herein. But, at the same time, I defy anyone to say that any of the Enloe or Enlow subjects herein are not real and remarkable role models, past and present the very best I could find.

Now, I will provide the names, vocations and places (below) of a few other Enloe, Enlow, (et al) people. My source for these additions totally has been from Who's Who volumes. I am adding them, not in any organized way, to document the broad scope of jobs and professions of our family members down through the years and generations. And I want to remind you that all but a few individuals cited were from a population of about 3,000 of this U. S. family, based largely on the 1930s-1950s studies by the late E.E. Enlow of California, and the late Col. Thomas Enloe of Virginia.

I love you Aunt Louicie. Thanks for helping write WHETSTONES.

Sincerely,

Bob "Workman" Enlow.

P.S. I almost forgot to tell you a quickie story in return for at least one of your many funny ones in your past letters. It's about a five-year-old daughter of the Markley family, then of the Washington D. C. area. It was bedtime and her mamma had just said prayers with her and was leaving the room when she stepped on something sticky on a small bedside rug.

"What in the Lord's name is that?" her mama asked, and daughter answered: "The Lord says it's 'jeddy'."

*

Now for a few more Enloe, Enlow (et al) and occupations:

- Cinthia Holden Enloe, political science educator, writer; daughter of Cortez and Harriet, born July 16, 1936 in N.Y.C.
- Robert Ted Enlow, III, financial services executive, born October 31, 1938 at Mansfield, La. to Robert, Jean (McLaurin).
- Jeff H. Enloe, Jr., a North Carolina State Representative born at Franklin, N. C., Sept. 2, 1914 to Jeff H., Jessie Hester.
- Robert Ambrose Enlow, newspaper association executive, born Boone, Iowa, Nov. 15, 1917 to Frank and Bertha (Tams).
- Helen (Hahn) Enlow, biologist-librarian at university levels; born at Edgeworth, Penn., Sept. 14, 1904. (Parents not listed).
- Fred Clark Enlow, banker and university banking instructor; born at Lewistown, Mont., April 15, 1940 to Guy and Jewel.
- Ella Morgan Austin Enlows, physician, bacteriologist, serologist, otologist and writer; born W. Va., August 21, 1889 to Dr. Thomas Morgan and Mary Susan (Auvil).
- Hansell Porter Enloe, architect; born Atlanta, Georgia, on May 6, 1928 to Van Porter and Caroline (Hansell).
- Louis Henry Enloe, electrical engineering, communications; born Eldorado Springs, Mo., March 4, 1933 (parents not listed).
- Rebecca Lynn Enloe, educator, university faculty; born at Magnolia, Ark. April 11, 1949 to Russell and Jamie Eshenbaugh.
- Joseph R. Enloe, Jr., oil company executive, petroleum engineer; born at Seymour Texas, Sept. 9, 1924 to Joseph R. and Bessie (Taylor).
- Donald Hugh Enlow, professor of anatomy; born Jan 22, 1927 at Mosquero, N. M., (Parents not listed).
- Ridley Madison Enslow, Jr., book publisher; born Orange, N. J. on March 13, 1926 to Ridley Madison and Virginia E.
- Philip Harrison Enslow, Jr., electrical engineer and government executive; born Richmond Va., March 2, 1933 to Philip and Charlotte Eucebia (Coalter).
- Harold Eugene Enlows, professor and chairman of the department of geology, Oregon State Univ.; born Mason City, Ill. on March 13, 1926. (Parents not listed).

Did descendants ever amount to much?

REFERENCE QUIZ:
No dreams herein, but ...
Don't forget, Whetstones is part spun-funnery.

Some of my scientist friends whom I have interviewed over the years will cringe and say, "Enlow, this book is not traditional. In fact, it's 'bibliography' is irreverent considering scientific standards." One scientist already has cringed over the fact that he couldn't tell the difference between fact and fiction in a chapter he reviewed. I was genuinely pleased to hear that. It was one of my goals as, I believe, a fact-in-fiction writer.

WHETSTONES is based on actual historical threads, happenings and conditions of the times and locations. Those that are not, mimic true happenings and times.

To get a genuine feel for settlers and their trials, the author read *The Australians*, a series of seven volumes (about 4,000 pages in total) to get the full feeling of settling a new land. Each volume was written by William Stuart Long, published by A Dell Publishing Company, New York City, N.Y., (1980 to 1985) and designed by BCI. Executive producer was Lyle Kenyon Engel. These books detail the exploring and settling of Australia where the author began serving overseas in the U.S. Air Force, spending most of 3 years island hopping in the South Pacific.

If it helps, I'm calling the following a reference quiz, including questions, that are not traditional, but functional.

(1) Was Plowman Hill, I mean, Enlow Hill, really the community's founding name? See page 33 of Jasper Area History, which was written mostly by assigned authors chosen by Historic Jasper, Inc., this author included. The book (384 pages) was designed and published by Turner Publishing Company, Paducah, Kentucky and copyrighted in 1989 by the incorporated group.

(2) Did Capt. John Enlow actually chase a group of Indians or was it the other way around? See page 289 of *The History of Dubois County*

(Indiana) written and copyrighted by George R. Wilson and published in 1910 as a Whippoorwill Publication.

(3) Did Andrew and Mary Evans own their land on which they built their mill, or did they squat it and lose it? See page 33 ibid (1) *Jasper Area History*. (If you're not a technical writer or editor, ibid means ditto, and see above.)

(4) Were Indian prisoners killed and tossed into the Patoka River? Surely not. Or, were they? Ibid (2), page 289.

(5) Did Salem later become Bardstown, Kentucky, or was it vice versa? See pages 16-17, Historic Nelson County, by Sarah B. Smith, published in 1971 by Gateway Press, Louisville, Kentucky.

(6) On second thought, did an Enlow buy the Evan's mill or just the land from under his mill? Ibid (1), page 33.

(7) Who was "The Prophet?" (Absolutely and totally unlike Jesus Christ, you can be certain.) Ibid (2), page 398.

(8) Why did Tom Penn issue his decree to give unowned land back to the Indians? Did he really mean it? A hint: Frontier families had grit. See page 117, *History of Indian Villages and Place Names In Pennsylvania*, with Numerous Historical Notes and Reference, by George P. Donehoo, published by The Telegraph Press, Harrisburg, Pa., copyright assumed.

(9) Are these Enlow people from the Lake district of NW England or part of a Scottish highland fling? Various Enloe-Enlow people claim Scotland as their earliest origin. See Harper Row's *New Dictionary of American Family Names*, Eldson C. Smith, 1973.

(10) Some of the Enloes' families moved from Deleware Bay to the Province of Maryland and later to Penn Province . . . Why? Land ahoy, of course. See page 35 of *The Enlow Family of America* (1941), written, prepared and distributed by E. E. Enlow, Sabastopol, California. (In today's lingo, it was a desktop job, very thorough and accurate, from start to finish.)

(11) Were the Iroquois Indians friends of the Cherokee? Do brothers never quarrel? Ibid (8), page 117.

(12) Why did the English fight in straight lines at Fort Necessity? (To be killed! . . . Oh my, just joshing!) See Vol. 3, page 782, *The Book of Knowledge*; E.V. McLoughlin, editor and chief; copyrighted by Groiler Society, publisher, in 1949.

(13) Was Turkey Foot really the name of the home territory of Henry, George and John Enslow? (Enslow? A county clerk's slip up?) See page 3, *Listing of Inhabitants of Bedford County, Pennsylvania*, compiled by Shirley G. M. Iscrup, copyrighted by S.W. Penn Genealogical Services, Laughlintown, Pennsylvania.

(14) Joseph Enlow was an ensign in Washington County, Maryland in Capt. Cresap's company during the American Revolutionary War. Ibid (10),

ROBERT E. ENLOW

Page 39. (Ignore page 43. It cites this Joseph as being an "Inslow".)

(15) Did Chief Pisquetomen actually give his horse to Jenny Frazer? Was it vice versa? See page 565-566, *History of Somerset County, Pennsylvania*, by I. D. Rupp, reprinted as a leaflet from Rupp's 1948 History by the S.W. Pennsylvania Genealogical Society, Laughlintown, Penn.

(16) Did Dunmore's War include the dark country? Did the name come from dense forests and wild animals? See page 46, *A History of the Middle West* by Kenneth L. Walker, professor of History, Arkansas Polytechnic Institute, copyrighted, 1972.

(17) Why, oh why, did Chief Greathouse and men kill nine Indians, including a sister of Mingo Chief Logan? Ibid (16), page 47.

(18) Did Isaac Cox and his two brothers build forts along the Monongahela River? They had grit. Ibid (5), page 18.

(19) Did George Washington lose three-fourths of his troops at Ft. Necessity? Or was it the French? Ibid (8), page 117.

(20) Why were the waters of the Menaungehilla (earliest spelling) traced readily? From blood of battles? Ibid (8), page 113.

(21) Were the dimensions of Isaac Cox's flatboats correct? Why were they flat? Ibid (2), page 149.

(22) Did the pilot of the flatboats grease the anchor? If so, why? Ibid (2), page 152.

(23) Were turkey calls false; was Isaac Cox's brother killed? Ibid? Aw, hell. Ditto (5), pages 17 and 18.

(24) Did the Bogardus estate include King's Farm, later to become King's Park on Manhattan Island? Ditto (10), page 52.

(25) Was the grant of land patented? Can the deed be found on pages 28-30, Book 4 of Patents, at the Secretary of State Office, Albany, New York? Ditto (10), page 51.

(26) Can one be sure all Indian names, except Pisquetomen, are fictitious herein? Yes! Ditto (8), pages 565 and 566.

(27) Was a fort or station built at Cox's Creek? Was there a difference? Ditto (5), page 17.

(28) How can one find honey stores? By melting honey in the woods? Ditto (2), page 82.

(29a-b) Who really invented the steamboat? Robert Fulton or John Fitch? (a) *The Book of Knowledge*, Vol. 4, page 528; (b) Groliers, Vol 17, Page 6399. Both were published by the Grolier Society, Inc., New York City, New York in 1949 or 1950 editions.

(30) Did John Fitch sell land to Joseph Enlow, Sr? Was the land flooded by Cox's Creek and no steamboat at hand? No! See deed of sale on November 8, 1796 when Benjamin Grason, clerk of the court, Hardin County, Kentucky signed a deed of sale of 300 acres by John Fitch to

Enlow, not to be confused with Josh Enlow, Jr. in Chapter I.

(31) Are there really false birthing contractions? See Maternity Nursing (11th ed.) by Fitzpatrick, Eastmann, Reeder; copyrighted (1960) and published by T. P. Lippincott Co., Philadelphia, Penn., Pages 482-4.

(32) Was there such a medical practice as blood letting because of an imbalance of humors? See A Midwife Tale by Laurel Thatcher Ulrich, published by Alfred A. Knopf, New York, N.Y. and copyrighted in 1990, page 55-6.

(33) Did barber "doctors" use blood from black cats for healing? Did the cats dare to have white hairs? Ditto (32), page 51.

(34) Did Mary LaRue marry Isom Enlow in 1792 at the time Isom was sheriff or justice of the peace of Hardin County? See page 13 of The Mather Papers, published June 15, 1968 by The Herald News, Hodgenville, Kentucky.

(35) How many children did Mary and Isom have? Was it twelve? See pages 97-8 of Six Generations of LaRues and Allied Families, copyrighted and published in 1921 by Otis M. Mather, Hodgenville, Kentucky., a former vice president of the Ky. State Bar Assoc.

(36) Was Tom Lincoln's South Fork farm also called Sinking Spring farm? How much more will the spring sink? The author and Mrs. Enlow found it a deep sink; one shouldn't lean too far over the brink for a cool drink. Ditto (35), page 13.

(37) Can false contractions really be stopped by telling tales to a patient? Ditto (31), pages 483-4.

(38) Was Mary LaRue Enlow the midwife at the birth of Abraham Lincoln? Or was she at a quilting bee? Ditto (34), page 13.

(39) Did Abraham Enlow fetch his mother by horseback as midwife for the birthing of Abraham Lincoln? If so, did she arrive on time? Ditto (35), page 158.

(40) How far was the farm of Mary and Isom Enlow from Hodgen's mill? Way yonder? Or closer? Ditto (34), page 13.

(41) Why did neighbors think Abraham Lincoln was named after (not before) Abraham Enlow? Ditto (35), page 158.

(42) Was Tom Lincoln a wanderer or a wonderer, or both? Ditto (29-a), page 1649.

(43) Did Tom Lincoln face land problems? Or, is the question, how many? Ditto (35), Page 155-7.

(44) Did Mordecai kill an Indian who killed Tom Lincoln's father, Abraham? See page 17 of Carl Sandburg's Prairie Years, published in 1970 by The Reader's Digest Association, Inc.

(45) When did John Fitch die? How did he die? Was it by his own hand in "the dark country?" Ditto (29-b), Vol 4, page 528.

(46a-b) How could an Abraham Enloe of North Carolina have fathered

Nancy Lincoln's child, Abraham? (a) See page 11, "Abraham Lincoln: North Carolinian?" by Virgie Pittman, the State magazine, February 1989, published by Shaw Publishing, Inc., Charlotte, N.C. (b) See also "Enloe Family Touched By Many Legends", page 9A, Feb. ll, 1988, by John Parris of The Ashville (N.C.) Citizen.

(47) Did John Enlow marry Elizabeth Frazee, a descendant of Polly Bogardus? Ditto (10), page 15.

(48) Who was the first Dutch minister of Manhattan? Ditto (10), pages 49-50.

(49) Did Hyman Gerson Enelow, rabbi, come to this country from Russia or Hawaii? See Who's Who in America, 1932-33.

(50) Did Abraham Enloes say this in his will? "I have given them (their slaves) to my wife . . . " Ditto (10), pages 12-14.

(51) Who in this book got the highest tribute from Gov. Helm? None other than Mary Brooks LaRue Enlow. See "Who was who in Hardin County," an undated printed sheet by the Hardin County Historical Society, Hodgenville, Ky.

(52) Did Mary LaRue (later, Enlow) actually bring 1,000 converts to Baptist churches? For bingo? Ditto (51).

(53) Did Mary LaRue Enlow really hold a slave named Nancy? Was this Nancy's name confused with Nancy Lincoln's? Ditto (51).

(54) Did Nancy really work for Josh and Nelly? No!

(55) Did Aaron B. McCrillus and Benjamin Workman (Enlow) share a pulpit? Ditto (2), page 235.

(56) Why did Tecumseh and his brother, The Profit, stir up the Indians? Ditto (2), page 398.

(57) Was Henry Young Workman actually an Enlow? You guess.

(58) Was Indian land considered common? Ditto (2), page 398.

(59) Did Hill Creek actually intersect the buffalo trace? Ditto (2), page 163 (map).

(60) Did The Profit really have a town named for him? Ditto 2, page 398.

(61) Were there actually swarms upon swarms of pigeons? Ditto (2), page 81.

(62) Did Carolina paraquets really reside in Indiana? Ditto 2, page 80.

(63) Who led the Yellow Jackets? Ditto (2), page 404.

(64) Was Toussaint actually Dubois' first name? Yes!

(65) Did General Harrison lose 37 or 67 men to deaths? Ditto (2), page 402.

(66) Was a survey made of judges? Ditto (10), page 46.

About the Author

The author, assisted by first reviewer-editor Helen T. Enlow, has experience and education strongly supportive of writing the narrative-biographical novel, *WHETSTONES*. The book is heavily intertwined in farm family living. As examples, he has hands-on experience in horse-powered and lantern-lit farming during summers in Kansas and Idaho, is a journalism graduate with a minor in agriculture and has 30+ years of reporting, writing and editing, mostly in fields of farming and agriculture.

He is a graduate of the University of Minnesota where he majored in journalism and minored in agricultural economics, plus a mix of courses in rural sociology, agronomy (near minor), dairy husbandry and entomology, to name those recalled.

His experience and education provided background in farming and farm family life. He has 8 years experience (off and on) in genealogical research; 25 years of agricultural research reporting, writing and editing, including being editor of USDA's Agricultural Research magazine and 4 years a farm reporter for the Battle Creek (Michigan) Enquirer and News (now B.C. Enquirer); a year as editor of the Mississippi Farmer magazine; 4 years as editor of Helping Build Mississippi; and 4 years as a volunteer and a year full time in Mississippi politics.

During this time, the author received five significant recognitions, among other writing awards:

- An honorary member of the Bellevue, Michigan, Future Farmers of America in the early 1950s for reporting farm and farm family articles for the Battle Creek Enquirer and News.
- Outstanding newspaper reporter award in 1950 by the Michigan Association of Soil Conservation Districts, again with the Enquirer and News.
- One of the top 10 agricultural writers' awards of the nation in 1957 by the American Seed Trade Association, as an associate editor of Capper's Farmer magazine.

ROBERT E. ENLOW

- An Award of Distinction for "outstanding technical communication" in 1972 from the Central Illinois Chapter of the Society for Technical Communication.
- A USDA's Superior Service Award in 1974 for leadership, signed and presented to the author by Secretary of Agriculture Earl L. Butz at ceremonies in Washington, D.C.
- And he was clerk of the Mission Commission, Jackson, Mississippi, for the establishment of a new church, St. Philips, which later became the diocesan cathedral. Chairman of the commission was the Rt. Rev. John M. Allin, then bishop coadjutor who later became presiding bishop of the U. S. Episcopal Church.